John Addington Symonds, Ben Jonson

The Dramatic Works and Lyrics of Ben Jonson

With an Essay, Biographical and Critical

John Addington Symonds, Ben Jonson

The Dramatic Works and Lyrics of Ben Jonson
With an Essay, Biographical and Critical

ISBN/EAN: 9783744782524

Printed in Europe, USA, Canada, Australia, Japan

Cover: Foto ©Andreas Hilbeck / pixelio.de

More available books at **www.hansebooks.com**

THE DRAMATIC WORKS AND LYRICS

OF

BEN JONSON

[SELECTED]

With an Essay, Biographical and Critical,

BY

JOHN ADDINGTON SYMONDS.

LONDON:
Walter Scott, 24 Warwick Lane, Paternoster Row,
AND NEWCASTLE-ON-TYNE.
1886.

CONTENTS.

Lyrics and Occasional Pieces.

Introduction.

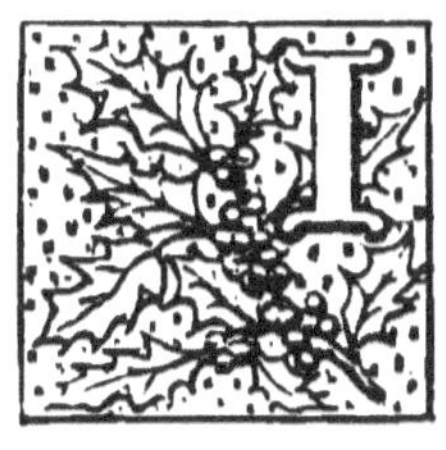IN the reign of Henry VIII. a member of the Border family of Johnston emigrated from Annandale to Carlisle. He became a servant of the English king, and was, according to the language of that time, a gentleman ; that is to say, one who could prove his right to bear coat armour. His son suffered religious persecution in the reign of Queen Mary, lost his estates, and adopted the profession of Protestant minister. He had married in England ; and one month after his decease his widow bore a son, whom she christened Benjamin. This boy, who subsequently spelled his family name Jonson, is the subject of the present volume. We know him as Rare Ben Jonson, one of the brightest ornaments of English literature in the age of Elizabeth, James, and Charles I. The widow Jonson, not long after her

son's birth, made a second marriage, this time with a master mason or bricklayer. We do not know his name. But he seems to have been a worthy man ; for he put his little step-son, Benjamin, to school, providing for the first stage of a training which was destined to produce one of the wisest scholars and most learned poets whom English annals can boast.

William Camden, the great antiquary, was at this time second master of Westminster School. It seems that he had been a friend of Ben Jonson's deceased father, or at all events that he was interested in the boy's family. Owing to this illustrious man's kindness, the little Ben was admitted to that noble nursery of English youth ; and the future of his life was fixed on the day when he entered Westminster. In after years he addressed the patron of his boyhood in verses which bear all the marks of sincere gratitude—

> " Camden ! most reverend head, to whom I owe
>   All that I am in arts, all that I know."

Ben was an apt pupil, and well repaid the generosity of his protector. He was gifted with a prodigious memory, and with a peculiar aptitude for appropriating all the stores of knowledge opened to him, and for vivifying these in his own brain by the mental force of one to whom the past was equally real with the present of human nature.

In person he was an ungainly lad ; big-boned, of large stature, but clumsy in his gait, not quite

healthy, and with features somewhat repellant in
their harsh and saturnine force of expression.
During the years he spent at Westminster we must
imagine him absorbing all the new learning of the
Greeks and Romans which England had derived
from Italian humanism, drinking in knowledge at
every sense, and, after books were cast aside,
indulging his leisure in studying the humours of
the town which lay around him. The main point
to notice in the accomplished man of letters, Rare
Ben, as his printed works declare him to us, is the
blending of vast and precisely assimilated erudition with the most acutely realistic sense of men
and women as he saw them in the world of actual
experience. His boyhood stamped this double
character upon the dramatist. Westminster made
him what he was to be, no less surely than the
water-meadows by the shores of Avon and the
deer-park of Charlcote created Shakespeare. This
raw observant boy, his head crammed with Tacitus
and Livy, Aristophanes and Thucydides, sallied
forth from the class-room, when the hours of study
were over, into the slums of suburban London,
lounged around the water-stairs of the Thames,
threaded the purlieus of Cheapside and Smithfield,
drank with 'prentices and boxed with porters,
learned the slang of the streets, and picked up
insensibly that inexhaustible repertory of contemporary manners which makes his comedies our
most prolific source of information on the life of
London in the sixteenth century.

What became of him when he left Westminster

is uncertain.   Tradition of some value reports that
he matriculated at Cambridge.   But we have no
record of his residence there ; and his own state-
ments make it more than probable that he did not
profit by any course of reading at the University.
It is at any rate certain that the degrees which both
Oxford and Cambridge afterwards conferred on
him were honorary, due not to his studies but
to the admiration which his plays inspired.   On
the whole we may assume that he went straight
from school into the office of his step-father, the
builder or bricklayer.   How he was employed
there, whether as a clerk or as an actual apprentice
to the trade, cannot now be decided.   But when he
became famous, his enemies often taunted him with
having been a mason ; and on this fact of his early
manhood the legend has been based of a marvellous
workman, who studied Juvenal and Horace while
carrying his hod up ladders or plastering walls
with mortar.

However he may have entered into his step-
father's trade, the occupation proved distasteful to
him.   He felt called to be a scholar and a poet ;
and there was, moreover, something of the
Bohemian in his nature which ill brooked life-
long devotion to handicraft.   In order to break the
chains of business which seemed to bind him down,
Jonson ran away and joined an English force in
the Low Countries.   One exploit of his campaign
there has been handed down to us through his own
lips.   He says that he fought in single combat
with a champion of the enemy in the face of both

camps, killed his man, and stripped him of his armour. That he should have done so is quite consistent with what we know about his character, with his intense thirst for distinction, his personal courage, and something arrogant in his self-assertion. Perhaps it was in the Low Countries, like others after him, that he learned to drink deep and to swear. Certainly, when he returned from military service, he was not unaccomplished in these arts.

When he was about twenty years of age, that is to say probably in the year 1592, he married an English wife. He tells us that she was "a shrew, yet honest." By this wife he had several children, all of whom he survived. He was not in any eminent degree a domestic man. Talking to his friend Drummond at Hawthornden in 1619, he mentioned that he had lived five years apart from his family, and he told several stories, which do not bear repetition, arguing no great fidelity to the marriage tie on his own part. Yet he was attached to his children. For two of them he wrote elegiac verses which we still possess ; and he narrated the singular circumstance of his eldest son's ghost appearing to him at the moment when the boy died of plague in London. From his plays it is clear that Jonson never felt the finer charms of womanhood ; for we cannot find in any of them a female character to match the least attractive of Shakespeare's. If we seek truly to comprehend the man, we must conceive of him as one in whom the natural instincts were partially controlled by a strong will and sound intellect, who regarded matrimony as a useful institution, and who felt strongly toward his offspring, but in whom the ideal sentiment of love, the worship of woman, was absent. This will enable us not only to penetrate his biography, but also to judge his attitude as a dramatic artist with correctness.

He took to writing for the stage soon after his return from the Low Countries and his marriage, apparently with the object of gaining a livelihood. Nothing proves that he felt a real vocation for this branch of literature. But it was the readiest for a man of his breeding to engage in. His predecessors, Greene, Peele, Lodge, Nash, and Marlowe, had been scholars, more or less accomplished. They had created the profession of educated playwrights ; and the greatest of them, Marlowe, had determined the style of drama which we call Elizabethan. Shakespeare was content to follow in Marlowe's wake, and to render perfect what that ill-starred pioneer had left rough-hewn. Classical traditions, in spite of Sidney and the courtiers, were abandoned ; and the English people declared itself with unanimous and enthusiastic instinct for the romantic drama. When Jonson then joined the company of playwrights and actors—for it appears that, like most of his contemporaries, he acted on the stage—he found himself at first compelled to adopt the prevailing fashion. His years of apprenticeship to the dramatic craft were spent in furbishing up old plays, collaborating with comrades in the production of new ones, and studying his trade in the romantic school. From that epoch of his life nothing remains to us. But we know, from the still existing titles of some pieces, that he must have employed his pen in the concoction of sensational dramas calculated for the public taste. The Additions he furnished so late as 1601 to Kyd's Spanish Tragedy, which I should have liked to print among the specimens of his work, prove with what energy he could command the purest romantic style. Doubts have been cast upon his authorship of those striking scenes ; and yet the external evidence in favour of it is too strong to be resisted. Until the scenes in question can be assigned with any show of certainty to some named author of the time, Jonson, and only Jonson, claims them. And in tracing the evolution of his genius they have a capital importance, for they show that, when he deserted the romantic manner for his own style, which he did in 1598, he must have done this on deliberate choice.

Jonson worked in the way I have described for the theatrical manager and money-lender, Henslow, between 1593 and 1598. In the autumn of the latter year he had a duel with one of Henslow's actors, Gabriel Spencer. They fought in Hogsden Fields, and Jonson was so unlucky as to kill his antagonist. He was thrown into prison, and narrowly escaped hanging. Indeed, it is now proved by a document brought recently to light that he was tried and convicted of felony, that he pleaded guilty, claimed benefit of clergy, and was set at large with the letter T branded on his left thumb. The peril he then ran seems to have made a deep impression on his conscience ; for when he quitted Newgate he had changed his religion, having been converted to Catholicism by a priest. Three years later he recanted Popery, and rejoined the Church of England. On this occasion, in order to demonstrate his sincerity, he took the sacrament, and signalised his zeal by draining the communion cup of all the wine which it contained. The anecdote is from his own life ; and instead of being any evidence of a ribald disposition, we must take it as he meant it, to indicate a firm conviction. Anyhow he died faithful to Protestantism, and there is nothing to show that his changes of religion were influenced, as Dryden's may have been, by a sense of interest. Indeed, he suffered in 1603 for his Papistical opinions, just as his father under Mary had suffered for the Protestant cause, and his reconversion brought him no special advancement.

The duel with Gabriel Spencer caused a breach between Jonson and his employer, Henslow. This, which at the moment may have seemed to him a disaster, was the occasion of his first eminent success as playwright. Shakespeare, who belonged to the acting company which then divided London with Henslow's, accepted a comedy from Jonson's pen, and put it on the stage. The play was *Every Man in his Humour.* Here Jonson displayed his own peculiar manner for the first time. The prologue sounds a note of defiance to romantic playwrights, repeating the tone of Sidney's attack on them in his Defence of Poetry. Romance, adapted to the stage by Marlowe's predecessors, by Marlowe himself, and by Shakespeare, now in the morning of his glory, neglected classical rules of art. To time and space the romantic muse had proved herself indifferent. Upon the narrow room of a wooden theatre in the suburbs, with somewhat less than three hours for "the traffic of the stage," she represented the lives of heroes from their cradle to the grave, and the catastrophes of empires under the "drums and tramplings of three conquests." Romantic poets calmly ignored the unities of Aristotelian tradition. For them a story translated into action was the main point ; and the conditions of the English theatres, devoid of scenery, dependent upon vivid movement in the players for effect, and on keen imaginative sympathies in the audience for approval, assisted them to such a point that the magnificent artistic licences of *Pericles* and *A Winter's Tale* were rendered possible. Against all this Jonson, the Westminster scholar, the bluff rebellious personage who had killed his two men in single combat, and who felt pugnaciously inclined to challenge all the world, rebelled. He declared himself for unity of action, unity of time, unity of place, and unity of subject. He produced a masterpiece which preserved these decencies of art, and which borrowed something from the Latin classics. At the same time he took pains to prove that the follies of the town might be acutely seized and vividly presented in accordance with the stricter rules of drama, and that comedy might be made to serve a moral purpose by delineating foibles common to humanity. *Every Man in his Humour* was the highly original work which demonstrated his divergence from the style in vogue and the soundness of his method. It was to the credit of Shakespeare that he recognised its merit, had it acted, and took part himself in the performance.

This comedy had a great success. It started Jonson upon a cycle of plays, in which he strove to delineate the humours of society, or, in other words, to portray the peculiarities of character which make men and women laughable. Humour he conceived to be something dependent upon the physical constitution of the individual, which provokes a habit, constitutes a ruling foible, and diverts the action of its subject into courses which move mirth. In seizing these ruling follies by observation of the motley London crowd, he was eminently happy. His comedies form an inexhaustible Hogarthian picture-gallery of sixteenth-century oddities. But he was too profound a student of human nature to stop here. He knew the point at which eccentricity shades off into vice, and discerned the subtle links whereby crime is connected with moral weakness. Therefore, in the noblest of his plays, dominant passions tower above the undergrowth of humours. Lust, hunger for gold, jealousy, brutal egotism, vulgar ambition, control and sway the multiform kaleidoscope of minor aberrations brought before our notice in bewildering profusion. It was granted to him by nature in no small measure to preserve right relations between the criminal, the vicious, the passionate, and the merely foolish ; so that a steady study of his work is equal to a lesson in ethics. Each figment of his brain assumes its proper distance and perspective ; each is endowed with specific vitality.　As in a bas-relief, the larger persons of his art stand prominently forward, the lesser retreat into the background ; but all alike are firmly outlined, unmistakable in individuality. This robust power of characterisation and of maintaining the gradations of dramatic interest is Jonson's highest quality.　But it has a corresponding defect.　There is no atmosphere, nothing unexpected, nothing unforeseen, no overshadowing mystery of fate, no delicate revealing of complexities of character, in his stupendous craftsmanship. The romantic poets, whom he despised, created human beings more realistically natural in their mingled good and evil, than these vigorously conceived and Titanically projected creatures of his understanding.　Though we retire from his theatre, overwhelmed by the man's prodigious inventive and delineative force, we feel that we have been, after all, at a marionette show, where the puppets are moved by wires.

The satiric impulse was strong in Jonson.　He felt called upon to lash the errors and the vices of his age ; and he boasted that he took Horace for his model.　Yet he had neither the irony nor the urbanity of the Augustan poet.　His blows fell as hard upon the backs of people he chastised, as his translations from smooth Latin verse fall harsh upon our modern ears.   Three comedies, composed between 1598 and 1600—*Every Man out of his Humour, The Case is Altered,* and *Cynthia's Revels* —roused society against him.   Whole classes, like the courtiers, the play-goers, the actors, bad poets, and fashionable fribblers, felt themselves attacked. Being men of flesh and blood, some of them turned in the dust, and stung Jonson.   He was lampooned in verses and caricatured upon the stage.   To bear these reprisals calmly, though he had provoked them, was not in his nature.   And in 1601 he summoned all his strength to give the foes, whose wrath he had aroused, a thorough drubbing.   For this purpose he selected two assailants—Tom Dekker, with whom he had previously worked upon a romantic tragedy, and John Marston, who afterwards professed himself his pupil and ad- mirer.   They were to be nailed up, like wild-cats on a keeper's back-door, to warn the common fry of scribblers that Ben Jonson was Apollo's darling.   The outcome of this literary squabble was a rare and singular production of his pen, called *The Poetaster.*   The scene of the play is laid in Rome at the time of Augustus, but the main characters are persons of Jonson's day presented under thin disguises.   Much of its gall and venom has doubtless grown stale ; but enough of curious quaintness and fine invention remains to furnish forth quotations which may still be read with pleasure.   Instead of crushing his antagonists by this " comical satire," as he would have called it, *The Poetaster* only brought down double fury on its author's head. At this point, Jonson took a manly resolution, and one that confirms our respect for the essential goodness of his nature. He published a dialogue in verse setting forth his case, and apologising where he thought apology was due. In the course of this self-vindication, he acknowledged that the Comic Muse had not been favourable to his satiric bent of mind, and proclaimed his intention of courting her severer Tragic sister.

Sejanus, produced in 1603, two years after *The Poetaster*, was Jonson's next venture on the public stage. It was brought out by Shakespeare's company, Shakespeare acting in it, and Shakespeare contributing (if an old tradition be correct) some passages to the play. When Jonson gave this tragedy to the press, he carefully omitted the additions, and bade his readers take note that he had done so. But who had helped him, he did not say ; only remarking that he would not "defraud so happy a genius of his right by my loathed usurpation." *Sejanus* proved that Jonson's conception of tragedy differed no less from the romantic ideal than his conception of comedy. It is a laboured, carefully-sententious transcript from classical authorities, so composed as to preserve a semblance of unity in time and place and action, and furnished with choruses after the manner of Seneca. Probably the author fondly imagined that it approached nearer to the type of a "high and lofty" tragedy than the *Antony and Cleopatra* which Shakespeare, so genially, and yet apparently so carelessly, evolved from North's translation of Plutarch. Posterity thinks otherwise, and condemns *Sejanus* as one of Jonson's meritorious failures.

The accession of James I. to the English throne in 1604 opened a new era for our poet. James loved nothing better than splendid shows, and he prized nothing more than erudition. So learned a bard as Jonson was sure of his patronage. But when it was discovered that this scholar-poet held within the vast mines of his intellect an inexhaustible vein of fancy, specially adapted for Masque and Pageant, his fortune was assured. From the specimens of his art previously given to the world, no one could have predicted that Jonson had it in him to furnish forth motives and lyrics for those gorgeous court-toys, resembling our panto-mimes and ballets, which then had the name of Masque. Yet so it was. Every year, until his genius sank in dotage, Jonson wrote libretti of rarest quality and most curious variety, for the court and noble folk of England. To dwell upon them here in detail would be to transcend the limits of an essay which has to deal with the main current of a great dramatist's life-work. It must suffice to mention that the peculiar aptitudes he displayed in composing Masques and entertain-ments, brought him into favour with the royal family, and made him personally acquainted with the chief members of the aristocracy. He was appointed Laureate, with an annual stipend, and in due course with a butt of Canary wine. James wished to dub him knight ; but, unlike artists of the present age, he laughingly put by the honour. He frequented the houses of the great, and spent many months of each year on visits to their country-seats, complimenting them with poems, and receiving from them in return the honoraria of timely presents. Lord Pembroke, for example, sent him each year £20 to buy books with. In this commerce with royalty and nobility I find that Jonson always maintained the dignified attitude of a self-respecting man. He never condescended to flattery. When he praised, he chose the point on which his patron deserved commendation. He dared to tell a pedant king that his manner of reciting verses was atrocious. He told the Prince of Wales, before the Court, that his favourite architect was an arch-scoundrel. This excursion into the particulars of Jonson's connection with the Court was necessary, because it forms a special feature in his biography, and distinguishes him from every poet of his time.

Meanwhile, Jonson did not neglect the public stage. Strangely enough, we next find him collaborating with Chapman and his old adversary, Marston, in a comedy called *Eastward Ho!* Some allusions in this play were thought to reflect upon the Scots. So precarious was the existence of a playwright in those days, and so vigorous was the censorship, that these three poor fellows met together in jail, with the prospect of having their noses and ears cut off. Chapman and Marston had been sent to prison. Jonson, hearing of their mischance, joined them of his own free will. The circumstance has to be dwelt on, since it illustrates the generous and reckless nature of the man. All three were eventually liberated ; and Jonson gave a supper party on the occasion. No less personages than Camden and Selden took their share in it ; which proves, I think, that Jonson's peril had been considerable. His old mother was also there. She showed the company a paper of poison, which she had meant to mix with her son's drink, in the event of his being sentenced ; and "since she was no churl," it had been her purpose to quaff the goblet with him. Whether she truly so intended, or whether the supper inspired her with bravado, cannot now be estimated. But at this point of Jonson's domestic history the good woman disappears.

Between the years 1609 and 1615 Jonson put forth all his strength, and produced the best work of his lifetime. That decade saw the appearance in rapid succession of *Volpone, The Silent Woman, The Alchemist, Catiline,* and *Bartholomew Fair. Volpone* is a comedy, less of humours than of character and manners. With grimmest satire it exposes the master vice of cupidity, that accursed hunger after gold which debases human nature below the brutes, supersedes domestic affection, obliterates the sense of honour, and swallows up such powerful passions even as jealousy. The construction of the mighty plot is masterly ; the interest never flags ; the art of *Volpone* throughout is burning and intense. Yet we rise from its perusal with the feeling that wickedness so un-mitigated, cynicism so crude, characters so utterly abandoned to evil, are not human. True perhaps in detail, piece by piece, and personage by person-age, these component parts exceed the truth when brought thus into combination. *The Silent Woman* shifts the scene from satire to humour, from comedy to farce. While *Volpone* is written in blank verse of highly sustained quality, *The Silent Woman* is in prose. Dryden esteemed this play not only as the most perfect of Jonson's works, but also as the most admirably constructed specimen of modern dramatic art. Coleridge reckoned it the most entertaining of its author's comedies. That *The Silent Woman* observes the rules of classical propriety, that the unities are maintained without sacrifice of ease and probability, that the threads of its simple but varied intrigue are skilfully twined into one knot, which is cut at last by a single dis-covery no less ingenious than unexpected, forms perhaps the slightest merit of this masterpiece. From beginning to ending, it provokes mirth, and the mirth increases as the situation deepens. The characters, moreover, are portrayed with inimitable freshness and vivacity. None of them are so bad as to stir loathing ; some are so foolish, others so eccentric, as to affect us with a lively sense of the ridiculous. Jonson conceived the character of a perverse old man, who spites his nephew. Morose has this weakness, that he cannot endure noise. His life is spent in preserving himself from the least disturbance. Yet he thinks of marriage, as the best means of disinheriting Dauphine. The young man casts a bait to catch his uncle in his own wiles. He introduces a boy dressed up in woman's clothes into the neighbourhood, who pretends to be almost incapable of speech. So rare a prodigy attracts Morose's notice. He marries Epicœne; but when the ceremony is completed, she finds her voice, welcomes all her noisiest acquaintances to a wedding feast, and drives her unfortunate bridegroom to distraction. The slow degrees whereby Morose is reduced to grant his nephew a fair allowance and the reversion of the estate, and the final discovery of Epicœne's real sex, constitute the plot and denouement of the comedy. In *The Alchemist* we return from farce to the graver ground of satire; but the satire is not so caustic as in *Volpone.* Jonson has here chosen for his theme the gullibility of human nature. His alchemist is a vulgar sharper who, aided by confederates, works upon the avarice and vanity of dupes. Blinded by their own greed, the lawyer's clerk, the petty shopman, the county squireen, the sanctimonious Puritan, and the blustering city knight, fall into the meshes of his coarse-spun net. Imposture practising on folly is so universal a feature of human society that, although alchemy has ceased to delude the world, this largely-planned and powerfully-executed comedy remains an allegory of the deepest moral significance. *Bartholomew Fair* does not take the same high rank in art. Yet to my mind it is of Jonson's works the one which I could least

afford to spare. It is a pure farce of the broadest
and most genial humour, photographically true
to the London life which Jonson had observed
from boyhood. With strong Hogarthian brush he
dashed upon his canvas a motley crowd of the
knaves, fools, hawkers, sharpers, showmen, cooks,
bum-bailiffs, costermongers, silly women, designing
men, loose-livers, lovers, simpletons, onlookers,
cockneys, and country folk of all descriptions, who
were wont to jostle together when the Bartlemas
fair was held in Smithfield. From the midst of
this rabble emerges into clear prominence the
inimitable portrait of the Puritan, Rabbi Busy.
This I hope to detach from its surroundings, and
to present it to the readers of my selections.

Catiline, like *Sejanus,* is a Roman tragedy,
studied with minute care from the original texts
of Sallust and Cicero. In spite of long-winded
orations, tedious monologues, and dry choruses, it
has more sustained interest than *Sejanus;* and its
characterisation is masterly. The whole play is
stretched out with robust and Roman touches ;
and the colouring is sombre, in harmony with the
grim subject. The first act, which I purpose to
include in the specimens of Jonson's dramatic work,
can easily be separated from the rest. It presents
a vivid picture of the various passions which move
conspirators against social order, according to their
several characters and temperaments. At the
same time, a comparison of these scenes with the
opening of *Volpone* will enable students to understand how Jonson treated the tragic as different

from the comic style of metre and of diction. Like
Milton, he held that tragedy should abound in
weighty sentences ; and he clearly aimed at loftier
imagery and more laboured elocution than befitted
the comic Muse.

After 1614 Jonson's powers declined in vigour.
The Devil is an Ass, which was produced in 1616,
already shows some signs of failing inspiration.
It is based upon the old Italian fable of Belphegor,
and tends to prove that human craft and folly
can teach the imps of darkness something in their
own line.   The special foible here selected is that
mania for speculation which in another century
possessed France and England at the time of the
South Sea Bubble.   Dryden called the last comedies of Ben Jonson his "dotages ;" and this name
must be given to *The Staple of News* (1625), *The
New Inn* (1629), *The Magnetic Lady* (1632), and
The Tale of a Tub (1633). To bestow criticism
upon each of these pieces, in the narrow room
allowed me, would be superfluous.   Yet some
passing observations may be made. In *The Staple
of News* Jonson combined an Aristophanic allegory,
borrowed from the *Plutus*, with satire upon the
town's avidity for printed gossip. A trifle more of
inspiration might have made this play symbolic for
the future.   In certain daily papers of the
present day, we have our Staple of News, pretend-
ing deep and moral doctrine, but really pandering
 o morbid curiosity. *The Magnetic Lady* is only
noteworthy, because in this comedy Jonson closed
his cycle of the humours. He made his bow of

exit to the public he had so long served. *The Tale of a Tub* attempts in vain to recapture the rollicking enthusiasm of *Bartholomew Fair.* It is meant to be a screaming farce. But it fails, and falls flat. And now, for antiquarians, it is chiefly interesting, because the author strove to vent an old grudge against Inigo Jones in some of its interpolated scenes. The quarrels of artists are so despicable that I do not care to dwell upon this warfare between the author of *Volpone* and the builder of Whitehall. Both were to blame, in the course of a long companionship of art together. Jones dealt Jonson cruel blows, when he thought the old lion was asleep upon his death-bed. Jonson roused himself to fury, parrying his foeman's thrust. But for us, the squabble is ignoble. We can pass it by. Of Jones remains the fragment of Whitehall ; of Jonson the immortal row of five comedies and one good tragedy. *The New Inn* deserves a separate commentary. Jonson wrote it when his health had failed, and his particular vein of fancy was exhausted. He strove to give the public something in the kind they cared for. It was meant to be a romantic comedy ; and the plot was so superfluously imaginative as to exceed the romantic measure. The habits of a lifetime were not, however, easily cast off. Taking his improbable, deliriously accidental plot to work upon, he delved deep lines for all the characters, introduced horse-play of out-worn humours, and upon this slender basis raised a superstructure of solid poetry. It is not difficult to excavate that vein of poetry from the unsuccessful play; and those who have taken the pains to do so, will perceive that, even to the last, the fire of genius burned in Jonson's brain. Yet the comedy was justly damned, on account of its absurd fable, frigid jokes, and ponderous declamatory passages. Indignation at this reception of his play called forth that haughty "Ode to Himself" which will be read among his lyrics.

Returning to the facts of Jonson's biography, it is worth notice that in 1618 he took a walking journey into Scotland, where he spent several weeks. Part of this time was passed at Hawthornden, with the poet William Drummond, to whose notes of the conversations they held on this occasion we owe one of our best sources of information regarding his life and opinions. In England he visited his noble friends and patrons in the country during part of every summer. But it was in the purlieus of Cheapside and Fleet Street that his burly figure might most frequently be seen, rolling from the Mermaid to the Dog, or Sun, or Triple Tun. Like his great namesake, Samuel Johnson, he felt himself nowhere so much at home as on the pavement of London, or in the sanded parlours of its taverns. Not that we have any right to think of Jonson as a sot or toper. It is true that he indulged too much in drink. The Laureate's famous butt of sherry dates from Ben's known partiality for sack. Many of the tales he told against himself to Drummond owe their point to a certain weakness for the bottle in his nature.

We learn, for instance, how one nobleman "drank him drowsy," and how Sir Walter Raleigh's son, with whom he went as governor to Paris, "caused him to be drunken and dead drunk," and drove him in a cart all round the town in that state. Yet this addiction to wine must not blind us to the fact that in the taverns he frequented were gathered round him the most famous wits of England. Beaumont's lines upon the Mermaid, and Fuller's description of the "wit-combats" between Jonson and Shakespeare, the one moving like a stately galleon under press of sail, the other shifting like a lighter and more nimble craft, have bequeathed lively pictures of the intellectual atmosphere of those Bohemian meetings. Herrick, writing with rapture of that society, describes the "lyric feasts"—

> " Where we such clusters had
> As made us nobly wild, not mad ;
> And yet each verse of thine
> Out-did the frolic wine."

Beaumont, meditating in absence on the vivid life of those convivial meetings, exclaims :

> " What things have we seen
> Done at the Mermaid ! heard words that have been
> So nimble and so full of subtle flame
> As if that every one from whom they came
> Had meant to put his whole wit in a jest,
> And had resolved to live a fool the rest
> Of his dull life."

After making experience of many such places of resort, Jonson finally settled down in the Old Devil Tavern at Temple Bar. In this house a club-room, called the Apollo, was reserved for his set. He wrote laws in terse Latin to regulate the conduct of its members ; and here, among the most distinguished men of intellect and fashion whom the town could show, it often happened that some youth of promise came forward, requesting to be " Sealed of the Tribe of Ben." Such candidates for his favour and intimacy, when they were approved, Jonson called his sons. And not a few of the best writers of the day felt honoured by this designation. ·

Though powerfully built, Jonson had never been a wholly healthy man. He suffered from scorbutic affections, inherited probably from his ancestors, and was subject to fits of abstraction bordering upon melancholy. Drummond significantly records of him that he was " oppressed with phantasy, which hath ever mastered his reason ; a general disease in many poets." Now that years increased, and sedentary habits grew upon him, these physical disabilities became more irksome. About 1626 he was stricken with paralysis. Between this date and 1637, when he died, his state of health gradually weakened. Dropsy was added to the palsy. His huge overgrown body, which he humorously compared to the Tun of Heidelberg, could scarcely be moved from the apartment where he dwelt, and at last he took to his bed. On the death of his royal master James, the court seemed for a while to have forgotten him, and the city of London, whom he served in the capacity of chronologer, withdrew their pension. Destitution, as well as sickness, threatened his declining age. Yet Jonson had too lastingly impressed the finer spirits of that epoch by the manliness of his character, the vastness of his learning, and the rarity of his genius to be long neglected. Noble friends, among whom the Duke of Newcastle deserves to be commemorated, bestowed pains on his comfort. Charles I. increased his Laureate's salary, and forced the city to renew their annual payments. After 1635 he wrote but little, unless we refer the prose notes called *Discoveries* to that period. But there is no reason to believe that his end, though irksome through manifold diseases, was either forlorn or unhappy. His death was greeted with a chorus of elegiac and panegyrical verses, poured forth by the best poets of the moment ; and he found an honourable resting place in Poets' Corner of Westminster Abbey. Money was collected to defray the expenses of a solemn monument. The disorders of the Great Rebellion interrupted this scheme ; and the marble tablet inscribed with the famous words, " O Rare Ben Jonson ! " is due to the piety of a friend, Sir John Young, of Great Milton, Oxfordshire.

When we review Ben Jonson's position among the poets of his age, the first thing which strikes us is the length of his career as a man of letters. He conquered fame in 1598, while Queen Elizabeth was yet alive, and Shakespeare had but recently begun to reap his laurels. He lived through the reign of James I., contributing more than any other poet to form the literary tone of that king's period. He was still a power in the world of learning and fine letters in the year when John Hampden refused to pay King Charles's ship-money. From his contemporaries he stood forth with singular distinctness. Of Shakespeare we know what is tantamount to nothing. Of Beaumont, of Fletcher, of Chapman, of Massinger, of Ford, of Webster, how very little can we say we know! But Jonson manifested his individuality in so many ways that it is easy to form a tolerably accurate conception of the man. Unlike the most illustrious of his brother playwrights, he was one of the ripest scholars of an age which produced great students ; in fact, he divides with Milton the honour of being the most learned among English poets. This distinction gave him a certain pre-eminence in literary circles, of which he was perhaps too conscious. He formed a high uncompromising ideal of the poet's vocation, felt himself bound to assert its dignity in his works, and from the first attempted to strike out a way of art different from that of his contemporaries. The independence which marked his personal character and his theory of poetry, expressed itself at times in arrogance and satire ; but the poems addressed to individuals, who might have been accounted rivals, exonerate him from the charge of envy and malignity. That he rated his own powers and achievements highly, cannot be denied ; yet he was not illiberal of praise to others. In his dealings with great folk, he showed a manly frankness, proclaiming his belief that " poets were rarer births than kings," and boasting with sincerity that he esteemed no man for the name of a lord. " Of all styles he loved most to be named honest," and honesty seems to have formed the basis of his character.

It is not easy to determine Jonson's place among the poets of his age, partly because of his stubborn opposition to their leading impulses, and partly because we suspect him to have followed a deliberately adopted theory rather than his natural bent of genius. If he really penned the Additions to Jeronymo, who was more capable of commanding the romantic drama than Ben Jonson? To say that he was not the author of those thrilling scenes, costs nothing ; but it contradicts the only direct evidence we have upon the subject. We must, therefore, accept them, in spite of their divergence from his well-known style, as specimens of what he could achieve in the romantic manner. Yet from the moment when *Every Man in His Humour* first saw the light in 1598, until 1633, when the last of Jonson's " dotages " was coldly received by court and public, he sustained a wholly different dramatic style. The specific marks of this style were sound sense rather than imagination, robust logic instead of fancy, a vigorous yet somewhat pedestrian march of blank verse, prose eminent for terse pregnancy and pith—much to impress us with the sense of power and sterling wisdom, little to fascinate us by vague unexpected charm or subtle beauty. Jonson's plays have been compared to substantial edifices from which the scaffolding has not been taken down. There is something cumbrous in their solidity, unfinished in their decorative details. We detect in them the hand of a craftsman working by rule, not following the suasion of instinct. Moreover, they are overweighted with ponderous erudition. It is true that Jonson gambols beneath loads of learning which would crush another playwright's back. Nothing in the most recondite classical and medieval sources comes amiss to him. He carries libraries as lightly as an elephant his howdar. But while we watch his "gigantic sport," and wonder, we feel that contemporary critics were not wrong in blaming him for indiscriminate use of antique texts, and in professing a distaste for his laboured translations.

He was not merely a comic and tragic dramatist. Among his papers at his death was found a half-completed pastoral. This fragment, entitled *The Sad Shepherd*, proves that he could blow the rustic pipe ; but he breathed upon it with the lungs of a cultured Polyphemus. How different is his touch to the far laxer yet more moving manner of Fletcher ! The specimens of his lyrics and occasional verses which I have selected, show that in these departments of poetry he attained to rare excellence. Yet they miss the fragrance of Beaumont's or of Fletcher's muse, the intensity of Webster's, the magic of Shakespeare's ; and the very best of them, " Drink to me only with thine eyes," is a supremely successful adaptation of fragments chosen for free translation from the prose of Philostratus.

Jonson again was not only a poet. He was also a great critic, a writer of majestic prose, and a philosophical observer of human nature. The lofty Dedication of *Volpone* to the Sister Universities and the *Discoveries*, in which he digested some of his ripest thoughts on men and art and statecraft, will repay persual by all who care to study the development of English style in prose. They show that the first half of the seventeenth century, so rich in works of creative genius, was not deficient in reflection upon the principles of life and art. Unfortunately, the larger bulk of Jonson's critical essays perished in a fire which destroyed his library at some uncertain date between 1619 and 1625.

If I were bound to offer in one sentence a definition of Ben Jonson's genius, I should be inclined to call him a poet of the understanding and of judgment, in whom vast erudition was combined with rarely acute faculties for studying and reproducing the distinctive marks of personal character, and who had overlaid a lively imaginative faculty with deliberately conceived ideals of the literary art. Fire of the imagination and fancy smouldered in the man without emerging into luminosity. He struggled under the weight of his encumbered memory ; and haughtily submitted to the fetters of a self-prescribed rule. Yet it was this central heat of a naturally poetic temperament which gave warmth and glow to his best work, even when we recognise it to be clumsy, and feel bound to acknowledge that it bears the aspect rather of constructive ability than of genial inspiration.

JOHN ADDINGTON SYMONDS.

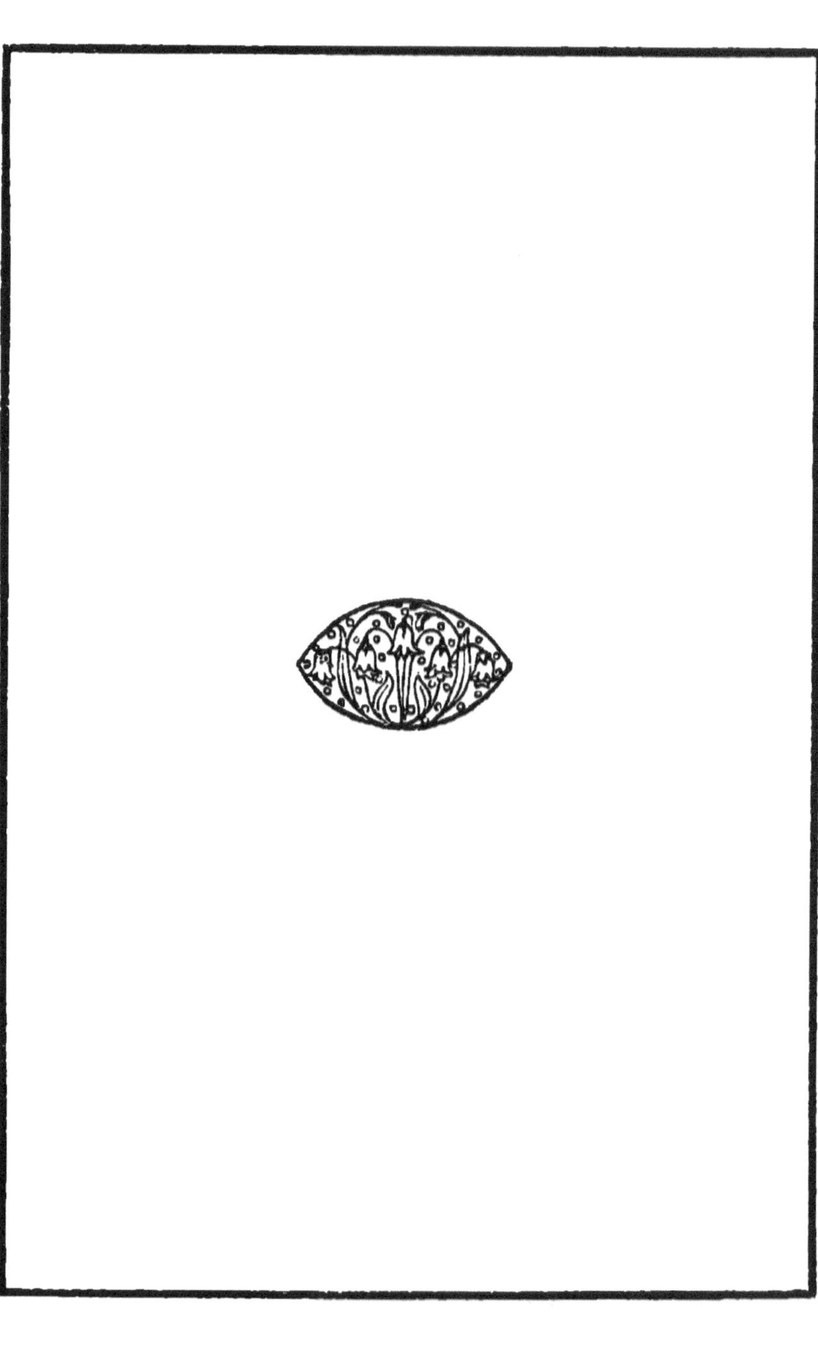

Epicœne; or, the Silent Woman.

DRAMATIS PERSONÆ.

Morose, *a gentleman that loves no noise.*
Sir Dauphine Eugenie, *a Knight, his Nephew.*
Ned Clerimont, *a Gentleman, his Friend.*
Truewit, *another Friend.*
Sir John Daw, *a Knight.*
Sir Amorous La-Foole, *a Knight also.*
Thomas Otter, *a Land and Sea Captain.*
Cutbeard, *a Barber.*
Mute, *one of* Morose's *Servants.*
Parson.

Page *to* Clerimont.

Epicœne, *supposed the* Silent Woman.
Lady Haughty,   } *Ladies*
Lady Centaure,   } *Collegi-*
Mistress Dol. Mavis, } *ates.*
Mistress Otter, *the Captain's Wife.*   } *Pre-*
Mistress Trusty, Lady Haughty's *Woman.* } *tenders*

Pages, Servants, etc.

Scene—LONDON.

EPICŒNE; OR, THE SILENT WOMAN.

ACT I.

Scene I.—*A Room in* Clerimont's *House.*

Enter Clerimont, *making himself ready, followed by his* Page.

Cler. Have you got the song yet perfect, I gave you, boy?

Page. Yes, sir.

Cler. Let me hear it.

Page. You shall, sir; but i'faith let nobody else.

Cler. Why, I pray?

Page. It will get you the dangerous name of a poet in town, sir; besides me a perfect deal of ill-will at the mansion you wot of, whose lady is the argument of it; where now I am the welcomest thing under a man that comes there.

Cler. I think; and above a man too, if the truth were rack'd out of you.

Page. No, faith, I'll confess before, sir. The gentlewomen play with me, and throw me on the bed, and carry me in to my lady: and she kisses me with her oil'd face, and puts a peruke on my head; and asks me an I will wear her gown? and I say no: and then she hits me a blow o' the ear, and calls me Innocent! and lets me go.

Cler. No marvel if the door be kept shut against your master, when the entrance is so easy to you—— well, sir, you shall go there no more, lest I be fain to seek your voice in my lady's rushes, a fortnight hence. Sing, sir.   [Page *sings.*

Still to be neat, still to be drest—

Enter TRUEWIT.

True. Why, here's the man that can melt away his time and never feels it! What between his mistress abroad and his ingle at home, high fare, soft lodging, fine clothes, and his fiddle; he thinks the hours have no wings, or the day no post-horse. Well, sir gallant, were you struck with the plague this minute, or condemn'd to any capital punishment to-morrow, you would begin then to think, and value every article of your time, esteem it at the true rate, and give all for it.

Cler. Why, what should a man do?

True. Why, nothing; or that which, when 'tis done, is as idle. Hearken after the next horse-race, or hunting-match, lay wagers, praise Puppy, or Peppercorn, White-foot, Franklin; swear upon Whitemane's party; speak aloud, that my lords may hear you; visit my ladies at night, and be able to give them the character of every bowler or better on the green. These be the things wherein your fashionable men exercise themselves, and I for company.

Cler. Nay, if I have thy authority, I'll not leave yet. Come, the other are considerations, when we come to have gray heads and weak hams, moist eyes and shrunk members.   We'll think on 'em then ; then we'll pray and fast.

True. Ay, and destine only that time of age to goodness, which our want of ability will not let us employ in evil !

Cler. Why, then 'tis time enough.

True. Yes ; as if a man should sleep all the term, and think to effect his business the last day.   O, Clerimont, this time, because it is an incorporeal thing, and not subject to sense, we mock ourselves the fineliest out of it, with vanity and misery indeed ! not seeking an end of wretchedness, but only changing the matter still.

Cler. Nay, thou'lt not leave now——

True. See but our common disease ! with what justice can we complain, that great men will not look upon us, nor be at leisure to give our affairs such dispatch as we expect, when we will never do it to ourselves ? nor hear, nor regard ourselves ?

Cler. Foh ! thou hast read Plutarch's morals, now, or some such tedious fellow; and it shews so vilely with thee ! 'fore God, 'twill spoil thy wit utterly.   Talk to me of pins, and feathers, and ladies, and rushes, and such things : and leave this Stoicity alone, till thou mak'st sermons.

True. Well, sir ; if it will not take, I have learn'd to lose as little of my kindness as I can ; I'll do good to no man against his will, certainly.   When were you at the college ?

Cler. What college ?

True. As if you knew not !

Cler. No, faith, I came but from court yesterday.

True. Why, is it not arrived there yet, the news ?   A new foundation, sir, here in the town, of ladies, that call themselves the collegiates, an order between courtiers and country-madams, that live from their husbands; and give entertainment to all the wits, and braveries of the time, as they call them: cry down, or up, what they like or dislike in a brain or a fashion, with most masculine, or rather hermaphroditical authority; and every day gain to their college some new probationer.

Cler. Who is the president?

True. The grave and youthful matron, the lady Haughty.

Cler. A pox of her autumnal face, her pieced beauty! there's no man can be admitted till she be ready, now-a-days, till she has painted, and perfumed, and wash'd, and scour'd, but the boy, here; and him she wipes her oil'd lips upon, like a sponge. I have made a song (I pray thee hear it) on the subject.   [*Page sings.*

> Still to be neat, still to be drest,
> As you were going to a feast;
> Still to be powder'd, still perfum'd:
> Lady, it is to be presumed,
> Though art's hid causes are not found,
> All is not sweet, all is not sound.
>
> Give me a look, give me a face,
> That makes simplicity a grace;
> Robes loosely flowing, hair as free:
> Such sweet neglect more taketh me,
> Than all the adulteries of art;
> They strike mine eyes, but not my heart.

True. And I am clearly on the other side: I love a good dressing before any beauty o' the world. O, a woman is then like a delicate garden; nor is there one kind of it; she may vary every hour; take often counsel of her glass, and choose the best. If she have good ears, shew them; good hair, lay it out; good legs, wear short clothes; a good hand, discover it often; practice any art to mend breath, cleanse teeth, repair eye-brows; paint, and profess it.

Cler. How! publicly?

True. The doing of it, not the manner: that must be private. Many things that seem foul in the doing, do please done. A lady should, indeed, study her face, when we thinks she sleeps; nor, when the doors are shut, should men be enquiring; all is sacred within, then. Is it for us to see their perukes put on, their false teeth, their complexion, their eye-brows, their nails? You see gilders will not work, but inclosed. They must not discover how little serves, with the help of art, to adorn a great deal. How long did the canvas hang afore Aldgate? Were the people suffered to see the city's Love and Charity, while they were rude stone, before they were painted and burnish'd? No; no more should servants approach their mistresses, but when they are complete and finish'd.

Cler. Well said, my Truewit.

True. And a wise lady will keep a guard always upon the place, that she may do things securely. I once followed a rude fellow into a chamber, where the poor madam, for haste, and troubled, snatch'd at her peruke to cover her baldness; and put it on the wrong way.

Cler. O prodigy!

True. And the unconscionable knave held her in compliment an hour with that reverst face, when I still look'd when she should talk from the t'other side.

Cler. Why, thou shouldst have relieved her.

True. No, faith, I let her alone, as we'll let this argument, if you please, and pass to another. When saw you Dauphine Eugenie?

Cler. Not these three days. Shall we go to him this morning? he is very melancholy, I hear.

True. Sick of the uncle, is he ?   I met that stiff piece of formality, his uncle, yesterday, with a huge turban of night-caps on his head, buckled over his ears.

Cler. O, that's his custom when he walks abroad. He can endure no noise, man.

True. So I have heard.   But is the disease so ridiculous in him as it is made ?   They say he has been upon divers treaties with the fish-wives and orange-women ; and articles propounded between them : marry, the chimney-sweepers will not be drawn in.

Cler. No, nor the broom-men : they stand out stiffly. He cannot endure a costard-monger, he swoons if he hear one.

True. Methinks a smith should be ominous.

Cler. Or any hammer-man.   A brasier is not suffer'd to dwell in the parish, nor an armourer.   He would have hang'd a pewterer's prentice once upon a Shrove-tuesday's riot, for being of that trade, when the rest were quit.

True. A trumpet should fright him terribly, or the hautboys.

Cler. Out of his senses.   The waights of the city have a pension of him not to come near that ward.   This youth practised on him one night like the bell-man ; and never left till he had brought him down to the door with a long sword ; and there left him flourishing with the air.

Page. Why, sir, he hath chosen a street to lie in so narrow at both ends, that it will receive no coaches, nor carts, nor any of these common noises : and therefore we that love him, devise to bring him in such as we may, now and then, for his exercise, to breathe him. He would grow resty else in his ease : his virtue would rust without action.   I entreated a bearward, one day, to come down with the dogs of some four parishes that

way, and I thank him he did ; and cried his games
under master Morose's window : till he was sent crying
away, with his head made a most bleeding spectacle to
the multitude. And, another time, a fencer marching
to his prize, had his drum most tragically run through,
for taking that street in his way at my request.

True. A good wag ! How does he for the bells ?

Cler. O, in the Queen's time, he was wont to go out
of town every Saturday at ten o'clock, or on holy day
eves. But now, by reason of the sickness, the perpetuity
of ringing has made him devise a room, with double
walls and treble ceilings ; the windows close shut and
caulk'd : and there he lives by candle-light. He turn'd
away a man, last week, for having a pair of new shoes
that creak'd. And this fellow waits on him now in
tennis-court socks, or slippers soled with wool : and they
talk each to other in a trunk. See, who comes here !

Enter Sir DAUPHINE EUGENIE.

Daup. How now ! what ail you, sirs ? dumb ?

True. Struck into stone, almost, I am here, with
tales o' thine uncle. There was never such a prodigy
heard of.

Daup. I would you would once lose this subject,
my masters, for my sake. They are such as you are,
that have brought me into that predicament I am with
him.

True. How is that ?

Daup. Marry, that he will disinherit me ; no more.
He thinks, I and my company are authors of all the
ridiculous Acts and Monuments are told of him.

True. 'Slid, I would be the author of more to vex him;
that purpose deserves it ; it gives thee law of plaguing
him. I'll tell thee what I would do. I would make a
false almanack, get it printed ; and then have him

drawn out on a coronation day to the Tower-wharf, and kill him with the noise of the ordnance. Disinherit thee ! he cannot, man. Art not thou next of blood, and his sister's son ?

Daup. Ay, but he will thrust me out of it, he vows, and marry.

True. How ! that's a more portent. Can he endure no noise, and will venture on a wife ?

Cler. Yes: why, thou art a stranger, it seems, to his best trick, yet. He has employed a fellow this half-year all over England to hearken him out a dumb woman ; be she of any form, or any quality, so she be able to bear children : her silence is dowry enough, he says.

True. But I trust to God he has found none.

Cler. No ; but he has heard of one that's lodged in the next street to him, who is exceedingly soft-spoken ; thrifty of her speech ; that spends but six words a day. And her he's about now, and shall have her.

True. Is't possible ! who is his agent in the business ?

Cler. Marry, a barber, one Cutbeard ; an honest fellow, one that tells Dauphine all here.

True. Why you oppress me with wonder : a woman, and a barber, and love no noise !

Cler. Yes, faith. The fellow trims him silently, and has not the knack with his sheers or his fingers : and that continence in a barber he thinks so eminent a virtue, as it has made him chief of his counsel.

True. Is the barber to be seen, or the wench ?

Cler. Yes, that they are.

True. I prithee, Dauphine, let's go thither.

Daup. I have some business now : I cannot, i' faith.

True. You shall have no business shall make you neglect this, sir : we'll make her talk, believe it ; or, if she will not, we can give out at least so much as shall interrupt the treaty ; we will break it. Thou art bound in conscience, when he suspects thee without cause, to torment him.

Daup. Not I, by any means. I'll give no suffrage to't. He shall never have that plea against me, that I opposed the least phant'sy of his. Let it lie upon my stars to be guilty, I'll be innocent.

True. Yes, and be poor, and beg; do, innocent: when some groom of his has got him an heir, or this barber, if he himself cannot. *Innocent!*—I prithee, Ned, where lies she? let him be innocent still.

Cler. Why, right over against the barber's; in the house where sir John Daw lies.

True. You do not mean to confound me!

Cler. Why?

True. Does he that would marry her know so much?

Cler. I cannot tell.

True. 'Twere enough of imputation to her with him.

Cler. Why?

True. The only talking sir in the town! Jack Daw! and he teach her not to speak!—God be wi' you. I have some business, too.

Cler. Will you not go thither, then?

True. Not with the danger to meet Daw, for mine ears.

Cler. Why, I thought you two had been upon very good terms.

True. Yes, of keeping distance.

Cler. They say, he is a very good scholar.

True. Ay, and he says it first. A pox on him, a fellow that pretends only to learning, buys titles, and nothing else of books in him!

Cler. The world reports him to be very learned.

True. I am sorry the world should so conspire to belie him.

Cler. Good faith, I have heard very good things come from him.

True. You may ; there's none so desperately ignorant to deny that : would they were his own ! God be wi' you, gentlemen.   [*Exit hastily.*

Cler. This is very abrupt !

Daup. Come, you are a strange, open man, to tell everything thus.

Cler. Why, believe it, Dauphine, Truewit's a very honest fellow.

Daup. I think no other : but this frank nature of his is not for secrets.

Cler. Nay, then, you are mistaken. Dauphine : I know where he has been well trusted, and discharged the trust very truly, and heartily.

Daup. I contend not, Ned ;. but with the fewer a business is carried, it is ever the safer. Now we are alone, if you'll go thither, I am for you.

Cler. When were you there ?

Daup. Last night : and such a Decameron of sport fallen out ! Boccace never thought of the like. Daw does nothing but court her ; and the wrong way. He would lie with her, and praises her modesty ; desires that she would talk and be free, and commends her silence in verses ; which he reads, and swears are the best that ever man made. Then rails at his fortunes, stamps, and mutines, why he is not made a counsellor, and call'd to affairs of state.

Cler. I prithee let's go. I would fain partake this.— Some water, boy.   [*Exit* Page.

Daup. We are invited to dinner together, he and I, by one that came thither to him, sir La-Foole.

Cler. O, that's a precious mannikin !

Daup. Do you know him ?

Cler. Ay, and he will know you too, if e'er he saw you but once, though you should meet him at church in the midst of prayers. He is one of the braveries,

though he be none of the wits. He will salute a judge
upon the bench, and a bishop in the pulpit, a lawyer
when he is pleading at the bar, and a lady when she is
dancing in a masque, and put her out. He does give
plays, and suppers, and invites his guests to them,
aloud, out of his window, as they ride by in coaches.
He has a lodging in the Strand for the purpose : or to
watch when ladies are gone to the china-houses, or the
Exchange, that he may meet them by chance, and give
them presents, some two or three hundred pounds'
worth of toys, to be laugh'd at. He is never without a
spare banquet, or sweet-meats in his chamber, for their
women to alight at, and come up to for a bait.

Daup. Excellent ! he was a fine youth last night ; but
now he is much finer ! what is his Christian name ? I
have forgot.

Re-enter Page.

Cler. Sir Amorous La-Foole.

Page. The gentleman is here below that owns that
name.

Cler. 'Heart, he's come to invite me to dinner, I hold
my life.

Daup. Like enough : prithee, let's have him up.

Cler. Boy, marshal him.

Page. With a truncheon, sir ?

Cler. Away, I beseech you. [*Exit* Page.]—I'll make
him tell us his pedigree now ; and what meat he has to
dinner ; and who are his guests ; and the whole course
of his fortunes ; with a breath.

Enter Sir AMOROUS LA-FOOLE.

La-F. 'Save, dear sir Dauphine ! honoured master
Clerimont !

Cler. Sir Amorous! you have very much honested my lodging with your presence.

La-F. Good faith, it is a fine lodging: almost as delicate a lodging as mine.

Cler. Not so, sir.

La-F. Excuse me, sir, if it were in the Strand, I assure you. I am come, master Clerimont, to entreat you to wait upon two or three ladies, to dinner, to-day.

Cler. How, sir! wait upon them? did you ever see me carry dishes?

La-F. No, sir, dispense with me; I meant, to bear them company.

Cler. O, that I will, sir: the doubtfulness of your phrase, believe it, sir, would breed you a quarrel once an hour, with the terrible boys, if you should but keep them fellowship a day.

La-F. It should be extremely against my will, sir, if I contested with any man.

Cler. I believe it, sir. Where hold you your feast?

La-F. At Tom Otter's, sir.

Daup. Tom Otter! what's he?

La-F. Captain Otter, sir; he is a kind of gamester, but he has had command both by sea and by land.

Daup. O, then he is *animal amphibium?*

La-F. Ay, sir: his wife was the rich china-woman, that the courtiers visited so often; that gave the rare entertainment. She commands all at home.

Cler. Then she is captain Otter.

La-F. You say very well, sir; she is my kinswoman, a La-Foole by the mother-side, and will invite any great ladies for my sake.

Daup. Not of the La-Fooles of Essex?

La-F. No, sir, the La-Fooles of London.

Cler. Now, he's in.   [*Aside.*

La-F. They all come out of our house, the La-Fooles

of the north, the La-Fooles of the west, the La-Fooles of the east and south—we are as ancient a family as any is in Europe—but I myself am descended lineally of the French La-Fooles—and, we do bear for our coat yellow, or *or*, checker'd *azure*, and *gules*, and some three or four colours more, which is a very noted coat, and has, sometimes, been solemnly worn by divers nobility of our house—but let that go, antiquity is not respected now.— I had a brace of fat does sent me, gentlemen, and half-a-dozen of pheasants, a dozen or two of godwits, and some other fowl, which I would have eaten, while they are good, and in good company :—there will be a great lady or two, my lady Haughty, my lady Centaure, mistress Dol Mavis—and they come o' purpose to see the silent gentlewoman, mistress Epicœne, that honest sir John Daw has promised to bring thither—and then, mistress Trusty, my lady's woman, will be there too, and this honourable knight, sir Dauphine, with yourself, master Clerimont—and we'll be very merry, and have fiddlers, and dance.—I have been a mad wag in my time, and have spent some crowns since I was a page in court, to my lord Lofty, and after, my lady's gentleman-usher, who got me knighted in Ireland, since it pleased my elder brother to die.—I had as fair a gold jerkin on that day, as any worn in the island voyage, or at Cadiz, none dispraised ; and I came over in it hither, show'd myself to my friends in court, and after went down to my tenants in the country, and surveyed my lands, let new leases, took their money, spent it in the eye o' the land here, upon ladies :—and now I can take up at my pleasure.

Daup. Can you take up ladies, sir ?

Cler. O, let him breathe, he has not recover'd.

Daup. Would I were your half in that commodity !

La-F. No, sir, excuse me : I meant money, which

can take up any thing. I have another guest or two, to invite, and say as much to, gentlemen. I'll take my leave abruptly, in hope you will not fail——Your servant.   [*Exit.*

Daup. We will not fail you, sir precious La-Foole ; but she shall, that your ladies come to see, if I have credit afore sir Daw.

Cler. Did you ever hear such a wind-sucker, as this ?

Daup. Or such a rook as the other, that will betray his mistress to be seen ! Come, 'tis time we prevented it.

Cler. Go.   [*Exeunt.*

ACT II.

SCENE I.—*A Room in* MOROSE'S *House.*

Enter MOROSE, *with a tube in his hand, followed by* MUTE.

Mor. Cannot I, yet, find out a more compendious method, than by this trunk, to save my servants the labour of speech, and mine ears the discords of sounds ? Let me see : all discourses but my own afflict me ; they seem harsh, impertinent, and irksome. Is it not possible, that thou shouldst answer me by signs, and I apprehend thee, fellow ? Speak not, though I question you. You have taken the ring off from the street door, as I bade you ? answer me not by speech, but by silence ; unless it be otherwise [MUTE *makes a leg.*]—very good. And you have fastened on a thick quilt, or flock-bed, on the outside of the door ; that if they knock with their daggers, or with brick-bats, they can make no noise ?— But with your leg, your answer, unless it be otherwise [*makes a leg*].—Very good. This is not only fit modesty in a servant, but good state and discretion in a master. And you have been with Cutbeard the barber, to have

him come to me ? [*makes a leg.*]—Good.   And, he will
come presently ?   Answer me not but with your leg,
unless it be otherwise, shake your head, or shrug [*makes
a leg*].   So !   Your Italian and Spaniard are wise in
these : and it is a frugal and comely gravity.   How long
will it be ere Cutbeard come ?   Stay ; if an hour, hold
up your whole hand ; if half an hour, two fingers ; if a
quarter, one ; [*holds up a finger bent.*]—Good : half a
quarter ? tis well.   And have you given him a key, to
come in without knocking ? [*makes a leg.*]—good.   And,
is the lock oil'd, and the hinges, to-day ? [*makes a leg.*]
—good.   And the quilting of the stairs no where worn
out and bare ? [*makes a leg.*]—Very good.   I see, by
much doctrine, and impulsion, it may be effected ; stand
by.   The Turk, in this divine discipline, is admirable,
exceeding all the potentates of the earth ; still waited
on by mutes ; and all his commands so executed ; yea,
even in the war, as I have heard, and in his marches,
most of his charges and directions given by signs, and
with silence : an exquisite art ! and I am heartily
ashamed, and angry oftentimes, that the princes of
Christendom should suffer a barbarian to transcend them
in so high a point of felicity.   I will practise it hereafter.   [*A horn winded within.*]—How now ? oh ! oh !
what villain, what prodigy of mankind is that ? look.
[*Exit* MUTE.]—[*Horn again.*]—Oh ? cut his throat, cut
his throat ! what murderer, hell-hound, devil can this
be ?

Re-enter MUTE.

Mute. It is a post from the court——
Mor. Out, rogue ! and must thou blow thy horn too ?
Mute. Alas, it is a post from the court, sir, that says,
he must speak with you, pain of death——
Mor. Pain of thy life, be silent !

...2...

Enter TRUEWIT *with a post-horn, and a halter in his hand.*

True. By your leave, sir ;—I am a stranger here :—Is your name master Morose ? is your name master Morose ? Fishes ! Pythagoreans all ! This is strange. What say you, sir? nothing ! Has Harpocrates been here with his club, among you? Well, sir, I will believe you to be the man at this time : I will venture upon you, sir. Your friends at court commend them to you, sir——

Mor. O men ! O manners ! was there ever such an impudence ?

True. And are extremely solicitous for you, sir.

Mor. Whose knave are you ?

True. Mine own knave, and your compeer, sir.

Mor. Fetch me my sword——

True. You shall taste the one half of my dagger, if you do, groom ; and you the other, if you stir, sir : Be patient, I charge you, in the king's name, and hear me without insurrection. They say, you are to marry ; to marry ; do you mark, sir ?

Mor. How then, rude companion !

True. Marry, your friends do wonder, sir, the Thames being so near, wherein you may drown, so handsomely ; or London Bridge, at a low fall, with a fine leap, to hurry you down the stream ; or, such a delicate steeple in the town, as Bow, to vault from ; or, a braver height, as Paul's : Or, if you affected to do it nearer home, and a shorter way, an excellent garret-window into the street ; or, a beam in the said garret, with this halter [*shows him the halter*]—which they have sent, and desire that you would sooner commit your grave head to this knot, than to the wedlock noose ; or, take a little sublimate, and go out of the world like a rat ; or a fly, as one said, with a straw in your arse : any way, rather than follow this goblin Matrimony. Alas, sir, do you ever think to find a chaste wife in these times? now, when there are so many masques, plays, Puritan preachings, mad folks, and other strange sights to be seen daily, private and public? If you had lived in king Etheldred's time, sir, or Edward the Confessor, you might, perhaps, have found one in some cold country hamlet, then, a dull frosty wench, would have been contented with one man : now, they will as soon be pleased with one leg, or one eye. I'll tell you, sir, the monstrous hazards you shall run with a wife.

Mor. Good sir, have I ever cozen'd any friends of yours of their land? bought their possessions? taken forfeit of their mortgage? begg'd a reversion from them? bastarded their issue? What have I done, that may deserve this?

True. Nothing, sir, that I know, but your itch of marriage.

Mor. Why, if I had made an assassinate upon your father, vitiated your mother, ravished your sisters——

True. I would kill you, sir, I would kill you, if you had.

Mor. Why, you do more in this, sir : it were a vengeance centuple, for all facinorous acts that could be named, to do that you do.

True. Alas, sir, I am but a messenger: I but tell you, what you must hear. It seems your friends are careful after your soul's health, sir, and would have you know the danger : (but you may do your pleasure for all them, I persuade not, sir). If, after you are married, your wife do run away with a vaulter, or the Frenchman that walks upon ropes, or him that dances the jig, or a fencer for his skill at his weapon ; why it is not their fault, they have discharged their consciences ; when you know what may happen. Nay, suffer valiantly, sir, for I must tell you all the perils that you are obnoxious to. If she be fair, young and vegetous, no sweetmeats ever drew more flies; all the yellow doublets and great roses in the town will be there. If foul and crooked, she'll be with them, and buy those doublets and roses, sir. If rich, and that you marry her dowry, not her, she'll reign in your house as imperious as a widow. If noble, all her kindred will be your tyrants. If fruitful, as proud as May, and humorous as April; she must have her doctors, her midwives, her nurses, her longings every hour; though it be for the dearest morsel of man. If learned, there was never such a parrot; all your patrimony will be too little for the guests that must be invited to hear her speak Latin and Greek; and you must lie with her in those languages too, if you will please her. If precise, you must feast all the silenced brethen, once in three days; salute the sisters; entertain the whole family, or wood of them; and hear long-winded exercises, singings and catechisings, which you are not given to, and yet must give for; to please the zealous matron your wife, who for the holy cause, will cozen you over and above. You begin to sweat, sir! but this is not half, i'faith: you may do your pleasure, notwithstanding, as I said before: I come not to persuade you. [MUTE *is stealiny away.*]—Upon my faith, master serving-man, if you do stir, I will beat you.

Mor. O, what is my sin! what is my sin!

True. Then, if you love your wife, or rather dote on her, sir; O, how she'll torture you, and take pleasure in your torments! you shall lie with her but when she lists; she will not hurt her beauty, her complexion; or it must be for that jewel, or that pearl, when she does: every half hour's pleasure must be bought anew, and with the same pain and charge you woo'd her at first. Then you must keep what servants she please; what company she will; that friend must not visit you without her license; and him she loves most, she will seem to hate eagerliest, to decline your jealousy ; or, feign to be jealous of you first ; and for that cause go live with her she-friend, or cousin at the college, that can instruct her in all the mysteries of writing letters, corrupting servants, taming spies ; where she must have that rich gown for such a great day ; a new one for the next ; a richer for the third ; be served in silver ; have the chamber fill'd with a succession of grooms, footmen, ushers, and other messengers ; besides embroiderers, jewellers, tire-women, sempsters, feathermen, perfumers ; whilst she feels not how the land drops away, nor the acres melt ; nor foresees the change, when the mercer has your woods for her velvets ; never weighs what her pride costs, sir ; so she may kiss a page, or a smooth chin, that has the despair of a beard : be a stateswoman, know all the news, what was done at Salisbury, what at the Bath, what at court, what in progress ; or, so she may censure poets, and authors, and styles, and compare them ; Daniel with Spenser, Jonson with the t'other youth, and so forth : or be thought cunning in controversies, or the very knots of divinity : and have often in her mouth the state of the question ; and then skip to the mathematics, and demonstration ; and answer in religion to one, in state to another, in bawdry to a third.

Mor. O, O !

True. All this is very true, sir. And then her going in disguise to that conjurer, and this cunning woman : where the first question is, how soon you shall die ? next, if her present servant love her ? next, if she shall have a new servant ? and how many ? which of her family would make the best bawd, male or female ? what precedence she shall have by her next match ? and sets down the answers, and believes them above the scriptures. Nay, perhaps she'll study the art.

Mor. Gentle sir, have you done? have you had your pleasure of me? I'll think of these things.

True. Yes, sir: and then comes reeking home of vapour and sweat, with going a foot, and lies in a month of a new face, all oil and birdlime; and rises in asses' milk, and is cleansed with a new fucus; God be wi' you, sir. One thing more, which I had almost forgot. This too, with whom you are to marry, may have made a conveyance of her virginity afore hand, as your wise widows do of their states, before they marry, in trust to some friend, sir: Who can tell? Or if she have not done it yet, she may do, upon the wedding-day, or the night before, and antedate you cuckold. The like has been heard of in nature. 'Tis no devised, impossible thing, sir. God be wi' you: I'll be bold to leave this rope with you, sir, for a remembrance.—Farewell, Mute! [*Exit.*

Mor. Come, have me to my chamber: but first shut the door. [Truewit *winds the horn without.*] O, shut the door, shut the door! is he come again?

Enter Cutbeard.

Cut. 'Tis I, sir, your barber.

Mor. O, Cutbeard, Cutbeard, Cutbeard! here has been a cut-throat with me: help me in to my bed, and give me physic with thy counsel.   [*Exeunt.*

Scene II.—*A Room in* Sir John Daw's *House.*

Enter Daw, Clerimont, Dauphine, *and* Epicœne.

Daw. Nay, an she will, let her refuse at her own charges; 'tis nothing to me, gentlemen: but she will not be invited to the like feasts or guests every day.

Cler. O, by no means, she may not refuse——to stay at home, if you love your reputation: 'Slight, your are invited thither o' purpose to be seen, and laughed at by the lady of the college, and her shadows. This trumpeter bath proclaim'd you.   *[Aside to* Epi.

Daup. You shall not go; let him be laugh'd at in your stead, for not bringing you: and put him to his extemporal faculty of fooling and talking loud, to satisfy the company.   *[Aside to* Epi.

Cler. He will suspect us; talk aloud.—'Pray, mistress Epicœne, let's see your verses; we have sir John Daw's leave; do not conceal your servant's merit, and your own glories.

Epi. They'll prove my servant's glories, if you have his leave so soon.

Daup. His vain-glories, lady!

Daw. Shew them, shew them, mistress; I dare own them.

Epi. Judge you, what glories.

Daw. Nay, I'll read them myself too: an author must recite his own works. It is a madrigal of Modesty.

> *Modest and Fair, for fair and good are near*
> > *Neighbours, howe'er.—*

Daup. Very good.

Cler. Ay, is't not?

Daw.   *No noble virtue ever was alone,*
> > *But two in one.*

Daup. Excellent!

Cler. That again, I pray, sir John.

Daup. It has something in't like rare wit and sense.

Cler. Peace.

Daw.   *No noble virtue ever was alone,*
> > *But two in one.*
> *Then, when I praise sweet modesty, I praise*
> > *Bright beauty's rays:*
> *And having praised both beauty and modesty,*
> > *I have praised thee.*

Daup. Admirable !

Cler. How it chimes, and cries tink in the close, divinely !

Daup. Ay, 'tis Seneca.

Cler. No, I think 'tis Plutarch.

Daw. The dor on Plutarch and Seneca ! I hate it: they are mine own imaginations, by that light. I wonder those fellows have such credit with gentlemen.

Cler. They are very grave authors.

Daw. Grave asses ! mere essayists : a few loose sentences, and that's all. A man would talk so, his whole age : I do utter as good things every hour, if they were collected and observed, as either of them.

Daup. Indeed, sir John !

Cler. He must needs ; living among the wits and braveries too.

Daup. Ay, and being president of them, as he is.

Daw. There's Aristotle, a mere common-place fellow ; Plato, a discourser ; Thucydides and Livy, tedious and dry ; Tacitus, an entire knot : sometimes worth the untying, very seldom.

Cler. What do you think of the poets, sir John ?

Daw. Not worthy to be named for authors. Homer, an old tedious, prolix ass, talks of curriers, and chines of beef ; Virgil of dunging of land, and bees ; Horace, of I know not what.

Cler. I think so.

Daw. And so, Pindarus, Lycophron, Anacreon, Catullus, Seneca the tragedian, Lucan, Propertius, Tibullus, Martial, Juvenal, Ausonius, Statius, Politian, Valerius Flaccus, and the rest——

Cler. What a sack full of their names he has got !

Daup. And how he pours them out ! Politian with Valerius Flaccus !

Cler. Was not the character right of him ?

Daup. As could be made, i'faith.

Daw. And Persius, a crabbed coxcomb, not to be endured.

Daup. Why, whom do you account for authors, sir John Daw?

Daw. Syntagma juris civilis; Corpus juris civilis; Corpus juris canonici; the king of Spain's bible——

Daup. Is the king of Spain's bible an author?

Cler. Yes, and Syntagma.

Daup. What was that Syntagma, sir?

Daw. A civil lawyer, a Spaniard.

Daup. Sure, Corpus was a Dutchman.

Cler. Ay, both the Corpuses, I knew 'em: they were very corpulent authors.

Daw. And then there's Vatablus, Pomponatius, Symancha: the other are not to be received, within the thought of a scholar.

Daup. 'Fore God, you have a simple learned servant, lady,—in titles.   [*Aside.*

Cler. I wonder that he is not called to the helm, and made a counsellor.

.Daup. He is one extraordinary.

Cler. Nay, but in ordinary: to say truth, the state wants such.

Daup. Why that will follow.

Cler. I muse a mistress can be so silent to the dotes of such a servant.

Daw. 'Tis her virtue, sir. I have written somewhat of her silence too.

Daup. In verse, sir John?

Cler. What else?

Daup. Why, how can you justify your own being of a poet, that so slight all the old poets?

Daw. Why, every man that writes in verse is not a poet; you have of the wits that write verses, and yet are no poets : they are poets that live by it, the poor fellows that live by it.

Daup. Why, would not you live by your verses, sir John ?

Cler. No, 'twere pity he should. A knight live by his verses ! he did not make them to that end, I hope.

Daup. And yet the noble Sidney lives by his, and the noble family not ashamed.

Cler. Ay, he profest himself ; but sir John Daw has more caution : he'll not hinder his own rising in the state so much. Do you think he will ? Your verses, good sir John, and no poems.

Daw. Silence in woman, is like speech in man ;
     Deny't who can.

Daup. Not I, believe it : your reason, sir.
Daw.   *Nor is't a tale,*
 That female vice should be a virtue male,
 Or masculine vice a female virtue be :
     You shall it see
     Prov'd with increase ;
 I know to speak, and she to hold her peace.
Do you conceive me, gentlemen ?

Daup. No, faith ; how mean you *with increase,* sir John ?

Daw. Why, with increase is, when I court her for the common cause of mankind, and she says nothing, but *consentire videtur ;* and in time is *gravida.*

Daup. Then this is a ballad of procreation ?

Cler. A madrigal of procreation ; you mistake.

Epi. 'Pray give me my verses again, servant.

Daw. If you'll ask them aloud, you shall.
       [*Walks aside with the papers.*

Enter TRUEWIT *with his horn.*

Cler. See, here's Truewit again !—Where hast thou

been, in the name of madness, thus accoutred with thy horn?

True. Where the sound of it might have pierced your senses with gladness, had you been in ear-reach of it. Dauphine, fall down and worship me; I have forbid the banns, lads: I have been with thy virtuous uncle, and have broke the match.

Daup. You have not, I hope.

True. Yes, faith; an thou shouldst hope otherwise, I should repent me: this horn got me entrance; kiss it. I had no other way to get in, but by feigning to be a post; but when I got in once, I proved none, but rather the contrary, turn'd him into a post, or a stone, or what is stiffer, with thundering into him the incommodities of a wife, and the miseries of marriage. If ever Gorgon were seen in the shape of a woman, he hath seen her in my description: I have put him off o' that scent for ever.—Why do you not applaud and adore me, sirs? why stand you mute? are you stupid? You are not worthy of the benefit.

Daup. Did not I tell you? Mischief!——

Cler. I would you had placed this benefit somewhere else.

True. Why so?

Cler. 'Slight, you have done the most inconsiderate, rash, weak thing, that ever man did to his friend.

Daup. Friend! if the most malicious enemy I have, had studied to inflict an injury upon me, it could not be a greater.

True. Wherein, for God's sake? Gentlemen, come to yourselves again.

Daup. But I presaged thus much afore to you.

Cler. Would my lips had been solder'd when I spake on't! Slight, what moved you to be thus impertinent?

True. My masters, do not put on this strange face to

pay my courtesy : off with this vizor.   Have good turns done you, and thank' em this way !

Daup. 'Fore heaven, you have undone me.   That which I have plotted for, and been maturing now these four months, you have blasted in a minute : Now I am lost, I may speak.   This gentlewoman was lodged here by me o' purpose, and, to be put upon my uncle, hath profest this obstinate silence for my sake ; being my entire friend, and one that for the requital of such a fortune as to marry him, would have made me very ample conditions ; where now, all my hopes are utterly miscarried by this unlucky accident.

Cler. Thus 'tis when a man will be ignorantly officious, do services, and not know his why : I wonder what courteous itch possest you.   You never did absurder part in your life, nor a greater trespass to friendship or humanity.

Daup. Faith, you may forgive it best ; 'twas your cause principally.

Cler. I know it ; would it had not.

Enter CUTBEARD.

Daup. How now, Cutbeard ! what news ?

Cut. The best, the happiest that ever was, sir.   There has been a mad gentleman with your uncle this morning, [*seeing* TRUEWIT.]—I think this be the gentleman —that has almost talk'd him out of his wits, with threatening him from marriage——

Daup. On, I prithee.

Cut. And your uncle, sir, he thinks 'twas done by your procurement ; therefore he will see the party you wot of presently ; and if he like her, he says, and that she be so inclining to dumb as I have told him, he swears he will marry her to-day, instantly, and not defer it a minute longer.

Daup. Excellent ! beyond our expectation !

True. Beyond our expectation ! By this light, I knew it would be thus.

Daup. Nay, sweet Truewit, forgive me.

True. No, I was *ignorantly officious, impertinent ;* this was the *absurd, weak part.*

Cler. Wilt thou ascribe that to merit now, was mere fortune !

True. Fortune ! mere providence. Fortune had not a finger in't. I saw it must necessarily in nature fall out so : my genius is never false to me in these things. Shew me how it could be otherwise.

Daup. Nay, gentlemen, contend not ; 'tis well now.

True. Alas, I let him go on with *inconsiderate,* and *rash,* and what he pleased.

Cler. Away, thou strange justifier of thyself, to be wiser than thou wert, by the event !

True. Event ! by this light, thou shalt never persuade me, but I foresaw it as well as the stars themselves.

Daup. Nay, gentlemen, 'tis well now. Do you two entertain sir John Daw with discourse, while I send her away with instructions.

True. I'll be acquainted with her first, by your favour.

Cler. Master Truewit, lady, a friend of ours.

True. I am sorry I have not known you sooner, lady, to celebrate this rare virtue of your silence.

            [*Exeunt* DAUP., EPI., *and* CUTBEARD.

Cler. Faith, and you had come sooner, you should have seen and heard her well celebrated in sir John Daw's madrigals.

True. [*advances to* DAW.] Jack Daw, God save you ! when saw you La-Foole ?

Daw. Not since last night, master Truewit.

True. That's a miracle! I thought you two had been inseparable.

Daw. He's gone to invite his guests.

True. 'Odso! 'tis true! What a false memory have I towards that man! I am one: I met him even now, upon that he calls his delicate fine black horse, rid into foam, with posting from place to place, and person to person, to give them the cue——

Cler. Lest they should forget?

True. Yes: There was never poor captain took more pains at a muster to show men, than he, at this meal, to show friends.

Daw. It is his quarter-feast, sir.

Cler. What! do you say so, sir John?

True. Nay, Jack Daw will not be out, at the best friends he has, to the talent of his wit: Where's his mistress, to hear and applaud him? is she gone!

Daw. Is mistress Epicœne gone?

Cler. Gone afore, with sir Dauphine, I warrant, to the place.

True. Gone afore! that were a manifest injury, a disgrace and a half; to refuse him at such a festival-time at this, being a bravery, and a wit too!

Cler. Tut, he'll swallow it like cream: he's better read in Jure civili, than to esteem anything a disgrace, is offer'd him from a mistress.

Daw. Nay, let her e'en go; she shall sit alone, and be dumb in her chamber a week together, for John Daw, I warrant her. Does she refuse me?

Cler. No, sir, do not take it so to heart; she does not refuse you, but a little neglects you. Good faith, Truewit, you are to blame, to put it into his head, that she does refuse him.

True. Sir, she does refuse him palpably, however you

mince it. An I were as he, I would swear to speak ne'er a word to her to-day for't.

Daw. By this light, no more I will not.

True. Nor to any body else, sir.

Daw. Nay, I will not say so, gentlemen.

Cler. It had been an excellent happy condition for the company, if you could have drawn him to it. [*Aside.*

Daw. I'll be very melancholy, i'faith.

Cler. As a dog, if I were as you, sir John.

True. Or a snail, or a hog-louse; I would roll myself up for this day; in troth, they should not unwind me.

Daw. By this pick-tooth, so I will.

Cler. 'Tis well done: He begins already to be angry with his teeth.

Daw. Will you go, gentlemen?

Cler. Nay, you must walk alone, if you be right melancholy, sir John.

True. Yes, sir, we'll dog you, we'll follow you afar off.   [*Exit* DAW.

Cler. Was there ever such a two yards of knighthood measured out by time, to be sold to laughter?

True. A mere talking mole, hang him! no mushroom was ever so fresh. A fellow so utterly nothing, as he knows not what he would be.

Cler. Let's follow him: but first let's go to Dauphine, he's hovering about the house to hear what news.

True. Content.   [*Exeunt.*

SCENE III.—A Room in MOROSE'S House.

Enter MOROSE and MUTE, followed by CUTBEARD with EPICŒNE.

Mor. Welcome, Cutbeard! draw near with your fair charge: and in her ear softly entreat her to unmask.

[Epi. *takes off her mask.*]—So! Is the door shut?
[Mute *makes a leg.*]—Enough. Now, Cutbeard, with
the same discipline I use to my family, I will question
you. As I conceive, Cutbeard, this gentlewoman is she
you have provided, and brought, in hope she will fit me
in the place and person of a wife? Answer me not but
with your leg, unless it be otherwise: [Cut. *makes
a leg.*]—Very well done, Cutbeard. I conceive besides,
Cutbeard, you have been pre-acquainted with her birth,
education, and qualities, or else you would not prefer
her to my acceptance, in the weighty consequence
of marriage. [*makes a leg.*]—This I conceive, Cutbeard.
Answer me not but with your leg, unless it be otherwise. [*bows again.*]—Very well done, Cutbeard. Give
aside now a little, and leave me to examine her
condition, and aptitude to my affection. [*goes about
her and views her.*]—She is exceeding fair, and of a
special good favour; a sweet composition or harmony of
limbs; her temper of beauty has the true height of my
blood. The knave hath exceedingly well fitted me
without: I will now try her within.—Come near, fair
gentlewoman; let not my behaviour seem rude, though
unto you, being rare, it may haply appear strange.
(Epicœne *curtsies.*] Nay, lady, you may speak, though
Cutbeard and my man might not; for of all sounds,
only the sweet voice of a fair lady has the just length of
mine ears. I beseech you, say, lady; out of the first
fire of meeting eyes, they say, love is stricken: do you
feel any such motion suddenly shot into you, from
any part you see in me? ha, lady? [Epi. *curtsies.*]—
Alas, lady, these answers by silent curtsies from you are
too courtless and simple. I have ever had my breeding
in court; and she that shall be my wife, must be
accomplished with courtly and audacious ornaments.
Can you speak, lady?

Epi. [*softly.*] Judge you, forsooth.

Mor. What say you, lady? Speak out, I beseech you.

Epi. Judge you, forsooth.

Mor. On my judgment, a divine softness! But can you naturally, lady, as I enjoin these by doctrine and industry, refer yourself to the search of my judgment, and, not taking pleasure in your tongue, which is a woman's chiefest pleasure, think it plausible to answer me by silent gestures, so long as my speeches jump right with what you conceive? [*Epi. curtsies.*] —Excellent! divine! if it were possible she should hold out thus!—Peace, Cutbeard, thou art made for ever, as thou hast made me, if this felicity have lasting: but I will try her further. Dear lady, I am courtly, I tell you, and I must have mine ears banquetted with pleasant and witty conferences, pretty girds, scoffs, and dalliance in her that I mean to choose for my bed-phere. The ladies in court think it a most desperate impair to their quickness of wit, and good carriage, if they cannot give occasion for man to court 'em; and when an amorous discourse is set on foot, minister as good matter to continue it, as himself: And do you alone so much differ from all them, that what they, with so much circumstance, affect and toil for, to seem learn'd, to seem judicious, to seem sharp and conceited, you can bury in yourself with silence, and rather trust your graces to the fair conscience of virtue, than to the world's or your own proclamation?

Epi. [*softly.*] I should be sorry else.

Mor. What say you, lady? good lady, speak out.

Epi. I should be sorry else.

Mor. That sorrow doth fill me with gladness. O Morose, thou art happy above mankind! pray that thou mayest contain thyself. I will only put her to it once more, and it shall be with the utmost touch and test of their sex. But hear me, fair lady; I do also love to see her whom I shall choose for my heifer, to be the first and principal in all fashions, precede all the dames at court by a fortnight, have council of tailors, lineners, lace-women, embroiderers; and sit with them sometimes twice a day upon French intelligences, and then come forth varied like nature, or oftener than she, and better by the help of art, her emulous servant. This do I affect: and how will you be able, lady, with this frugality of speech, to give the manifold but necessary instructions, for that bodice, these sleeves, those skirts, this cut, that stitch, this embroidery, that lace, this wire, those knots, that ruff, those roses, this girdle, that fan, the t'other scarf, these gloves ? Ha ! what say you, lady ?

Epi. [*softly.*] I'll leave it to you, sir.

Mor. How, lady ? pray you rise a note.

Epi. I leave it to wisdom and you, sir.

Mor. Admirable creature ! I will trouble you no more : I will not sin against so sweet a simplicity. Let me now be bold to print on those divine lips the seal of being mine.—Cutbeard, I give thee the lease of thy house free ; thank me not but with thy leg. [CUTBEARD *shakes his head.*]—I know what thou wouldst say, she's poor, and her friends deceased. She has brought a wealthy dowry in her silence, Cutbeard ; and in respect of her poverty, Cutbeard, I shall have her more loving and obedient, Cutbeard. Go thy ways, and get me a minister presently, with a soft low voice, to marry us ; and pray him he will not be impertinent, but brief as he can ; away: softly, Cutbeard. [*Exit* CUT.]—Sirrah, conduct your mistress into the dining-room, your now mistress. [*Exit* MUTE, *followed by* EPI.]—O my felicity ! how shall I be revenged on mine insolent kinsman, and his plots to fright me from marrying ! This

night I will get an heir, and thrust him out of my
blood, like a stranger.   He would be knighted, forsooth,
and thought by that means to reign over me; his title
must do it : No, kinsman, I will now make you bring
me the tenth lord's and the sixteenth lady's letter,
kinsman ; and it shall do you no good, kinsman.   Your
knighthood itself shall come on its knees, and it shall be
rejected ; it shall be sued for its fees to execution,
and not be redeem'd ; it shall cheat at the twelve-penny
ordinary, it knighthood, for its diet, all the term-
time, and tells tales for it in the vacation to the hostess ;
or it knighthood shall do worse, take sanctuary in
Cole-harbour, and fast.   It shall fright all it friends
with borrowing letters ; and when one of the fourscore
hath brought it knighthood ten shillings, it knighthood
shall go to the Cranes, or the Bear at the Bridgefoot,
and be drunk in fear ; it shall not have money to
discharge one tavern-reckoning, to invite the old
creditors to forbear it knighthood, or the new, that
should be, to trust it knighthood.   It shall be the
tenth name in the bond to take up the commodity of
pipkins and stone-jugs : and the part thereof shall
not furnish it knighthood forth for the attempting of a
baker's widow, a brown baker's widow.   It shall give it
knighthood's name for a stallion, to all gamesome
citizens wives, and be refused, when the master of
a dancing-school, or how do you call him, the worst
reveller in the town is taken : it shall want clothes, and
by reason of that, wit, to fool to lawyers.   It shall
not have hope to repair itself by Constantinople,
Ireland, or Virginia ; but the best and last fortune to it
knighthood shall be to make Dol Tear-sheet, or Kate
Common a lady, and so it knighthood may eat.

[Exit.

SCENE IV.—*A Lane, near* MOROSE'S *House.*

Enter TRUEWIT, DAUPHINE, *and* CLERIMONT.

True. Are you sure he is not gone by?

Daup. No, I staid in the shop ever since.

Cler. But he may take the other end of the lane.

Daup. No, I told him I would be here at this end: I appointed him hither.

True. What a barbarian it is to stay then!

Daup. Yonder he comes.

Cler. And his charge left behind him, which is a very good sign, Dauphine.

Enter CUTBEARD.

Daup. How now, Cutbeard! succeeds it, or no?

Cut. Past imagination, sir, *omnia secunda;* you could not have pray'd to have had it so well. *Saltat senex,* as it is in the proverb; he does triumph in his felicity, admires the party! he has given me the lease of my house too! and I am now going for a silent minister to marry them, and away.

True. 'Slight! get one of the silenced ministers; a zealous brother would torment him purely.

Cut. Cum privilegio, sir.

Daup. O, by no means; let's do nothing to hinder it now: when 'tis done and finished, I am for you, for any device of vexation.

Cut. And that shall be within this half hour, upon my dexterity, gentlemen. Contrive what you can in the mean time, *bonis avibus.*   *[Exit.*

Cler. How the slave doth Latin it!

True. It would be made a jest to posterity, sirs, this day's mirth, if ye will.

Cler. Beshrew his heart that will not, I pronounce.

Daup. And for my part. What is it?

True. To translate all La-Foole's company, and his feast thither, to-day, to celebrate this bride-ale.

Daup. Ay, marry ; but how will't be done ?

True. I'll undertake the directing of all the lady-guests thither, and then the meat must follow.

Cler. For God's sake, let's effect it ; it will be an excellent comedy of affliction, so many several noises.

Daup. But are they not at the other place, already, think you.

True. I'll warrant you for the college-honours : one of their faces has not the priming colour laid on yet, nor the other her smock sleek'd.

Cler. O, but they'll rise earlier than ordinary to a feast.

True. Best go see, and assure ourselves.

Cler. Who knows the house ?

True. I'll lead you : Were you never there yet ?

Daup. Not I.

Cler. Nor I.

True. Where have you lived then ? not know Tom Otter !

Cler. No : for God's sake, what is he ?

True. An excellent animal, equal with your Daw or La-Foole, if not transcendent ; and does Latin it as much as your barber : He is his wife's subject ; he calls her princess, and at such times as these follows her up and down the house like a page, with his hat off, partly for heat, partly for reverence. At this instant he is marshalling of his bull, bear, and horse.

Daup. What be those, in the name of Sphynx ?

True. Why, sir, he has been a great man at the Bear-garden in his time ; and from that subtle sport has ta'en the witty denomination of his chief carousing cups. One he calls his bull, another his bear, another his horse. And then he has his lesser glasses, that he calls his deer and his ape; and several degrees of them too; and never is well, nor thinks any entertainment perfect, till these be brought out, and set on the cupboard.

Cler. For God's love!—we should miss this, if we should not go.

True. Nay, he has a thousand things as good, that will speak him all day. He will rail on his wife, with certain common places, behind her back; and to her face——

Daup. No more of him. Let's go see him, I petition you.   [*Exeunt.*

ACT III.

Scene I.—*A Room in* Otter's *House.*

Enter Captain Otter *with his cups, and* Mistress Otter.

Ott. Nay, good princess, hear me *pauca verba.*

Mrs. Ott. By that light, I'll have you chain'd up, with your bull-dogs and bear-dogs, if you be not civil the sooner. I'll send you to kennel, i'faith. You were best bait me with your bull, bear, and horse. Never a time that the courtiers or collegiates come to the house, but you make it a Shrove-tuesday! I would have you get your Whitsuntide velvet cap, and your staff in your hand, to entertain them: yes, in troth, do.

Ott. Not so, princess, neither; but under correction, sweet princess, give me leave.——These things I am known to the courtiers by: It is reported to them for my humour, and they receive it so, and do expect it. Tom Otter's bull, bear, and horse is known all over England, *in rerum natura.*

Mrs. Ott. 'Fore me, I will *na-ture* them over to Paris-garden, and *na-ture* you thither too, if you pronounce them again. Is a bear a fit beast, or a bull, to mix in society with great ladies? think in your discretion, in good policy.

Ott. The horse then, good princess.

Mrs. Ott. Well, I am contented for the horse; they love to be well horsed, I know: I love it myself.

Ott. And it is a delicate fine horse this: *Poetarum Pegasus.* Under correction, princess, Jupiter did turn himself into a—*taurus*, or bull, under correction, good princess.

Enter Truewit, Clerimont, *and* Dauphine, *behind.*

Mrs. Ott. By my integrity, I'll send you over to the Bank-side; I'll commit you to the master of the Garden, if I hear but a syllable more. Must my house or my roof be polluted with the scent of bears and bulls, when it is perfumed for great ladies? Is this according to the instrument, when I married you? that I would be princess, and reign in mine own house; and you would be my subject, and obey me? What did you bring me, should make you thus peremptory? do I allow you your half-crown a-day, to spend where you will, among your gamesters, to vex and torment me at such times as these? Who gives you your maintenance, I pray you? who allows you your horse-meat and man's meat? your three suits of apparel a-year? your four pair of stockings, one silk, three worsted? your clean linen, your bands and cuffs, when I can get you to wear them?—'tis marle you have them on now.—Who graces you with courtiers or great personages, to speak to you out of their coaches, and come home to your house? Were you ever so much as look'd upon by a lord or a lady, before I married you, but on the Easter or Whitsun-holidays? and then out at the banqueting-house window, when Ned Whiting or George Stone were at the stake?

True. For God's sake, let's go stave her off him.

Mrs. Ott. Answer me to that. And did not I take you up from thence, in an old greasy buff-doublet, with points, and green velvet sleeves, out at the elbows? you forget this.

True. She'll worry him, if we help not in time.

                         [*They come forward.*

Mrs. Ott. O, here are some of the gallants! Go to, behave yourself distinctly, and with good morality; or, I protest, I'll take away your exhibition.

True. By your leave, fair mistress Otter, I'll be bold to enter these gentlemen in your acquaintance.

Mrs. Ott. It shall not be obnoxious, or difficil, sir.

True. How does my noble captain? is the bull, bear, and horse in *rerum natura* still?

Ott. Sir, *sic visum superis.*

Mrs. Ott. I would you would but intimate them, do. Go your ways in, and get toasts and butter made for the woodcocks: that's a fit province for you.

                         [*Drives him off.*

Cler. Alas, what a tyranny is this poor fellow married to.

True. O, but the sport will be anon, when we get him loose.

Daup. Dares he ever speak?

True. No Anabaptist ever rail'd with the like license: but mark her language in the mean time, I beseech you.

Mrs. Ott. Gentlemen, you are very aptly come. My cousin, sir Amorous, will be here briefly.

True. In good time, lady. Was not sir John Daw here, to ask for him, and the company?

Mrs. Ott. I cannot assure you, master Truewit. Here was a very melancholy knight in a ruff, that demanded my subject for somebody, a gentleman, I think.

Cler. Ay, that was he, lady.

Mrs. Ott. But he departed straight, I can resolve you.

Daup. What an excellent choice phrase this lady expresses in.

Truc. O, sir, she is the only authentical courtier, that is not naturally bred one, in the city.

Mrs. Ott. You have taken that report upon trust, gentlemen.

True. No, I assure you, the court governs it so, lady, in your behalf.

Mrs. Ott. I am the servant of the court and courtiers, sir.

True. They are rather your idolaters.

Mrs. Ott. Not so, sir.

Enter CUTBEARD.

Daup. How now, Cutbeard! any cross?

Cut. O no, sir, *omnia bene.* 'Twas never better on the hinges; all's sure. I have so pleased him with a curate, that he's gone to't almost with the delight he hopes for soon.

Daup. What is he for a vicar?

Cut. One that has catch'd a cold, sir, and can scarce be heard six inches off; as if he spoke out of a bulrush that were not pick'd, or his throat were full of pith: a fine quick fellow, and an excellent barber of prayers. I came to tell you, sir, that you might *omnem movere lapidem*, as they say, be ready with your vexation.

Daup. Gramercy, honest Cutbeard! be thereabouts with thy key, to let us in.

Cut. I will not fail you, sir; *ad manum.*   [*Exit.*

True. Well, I'll go watch my coaches.

Cler. Do; and we'll send Daw to you, if you meet him not.   [*Exit* TRUEWIT.

Mrs. Ott. Is master Truewit gone?

Daup. Yes, lady, there is some unfortunate business fallen out.

Mrs. Ott. So I adjudged by the physiognomy of the fellow that came in ; and I had a dream last night too of the new pageant, and my lady mayoress, which is always very ominous to me. I told it my lady Haughty t'other day, when her honour came hither to see some China stuffs ; and she expounded it out of Artemidorus, and I have found it since very true. It has done me many affronts.

Cler. Your dream, lady ?

Mrs. Ott. Yes, sir, any thing I do but dream of the city. It stain'd me a damask table-cloth, cost me eighteen pound, at one time ; and burnt me a black satin gown, as I stood by the fire, at my lady Centaure's chamber in the college, another time. A third time, at the lords' masque, it dropt all my wire and my ruff with wax candle, that I could not go up to the banquet. A fourth time, as I was taking coach to go to Ware, to meet a friend, it dash'd me a new suit all over (a crimson satin doublet, and black velvet skirts) with a brewer's horse, that I was fain to go in and shift me, and kept my chamber a leash of days for the anguish of it.

Daup. These were dire mischances, lady.

Cler. I would not dwell in the city, an 'twere so fatal to me.

Mrs. Ott. Yes, sir ; but I do take advice of my doctor to dream of it as little as I can.

Daup. You do well, mistress Otter.

Enter Sir JOHN DAW, *and is taken aside by* CLERIMONT.

Mrs. Ott. Will it please you to enter the house farther, gentlemen ?

Daup. And your favour, lady : but we stay to speak

with a knight, sir John Daw, who is here come. We shall follow you, lady.

Mrs. Ott. At your own time, sir. It is my cousin sir Amorous his feast——

Daup. I know it, lady.

Mrs. Ott. And mine together. But it is for his honour, and therefore I take no name of it, more than of the place.

Daup. You are a bounteous kinswoman.

Mrs. Ott. Your servant, sir.   [*Exit.*

Cler. [*coming forward with* DAW.] Why, do you not know it, sir John Daw?

Daw. No, I am a rook if I do.

Cler. I'll tell you, then; she's married by this time. And, whereas you were put in the head, that she was gone with sir Dauphine, I assure you, sir Dauphine has been the noblest, honestest friend to you, that ever gentleman of your quality could boast of. He has discover'd the whole plot, and made your mistress so acknowledging, and indeed so ashamed of her injury to you, that she desires you to forgive her, and but grace her wedding with your presence to-day—She is to be married to a very good fortune, she says, his uncle, old Morose; and she will'd me in private to tell you, that she shall be able to do you more favours, and with more security now than before.

Daw. Did she say so, i'faith?

Cler. Why, what do you think of me, sir John? Ask sir Dauphine.

Daw. Nay, I believe you.—Good sir Dauphine, did she desire me to forgive her?

Daup. I assure you, sir John, she did.

Daw. Nay, then, I do with all my heart, and I'll be jovial.

Cler. Yes, for look you, sir, this was the injury to

you.   La-Foole intended this feast to honour her bridal day, and made you the property to invite the college ladies, and promise to bring her; and then at the time she would have appear'd, as his friend, to have given you the dor.   Whereas now, sir Dauphine has brought her to a feeling of it, with this kind of satisfaction, that you shall bring all the ladies to the place where she is, and be very jovial; and there, she will have a dinner, which shall be in your name: and so disappoint La-Foole, to make you good again, and, as it were, a saver in the main.

Daw. As I am a knight, I honour her; and forgive her heartily.

Cler. About it then presently.   Truewit has gone before to confront the coaches, and to acquaint you with so much, if he meet you.   Join with him, and 'tis well.——

Enter Sir Amorous La-Foole.

See; here comes your antagonist; but take you no notice, but be very jovial.

La-F. Are the ladies come, sir John Daw, and your mistress? [*Exit* Daw.]—Sir Dauphine! you are exceeding welcome, and honest master Clerimont.   Where's my cousin? did you see no collegiates, gentlemen?

Daup. Collegiates! do you not hear, sir Amorous, how you are abused?

La-F. How, sir!

Cler. Will you speak so kindly to sir John Daw, that has done you such an affront?

La-F. Wherein, gentlemen? let me be a suitor to you to know, I beseech you.

Cler. Why, sir, his mistress is married to-day to sir Dauphine's uncle, your cousin's neighbour, and he has diverted all the ladies, and all your company thither, to frustrate your provision, and stick a disgrace upon you. He was here now to have enticed us away from you too : but we told him his own, I think.

La-F. Has sir John Daw wrong'd me so inhumanly ?

Daup. He has done it, sir Amorous, most maliciously and treacherously : but if you'll be ruled by us, you shall quit him, i'faith.

La-F. Good gentlemen, I'll make one, believe it. How, I pray ?

Daup. Marry, sir, get me your pheasants, and your godwits, and your best meat, and dish it in silver dishes of your cousin's presently ; and say nothing, but clap me a clean towel about you, like a sewer ; and, bareheaded, march afore it with a good confidence ('tis but over the way, hard by), and we'll second you, where you shall set it on the board, and bid them welcome to't, which shall shew 'tis yours, and disgrace his preparation utterly : and for your cousin, whereas she should be troubled here at home with care of making and giving welcome, she shall transfer all that labour thither, and be a principal guest herself ; sit rank'd with the college-honours, and be honour'd, and have her health drunk as often, as bare, and as loud as the best of them.

La-F. I'll go tell her presently. It shall be done, that's resolved. *[Exit.*

Cler. I thought he would not hear it out, but 'twould take him.

Daup. Well, there be guests and meat now ; how shall we do for music ?

Cler. The smell of the venison, going through the street, will invite one noise of fiddlers or other.

Daup. I would it would call the trumpeters hither !

Cler. Faith, there is hope ; they have intelligence of all feasts. There's good correspondence betwixt them and the London cooks : 'tis twenty to one but we have them. ,

Daup. 'Twill be a most solemn day for my uncle, and an excellent fit of mirth for us.

Cler. Ay, if we can hold up the emulation betwixt Foole and Daw, and never bring them to expostulate.

Daup. Tut, flatter them both, as Truewit says, and you may take their understandings in a purse-net. They'll believe themselves to be just such men as we make them, neither more nor less. They have nothing, not the use of their senses, but by tradition.

Re-enter LA-FOOLE, *like a Sewer.*

Cler. See ! sir Amorous has his towel on already. Have you persuaded your cousin ?

La-F. Yes, 'tis very feasible : she'll do anything, she says, rather than the La-Fooles shall be disgraced.

Daup. She is a noble kinswoman. It will be such a pestling device, sir Amorous ; it will pound all your enemy's practices to powder, and blow him up with his own mine, his own train.

La-F. Nay, we'll give fire, I warrant you.

Cler. But you must carry it privately, without any noise, and take no notice by any means——

Re-enter Captain OTTER.

Ott. Gentlemen, my princess says you shall have all her silver dishes, *festinate :* and she's gone to alter her tire a little, and go with you——

Cler. And yourself too, captain Otter ?

Daup. By any means, sir.

Ott. Yes, sir, I do mean it : but I would entreat my cousin sir Amorous, and you, gentlemen, to be suitors to my princess, that I may carry my bull and my bear, as well as my horse.

Cler. That you shall do, captain Otter.

La-F. My cousin will never consent, gentlemen.

Daup. She must consent, sir Amorous, to reason.

La-F. Why, she says they are no decorum among ladies.

Ott. But they are *decora*, and that's better, sir.

Cler. Ay, she must hear argument. Did not Pasiphaë, who was a queen, love a bull? and was not Calisto, the mother of Arcas, turn'd into a bear, and made a star, mistress Ursula, in the heavens?

Ott. O lord! that I could have said as much! I will have these stories painted in the Bear-garden, *ex Ovidii metamorphosi.*

Daup. Where is your princess, captain? pray, be our leader.

Ott. That I shall, sir.

Cler. Make haste, good sir Amorous.   [*Exeunt.*

SCENE II.—*A room in* MOROSE'S *House.*

Enter MOROSE, EPICŒNE, Parson, *and* CUTBEARD.

Mor. Sir, there's an angel for yourself. and a brace of angels for your cold. Muse not at this manage of my bounty. It is fit we should thank fortune, double to nature, for any benefit sLe confers upon us; besides, it is your imperfection, but my solace.

Par. [*speaks as having a cold.*] I thank your worship; so it is mine, now.

Mor. What says he, Cutbeard?

Cut. He says *præsto*, sir, whensoever your worship needs him, he can be ready with the like. He got this cold with sitting up late, and singing catches with cloth-workers.

Mor. No more. I thank him.

Par. God keep your worship, and give you much joy
with your fair spouse !—uh ! uh ! uh !

Mor. O, O ! stay, Cutbeard ! let him give me five
shillings of my money back.   As it is bounty to reward
benefits, so it is equity to mulct injuries.   I will have
it.   What says he ?

Cler. He cannot change it, sir

Mor. It must be changed.

Cut. Cough again.　　　　　　　　　*[Aside to* Parson.

Mor. What says he ?

Cut. He will cough out the rest, sir.

Par. Uh, uh, uh !

Mor. Away, away with him ! stop his mouth ! away !
I forgive it.——

　　　　　　　　　[Exit Cut. *thrusting out the* Par.

Epi. Fie, master Morose, that you will use this
violence to a man of the church.

Mor. How !

Epi. It does not become your gravity, or breeding, as
you pretend, in court, to have offer'd this outrage on a
waterman, or any more boisterous creature, much less on
a man of his civil coat.

Mor. You can speak then !

Epi. Yes, sir.

Mor. Speak out, I mean.

Epi. Ay, sir.   Why, did you think you had married
a statue, or a motion only ? one of the French puppets,
with the eyes turn'd with a wire ? or some innocent out
of the hospital, that would stand with her hands thus,
and a plaise mouth, and look upon you ?

Mor. O immodesty ! a manifest woman ! What, Cutbeard !

Epi. Nay never quarrel with Cutbeard, sir ; it is too
late now.   I confess it doth bate somewhat of the
modesty I had, when I writ simply maid : but I hope I

shall make it a stock still competent to the estate and dignity of your wife.

Mor. She can talk !

Epi. Yes, indeed, sir.

Enter Mute.

Mor. What sirrah ! None of my knaves there ! where is this impostor Cutbeard ?

           [Mute *makes signs.*

Epi. Speak to him, fellow, speak to him! I'll have none of this coacted, unnatural dumbness in my house, in a family where I govern.   [*Exit* Mute.

Mor. She is my regent already ! I have married a Penthesilea, a Semiramis; sold my liberty to a distaff.

Enter Truewit.

True. Where's master Morose ?

Mor. Is he come again ! Lord have mercy upon me !

True. I wish you all joy, mistress Epicœne, with your grave and honourable match.

Epi. I return you the thanks, master Truewit, so friendly a wish deserves.

Mor. She has acquaintance, too !

True. God save you, sir, and give you all contentment in your fair choice, here ! Before, I was the bird of night to you, the owl ; but now I am the messenger of peace, a dove, and bring you the glad wishes of many friends to the celebration of this good hour.

Mor. What hour, sir ?

True. Your marriage hour, sir. I commend your resolution, that, notwithstanding all the dangers I laid afore you, in the voice of a night-crow, would yet go on, and be yourself. It shews you are a man constant to your own ends, and upright to your purposes, that would not be put off with left-handed cries.

Mor. How should you arrive at the knowledge of so much?

True. Why, did you ever hope, sir, committing the secrecy of it to a barber, that less than the whole town should know it? you might as well have told it the conduit, or the bake-house, or the infantry that follow the court, and with more security. Could your gravity forget so old and noted a remnant, as, *lippis et tonsoribus notum?* Well, sir, forgive it yourself now, the fault, and be communicable with your friends. Here will be three or four fashionable ladies from the college to visit you presently, and their train of minions and followers.

Mor. Bar my doors! bar my doors! Where are all my eaters? my mouths, now?——

Enter Servants.

Bar up my doors, you varlets!

Epi. He is a varlet that stirs to such an office. Let them stand open. I would see him that dares move his eyes toward it. Shall I have a barricade made against my friends, to be barr'd of any pleasure they can bring in to me with their honourable visitation! [*Exeunt* Ser.

Mor. O Amazonian impudence!

True. Nay, faith, in this, sir, she speaks but reason; and, methinks, is more continent than you. Would you go to bed so presently, sir, afore noon? a man of your head and hair should owe more to that reverend ceremony, and not mount the marriage-bed like a town-bull, or a mountain-goat; but stay the due season; and ascend it then with religion and fear. Those delights are to be steeped in the humour and silence of the night; and give the day to other open pleasures, and jollities of feasting, of music, of revels, of discourse: we'll have all, sir, that may make your Hymen high and happy.

Mor. O my torment, my torment!

True. Nay if you endure the first half hour, sir, so tediously, and with this irksomeness; what comfort or hope can this fair gentlewoman make to herself hereafter, in the consideration of so many years as are to come——

Mor. Of my affliction. Good sir, depart, and let her do it alone.

True. I have done, sir.

Mor. That cursed barber.

True. Yes, faith, cursed wretch indeed, sir.

Mor. I have married his cittern, that's common to all men. Some plague above the plague——

True. All Egypt's ten plagues.

Mor. Revenge me on him!

True. 'Tis very well, sir. If you laid on a curse or two more, I'll assure you he'll bear them. As, that he may get the pox with seeking to cure it, sir; or, that while he is curling another man's hair, his own may drop off; or, for burning some male-bawd's lock, he may have his brain beat out with the curling iron.

Mor. No, let the wretch live wretched. May he get the itch, and his shop so lousy, as no man dare come at him, nor he come at no man!

True. Ay, and if he would swallow all his balls for pills, let not them purge him.

Mor Let his warming-pan be ever cold.

True. A perpetual frost underneath it, sir.

Mor. Let him never hope to see fire again.

True. But in hell, sir.

Mor. His chairs be always empty, his scissors rust, and his combs mould in their cases.

True. Very dreadful that! And may he lose the invention, sir, of carving lanterns in paper.

Mor. Let there be no bawd carted that year; to

employ a bason of his : but let him be glad to eat his sponge for bread.

True. And drink lotium to it, and much good do him.

Mor. Or, for want of bread——

True. Eat ear-wax, sir. I'll help you. Or, draw his own teeth, and add them to the lute-string.

Mor. No, beat the old ones to powder, and make bread of them.

True. Yes, make meal of the mill-stones.

Mor. May all the botches and burns that he has cured on others break out upon him.

True. And he now forget the cure of them in himself, sir ; or, if he do remember it, let him have scraped all his linen into lint for't, and have not a rag left him for to set up with.

Mor. Let him never set up again, but have the gout in his hands for ever !—Now, no more, sir.

True. O, that last was too high set ; you might go less with him, i'faith, and be revenged enough : as, that he be never able to new-paint his pole——

Mor. Good sir, no more, I forgot myself.

True. Or, want credit to take up with a comb-maker——

Mor. No more, sir.

True. Or, having broken his glass in a former despair, fall now into a much greater, of ever getting another——

Mor. I beseech you, no more.

True. Or, that he never be trusted with trimming of any but chimney-sweepers——

Mor. Sir——

True. Or, may he cut a collier's throat with his razor, by chance-medley, and yet be hanged for't.

Mor. I will forgive him, rather than hear any more. I beseech you, sir.

Enter DAW, *introducing* Lady HAUGHTY, CENTAURE, MAVIS, *and* TRUSTY.

Daw. This way, madam.

Mor. O, the sea breaks in upon me! another flood! an inundation! I shall be overwhelmed with noise. It beats already at my shores. I feel an earthquake in my self for't.

Daw. 'Give you joy, mistress.

Mor. Has she servants too!

Daw. I have brought some ladies here to see and know you. My lady Haughty—[*as he presents them severally,* EPI. *kisses them.*] this is my lady Centaure—mistress Dol Mavis—mistress Trusty, my lady Haughty's woman. Where's your husband? let's see him: can he endure no noise? let me come to him.

Mor. What nomenclator is this!

True. Sir John Daw, sir, your wife's servant, this.

Mor. A Daw, and her servant! O, 'tis decreed, 'tis decreed of me, an she have such servants.   [*Going.*

True. Nay, sir, you must kiss the ladies; you must not go away, now: they come toward you to seek you out.

Hau. I' faith, master Morose, would you steal a marriage thus, in the midst of so many friends, and not acquaint us? Well, I'll kiss you, notwithstanding the justice of my quarrel: you shall give me leave, mistress, to use a becoming familiarity with your husband.

Epi. Your ladyship does me an honour in it, to let me know he is so worthy your favour: as you have done both him and me grace to visit so unprepared a pair to entertain you,

Mor. Compliment! compliment!

Epi. But I must lay the burden of that upon my servant here.

Hau. It shall not need, mistress Morose ; we will all bear, rather than one shall be opprest.

Mor. I know it : and you will teach her the faculty, if she be to learn it.

        [*Walks aside while the rest talk apart.*

Hau. Is this the silent woman ?

Cen. Nay, she has found her tongue since she was married, master Truewit says.

Hau. O, master Truewit ! 'save you. What kind of creature is your bride here ? she speaks, methinks !

True. Yes, madam, believe it, she is a gentlewoman of very absolute behaviour, and of a good race.

Hau. And Jack Daw told us she could not speak !

True. So it was carried in plot, madam, to put her upon this old fellow, by sir Dauphine, his nephew, and one or two more of us : but she is a woman of an excellent assurance, and an extraordinary happy wit and tongue. You shall see her make rare sport with Daw ere night.

Hau. And he brought us to laugh at her !

True. That falls out often, madam, that he that thinks himself the master-wit, is the master-fool. I assure your ladyship, ye cannot laugh at her.

Hau. No, we'll have her to the college : An she have wit, she shall be one of us, shall she not, Centaure ? we'll make her a collegiate.

Cen. Yes, faith, madam, and Mavis and she will set up a side.

True. Believe it, madam, and mistress Mavis she will sustain her part.

Mav. I'll tell you that, when I have talk'd with her, and tried her.

Hau. Use her very civilly, Mavis.

Mav. So I will, madam.   [*Whispers her.*

Mor. Blessed minute ! that they would whisper thus
ever !   [*Aside.*

True. In the mean time, madam, would but your
ladyship help to vex him a little : you know his disease,
talk to him about the wedding ceremonies, or call for
your gloves, or——

Hau. Let me alone. Centaure, help me.—Master
bridegroom, where are you ?

Mor. O, it was too miraculously good to last !
                                                  [*Aside.*

Hau. We see no ensigns of a wedding here ; no
character of a bride-ale : where be our scarves and our
gloves ? I pray you, give them us. Let us know your
bride's colours, and yours at least.

Cen. Alas, madam, he has provided none.

Mor. Had I known your ladyship's painter, I would.

Hau. He has given it you, Centaure, i'faith. But do
you hear, master Morose ? a jest will not absolve you in
this manner. You that have suck'd the milk of the
court, and from thence have been brought up to the very
strong meats and wine of it ; been a courtier from the
biggen to the nightcap, as we may say, and you to
offend in such a high point of ceremony as this, and let
your nuptials want all marks of solemnity ! How much
plate have you lost to-day (if you had but regarded your
profit), what gifts, what friends, through your mere
rusticity ?

Mor. Madam——

Hau. Pardon me, sir, I must insinuate your errors
to you ; no gloves ? no garters ? no scarves ? no
epithalamium ? no masque ?

Daw. Yes, madam, I'll make an epithalamium, I
promise my mistress ; I have begun it already : will
your ladyship hear it ?

Hau. Ay, good Jack Daw.

Mor. Will it please your ladyship command a chamber, and be private with your friend ? you shall have your choice of rooms to retire to after : my whole house is yours. I know it hath been your ladyship's errand into the city at other times, however now you have been unhappily diverted upon me ; but I shall be loth to break any honourable custom of your ladyship's. And therefore, good madam——

Epi. Come, you are a rude bridegroom, to entertain ladies of honour in this fashion.

Cen. He is a rude groom indeed.

True. By that light you deserve to be grafted, and have your horns reach from one side of the island to the other.—Do not mistake me, sir; I but speak this to give the ladies some heart again, not for any malice to you.

Mor. Is this your bravo, ladies ?

True. As God [shall] help me, if you utter such another word, I'll take mistress bride in, and begin to you in a very sad cup; do you see ? Go to, know your friends, and such as love you.

Enter CLERIMONT, *followed by a number of* Musicians.

Cler. By your leave, ladies. Do you want any music ? I have brought you variety of noises. Play, sirs, all of you.

[*Aside to the* Musicians, *who strike up altogether.*]

Mor. O, a plot, a plot, a plot, a plot, upon me ! this day I shall be their anvil to work on, they will grate me asunder. 'Tis worse than the noise of a saw.

Cler. No, they are hair, rosin, and guts: I can give you the receipt.

True. Peace, boys !

Cler. Play ! I say.

True. Peace, rascals ! You see who's your friend now, sir : take courage, put on a martyr's resolution. Mock down all their attemptings with patience : 'tis but a day, and I would suffer heroically. Should an ass exceed me in fortitude ? no. You betray your infirmity with your hanging dull ears, and make them insult : bear up bravely, and constantly. [LA-FOOLE *passes over the stage as a Sewer, followed by Servants carrying dishes, and* Mistress OTTER.]—Look you here, sir, what honour is done you unexpected, by your nephew ; a wedding-dinner come, and a knight-sewer before it, for the more reputation : and fine mistress Otter, your neighbour, in the rump or tail of it.

Mor. Is that Gorgon, that Medusa come ! hide me, hide me.

True. I warrant you, sir, she will not transform you. Look upon her with a good courage. Pray you entertain her, and conduct your guests in. No !—Mistress bride, will you entreat in the ladies ? your bridegroom is so shame-faced, here.

Epi. Will it please your ladyship, madam ?

Hau. With the benefit of your company, mistress.

Epi. Servant, pray you perform your duties.
Daw. And glad to be commanded, mistress.
Cen. How like you her wit, Mavis?
Mav. Very prettily, absolutely well.
Mrs. Ott. 'Tis my place.
Mav. You shall pardon me, mistress Otter.
Mrs. Ott. Why, I am a collegiate.
Mav. But not in ordinary.
Mrs. Ott. But I am.
Mav. We'll dispute that within.   [*Exeunt* Ladies.
Cler. Would this had lasted a little longer.
True. And that they had sent for the heralds.

Enter CAPTAIN OTTER.

—Captain Otter ! what news ?

Ott. I have brought my bull, bear, and horse, in private, and yonder are the trumpeters without, and the drum, gentlemen.

        [*The drum and trumpets sound within.*

Mor. O, O, O !

Ott. And we will have a rouse in each of them, anon, for bold Britons, i'faith.   [*They sound again.*

Mor. O, O, O !   [*Exit hastily.*

Omnes. Follow, follow, follow !   [*Exeunt.*

ACT IV.

SCENE 1.—*A Room in* MOROSE'S *House.*

Enter TRUEWIT *and* CLERIMONT.

True. Was there ever poor bridegroom so tormented ? or man, indeed ?

Cler. I have not read of the like in the chronicles of the land.

True. Sure, he cannot but go to a place of rest, after all this purgatory.

Cler. He may presume it, I think.

True. The spitting, the coughing, the laughter, the sneezing, the farting, dancing, noise of the music, and her masculine and loud commanding, and urging the whole family, makes him think he has married a fury.

Cler. And she carries it up bravely.

True. Ay, she takes any occasion to speak : that's the height on't.

Cler. And how soberly Dauphine labours to satisfy him, that it was none of his plot !

True. And has almost brought him to the faith, in the article.   Here he comes.—

Enter Sir DAUPHINE.

Where is he now? what's become of him, Dauphine?

Daup. O, hold me up a little, I shall go away in the jest else.   He has got on his whole nest of night-caps, and lock'd himself up in the top of the house, as high as ever he can climb from the noise.   I peep'd in at a cranny, and saw him sitting over a cross-beam of the roof, like him on the saddler's horse in Fleet-street, upright : and he will sleep there.

Cler. But where are your collegiates?

Daup. Withdrawn with the bride in private.

True. O, they are instructing her in the college-grammar.   If she have grace with them, she knows all their secrets instantly.

Cler. Methinks the lady Haughty looks well to-day, for all my dispraise of her in the morning.   I think, I shall come about to thee again, Truewit.

True. Believe it, I told you right.   Women ought to repair the losses time and years have made in their features, with dressings.   And an intelligent woman, if she know by herself the least defect, will be most curious to hide it : and it becomes her.   If she be short, let her sit much, lest, when she stands, she be thought to sit.   If she have an ill foot, let her wear her gown the longer, and her shoe the thinner.   If a fat hand, and scald nails, let her carve the less, and act in gloves.   If a sour breath, let her never discourse fasting, and always talk at her distance.   If she have black and rugged teeth, let her offer the less at laughter, especially if she laugh wide and open.

Cler. O, you shall have some women, when they laugh, you would think they brayed, it is so rude and——

True. Ay, and others, that will stalk in their gait like an estrich, and take huge strides. I cannot endure such a sight. I love measure in the feet, and number in the voice : they are gentlenesses, that oftentimes draw no less than the face.

Daup. How camest thou to study these creatures so exactly? I would thou wouldst make me a proficient.

True. Yes, but you must leave to live in your chamber, then, a month together upon Amadis de Gaul, or Don Quixote, as you are wont ; and come abroad where the matter is frequent, to court, to tiltings, public shows and feasts, to plays, and church sometimes : thither they come to shew their new tires too, to see, and to be seen. In these places a man shall find whom to love, whom to play with, whom to touch once, whom to hold ever. The variety arrests his judgment. A wench to please a man comes not down dropping from the ceiling, as he lies on his back droning a tobacco-pipe. He must go where she is.

Daup. Yes, and be never the nearer.

True. Out, heretic ! That diffidence makes thee worthy it should be so.

Cler. He says true to you, Dauphine.

Daup. Why ?

True. A man should not doubt to overcome any woman. Think he can vanquish them, and he shall : for though they deny, their desire is to be tempted. Penelope herself cannot hold out long. Ostend, you saw, was taken at last. You must perséver, and hold to your purpose. They would solicit us, but that they are afraid. Howsoever, they wish in their hearts we should solicit them. Praise them, flatter them, you shall never want eloquence or trust : even the chastest delight to feel themselves that way rubb'd. With praises you must mix kisses too : if they take them, they'll take more—though they strive, they would be overcome.

Cler. O, but a man must beware of force.

True. It is to them an acceptable violence, and has oft-times the place of the greatest courtesy. She that might have been forced, and you let her go free without touching, though then she seem to thank you, will ever hate you after ; and glad in the face, is assuredly sad at the heart.

Cler. But all women are not to be taken all ways.

True. 'Tis true ; no more than all birds, or all fishes. If you appear learned to an ignorant wench, or jocund to a sad, or witty to a foolish, why she presently begins to mistrust herself. You must approach them in their own height, their own line ; for the contrary makes many, that fear to commit themselves to noble and worthy fellows, run into the embraces of a rascal. If she love wit, give verses, though you borrow them of a friend, or buy them, to have good. If valour, talk of your sword, and be frequent in the mention of quarrels, though you be staunch in fighting. If activity, be seen on your barbary often, or leaping over stools, for the credit of your back. If she love good clothes or dressing, have your learned council about you every morning, your French tailor, barber, linener, etc. Let your powder, your glass, and your comb be your dearest acquaintance. Take more care for the ornament of your head, than the safety ; and wish the commonwealth rather troubled, than a hair about you. That will take her. Then, if she be covetous and craving, do you promise any thing, and perform sparingly ; so shall you keep her in appetite still. Seem as you would give, but be like a barren field, that yields little ; or unlucky dice to foolish and hoping gamesters. Let your gifts be slight and dainty, rather than precious. Let cunning be above cost. Give cherries at time of year, or apricots : and say, they were sent you out of the country, though you bought them in Cheapside. Admire her tires : like her in all fashions; compare her in every habit to some deity ; invent excellent dreams to flatter her, and riddles ; or, if she be a great one, perform always the second parts to her : like what she likes, praise whom she praises, and fail not to make the household and servants yours, yea the whole family, and salute them by their names, ('tis but light cost, if you can purchase them so,) and make her physician your pensioner, and her chief woman. Nor will it be out of your gain to make love to her too, so she follow, not usher her lady's pleasure. All blabbing is taken away, when she comes to be a part of the crime.

Daup. On what courtly lap hast thou late slept, to come forth so sudden and absolute a courtling ?

True. Good faith, I should rather question you, that are so hearkening after these mysteries. I begin to suspect your diligence, Dauphine. Speak, art thou in love in earnest ?

Daup. Yes, by my troth, am I ; 'twere ill dissembling before thee.

True. With which of them, I prithee ?

Daup. With all the collegiates.

Cler. Out on thee ! We'll keep you at home, believe it, in the stable, an you be such a stallion.

True. No ; I like him well. Men should love wisely, and all women ; some one for the face, and let her please the eye ; another for the skin, and let her please the touch ; a third for the voice, and let her please the ear ; and where the objects mix, let the senses so too. Thou would'st think it strange, if I should make them all in love with thee afore night !

Daup. I would say, thou hadst the best philtre in the

world, and couldst do more than madam Medea, or doctor Foreman.

True. If I do not, let me play the mountebank for my meat, while I live, and the bawd for my drink.

Daup. So be it, I say.

Enter OTTER, *with his three Cups,* DAW, *and* LA-FOOLE.

Ott. O lord, gentlemen, how my knights and I have mist you here!

Cler. Why, captain, what service, what service?

Ott. To see me bring up my bull, bear, and horse to fight.

Daw. Yes, faith, the captain says we shall be his dogs to bait them.

Daup. A good employment.

True. Come on, let's see you course, then.

La-F. I am afraid my cousin will be offended, if she come.

Ott. Be afraid of nothing.—Gentlemen, I have placed the drum and the trumpets, and one to give them the sign when you are ready. Here's my bull for myself, and my bear for sir John Daw, and my horse for sir Amorous. Now set your foot to mine, and yours to his, and——

La-F. Pray God my cousin come not.

Ott. St. George, and St. Andrew, fear no cousins. Come, sound, sound! [*Drum and trumpets sound.*] *Et rauco strepuerunt cornua cantu.* [*They drink.*

True. Well said, captain, i'faith; well fought at the bull.

Cler. Well held at the bear.

True. Low, low! captain.

Daup. O, the horse has kick'd off his dog already.

La-F. I cannot drink it, as I am a knight.

True. Ods so! off with his spurs, somebody.

La-F. It goes against my conscience.　My cousin will be angry with it.

Daw. I have done mine.

True. You fought high and fair, sir John.

Cler. At the head.

Daup. Like an excellent bear-dog.

Cler. You take no notice of the business, I hope?

Daw. Not a word, sir : you see we are jovial.

Ott. Sir Amorous, you must not equivocate.　It must be pull'd down, for all my cousin.

Cler. 'Sfoot, if you take not your drink, they'll think you are discontented with something; you'll betray all, if you take the least notice.

La-F. Not I; I'll both drink and talk then.

Ott. You must pull the horse on his knees, sir Amorous; fear no cousins.　*Jacte est alea.*

True. O, now he's in his vein, and bold.　The least hint given him of his wife now, will make him rail desperately.

Cler. Speak to him of her.

True. Do you, and I'll fetch her to the hearing of it.

　　　　　　　　　　　　　　　　　[Exit.

Daup. Captain He-Otter, your She-Otter is coming, your wife.

Ott. Wife! buz? *titivilitium!*　There's no such thing in nature.　I confess, gentlemen, I have a cook, a laundress, a house-drudge, that serves my necessary turns, and goes under that title; but he's an ass that will be so uxorious to tie his affections to one circle. Come, the name dulls appetite.　Here, replenish again ; another bout.　[*Fills the cups again.*]　Wives are nasty, sluttish animals.

Daup. O, captain.

Ott. As ever the earth bare, *tribus verbis.*—Where's Master Truewit?

Daw. He's slipt aside, sir.

Cler. But you must drink and be jovial.

Daw. Yes, give it me.

La-F. And me too.

Daw. Let's be jovial.

La-F. As jovial as you will.

Ott. Agreed. Now you shall have the bear, cousin, and sir John Daw the horse, and I'll have the bull still. Sound, Tritons of the Thames! [*Drum, and trumpets sound again.*] *Nunc est bibendum, nunc pede libero——*

Mor. [*above.*] Villains, murderers, sons of the earth, and traitors, what do you there?

Cler. O, now the trumpets have waked him, we shall have his company.

Ott. A wife is a scurvy clogdogdo, an unlucky thing, a very foresaid bear-whelp, without any good fashion or breeding, *mala bestia.*

Re-enter TRUEWIT *behind, with* Mistress OTTER.

Daup. Why did you marry one then, captain?

Ott. A pox!——I married with six thousand pound, I. I was in love with that. I have not kissed my Fury these forty weeks.

Cler. The more to blame you, captain.

True. Nay, mistress Otter, hear him a little first.

Ott. She has a breath worse than my grandmother's, *profecto.*

Mrs. Ott. O treacherous liar! kiss me, sweet master Truewit, and prove him a slandering knave.

True. I'll rather believe you, lady.

Ott. And she has a peruke that's like a pound of hemp, made up in shoe-threads.

Mrs. Ott. O viper, mandrake!

Ott. A most vile face! and yet she spends me forty pound a year in mercury and hogs-bones. All her teeth were made in the Black-friars, both her eye-brows in the Strand, and her hair in Silver-street. Every part of the town owns a piece of her.

Mrs. Ott. [*comes forward.*] I cannot hold.

Ott. She takes herself asunder still when she goes to bed, into some twenty boxes; and about next day noon is put together again, like a great German clock : and so comes forth, and rings a tedious larum to the whole house, and then is quiet again for an hour, but for her quarters.—Have you done me right, gentlemen ?

Mrs. Ott. [*falls upon him and beats him.*] No, sir, I'll do you right with my quarters, with my quarters.

Ott. O, hold, good princess.

True. Sound, sound ! [*Drum and trumpets sound.*

Cler. A battle, a battle !

Mrs. Ott. You notorious stinkardly bearward, does my breath smell ?

Ott. Under correction, dear princess.—Look to my bear and my horse, gentlemen.

Mrs. Ott. Do I want teeth, and eyebrows, thou bull-dog ?

True. Sound, sound still. [*They sound again.*

Ott. No, I protest, under correction——

Mrs. Ott. Ay, now you are under correction, you protest : but you did not protest before correction, sir. Thou Judas, to offer to betray thy princess ! I'll make thee an example—— [*Beats him.*

Enter MOROSE *with his long sword.*

Mor. I will have no such examples in my house, lady Otter.

Mrs. Ott. Ah !——

[Mrs. OTTER, DAW, *and* LA-FOOLE *run off.*

Mor. Mistress Mary Ambree, your examples are dangerous.—Rogues, hell-hounds, Stentors ! out of my doors, you sons of noise and tumult, begot on an ill May-day, or when the galley-foist is afloat to Westminster! [*Drives out the musicians.*]   A trumpeter could not be conceived but then.

Daup. What ails you, sir?

Mor. They have rent my roof, walls, and all my windows asunder, with their brazen throats.   [*Exit.*

True. Best follow him, Dauphine.

Daup. So I will.   [*Exit.*

Cler. Where's Daw and La-Foole?

Ott. They are both run away, sir.   Good gentlemen, help to pacify my princess, and speak to the great ladies for me.   Now must I go lie with the bears this fort-night, and keep out of the way, till my peace be made, for this scandal she has taken.   Did you not see my bull-head, gentlemen?

Cler. Is't not on, captain?

True. No; but he may make a new one, by that is on.

Ott. O, here it is.   An you come over, gentlemen, and ask for Tom Otter, we'll go down to Ratcliff, and have a course i'faith, for all these disasters.   There is *bona spes* left.

True. Away, captain, get off while you are well.
[*Exit* OTTER.

Cler. I am glad we are rid of him.

True. You had never been, unless we had put his wife upon him.   His humour is as tedious at last, as it was ridiculous at first.   [*Exeunt.*

SCENE II.—*A long open Gallery in the same.*

Enter Lady HAUGHTY, Mistress OTTER, MAVIS, DAW,
LA-FOOLE, CENTAURE, *and* EPICŒNE.

Hau. We wonder'd why you shriek'd so, mistress Otter.

Mrs. Ott. O lord, madam, he came down with a huge long naked weapon in both his hands, and look'd so dreadfully ! sure he's beside himself.

Mav. Why, what made you there, mistress Otter?

Mrs. Ott. Alas, mistress Mavis, I was chastising my subject, and thought nothing of him.

Daw. Faith, mistress, you must do so too : learn to chastise.　Mistress Otter corrects her husband so, he dares not speak but under correction.

La-F. And with his hat off to her : 'twould do you good to see.

Hau. In sadness, 'tis good and mature counsel ; practise it, Morose.　I'll call you Morose still now, as I call Centaure and Mavis ; we four will be all one.

Cen. And you'll come to the college, and live with us?

Hau. Make him give milk and honey.

Mav. Look how you manage him at first, you shall have him ever after.

Cen. Let him allow you your coach, and four horses, your woman, your chamber-maid, your page, your gentleman-usher, your French cook, and four grooms.

Hau. And go with us to Bedlam, to the china-houses, and to the Exchange.

Cen. It will open the gate to your fame.

Hau. Here's Centaure has immortalised herself, with taming of her wild male.

Mav. Ay, she has done the miracle of the kingdom.

Enter CLERIMONT *and* TRUEWIT.

Epi. But, ladies, do you count it lawful to have such plurality of servants, and do them all graces ?

Hau. Why not ? why should women deny their favours to men ? are they the poorer or the worse ?

Daw. Is the Thames the less for the dyers' water, mistress ?

La-F. Or a torch for lighting many torches?

True. Well said, La-Foole; what a new one he has got!

Cen. They are empty losses women fear in this kind.

Hau. Besides, ladies should be mindful of the approach of age, and let no time want his due use. The best of our days pass first.

Mav. We are rivers, that cannot be call'd back, madam: she that now excludes her lovers, may live to lie a forsaken beldame, in a frozen bed.

Cen. 'Tis true, Mavis: and who will wait on us to coach then? or write, or tell us the news then, make anagrams of our names, and invite us to the Cockpit, and kiss our hands all the play-time, and draw their weapons for our honours?

Hau. Not one.

Daw. Nay, my mistress is not altogether unintelligent of these things; here be in presence have tasted of her favours.

Cler. What a neighing hobby-horse is this!

Epi. But not with intent to boast them again, servant.—And have you those excellent receipts, madam, to keep yourselves from bearing of children?

Hau. O yes, Morose: how should we maintain our youth and beauty else? Many births of a woman make her old, as many crops make the earth barren.

Enter MOROSE *and* DAUPHINE.

Mor. O my cursed angel, that instructed me to this fate!

Daup. Why, sir?

Mor. That I should be seduced by so foolish a devil as a barber will make!

Daup. I would I had been worthy, sir, to have

partaken your counsel; you should never have trusted it to such a minister.

Mor. Would I could redeem it with the loss of an eye, nephew, a hand, or any other member.

Daup. Marry, God forbid, sir, that you should geld yourself, to anger your wife.

Mor. So it would rid me of her!—and, that I did supererogatory penance in a belfry, at Westminster-hall, in the Cockpit, at the fall of a stag, the Tower-wharf—what place is there else?—London-bridge, Paris-garden, Billinsgate, when the noises are at their height, and loudest. Nay, I would sit out a play, that were nothing but fights at sea, drum, trumpet, and target.

Daup. I hope there shall be no such need, sir. Take patience, good uncle. This is but a day, and 'tis well worn too now.

Mor. O, 'twill be so for ever, nephew, I foresee it, for ever. Strife and tumult are the dowry that comes with a wife.

True. I told you so, sir, and you would not believe me.

Mor. Alas, do not rub those wounds, master Truewit, to blood again: 'twas my negligence. Add not affliction to affliction. I have perceived the effect of it too late, in madam Otter.

Epi. How do you, sir?

Mor. Did you ever hear a more unnecessary question? as if she did not see! Why, I do as you see, empress, empress.

Epi. You are not well, sir; you look very ill: something has distemper'd you.

Mor. O horrible, monstrous impertinencies! would not one of these have served, do you think, sir? would not one of these have served!

True. Yes, sir; but these are but notes of female kindness, sir; certain tokens that she has a voice, sir.

Mor. O, is it so! Come, an't be no otherwise—— What say you?

Epi. How do you feel yourself, sir?

Mor. Again that!

True. Nay, look you, sir, you would be friends with your wife upon unconscionable terms; her silence.

Epi. They say you are run mad, sir.

Mor. Not for love, I assure you, of you; do you see?

Epi. O lord, gentlemen! lay hold on him, for God's sake. What shall I do? who's his physician, can you tell, that knows the state of his body best, that I might send for him? Good sir, speak; I'll send for one of my doctors else.

Mor. What, to poison me, that I might die intestate, and leave you possest of all!

Epi. Lord, how idly he talks, and how his eyes sparkle! he looks green about the temples! do you see what blue spots he has!

Cler. Ay, tis melancholy.

Epi. Gentlemen, for Heaven's sake, counsel me. Ladies;—servant, you have read Pliny and Paracelsus; ne'er a word now to comfort a poor gentlewoman? Ay me, what fortune had I, to marry a distracted man!

Daw. I'll tell you, mistress——

True. How rarely she holds it up! [*Aside to* CLER.

Mor. What mean you, gentlemen?

Epi. What will you tell me, servant?

Daw. The disease in Greek is called μανια, in Latin, *insania, furor, vel ecstasis melancholica,* that is, *egressio,* when a man *ex melancholico evadit fanaticus.*

Mor. Shall I have a lecture read upon me alive?

Daw. But he may be but *phreneticus* yet, mistress; and *phrenctis* is only *delirium,* or so.

Epi. Ay, that is for the disease, servant ; but what is this to the cure ?   We are sure enough of the disease.

Mor. Let me go.

True. Why, we'll entreat her to hold her peace, sir.

Mor. O no, labour not to stop her.   She is like a conduit-pipe, that will gush out with more force when she opens again.

Hau. I'll tell you, Morose, you must talk divinity to him altogether, or moral philosophy.

La-F. Ay, and there's an excellent book of moral philosophy, madam, of Reynard the Fox, and all the beasts, called Doni's Philosophy.

Cen. There is, indeed, sir Amorous La-Foole.

Mor. O misery !

La-F. I have read it, my lady Centaure, all over, to my cousin here.

Mrs. Ott. Ay, and 'tis a very good book as any is, of the moderns.

Daw. Tut, he must have Seneca read to him, and Plutarch, and the ancients ; the moderns are not for this disease.

Cler. Why, you discommended them too, to-day, sir John.

Daw. Ay, in some cases : but in these they are best, and Aristotle's ethics.

Mav. Say you so, sir John ?   I think you are deceived; you took it upon trust.

Hau. Where's Trusty, my woman ?   I'll end this difference.   I prithee, Otter, call her.   Her father and mother were both mad, when they put her to me.

Mor. I think so.—Nay, gentlemen, I am tame.   This is but an exercise, I know, a marriage ceremony, which I must endure.

Hau. And one of them, I know not which, was cured

with the Sick Man's Salve, and the other with Green's
Groat's-worth of Wit.

True. A very cheap cure, madam.

Enter TRUSTY.

Hau. Ay, 'tis very feasible.

Mrs. Ott. My lady call'd for you, mistress Trusty :
you must decide a controversy.

Hau. O, Trusty, which was it you said, your father,
or your mother, that was cured with the Sick Man's
Salve ?

Trus. My mother, madam, with the Salve.

True. Then it was the sick woman's salve ?

Trus. And my father with the Groat's-worth of Wit.
But there was other means used : we had a preacher that
would preach folk asleep still ; and so they were pre-
scribed to go to church, by an old woman that was their
physician, thrice a-week——

Epi. To sleep ?

Trus. Yes, forsooth : and every night they read
themselves asleep on those books.

Epi. Good faith, it stands with great reason. I would
I knew where to procure those books.

Mor. Oh !

La-F. I can help you with one of them, mistress
Morose, the Groat's-worth of Wit.

Epi. But I shall disfurnish you, sir Amorous : can
you spare it ?

La-F. O yes, for a week, or so ; I'll read it myself to
him.

Epi. No, I must do that, sir ; that must be my
office.

Mor. Oh, oh !

Epi. Sure he would do well enough, if he could sleep.

Mor. No, I should do well enough, if you could sleep.

Have I no friend that will make her drunk, or give her a little laudanum, or opium ?

True. Why, sir, she talks ten times worse in her sleep.

Mor. How !

Cler. Do you know that, sir ? never ceases all night.

True. And snores like a porpoise.

Mor. O redeem me, fate ; redeem me, fate ! For how many causes may a man be divorced, nephew?

Daup. I know not, truly, sir.

True. Some divine must resolve you in that, sir, or canon-lawyer.

Mor. I will not rest, I will not think of any other hope or comfort, till I know.

[*Exit with* DAUPHINE.

Cler. Alas, poor man !

True. You'll make him mad indeed, ladies, if you pursue this.

Hau. No, we'll let him breathe now, a quarter of an hour or so.

Cler. By my faith, a large truce !

Hau. Is that his keeper, that is gone with him ?

Daw. It is his nephew, madam.

La-F. Sir Dauphine Eugenie.

Cen. He looks like a very pitiful knight——

Daw. As can be. This marriage has put him out of all.

La-F. He has not a penny in his purse, madam.

Daw. He is ready to cry all this day.

La-F. A very shark ; he set me in the nick t'other night at Primero.

True. How these swabbers talk !

Cler. Ay, Otter's wine has swell'd their humours above a spring-tide.

Hau. Good Morose, let's go in again. I like your couches exceeding well ; we'll go lie and talk there.

[*Exeunt* HAU. CEN. MAV. TRUS. LA-FOOLE, *and* DAW.

Epi. [*following them.*] I wait on you, madam.

True. [*stopping her.*] 'Slight, I will have them as silent as signs, and their post too, ere I have done. Do you hear, lady-bride ! I pray thee now, as thou art a noble wench, continue this discourse of Dauphine within ; but praise him exceedingly : magnify him with all the height of affection thou canst ;—I have some purpose in't : and but beat off these two rooks, Jack Daw and his fellow, with any discontentment, hither, and I'll honour thee for ever.

Epi. I was about it here. It angered me to the soul, to hear them begin to talk so malépert.

True. Pray thee perform it, and thou winn'st me an idolater to thee everlasting.

Epi. Will you go in and hear me do't ?

True. No, I'll stay here. Drive them out of your company, 'tis all I ask ; which cannot be any way better done, than by extolling Dauphine, whom they have so slighted.

Epi. I warrant you : you shall expect one of them presently. [*Exit.*

Cler. What a cast of kestrils are these, to hawk after ladies, thus !

True. Ay, and strike at such an eagle as Dauphine.

Cler. He will be mad when we tell him. Here he comes.

Re-enter DAUPHINE.

Cler. O sir, you are welcome.

True. Where's thine uncle !

Daup. Run out of doors in his night-caps, to talk with a casuist about his divorce. It works admirably.

True. Thou wouldst have said so, an thou hadst been here! The ladies have laugh'd at thee most comically, since thou went'st, Dauphine.

Cler. And ask'd, if thou wert thine uncle's keeper.

True. And the brace of baboons answer'd, Yes; and said thou wert a pitiful poor fellow, and didst live upon posts, and hadst nothing but three suits of apparel, and some few benevolences that the lords gave thee to fool to them, and swagger.

Daup. Let me not live, I'll beat them: I'll bind them both to grand-madam's bed-posts, and have them baited with monkies.

True. Thou shalt not need, they shall be beaten to thy hand, Dauphine. I have an execution to serve upon them, I warrant thee, shall serve; trust my plot.

Daup. Ay, you have many plots! so you had one to make all the wenches in love with me.

True. Why, if I do it not yet afore night, as near as 'tis, and that they do not every one invite thee, and be ready to scratch for thee, take the mortgage of my wit.

Cler. 'Fore God, I'll be his witness thou shalt have it, Dauphine: thou shalt be his fool for ever, if thou dost not.

True. Agreed. Perhaps 'twill be the better estate. Do you observe this gallery, or rather lobby, indeed? Here are a couple of studies, at each end one: here will I act such a tragi-comedy between the Guelphs and the Ghibellines, Daw and La-Foole——which of them comes out first, will I seize on;—you two shall be the chorus behind the arras, and whip out between the acts and speak—If I do not make them keep the peace for this remnant of the day, if not of the year. I have failed once——I hear Daw coming: hide, [*they withdraw*] and do not laugh, for God's sake.

Re-enter DAW.

Daw. Which is the way into the garden, trow?

True. O, Jack Daw! I am glad I have met with you. In good faith, I must have this matter go no further between you : I must have it taken up.

Daw. What matter, sir? between whom?

True. Come, you disguise it : sir Amorous and you. If you love me, Jack, you shall make use of your philosophy now, for this once, and deliver me your sword. This is not the wedding the Centaurs were at, though there be a she one here. [*Takes his sword.*] The bride has entreated me I will see no blood shed at her bridal : you saw her whisper me erewhile.

Daw. As I hope to finish Tacitus, I intend uo muider.

True. Do you not wait for sir Amorous?

Daw. Not I, by my knighthood.

True. And your scholarship too.

Daw. And my scholarship too.

True. Go to, then I return you your sword, and ask you mercy ; but put it not up, for you will be assaulted. I understood that you had apprehended it, and walked here to brave him ; and that you had held your life contemptible, in regard of your honour.

Daw. No, no ; no such thing, I assure you.　He and I parted now, as good friends as could be.

True. Trust not you to that visor.　I saw him since dinner with another face : I have known many men in my time vex'd with losses, with deaths, and with abuses ; but so offended a wight as sir Amorous, did I never see or read of.　For taking away his guests, sir, to-day, that's the cause ; and he declares it behind your back with such threatenings and contempts——He said to Dauphine, you were the arrant'st ass——

Daw. Ay, he may say his pleasure,

True. And swears you are so protested a coward, that he knows you will never do him any manly or single right; and therefore he will take his course.

Daw. I'll give him any satisfaction sir—but fighting.

True. Ay, sir: but who knows what satisfaction he'll take: blood he thirsts for, and blood he will have; and whereabouts on you he will have it, who knows but himself!

Daw. I pray you, master Truewit, be you a mediator.

True. Well, sir, conceal yourself then in this study till I return. [*Puts him into the study.*] Nay, you must be content to be lock'd in; for, for mine own reputation, I would not have you seen to receive a public disgrace, while I have the matter in managing. Ods so, here he comes; keep your breath close, that he do not hear you sigh. In good faith, sir Amorous, he is not this way; I pray you be merciful, do not murder him? he is a Christian, as good as you: you are arm'd as if you sought revenge on all his race. Good Dauphine, get him away from this place. I never knew a man's choler so high, but he would speak to his friends, he would hear reason.—Jack Daw, Jack! asleep!

Daw. [*within.*] Is he gone, master Truewit?

True. Ay; did you hear him?

Daw. O lord! yes.

True. What a quick ear fear has!

Daw. [*comes out of the closet.*] But is he so arm'd, as you say?

True. Arm'd! did you ever see a fellow set out to take possession?

Daw. Ay, sir.

True. That may give you some light to conceive of him; but 'tis nothing to the principal. Some false brother in the house has furnish'd him strangely ; or, if it were out of the house, it was Tom Otter.

Daw. Indeed, he's a captain, and his wife is his kinswoman.

True. He has got some body's old two-hand sword, to mow you off at the knees ; and that sword hath spawn'd such a dagger !—But then he is so hung with pikes, halberds, petronels, calivers and muskets, that he looks like a justice of peace's hall ; a man of two thousand a-year is not cess'd at so many weapons as he has on. There was never fencer challenged at so many several foils. You would think he meant to murder all St. Pulchre's parish. If he could but victual himself for half a-year in his breeches, he is sufficiently arm'd to over-run a country.

Daw. Good lord ! what means he, sir ? I pray you, master Truewit, be you a mediator.

True. Well, I'll try if he will be appeased with a leg or an arm ; if not you must die once.

Daw. I would be loth to lose my right arm, for writing madrigals.

True. Why, if he will be satisfied with a thumb or a little finger, all's one to me. You must think, I'll do my best.   [*Shuts him up again.*

Daw. Good sir, do.

[CLERIMONT *and* DAUPHINE *come forward.*

Cler. What hast thou done ?

True. He will let me do nothing, he does all afore ; he offers his left arm.

Cler. His left wing for a Jack Daw.

Daup. Take it by all means.

True. How ! maim a man for ever, for a jest ? What a conscience hast thou !

Daup. 'Tis no loss to him ; he has no employment for

his arms, but to eat spoon-meat.   Beside, as good maim his body as his reputation.

True. He is a scholar and a wit, and yet he does not think so.   But he loses no reputation with us; for we all resolved him an ass before.   To your places again.

Cler. I pray thee, let be me in at the other a little.

True. Look, you'll spoil all; these be ever your tricks.

Cler. No, but I could hit of some things that thou wilt miss, and thou wilt say are good ones.

True. I warrant you.   I pray forbear, I'll leave it off, else.

Daup. Come away, Clerimont.

[DAUP. *and* CLER. *withdraw as before.*

Enter LA-FOOLE.

True. Sir Amorous !

La-F. Master Truewit.

True. Whither were you going ?

La-F. Down into the court to make water.

True. By no means, sir ; you shall rather tempt your breeches.

La-F. Why, sir ?

True. Enter here, if you love your life.

[*Opening the door of the other study.*

La-F. Why ? why ?

True. Question till your throat be cut, do: dally till the enraged soul find you.

La-F. Who is that ?

True. Daw it is : will you in ?

La-F. Ay, ay, I'll in : what's the matter ?

True. Nay, if he had been cool enough to tell us that, there had been some hope to atone you ; but he seems so implacably enraged !

La-F. 'Slight, let him rage ! I'll hide myself,

True. Do, good sir. But what have you done to him within, that should provoke him thus ? You have broke some jest upon him afore the ladies.

La-F. Not I, never in my life, broke jest upon any man. The bride was praising sir Dauphine, and he went away in snuff, and I followed him ; unless he took offence at me in his drink erewhile, that I would not pledge all the horse full.

True. By my faith, and that may be ; you remember well : but he walks the round up and down, through every room o' the house, with a towel in his hand, crying, *Where's La-Foole ? Who saw La-Foole ?* And when Dauphine and I demanded the cause, we can force no answer from him, but—*O revenge, how sweet art thou ! I will strangle him in this towel*—which leads us to conjecture that the main cause of his fury is, for bringing your meat to-day, with a towel about you, to his discredit.

La-F. Like enough. Why, an he be angry for that, I'll stay here till his anger be blown over.

True. A good becoming resolution, sir ; if you can put it on o' the sudden.

La-F. Yes, I can put it on : or, I'll away into the country presently.

True. How will you go out of the house, sir ? he knows you are in the house, and he'll watch this se'ennight, but he'll have you : he'll outwait a serjeaut for you.

La-F. Why, then I'll stay here.

True. You must think how to victual yourself in time then.

La-F. Why, sweet master Truewit, will you entreat my cousin Otter to send me a cold venison pasty, a bottle or two of wine, and a chamber-pot ?

True. A stool were better, sir, of sir Ajax his invention.

La-F. Ay, that will be better, indeed; and a pallat to lie on.

True. O, I would not advise you to sleep by any means.

La-F. Would you not, sir? Why, then I will not.

True. Yet, there's another fear——

La-F. Is there! what is't?

True. No, he cannot break open this door with his foot, sure.

La-F. I'll set my back against it, sir. I have a good back.

True. But then if he should batter.

La-F. Batter! if he dare, I'll have an action of battery against him.

True. Cast you the worst. He has sent for powder already, and what he will do with it, no man knows: perhaps blow up the corner of the house where he suspects you are. Here he comes; in quickly. [*Thrusts in* La-Foole *and shuts the door.*]—I protest, sir John Daw, he is not this way: what will you do? Before God, you shall hang no petard here: I'll die rather. Will you not take my word? I never knew one but would be satisfied.—Sir Amorous [*speaks through the key hole*], there's no standing out: he has made a petard of an old brass pot, to force your door. Think upon some satisfaction, or terms to offer him.

La-F. [*within.*] Sir, I'll give him any satisfaction: I dare give any terms.

True. You'll leave it to me, then?

La-F. Ay, sir: I'll stand to any conditions.

True. [*beckoning forward* Cler. *and* Dauph.] How now, what think you, sirs? were't not a difficult thing to determine which of these two fear'd most?

Cler. Yes, but this fears the bravest: the other a whiniling dastard, Jack Daw! But La-Foole, a brave heroic coward! and is afraid in a great look and a stout accent; I like him rarely.

True. Had it not been pity these two should have been concealed?

Cler. Shall I make a motion?

True. Briefly: for I must strike while 'tis hot.

Cler. Shall I go fetch the ladies to the catastrophe?

True. Umph! ay, by my troth.

Daup. By no mortal means. Let them continue in the state of ignorance, and err still; think them wits and fine fellows, as they have done. 'Twere sin to reform them.

True. Well, I will have them fetch'd, now I think on't, for a private purpose of mine: do, Clerimont, fetch them, and discourse to them all that's past, and bring them into the gallery here.

Daup. This is thy extreme vanity, now: thou think'st thou wert undone, if every jest thou mak'st were not published.

True. Thou shalt see how unjust thou art presently. Clerimont, say it was Dauphine's plot. [*Exit* CLERIMONT.] Trust me not, if the whole drift be not for thy good. There is a carpet in the next room, put it on, with this scarf over thy face, and a cushion on thy head, and be ready when I call Amorous. Away! [*Exit* DAUP.] John Daw!

       [*Goes to* DAW's *closet and brings him out.*

Daw. What good news, sir?

True. Faith, I have followed and argued with him hard for you. I told him you were a knight, and a scholar, and that you knew fortitude did consist *magis patiendo quam faciendo, magis ferendo quam feriendo.*

Daw. It doth so indeed, sir.

True. And that you would suffer, I told him: so at first he demanded by my troth, iu my conceit, too much.

Daw. What was it, sir ?

True. Your upper lip, aud six of your fore-teeth.

Daw. 'Twas unreasonable.

True. Nay, I told him plainly, you could not spare them all. So after loug argument *pro et con.* as you know, I brought him down to your two butter-teeth, and them he would have.

Daw. O, did you so ? Why, he shall have them.

True. But he shall not, sir, by your leave. The conclusion is this, sir : because you shall be very good friends hereafter, and this never to be remembered or upbraided ; besides, that he may not boast he has done any such thing to you in his own person ; he is to come here in disguise, give you five kicks in private, sir, take your sword from you, and lock you up in that study during pleasure: which will bo but a little while, we'll get it released presently.

Daw. Five kicks ! he shall have six, sir, to be friends.

True. Believe me, you shall not over-shoot yourself, to send him that word by me.

Daw. Deliver it, sir; he shall have it with all my heart, to be friends.

True. Friends ! Nay, and he should not be so, and heartily too, upon these terms, he shall have me to enemy while I live. Come, sir, bear it bravely.

Daw. O lord, sir, 'tis nothing.

True. True: what's six kicks to a man that reads Seneca ?

Daw. I have had a hundred, sir.

True. Sir Amorous !

Re-enter DAUPHINE, *disguised.*

No speaking one to another, or rehearsing old matters.

Daw. [*as* DAUP. *kicks him.*] One, two, three, four, five. I protest, sir Amorous, you shall have six.

True. Nay, I told you, you should not talk. Come, give him six, an he will needs. [DAUPHINE *kicks him again.*]—Your sword. [*takes his sword.*] Now return to your safe custody; you shall presently meet afore the ladies, and be the dearest friends one to another. [*Puts* DAW *into the study.*]—Give me the scarf now, thou shalt beat the other bare-faced. Stand by : [DAUPHINE *retires, and* TRUEWIT *goes to the other closet, and releases* LA-FOOLE.]—Sir Amorous !

La-F. What's here ! A sword ?

True. I cannot help it, without I should take the quarrel upon myself. Here he has sent you his sword——

La-F. I'll receive none on't.

True. And he wills you to fasten it against a wall, and break your head in some few several places against the hilts.

La-F. I will not : tell him roundly. I cannot endure to shed my own blood.

True. Will you not ?

La-F. No. I'll beat it against a fair flat wall, if that will satisfy him : if not, he shall beat it himself, for Amorous.

True. Why, this is strange starting off, when a man undertakes for you ! I offer'd him another condition ; will you stand to that ?

La-F. Ay, what is't ?

True. That you will be beaten in private.

La-F. Yes, I am content, at the blunt.

Enter, above, HAUGHTY, CENTAURE, MAVIS, Mistress
OTTER, EPICŒNE, *and* TRUSTY.

True. Then you must submit yourself to be hood-
winked in this scarf, and be led to him, where he will
take your sword from you, and make you bear a blow
over the mouth, gules, and tweaks by the nose *sans
nombre.*

La-F. I am content. But why must I be blinded ?

True. That's for your good, sir ; because, if he should
grow insolent upon this, and publish it hereafter to
your disgrace (which I hope he will not do), you might
swear safely, and protest, he never beat you, to your
knowledge.

La-F. O, I conceive.

True. I do not doubt but you'll be perfect good
friends upon't, and not dare to utter an ill thought one
of another in future.

La-F. Not I, as God help me, of him.

True. Nor he of you, sir. If he should, [*binds his
eyes.*]—Come, sir. [*leads him forward.*]—*All* hid, sir
John !

Enter DAUPHINE, *and tweaks him by the nose.*

La-F. Oh, sir John, sir John ! Oh, o-o-o-o-o-Oh——
True. Good sir John, leave tweaking, you'll blow his
nose off.—'Tis sir John's pleasure, you should retire
into the study. [*Puts him up again.*]—Why, now you
are friends. All bitterness between you, I hope, is
buried ; you shall come forth by and by, Damon and
Pythias upon't, and embrace with all the rankness of
friendship that can be.—I trust, we shall have them
tamer in their language hereafter. Dauphine, I worship
thee.—God's will, the ladies have surprised us !

Enter HAUGHTY, CENTAURE, MAVIS, Mistress OTTER,
EPICŒNE, *and* TRUSTY, *behind.*

Hau. Centaure, how our judgments were imposed on
by these adulterate knights !

Cen. Nay, madam, Mavis was more deceived than we ;
'twas her commendation utter'd them in the college.

Mav. I commended but their wits, madam, and their
braveries.   I never look'd toward their valours.

Hau. Sir Dauphine is valiant, and a wit too, it
seems.

Mav. And a bravery too.

Hau. Was this his project ?

Mrs. Ott. So master Clerimont intimates, madam.

Hau. Good Morose, when you come to the college,
will you bring him with you ? he seems a very perfect
gentleman.

Epi. He is so, madam, believe it.

Cen. But when will you come, Morose ?

Epi. Three or four days hence, madam, when I have
got me a coach and horses.

Hau. No, to-morrow, good Morose ; Centaure shall
send you her coach.

Mav. Yes faith, do, and bring sir Dauphine with
you.

Hau. She has promised that, Mavis.

Mav. He is a very worthy gentleman in his exteriors,
madam.

Hau. Ay, he shows he is judicial in his clothes.

Cen. And yet not so superlatively neat as some,
madam, that have their faces set in a brake.

Hau. Ay, and have every hair in form.

Mav. That wear purer linen than ourselves, and
profess more neatness than the French hermaphrodite !

Epi. Ay, ladies, they, what they tell one of us, have

told a thousand ; and are the only thieves of our fame, that think to take us with that perfume, or with that lace, and laugh at us unconscionably when they have done.

Hau. But sir Dauphine's carelessness becomes him.

Cen. I could love a man for such a nose.

Mav. Or such a leg.

Cen. He has an exceeding good eye, madam.

Mav. And a very good lock.

Cen. Good Morose, bring him to my chamber first.

Mrs. Ott. Please your honours to meet at my house, madam.

True. See how they eye thee, man ! they are taken, I warrant thee. [HAUGHTY *comes forward.*

Hau. You have unbraced our brace of knights here, master Truewit.

True. Not I, madam ; it was Sir Dauphine's ingine : who, if we have disfurnish'd your ladyship of any guard or service by it, is able to make the place good again in himself.

Hau. There is no suspicion of that, sir.

Cen. God so, Mavis, Haughty is kissing.

Mav. Let us go too, and take part.

[*They come forward.*

Hau. But I am glad of the fortune (beside the discovery of two such empty caskets) to gain the knowledge of so rich a mine of virtue as sir Dauphine.

Cen. We would be all glad to style him of our friendship, and see him at the college.

Mav. He cannot mix with a sweeter society, I'll prophesy ; and I hope he himself will think so.

Daup. I should be rude to imagine otherwise, lady.

True. Did not I tell thee, Dauphine ! Why, all their actions are governed by crude opinion, without reason or cause ; they know not why they do any thing ; but, as they are inform'd, believe, judge, praise, condemn, love, hate, and in emulation one of another, do all these things alike. Only they have a natural inclination sways them generally to the worst, when they are left to themselves. But pursue it, now thou hast them.

Hau. Shall we go in again, Morose?

Epi. Yes, madam.

Cen. We'll entreat sir Dauphine's company. .

True. Stay, good madam, the interview of the two friends, Pylades and Orestes ; I'll fetch them out to you straight.

Hau. Will you, master Truewit ?

Daup. Ay, but noble ladies, do not confess in your countenance, or outward bearing to them, any discovery of their follies, that we may see how they will bear up again, with what assurance and erection.

Hau. We will not, sir Dauphine.

Cen. Mav. Upon our honours, sir Dauphine.

True. [*goes to the first closet.*] Sir Amorous, sir Amorous ! The ladies are here.

La-F. [*within.*] Are they?

True. Yes; but slip out by and by, as their backs are turn'd, and meet sir John here, as by chance, when I call you. [*Goes to the other.*].—Jack Daw.

Daw. [*within.*] What say you, sir ?

True. Whip out behind me suddenly, and no anger in your looks to your adversary. Now, now !

[LA-FOOLE *and* DAW *slip out of their respective closets, and salute each other.*

La-F. Noble sir John Daw, where have you been ?

Daw. To seek you, sir Amorous.

La-F. Me ! I honour you.

Daw. I prevent you, sir.

Cler. They have forgot their rapiers.

True. O, they meet in peace, man.

Daup. Where's your sword, sir John ?

Cler. And yours, sir Amorous ?

Daw. Mine ! my boy had it forth to mend the handle, e'en now.

La-F. And my gold handle was broke too, and my boy had it forth.

Daup. Indeed, sir !—How their excuses meet !

Cler. What a consent there is in the handles !

True. Nay, there is so in the points too, I warrant you.

Enter MOROSE, *with the two swords, drawn in his hands.*

Mrs. Ott. O me ! madam, he comes again, the madman ! Away !

        [Ladies, DAW, *and* LA-FOOLE, *run off.*

Mor. What make these naked weapons here, gentlemen ?

True. O sir ! here hath like to have been murder since you went ; a couple of knights fallen out about the bride's favours ! We were fain to take away their weapons ; your house had been begg'd by this time else.

Mor. For what ?

Cler. For manslaughter, sir, as being accessary.

Mor. And for her favours ?

True. Ay, sir, heretofore, not present—Clerimont, carry them their swords now. They have done all the hurt they will do.

       [*Exit* CLER. *with the two swords.*

Daup. Have you spoke with the lawyer, sir ?

Mor. O no ! there is such a noise in the court, that they have frighted me home with more violence than I went ! such speaking and counter-speaking, with their several voices of citations, appellations, allegations, certificates, attachments, intergatories, references, convictions, and afflictions indeed, among the doctors and proctors, that the noise here is silence to't, a kind of calm midnight!

True. Why, sir, if you would be resolved indeed, I can bring you hither a very sufficient lawyer, and a learned divine, that shall enquire into every least scruple for you.

Mor. Can you, master Truewit?

True. Yes, and are very sober, grave persons, that will despatch it in a chamber, with a whisper or two.

Mor. Good sir, shall I hope this benefit from you, and trust myself into your hands?

True. Alas, sir! your nephew and I have been ashamed and oft-times mad, since you went, to think how you are abused. Go in, good sir, and lock yourself up till we call you : we'll tell you more anon, sir.

Mor. Do your pleasure with me, gentlemen ; I believe in you, and that deserves no delusion.   [*Exit.*

True. You shall find none, sir;—but heap'd, heap'd plenty of vexation.

Daup. What wilt thou do now, Wit?

True. Recover me hither Otter and the barber, if you can, by any means, presently.

Daup. Why? to what purpose?

True. O, I'll make the deepest divine, and gravest lawyer, out of them two for him——

Daup. Thou canst not, man: these are waking dreams.

True. Do not fear me. Clap but a civil gown with a welt on the one, and a canonical cloke with sleeves on the other, and give them a few terms in their mouths, if there come not forth as able a doctor and complete a parson, for this turn, as may be wish'd, trust not my election ; and I hope, without wronging the dignity of either profession, since they are but persons put on, and

for mirth's sake, to torment him.   The barber smatters
Latin, I remember.

Daup. Yes, and Otter too.

True. Well then, if I make them not wrangle out this
case to his no comfort, let me be thought a Jack
Daw or La-Foole or anything worse.   Go you to your
ladies, but first send for them.

Daup. I will.   [*Exeunt.*

ACT V.

SCENE I.—*A Room in* MOROSE's *House.*

Enter LA-FOOLE, CLERIMONT, *and* DAW.

La-F. Where had you our swords, master Clerimont ?

Cler. Why, Dauphine took them from the madman.

La-F. And he took them from our boys, I warrant
you.

Cler. Very like, sir.

La-F. Thank you, good master Clerimont.   Sir John
Daw and I are both beholden to you.

Cler. Would I knew how to make you so, gentlemen !

Daw. Sir Amorous and I are your servants, sir.

Enter MAVIS.

Mav. Gentlemen, have any of you a pen and ink ?   I
would fain write out a riddle in Italian, for sir Dauphine
to translate.

Cler. Not I, in troth, lady ; I am no scrivener.

Daw. I can furnish you, I think, lady.
                              [*Exeunt* DAW *and* MAVIS.

Cler. He has it in the haft of a knife, I believe.

La-F. No, he has his box of instruments.

Cler. Like a surgeon !

La-F. For the mathematics : his square, his compasses, his brass pens, and black-lead, to draw maps of every place and person where he comes.

Cler. How, maps of persons !

La-F. Yes, sir, of Nomentack when he was here, and of the prince of Moldavia, and of his mistress, mistress Epicœne.

Re-enter DAW.

Cler. Away ! he hath not found out her latitude, I hope.

La-F. You are a pleasant gentleman, sir.

Cler. Faith, now we are in private, let's wanton it a little, and talk waggishly.—Sir John, I am telling sir Amorous here, that you two govern the ladies wherever you come ; you carry the feminine gender afore you.

Daw. They shall rather carry us afore them, if they will, sir.

Cler. Nay, I believe that they do, withal—but that you are the prime men in their affections, and direct all their actions——

Daw. Not I ; sir Amorous is.

La-F. I protest, sir John is.

Daw. As I hope to rise in the state, sir Amorous, you have the person.

La-F. Sir John, you have the person, and the discourse too.

Daw. Not I, sir, I have no discourse—and then you have activity beside.

La-F. I protest, sir John, you come as high from Tripoly as I do, every whit : and lift as many join'd stools, and leap over them, if you would use it.

Cler. Well, agree on't together, knights ; for between you, you divide the kingdom or commonwealth of ladies' affections : I see it, and can perceive a little how they observe you, and fear you, indeed,   You could tell strange stories, my masters, if you would, I know.

Daw. Faith, we have seen somewhat, sir.

La-F. That we have——velvet petticoats, and wrought smocks, or so.

Daw. Ay, and——

Cler. Nay, out with it, sir John ; do not envy your friend the pleasure of hearing, when you have had the delight of tasting.

Daw. Why—a—Do you speak, sir Amorous.

La-F. No, do you, sir John Daw.

Daw. I' faith, you shall.

La-F. I' faith, you shall.

Daw. Why, we have been——

La-F. In the great bed at Ware together in our time. On, sir John.

Daw. Nay, do you, sir Amorous.

Cler. And these ladies with you, knights ?

La-F. No, excuse us, sir.

Daw. We must not wound reputation.

La-F. No matter—they were these, or others.   Our bath cost us fifteen pound when we came home.

Cler. Do you hear, sir John ?   You shall tell me but one thing truly, as you love me.

Daw. If I can, I will, sir.

Cler. You lay in the same house with the bride here?

Daw. Yes, and conversed with her hourly, sir.

Cler. And what humour is she of ?   Is she coming and open, free ?

Daw. O, exceeding open, sir.   I was her servant, and sir Amorous was to be.

Cler. Come, you have both had favours from her : I know, and have heard so much.

Daw. O, no, sir.

La-F. You shall excuse us, sir ; we must not wound reputation.

Cler. Tut, she is married now, and you cannot hurt her with any report ; and therefore speak plainly : how many times, i'faith ? which of you led first ? ha !

La-F. Sir John had her maidenhead, indeed.

Daw. O, it pleases him to say so, sir ; but sir Amorous knows what's what, as well.

Cler. Dost thou, i' faith, Amorous ?

La-F. In a manner, sir.

Cler. Why, I commend you, lads. Little knows don Bridegroom of this ; nor shall he, for me.

Daw. Hang him, mad ox !

Cler. Speak softly ; here comes his nephew, with the lady Haughty ; he'll get the ladies from you, sirs, if you look not to him in time.

La-F. Why, if he do, we'll fetch them home again, I warrant you.   [*Exit with* DAW.   CLER. *walks aside.*

Enter DAUPHINE *and* HAUGHTY.

Hau. I assure you, sir Dauphine, it is the price and estimation of your virtue only, that hath embark'd me to this adventure ; and I could not but make out to tell you so: nor can I repent me of the act, since it is always an argument of some virtue in our selves, that we love and affect it so in others.

Daup. Your ladyship sets too high a price on my weakness.

Hau. Sir, I can distinguish gems from pebbles——

Daup. Are you so skilful in stones ?   [*Aside.*

Hau. And howsoever I may suffer in such a judgment as yours, by admitting equality of rank or society with Centaure or Mavis——

Daup. You do not, madam ; I perceive they are your mere foils.

Hau. Then, are you a friend to truth, sir; it makes me love you the more. It is not the outward, but the inward man that I affect. They are not apprehensive of an eminent perfection, but love flat and dully.

Cen. [*within.*] Where are you, my Lady Haughty?

Hau. I come presently, Centaure.—My chamber, sir, my page shall shew you; and Trusty, my woman, shall be ever awake for you: you need not fear to communicate any thing with her, for she is a Fidelia. I pray you wear, this jewel for my sake, sir Dauphine—

Enter CENTAURE.

Where's Mavis, Centaure?

Cen. Within, madam, a writing. I'll follow you presently: [*Exit* HAU.] I'll but speak a word with sir Dauphine.

Daup. With me, madam?

Cen. Good sir Dauphine, do not trust Haughty, nor make any credit to her whatever you do besides. Sir Dauphine, I give you this caution, she is a perfect courtier, and loves nobody but for her uses; and for her uses she loves all. Besides, her physicians give her out to be none o' the clearest, whether she pay them or no, heaven knows; and she's above fifty too, and pargets! See her in a forenoon. Here comes Mavis, a worse face than she! you would not like this by candle-light.

Re-enter MAVIS.

If you'll come to my chamber one o' these mornings early, or late in an evening, I'll tell you more. Where's Haughty, Mavis?

Mav. Within, Centaure.

Cen. What have you there?

Mav. An Italian riddle for sir Dauphine,—you shall

not see it, i'faith, Centaure.—[*Exit* CEN.] Good sir
Dauphine, solve it for me : I'll call for it anon.   [*Exit.*
   Cler. [*coming forward.*] How now, Dauphine ! how
dost thou quit thyself of these females ?
   Daup. 'Slight, they haunt me like fairies, and give me
jewels here ; I cannot be rid of them.
   Cler. O, you must not tell though.
   Daup. Mass, I forgot that : I was never so assaulted.
One loves for virtue, and bribes me with this ; [*shews
the jewel.*]—another loves me with caution, and so
would possess me ; a third brings me a riddle here : and
all are jealous, and rail each at other.
   Cler. A riddle ! pray let me see it.   [*Reads.*

   Sir Dauphine, I chose this way of intimation for privacy. The
ladies here, I know, have both hope and purpose to make
a collegiate and servant of you. If I might be so honoured, as
to appear at any end of so noble a work, I would enter into a
fame of taking physic to-morrow, and continue it four or five
days, or longer, for your visitation.
                                         MAVIS.

   By my faith, a subtle one? Call you this a riddle ?
what's their plain-dealing, trow ?
   Daup. We lack Truewit to tell us that.
   Cler. We lack him for somewhat else too : his knights
reformadoes are wound up as high and insolent as ever
they were.
   Daup. You jest.
   Cler. No drunkards, either with wine or vanity, ever
confess'd such stories of themselves. I would not give
a fly's leg in balance against all the women's reputations
here, if they could be but thought to speak truth : and
for the bride, they have made their affidavit against her
directly——
   Daup. What, that they have lain with her ?
   Cler. Yes ; and tell times and circumstances, with

the cause why, and the place where. I had almost brought them to affirm that they had done it to-day.

Daup. Not both of them?

Cler. Yes, faith; with a sooth or two more I had effected it. They would have set it down under their hands.

Daup. Why, they will be our sport, I see, still, whether we will or no.

Enter TRUEWIT.

True. O, are you here? Come, Dauphine; go call your uncle presently: I have fitted my divine and my canonist, dyed their beards and all. The knaves do not know themselves, they are so exalted and altered. Preferment changes any man. Thou shalt keep one door and I another, and then Clerimont in the midst, that he may have no means of escape from their cavilling, when they grow hot once again. And then the women, as I have given the bride her instructions, to break in upon him in the l'envoy. O, 'twill be full and twanging! Away! fetch him. [*Exit* DAUPHINE.

Enter OTTER *disguised as a divine, and* CUTBEARD *as a canon lawyer.*

Come, master doctor, and master parson, look to your parts now, and discharge them bravely; you are well set forth, perform it as well. If you chance to be out, do not confess it with standing still, or humming, or gaping one at another; but go on, and talk aloud and eagerly: use vehement action, and only remember your terms, and you are safe. Let the matter go where it will: you have many will do so. But at first be very solemn and grave, like your garments, though you loose yourselves after, and skip out like a brace of jugglers on a table. Here he comes: set your faces, and look superciliously, while I present you.

Re-enter MOROSE *with* DAUPHINE.

Mor. Are these the two learned men ?

True. Yes, sir; please you salute them.

Mor. Salute them ! I had rather do any thing, than wear out time so unfruitfully, sir. I wonder how these common forms, as *God save you,* and *You are welcome,* are come to be a habit in our lives : or, *I am glad to see you !* when I cannot see what the profit can be of these words, so long as it is no whit better with him whose affairs are sad and grievous, that he hears this salutation.

True. 'Tis true, sir; we'll go to the matter then.— Gentlemen, master doctor, and master parson, I have acquainted you sufficiently with the business for which you are come hither; and you are not now to inform yourselves in the state of the question, I know. This is the gentleman who expects your resolution, and therefore, when you please, begin.

Ott. Please you, master doctor.

Cut. Please you, good master parson.

Ott. I would hear the canon-law speak first.

Cut. It must give place to positive divinity, sir.

Mor. Nay, good gentlemen, do not throw me into circumstances. Let your comforts arrive quickly at me, those that are. Be swift in affording me my peace, if so I shall hope any. I love not your disputations, or your court-tumults. And that it be not strange to you, I will tell you : My father, in my education, was wont to advise me, that I should always collect and contain my mind, not suffering it to flow loosely; that I should look to what things were necessary to the carriage of my life, and what not ; embracing the one and eschewing the other : in short, that I should endear myself to rest, and avoid turmoil; which now is grown to be another nature to me. So that I come not to your public pleadings, or your places of noise; not that I neglect those things that make for the dignity of the commonwealth; but for the mere avoiding of clamours and impertineuces of orators, that know not how to be silent. And for the cause of noise, am I now a suitor to you. You do not know in what a misery I have been exercised this day, what a torrent of evil! my very house turns round with the tumult! I dwell in a windmill: the perpetual motion is here, and not at Eltham.

True. Well, good master doctor, will you break the ice? master parson will wade after.

Cut. Sir, though unworthy, and the weaker, I will presume.

Ott. 'Tis no presumption, *domine* doctor.

Mor. Yet again!

Cut. Your question is, For how many causes a man may have *divortium legitimum*, a lawful divorce? First, you must understand the nature of the word, divorce, *à divertendo*——

Mor. No excursions upon words, good doctor; to the question briefly.

Cut. I answer then, the canon law affords divorce but in few cases; and the priucipal is in the common case, the adulterous case: But there are *duodecim impedimenta*, twelve impediments, as we call them, all which do not *dirimere contractum*, but *irritum reddere matrimonium*, as we say in the canon law, *not take away the bond, but cause a nullity therein.*

Mor. I understood you before: good sir, avoid your impertineucy of translation.

Ott. He cannot open this too much, sir, by your favour.

Mor. Yet more!

True. O, you must give the learned men leave, sir.—To your impediments, master doctor.

Cut. The first is *impedimentum erroris.*

Ott. Of which there are several species.

Cut. Ay, as *error personæ.*

Ott. If you contract yourself to one person, thinking her another.

Cut. Then *error fortunæ.*

Ott. If she be a beggar, and you thought her rich.

Cut. Then, *error qualitatis.*

Ott. If she prove stubborn or head-strong, that you thought obedient.

Mor. How ! is that, sir, a lawful impediment ? One at once, I pray you, gentlemen.

Ott. Ay, *ante copulam*, but not *post copulam*, sir.

Cut. Master parson says right. *Nec post nuptiarum benedictionem.* It doth indeed but *irrita reddere sponsalia*, annul the contract ; after marriage it is of no obstancy.

True. Alas, sir, what a hope are we fallen from by this time !

Cut. The next is *conditio :* if you thought her free born, and she prove a bond-woman, there is impediment of estate and condition.

Ott. Ay, but, master doctor, those servitudes are *sublatæ* now, among us Christians.

Cut. By your favour, master parson——

Ott. You shall give me leave, master doctor.

Mor. Nay, gentlemen, quarrel not in that question ; it concerns not my case : pass to the third.

Cut. Well then, the third is *votum :* if either party have made a vow of chastity. But that practice, as master parson said of the other, is taken away among us, thanks be to discipline. The fourth is *cognatio ;* if the persons be of kin within the degrees.

Ott. Ay: do you know what the degrees are, sir?

Mor. No, nor I care not, sir; they offer me no comfort in the question, I am sure.

Cut. But there is a branch of this impediment may, which is *cognatio spiritualis:* if you were her godfather, sir, then the marriage is incestuous.

Ott. That comment is absurd and superstitious, master doctor: I cannot endure it. Are we not all brothers and sisters, and as much akin in that, as godfathers and goddaughters?

Mor. O me! to end the controversy, I never was a godfather, I never was a godfather in my life, sir. Pass to the next.

Cut. The fifth is *crimen adulterii;* the known case. The sixth, *cultus disparitas,* difference of religion: Have you ever examined her, what religion she is of?

Mor. No, I would rather she were of none, than be put to the trouble of it.

Ott. You may have it done for you, sir.

Mor. By no means, good sir; on to the rest: shall you ever come to an end, think you?

True. Yes, he has done half, sir. On to the rest.—Be patient, and expect, sir.

Cut. The seventh is *vis:* if it were upon compulsion or force.

Mor. O no, it was too voluntary, mine; too voluntary.

Cut. The eighth is *ordo;* if ever she have taken holy orders.

Ott. That's superstitious too.

Mor. No matter, master parson; would she would go into a nunnery yet.

Cut. The ninth is *ligamen;* if you were bound, sir, to any other before.

Mor. I thrust myself too soon into these fetters.

Cut. The tenth is *publica honestas;* which is *inchoata quædam affinitas.*

Ott. Ay, or *affinitas orta ex sponsalibus;* and is but *leve impedimentum.*

Mor. I feel no air of comfort blowing to me, in all this.

Cut. The eleventh is *affinitas ex fornicatione:*

Ott. Which is no less *vera affinitas,* than the other, master doctor.

Cut. True, *quæ oritur ex legitimo matrimonio.*

Ott. You say right, venerable doctor: and, *nascitur ex eo, quod per conjugium duæ personæ efficiuntur una caro——*

True. Hey-day, now they begin !

Cut. I conceive you, master parson : *ita per fornicationem æque est verus pater, qui sic generat——*

Ott. *Et vere filius qui sic generatur——*

Mor. What's all this to me ?

Cler. Now it grows warm.

Cut. The twelfth and last is, *si forte coire nequibis.*

Ott. Ay, this is *impedimentum gravissimum :* it doth utterly annul, and annihilate, that. If you have *manifestam frigiditatem,* you are well, sir.

True. Why, there is comfort come at length, sir. Confess yourself but a man unable, and she will sue to be divorced first.

Ott. Ay, or if there be *morbus perpetuus, et insanabilis;* as *paralysis, elephantiasis,* or so——

Daup. O, but *frigiditas* is the fairer way, gentlemen.

Ott. You say troth, sir, and as it is in the canon, master doctor——

Cut. I conceive you, sir.

Cler. Before he speaks !

Ott. That a boy, or child, under years, is not fit for

marriage, because he cannot *reddere debitum.*   So your *omnipotentes*——

True. Your *impotentes*, you whoreson lobster !

[*Aside to* OTT.

Ott. Your *impotentes*, I should say, are *minime apti ad contrahenda matrimonium.*

True. Matrimonium ! we shall have most unmatrimonial Latin with you : *matrimonia*, and be hang'd.

Daup. You put them out, man.

Cut. But then there will arise a doubt, master parson, in our case, *post matrimonium :* that *frigiditate præditus* —do you conceive me, sir ?

Ott. Very well, sir.

Cut. Who cannot *uti uxore pro uxore*, may *habere eam pro sorore.*

Ott. Absurd, absurd, absurd, and merely apostatical !

Cut. You shall pardon me, master parson, I can prove it.

Ott. You can prove a will, master doctor; you can prove nothing else.   Does not the verse of your own canon say,

Hæc socianda vetant connubia, facta retractant?

Cut. I grant you ; but how do they *retractare*, master parson.

Mor. O, this was it I feared.

Ott. In æternum, sir.

Cut. That's false in divinity, by your favour.

Ott. 'Tis false in humanity to say so.   Is he not *prorsus inutilis ad thorum?*   Can he *præstare fidem datam?*   I would fain know.

Cut. Yes ; how if he do *convalere ?*

Ott. He cannot *convalere*, it is impossible.

True. Nay, good sir, attend the learned men ; they'll think you neglect them else.

Cut. Or, if he do *simulare* himself *frigidum, odio uxoris,* or so ?

Ott. I say he is *adulter manifestus* then.

Daup. They dispute it very learnedly i' faith.

Ott. And *prostitutor uxoris ;* and this is positive.

Mor. Good sir, let me escape.

True. You will not do me that wrong, sir ?

Ott. And, therefore, if he be *manifeste frigidus,* sir——

Cut. Ay, if he be *manifeste frigidus,* I grant you——

Ott. Why, that was my conclusion.

Cut. And mine too.

True. Nay, hear the conclusion, sir.

Ott. Then, *frigiditatis causa*——

Cut. Yes, *causa frigiditatis*——

Mor. O, mine ears !

Ott. She may have *libellum divortii* against you.

Cut. Ay, *divortii libellum* she will sure have.

Mor. Good echoes, forbear.

Ott. If you confess it.——

Cut. Which I would do, sir——

Mor. I will do any thing.

Ott. And clear myself *in foro conscientiæ*——

Cut. Because you want indeed——

Mor. Yet more.

Ott. *Exercendi potestate.*

EPICŒNE *rushes in, followed by* HAUGHTY, CENTAURE, MAVIS, Mistress OTTER, DAW, *and* LA-FOOLE.

Epi. I will not endure it any longer. Ladies, I beseech you, help me. This is such a wrong as never was offered to poor bride before : upon her marriage-day to have her husband conspire against her, and a couple of mercenary companions to be brought in for form's sake, to persuade a separation ! If you had blood or virtue in you, gentlemen, you would not suffer such earwigs about a husband, or scorpions to creep between man and wife.

Mor. O the variety and changes of my torment !

Hau. Let them be cudgell'd out of doors by our grooms.

Cen. I'll lend you my footman.

Mav. We'll have our men blanket them in the hall.

Mrs. Ott. As there was one at our house, madam, for peeping in at the door.

Daw. Content, i' faith.

True. Stay, ladies and gentlemen ; you'll hear before you proceed.

Mav. I'd have the bridegroom blanketted too.

Cen. Begin with him first.

Hau. Yes, by my troth.

Mor. O mankind generation !

Daup. Ladies, for my sake forbear.

Hau. Yes, for sir Dauphine's sake.

Cen. He shall command us.

La-F. He is as fine a gentleman of his inches, madam, as any is about the town, and wears as good colours when he lists.

True. Be brief, sir, and confess your infirmity : she'll be a-fire to be quit of you, if she but hear that named once, you shall not entreat her to stay : she'll fly you like one that had the marks upon him.

Mor. Ladies, I must crave all your pardons——

True. Silence, ladies.

Mor. For a wrong I have done to your whole sex, in marrying this fair and virtuous gentlewoman——

Cler. Hear him, good ladies.

Mor. Being guilty of an infirmity, which, before I conferred with these learned men, I thought I might have concealed——

True. But now being better informed in his conscience

by them, he is to declare it, and give satisfaction, by asking your public forgiveness.

Mor. I am no man, ladies.

All. How !

Mor. Utterly unabled in nature, by reason of frigidity, to perform the duties, or any the least office of a husband.

Mav. Now, out upon him, prodigious creature.

Cen. Bridegroom uncarnate !

Hau. And would you offer it to a young gentlewoman ?

Mrs. Ott. A lady of her longings ?

Epi. Tut, a device, a device, this ! it smells rankly, ladies. A mere comment of his own.

True. Why, if you suspect that, ladies, you may have him search'd——

Daw. As the custom is, by a jury of physicians.

La-F. Yes, faith, 'twill be brave.

Mor. O me, must I undergo that ?

Mrs. Ott. No, let women search him, madam ; we can do it ourselves.

Mor. Out on me, worse !

Epi. No, ladies, you shall not need, I'll take him with all his faults.

Mor. Worst of all !

Cler. Why then, 'tis no divorce, doctor, if she consent not?

Cut. No, if the man be *frigidus*, it is *de parte uxoris*, that we grant *libellum divortii*, in the law.

Ott. Ay, it is the same in theology.

Mor. Worse, worse than worst !

True. Nay, sir, be not utterly disheartened ; we have yet a small relic of hope left, as near as our comfort is blown out. Clerimont, produce your brace of knights. What was that, master parson, you told me *in errore qualitatis*, e'en now ?—Dauphine, whisper the bride, that she carry it as if she were guilty, and ashamed. [*Aside.*

Ott. Marry, sir, *in errore qualitatis* (which master doctor did not forbear to urge), if she be found *corrupta*, that is, vitiated or broken up, that was *pro virgine desponsa*, espoused for a maid——

Mor. What then, sir?

Ott. It doth *dirimere contractum*, and *irritum reddere* too.

True. If this be true, we are happy again, sir, once more. Here are an honourable brace of knights, that shall affirm so much.

Daw. Pardon us, good master Clerimont.

La-F. You shall excuse us, master Clerimont.

Cler. Nay, you must make it good now, knights, there is no remedy; I'll eat no words for you, nor no men: you know you spoke it to me.

Daw. Is this gentleman-like, sir?

True. Jack Daw, he's worse than sir Amorous; fiercer a great deal. [*Aside to* DAW.]—Sir Amorous, beware, there be ten Daws in this Clerimont.

[Aside to LA-FOOLE.

La-F. I'll confess it, sir.

Daw. Will you, sir Amorous, will you wound reputation?

La-F. I am resolved.

True. So should you be too, Jack Daw: what should keep you off? she's but a woman, and in disgrace: he'll be glad on't.

Daw. Will he? I thought he would have been angry.

Cler. You will dispatch, knights; it must be done, i'faith.

True. Why, an it must, it shall, sir, they say: they'll ne'er go back.—Do not tempt his patience.

[Aside to them.

Daw. Is it true indeed, sir?

La-F. Yes, I assure you, sir.

Mor. What is true, gentlemen ? what do you assure me ?

Daw. That we have known your bride, sir——

La-F. In good fashion. She was our mistress, or so——

Cler. Nay, you must be plain, knights, as you were to me.

Ott. Ay, the question is, if you have *carnaliter*, or no ?

La-F. Carnaliter ! what else, sir ?

Ott. It is enough ; a plain nullity.

Epi. I am undone, I am undone !

Mor. O let me worship and adore you, gentlemen !

Epi. I am undone. [*Weeps.*

Mor. Yes, to my hand, I thank these knights. Master parson, let me thank you otherwise.

[*Gives him money.*

Cen. And have they confess'd ?

Mav. Now out upon them, informers !

True. You see what creatures you may bestow your favours on, madams.

Hau. I would except against them as beaten knights, wench, and not good witnesses in law.

Mrs. Ott. Poor gentlewoman, how she takes it !

Hau. Be comforted, Morose, I love you better for't.

Cen. So do I, I protest.

Cut. But, gentlemen, you have not known her since *matrimonium ?*

Daw. Not to-day, master doctor.

La-F. No, sir, not to-day.

Cut. Why, then I say, for any act before, the *matrimonium* is good and perfect ; unless the worshipful bridegroom did precisely, before witness, demand, if she were *virgo ante nuptias.*

Epi. No, that he did not, I assure you, master doctor.

Cut. If he cannot prove that, it is *ratum conjugium,* notwithstanding the premises; and they do no way *impedire.* And this is my sentence, this I pronounce.

Ott. I am of master doctor's resolution too, sir; if you made not that demand *ante nuptias.*

Mor. O my heart! wilt thou break? wilt thou break? this is worst of all worst worsts that hell could have devised! Marry a whore, and so much noise!

Daup. Come, I see now plain confederacy in this doctor and this parson, to abuse a gentleman. You study his affliction. I pray begone, companions.—And, gentlemen, I begin to suspect you for having parts with them.—Sir, will it please you hear me?

Mor. O do not talk to me; take not from me the pleasure of dying in silence, nephew.

Daup. Sir, I must speak to you. I have been long your poor despised kinsman, and many a hard thought has strengthened you against me: but now it shall appear if either I love you or your peace, and prefer them to all the world beside. I will not be long or grievous to you, sir. If I free you of this unhappy match absolutely, and instantly, after all this trouble, and almost in your despair, now——

Mor. It cannot be.

Daup. Sir, that you be never troubled with a murmur of it more, what shall I hope for, or deserve of you?

Mor. O, what thou wilt, nephew! thou shalt deserve me, and have me.

Daup. Shall I have your favour perfect to me, and love hereafter?

Mor. That, and any thing beside. Make thine own conditions. My whole estate is thine; manage it, I will become thy ward.

Daup. Nay, sir, I will not be so unreasonable.

Epi. Will sir Dauphine be mine enemy too?

Daup. You know I have been long a suitor to you, uncle, that out of your estate, which is fifteen hundred a-year, you would allow me but five hundred during life, and assure the rest upon me after; to which I have often, by myself and friends, tendered you a writing to sign, which you would never consent or incline to. If you please but to effect it now——

Mor. Thou shalt have it, nephew: I will do it, and more.

Daup. If I quit you not presently, and for ever, of this cumber, you shall have power instantly, afore all these, to revoke your act, and I will become whose slave you will give me to, for ever.

Mor. Where is the writing? I will seal to it, that, or to a blank, and write thine own conditions.

Epi. O me, most unfortunate, wretched gentlewoman!

Hau. Will sir Dauphine do this?

Epi. Good sir, have some compassion on me.

Mor. O, my nephew knows you, belike; away, crocodile!

Cen. He does it not sure without good ground.

Daup. Here, sir.   [*Gives him the parchments.*

Mor. Come, nephew, give me the pen; I will subscribe to any thing, and seal to what thou wilt, for my deliverance. Thou art my restorer. Here, I deliver it thee as my deed. If there be a word in it lacking, or writ with false orthography, I protest before [heaven] I will not take the advantage.

[*Returns the writings.*

Daup. Then here is your release, sir. [*takes off* EPICŒNE'S *peruke and other disguises.*] You have married a boy, a gentleman's son, that I have brought up this half year at my great charges, and for this composition, which I have now made with you.—What say you, master doctor? This is *justum impedimentum*, I hope, *error personæ?*

Ott. Yes, sir, *primo gradu.*

Cut. In primo gradu.

Daup. I thank you, good doctor Cutbeard, and parson Otter. [*pulls their false beards and gowns off.*] You are beholden to them, sir, that have taken this pains for you ; and my friend, master Truewit, who enabled them for the business. Now you may go in and rest ; be as private as you will, sir. [*Exit* Morose.] I'll not trouble you, till you trouble me with your funeral, which I care not how soon it come.—Cutbeard, I'll make your lease good. *Thank me not, but with your leg, Cutbeard.* And Tom Otter, your princess shall be reconciled to you.—How now, gentlemen, do you look at me?

Cler. A boy!

Daup. Yes, mistress Epicœne.

True. Well, Dauphine, you have lurch'd your friends of the better half of the garland, by concealing this part of the plot : but much good do it thee, thou deserv'st it, lad. And, Clerimont, for thy unexpected bringing these two to confession, wear my part of it freely. Nay, sir Daw and sir La-Foole, you see the gentlewoman that has done you the favours ! we are all thankful to you, and so should the woman-kind here, specially for lying on her, though not with her ! you meant so, I am sure. But that we have stuck it upon you to-day, in your own imagined persons, and so lately, this Amazon, this champion of the sex, should beat you now thriftily, for the common slanders which ladies receive from such cuckoos as you are. You are they that, when no merit or fortune can make you hope to enjoy their bodies, will yet lie with their reputations, and make their fame suffer. Away, you common moths of these, and all ladies' honours. Go, travel to make legs and faces, and come home with some new matter to be laugh'd at ; you deserve to live in an air as corrupted as that wherewith you feed rumour. [*Exeunt* DAW *and* LA-FOOLE.]— Madams, you are mute, upon this new metamorphosis ! But here stands she that has vindicated your fames. Take heed of such insectæ hereafter. And let it not trouble you, that you have discovered any mysteries to this young gentleman : he is almost of years, and will make a good visitant within this twelvemonth. In the mean time, we'll all undertake for his secrecy, that can speak so well of his silence. [*Coming forward.*]— *Spectators, if you like this comedy, rise cheerfully, and now Morose is gone in, clap your hands. It may be, that noise will cure him, at least please him.* [Exeunt.

The Alchemist.

DRAMATIS PERSONÆ.

—

Subtle, *the Alchemist.*
Face, *the Housekeeper.*
Dol Common, *their Colleague.*
Dapper, *a Lawyer's Clerk.*
Drugger, *a Tobacco Man.*
Lovewit, *Master of the House.*
Sir Epicure Mammon, *a Knight.*
Pertinax Surly, *a Gamester.*

Tribulation Wholesome, *a Pastor of Amsterdam.*
Ananias, *a Deacon there.*
Kastrill, *the angry Boy.*
Dame Pliant, *his Sister, a Widow.*
Neighbours.

Officers, Attendants, etc.

Scene—LONDON.

THE ALCHEMIST.

ACT I.

SCENE I.—*A Room in* LOVEWIT'S *House.*

Enter FACE, *in a captain's uniform, with his sword
drawn, and* SUBTLE *with a vial, quarrelling, and
followed by* DOL COMMON.

Face. Believe't, I will.
Sub. Thy worst.   I fart at thee.
Dol. Have you your wits? why, gentlemen! for love——
Face. Sirrah, I'll strip you——
Sub. What to do? lick figs
Out at my——
 Face. Rogue, rogue!—out of all your sleights.
 Dol. Nay, look ye, sovereign, general, are you mad-
men?
 Sub. O, let the wild sheep loose.   I'll gum your silks
With good strong water, an you come.
 Dol. Will you have
The neighbours hear you? will you betray all?
Hark! I hear somebody.
 Face. Sirrah——

Sub. I shall mar
All that the tailor has made, if you approach.
   Face. You most notorious whelp, you insolent slave,
Dare you do this?
   Sub. Yes, faith ; yes, faith.
   Face. Why, who
Am I, my mungrel? who am I?
   Sub. I'll tell you,
Since you know not yourself.
   Face. Speak lower, rogue.
   Sub. Yes, you were once (time's not long past) the
        good,
Honest, plain, livery-three-pound-thrum, that kept
Your master's worship's house here in the Friars,
For the vacations——
   Face. Will you be so loud ?
   Sub. Since, by my means, translated suburb-captain.
   Face. By your means, doctor dog!
   Sub. Within man's memory,
All this I speak of.
   Face. Why, I pray you, have I
Been countenanced by you, or you by me ?
Do but collect, sir, where I met you first.
   Sub. I do not hear well.
   Face. Not of this, I think it.
But I shall put you in mind, sir ;—at Pie-corner,
Taking your meal of steam in, from cooks' stalls,
Where, like the father of hunger, you did walk
Piteously costive, with your pinch'd-horn-nose,
And your complexion of the Roman wash,
Stuck full of black and melancholic worms,
Like powder corns shot at the artillery-yard.
   Sub. I wish you could advance your voice a little.
   Face. When you went pinn'd up in the several rags
You had raked and pick'd from dunghills, before day ;

Your feet in mouldy slippers, for your kibes ;
A felt of rug, and a thin threaden cloke,
That scarce would cover your no buttocks——
   Sub. So, sir !
   Face. When all your alchemy, and your algebra,
Your minerals, vegetals, and animals,
Your conjuring, cozening, and your dozen of trades,
Could not relieve your corps with so much linen
Would make you tinder, but to see a fire ;
I gave you countenance, credit for your coals,
Your stills, your glasses, your materials ;
Built you a furnace, drew you customers,
Advanced all your black arts ; lent you, beside,
A house to practise in——
   Sub. Your master's house !
   Face. Where you have studied the more thriving skill
Of bawdry since.
   Sub. Yes, in your master's house.
You and the rats here kept possession.
Make it not strange.   I know you were one could keep
The buttery-hatch still lock'd, and save the chippings,
Sell the dole beer to aqua-vitæ men,
The which, together with your Christmas vails
At post-and-pair, your letting out of counters,
Made you a pretty stock, some twenty marks,
And gave you credit to converse with cobwebs,
Here, since your mistress' death hath broke up house.
   Face. You might talk softlier, rascal.
   Sub. No, you scarab,
I'll thunder you in pieces : I will teach you
How to beware to tempt a Fury again,
That carries tempest in his hand and voice.
   Face The place has made you valiant.
   Sub. No, your clothes.—
Thou vermin, have I ta'en thee out of dung,

So poor, so wretched, when no living thing
Would keep thee company, but a spider, or worse !
Rais'd thee from brooms, and dust, and watering-pots,
Sublimed thee, and exalted thee, and fix'd thee
In the third region, call'd our state of grace ?
Wrought thee to spirit, to quintessence, with pains
Would twice have won me the philosopher's work ?
Put thee in words and fashion, made thee fit
For more than ordinary fellowships ?
Giv'n thee thy oaths, thy quarrelling dimensions,
Thy rules to cheat at horse-race, cock-pit, cards,
Dice, or whatever gallant tincture else ?
Made thee a second in mine own great art ?
And have I this for thanks !   Do you rebel,
Do you fly out in the projection ?
Would you be gone now ?
    Dol. Gentlemen, what mean you !
Will you mar all ?
    Sub. Slave, thou hadst had no name——
    Dol. Will you undo yourselves with civil war ?
    Sub. Never been known, past *equi clibanum,*
The heat of horse-dung, under ground, in cellars,
Or an ale-house darker than deaf John's ; been lost
To all mankind, but laundresses and tapsters,
Had not I been.
    Dol. Do you know who hears you, sovereign ?
    Face. Sirrah——
    Dol. Nay, general, I thought you were civil.
    Face. I shall turn desperate, if you grow thus loud
    Sub. And hang thyself, I care not.
    Face. Hang thee, collier,
And all thy pots, and pans, in picture, I will,
Since thou hast moved me——
    Dol. O, this will o'erthrow all.
    Face. Write thee up bawd in Paul's, have all thy tricks

Of cozening with a hollow cole, dust, scrapings,
Searching for things lost, with a sieve and sheers,
Erecting figures in your rows of houses,
And taking in of shadows with a glass,
Told in red letters ; and a face cut for thee,
Worse than Gamaliel Ratsey's.
   Dol. Are you sound ?
Have you your senses, masters ?
   Face. I will have
A book, but barely reckoning thy impostures,
Shall prove a true philosopher's stone to printers.
   Sub. Away, you trencher-rascal !
   Face. Out, you dog-leach !
The vomit of all prisons——
   Dol. Will you be
Your own destructions, gentlemen ?
   Face. Still spew'd out
For lying too heavy on the basket.
   Sub. Cheater !
   Face. Bawd !
   Sub. Cow-herd !
   Face. Conjurer !
   Sub. Cut-purse !
   Face. Witch !
   Dol. O me !
We are ruin'd, lost ! have you no more regard
To your reputations ? where's your judgment ? 'slight,
Have yet some care of me, of your republic——
   Face. Away, this brach ! I'll bring thee, rogue,
      within
The statute of sorcery, tricesimo tertio
Of Harry the Eighth : ay, and perhaps, thy neck
Within a noose, for laundring gold and barbing it.
   Dol. [*Snatches* FACE's *sword.*] You'll bring your head
      within a cockscomb, will you ?

And you, sir, with your menstrue—
                    [*Dashes* SUBTLE'S *vial out of his hand.*
                            Gather it up—
'Sdeath, you abominable pair of stinkards,
Leave off your barking, and grow one again,
Or, by the light that shines, I'll cut your throats.
I'll not be made a prey unto the marshal,
For ne'er a snarling dog-bolt of you both.
Have you together cozen'd all this while,
And all the world, and shall it now be said,
You've made most courteous shift to cozen yourselves?
You will accuse him! you will *bring him in*   [*To* FACE.
Within the statute!   Who shall take your word?
A whoreson, upstart, apocrýphal captain,
Whom not a Puritan in Blackfriars will trust
So much as for a feather: and you, too,   [*To* SUBTLE.
Will give the cause, forsooth! you will insult,
And claim a primacy in the divisions!
You must be chief! as if you only had
The powder to project with, and the work
Were not begun out of equality?
The venture tripartite? all things in common?
Without priority?   'Sdeath! you perpetual curs,
Fall to your couples again, and cozen kindly,
And heartily, and lovingly, as you should,
And lose not the beginning of a term,
Or, by this hand, I shall grow factious too,
And take my part, and quit you.
     Face. 'Tis his fault;
He ever murmurs, and objects his pains,
And says, the weight of all lies upon him.
     Sub. Why, so it does.
     Dol. How does it? do not we
Sustain our parts!
     Sub. Yes, but they are not equal.

Dol. Why, if your part exceed to-day, I hope
O urs may, to-morrow, match it.
Sub. Ay, they *may.*
Dol. May, murmuring mastiff! ay, and do.   Death
            on me !
Help me to throttle him.   [*Seizes* Sub. *by the throat.*
Sub. Dorothy ! mistress Dorothy !
'Ods precious, I'll do any thing.   What do you mean ?
Dol. Because o' your fermentation and cibation ?
Sub. Not I, by heaven——
Dol. Your Sol and Luna——help me.   [*To* Face.
Sub. Would I were hang'd then ! I'll conform
            myself.
Dol. Will you, sir ? do so then, and quickly : swear.
Sub. What should I swear ?
Dol. To leave your faction, sir,
And labour kindly in the common work.
Sub. Let me not breathe if I meant aught beside.
I only used these speeches as a spur
To him.
Dol. I hope we need no spurs, sir.   Do we ?
Face. 'Slid, prove to-day, who shall shark best.
Sub. Agreed.
Dol. Yes, and work close and friendly.
Sub. 'Slight, the knot
Shall grow the stronger for this breach, with me.
                                [*They shake hands.*
Dol. Why, so, my good baboons ! Shall we go make
A sort of sober, scurvy, precise neighbours,
That scarce have smiled twice since the king came in,
A feast of laughter at our follies ? Rascals,
Would run themselves from breath, to see me ride,
Or you t' have but a hole to thrust your heads in,
For which you should pay ear-rent ? No, agree.
And may don Provost ride a feasting long,

In his old velvet jerkin and stain'd scarfs,
My noble sovereign, and worthy general,
Ere we contribute a new crewel garter
To his most worsted worship.
  Sub. Royal Dol!
Spoken like Claridiana, and thyself.
  Face. For which at supper, thou shalt sit in triumph,
And not be styled Dol Common, but Dol Proper,
Dol Singular : the longest cut at night,
Shall draw thee for his Dol Particular.

                          [Bell rings without.
  Sub. Who's that? one rings. To the window, Dol:
      [Exit DOL.]—pray heaven,
The master do not trouble us this quarter.
  Face. O, fear not him. While there dies one a week
O' the plague, he's safe, from thinking toward London :
Beside, he's busy at his hop-yards now ;
I had a letter from him. If he do,
He'll send such word, for airing of the house,
As you shall have sufficient time to quit it :
Though we break up a fortnight, 'tis no matter.

            Re-enter DOL.

  Sub. Who is it, Dol?
  Dol. A fine young quodling.
  Face. O,
My lawyer's clerk, I lighted on last night,
In Holborn, at the Dagger. He would have
(I told you of him) a familiar,
To rifle with at horses, and win cups.
  Dol. O, let him in.
  Sub. Stay. Who shall do't?
  Face. Get you
Your robes on : I will meet him as going out.
  Dol. And what shall I do?

Face. Not be seen ; away !   [*Exit* DOL.
Seem you very reserv'd.
   Sub. Enough.   [*Exit.*
   Face. [*aloud and retiring.*] God be wi' you, sir,
I pray you let him know that I was here :
His name is Dapper.   I would gladly have staid, but—
   Dap. [*within.*] Captain, I am here.
   Face. Who's that ?—He's come, I think, doctor.

Enter DAPPER.

Good faith, sir, I was going away.
   Dap. In truth,
I am very sorry, captain.
   Face. But I thought
Sure I should meet you.
   Dap. Ay, I am very glad.
I had a scurvy writ or two to make,
And I had lent my watch last night to one
That dines to-day at the sheriff's, and so was robb'd
Of my past-time.

Re-enter SUBTLE, in his velvet Cap and Gown.

Is this the cunning man ?
   Face. This is his worship.
   Dap. Is he a doctor ?
   Face. Yes.
   Dap. And you have broke with him, captain ?
   Face. Ay.
   Dap. And how ?
   Face. Faith, he does make the matter, sir, so dainty
I know not what to say.
   Dap. Not so, good captain.
   Face. Would I were fairly rid of it, believe me.
   Dap. Nay, now you grieve me, sir.   Why should you
       wish so ?
I dare assure you, I'll not be ungrateful.

Face. I cannot think you will, sir.   But the law
Is such a thing——and then he says, Read's matter
Falling so lately.
    Dap. Read ! he was an ass,
And dealt, sir, with a fool.
    Face. It was a clerk, sir.
    Dap. A clerk !
    Face. Nay, hear me, sir, you know the law
Better, I think——
    Dap. I should, sir, and the danger :
You know I shew'd the statute to you.
    Face. You did so.
    Dap. And will I tell then ! By this hand of flesh,
Would it might never write good court-hand more,
If I discover.   What do you think of me,
That I am a chiaus ?
    Face. What's that ?
    Dap. The Turk was here.
As one would say, do you think I am a Turk ?
    Face. I'll tell the doctor so.
    Dap. Do, good sweet captain.
    Face. Come, noble doctor, pray thee let's prevail ;
This is the gentleman, and he has no chiaus.
    Sub. Captain, I have return'd you all my answer.
I would do much, sir, for your love——But this
I neither may, nor can.
    Face. Tut, do not say so.
You deal now with a noble fellow, doctor,
One that will thank you richly ; and he has no chiaus.
Let that, sir, move you.
    Sub. Pray you, forbear——
    Face. He has
Four angels here.
    Sub. You do me wrong, good sir.

Face. Doctor, wherein ? to tempt you with these
    spirits !
Sub. To tempt my art and love, sir, to my peril.
Fore heaven, I scarce can think you are my friend,
That so would draw me to apparent danger.
Face. I draw you ! a horse draw you, and a halter,
You, and your flies together——
Dap. Nay, good captain.
Face. That know no difference of men.
Sub. Good words, sir.
Face. Good deeds, sir, doctor dogs-meat. 'Slight, I
    bring you
No cheating Clim o' the Cloughs, or Claribels,
That look as big as five-and-fifty, and flush ;
And spit out secrets like hot custard——
Dap. Captain !
Face. Nor any melancholic under-scribe,
Shall tell the vicar ; but a special gentle,
That is the heir to forty marks a year,
Consorts with the small poets of the time,
Is the sole hope of his old grandmother ;
That knows the law, and writes you six fair hands,
Is a fine clerk, and has his cyphering perfect,
Will take his oath o' the Greek Testament,
If need be, in his pocket ; and can court
His mistress out of Ovid.
Dap. Nay, dear captain——
Face. Did you not tell me so ?
Dap. Yes ; but I'd have you
Use master doctor with some more respect.
Face. Hang him, proud stag, with his broad velvet
    head !—
But for your sake, I'd choak, ere I would change
An article of breath with such a puckfist :
Come, let's be gone.   *[Going.*

Sub. Pray you let me speak with you.
Dap. His worship calls you, captain.
Face. I am sorry
I e'er embark'd myself in such a business.
Dap. Nay, good sir ; he did call you.
Face. Will he take then ?
Sub. First, hear me——
Face. Not a syllable, 'less you take.
Sub. Pray you, sir——
Face. Upon no terms, but an *assumpsit.*
Sub. Your humour must be law.

        [*He takes the four angels.*

Face. Why now, sir, talk.
Now I dare hear you with mine honour. Speak.
So may this gentleman too.
Sub. Why, sir——   [*Offering to whisper* FACE.
Face. No whispering,
Sub. Fore heaven, you do not apprehend the loss
You do yourself in this.
Face. Wherein ? for what ?
Sub. Marry, to be so importunate for one,
That, when he has it, will undo you all :
He'll win up all the money in the town.
Face. How !
Sub. Yes, and blow up gamester after gamester,
As they do crackers in a puppet play.
If I do give him a familiar,
Give you him all you play for ; never set him :
For he will have it.
Face. You are mistaken, doctor.
Why he does ask one but for cups and horses,
A rifling fly ; none of your great familiars.
Dap. Yes, captain, I would have it for all games.
Sub. I told you so.   [business !
Face. [*Taking* DAP. *aside.*] 'Slight, that is a new

I understood you, a tame bird, to fly
Twice in a term, or so, on Friday nights,
When you had left the office, for a nag
Of forty or fifty shillings.
 Dap. Ay, 'tis true, sir ;
But I do think now I shall leave the law,
And therefore——
 Face. Why, this changes quite the case.
Do you think that I dare move him ?
 Dap. If you please, sir ;
All's one to him, I see.
 Face. What ! for that money ?
I cannot with my conscience ; nor should you
Make the request, methinks.
 Dap. No, sir, I mean
To add consideration.
 Face. Why then, sir,
I'll try.—[*Goes to* Subtle.] Say that it were for all
   games, doctor ?
 Sub. I say then, not a mouth shall eat for him
At any ordinary, but on the score,
That is a gaming mouth, conceive me.
 Face. Indeed !
 Sub. He'll draw you all the treasure of the realm,
If it be set him,
 Face. Speak you this from art ?
 Sub. Ay, sir, and reason too, the ground of art.
He is of the only best complexion,
The queen of Fairy loves.
 Face. What ! is he ?
 Sub. Peace.
He'll overhear you. Sir, should she but see him——
 Face. What ?
 Sub. Do not you tell him.
 Face. Will he win at cards too ?
...9...

Sub. The spirits of dead Holland, living Isaac,
You'd swear were in him ; such a vigorous luck
As cannot be resisted.   'Slight, he'll put
Six of your gallants to a cloke, indeed.
   Face. A strange success, that some man shall be born
      to ?
   Sub. He hears you, man——
   Dap. Sir, I'll not be ingrateful.
   Face. Faith, I have confidence in his good nature :
You hear, he says he will not be ingrateful.
   Sub. Why, as you please ; my venture follows yours.
   Face. Troth, do it, doctor ; think him trusty, and
      make him.
He may make us both happy in an hour ;
Win some five thousand pound, and send us two on't.
   Dap. Believe it, and I will, sir.
   Face. And you shall, sir.   *[Takes him aside.*
You haveheard all ?
   Dap. No, what was't ?   Nothing, I, sir.
   Face. Nothing !
   Dap. A little, sir.
   Face. Well, a rare star
Reign'd at your birth.
   Dap. At mine, sir !   No.
   Face. The doctor
Swears that you are——
   Sub. Nay, captain, you'll tell all now.
   Face. Allied to the queen of Fairy.
   Dap. Who ? that I am ?
Believe it, no such matter——
   Face. Yes, and that
You were born with a cawl on your head.
   Dap. Who says so ?
   Face. Come,
You know it well enough, though you dissemble it.

Dap. I' fac, I do not : you are mistaken.
Face. How !
Swear by your fac, and in a thing so known
Unto the doctor ?   How shall we, sir, trust you
In the other matter? can we ever think,
When you have won five or six thousand pound,
You'll send us shares in't, by this rate ?
Dap. By Jove, sir,
I'll win ten thousand pound, and send you half.
I' fac's no oath.
Sub. No, no, he did but jest.
Face. Go to.   Go thank the doctor : he's your friend,
To take it so.
Dap. I thank his worship.
Face. So !
Another angel.
Dap. Must I ?
Face. Must you ! 'slight,
What else is thanks? will you be trivial ?—Doctor.
                         [DAPPER *gives him the money.*
When must he come for his familiar ?
Dap. Shall I not have it with me ?
Sub. O, good, sir !
There must be a world of ceremonies pass ;
You must be bath'd and fumigated first :
Besides the queen of Fairy does not rise
Till it be noon.
Face Not, if she danced, to-night.
Sub. And she must bless it.
Face. Did you never see
Her royal grace yet ?
Dap. Whom ?
Face. Your aunt of Fairy ?
Sub. Not since she kist him in the cradle, captain :
I can resolve you that.

Face. Well, see her grace,
Whate'er it cost you, for a thing that I know.
It will be somewhat hard to compass ; but
However, see her.   You are made, believe it,
If you can see her.   Her grace is a lone woman,
And very rich ; and if she take a fancy,
She will do strange things.   See her, at any hand.
'Slid, she may hap to leave you all she has :
It is the doctor's fear.
    Dap. How will't be done, then ?
    Face. Let me alone, take you no thought.   Do you
But say to me, captain, I'll see her grace.
    Dap. Captain, I'll see her grace.
    Face. Enough.   [*Knocking within.*
    Sub. Who's there ?
Anon.—Conduct him forth by the back way.—
                                      [*Aside to* FACE.
Sir, against one o'clock prepare yourself ;
Till when you must be fasting ; only take
Three drops of vinegar in at your nose,
Two at your mouth, and one at either ear ;
Then bathe your fingers ends and wash your eyes,
To sharpen your five senses, and cry *hum*
Thrice, and then *buz* as often ; and then come.   [*Exit.*
    Face. Can you remember this ?
    Dap. I warrant you.
    Face. Well then, away.   It is but your bestowing
Some twenty nobles 'mong her grace's servants,
And put on a clean shirt : you do not know
What grace her grace may do you in clean linen.
                          [*Exeunt* FACE *and* DAPPER.
    Sub. [*within.*] Come in !   Good wives I pray you for-
            bear me now ;
Troth I can do you no good till afternoon——

Re-enters, followed by DRUGGER.
What is your name, say you, Abel Drugger?
  Drug. Yes, sir.
  Sub. A seller of tobacco?
  Drug. Yes, sir.
  Sub. Umph!
Free of the grocers?
  Drug. Ay, an't please you.
  Sub. Well——
Your business, Abel?
  Drug. This, an't please your worship;
I am a young beginner, and am building
Of a new shop, an't like your worship, just
At corner of a street:—Here is the plot on't—
And I would know by art, sir, of your worship,
Which way I should make my door, by necromancy,
And where my shelves; and which should be for boxes,
And which for pots.   I would be glad to thrive, sir:
And I was wish'd to your worship by a gentleman,
One captain Face, that says you know men's planets,
And their good angels, and their bad.
  Sub. I do,
If I do see them——

Re-enter FACE.
  Face. What! my honest Abel?
Thou art well met here.
  Drug. Troth, sir, I was speaking,
Just as your worship came here, of your worship:
I pray you speak for me to master doctor.
  Face. He shall do anything.—Doctor, do you hear!
This is my friend, Abel, an honest fellow;
He lets me have good tobacco, and he does not
Sophisticate it with sack-lees or oil,
Nor washes it in muscadel and grains,

Nor buries it in gravel, under ground,
Wrapp'd up in greasy leather, or piss'd clouts;
But keeps it in fine lily pots, that, opened,
Smell like conserve of roses, or French beans.
He has his maple block, his silver tongs,
Winchester pipes, and fire of Juniper:
A neat, spruce, honest fellow, and no goldsmith.
  Sub. He is a fortunate fellow, that I am sure on.
  Face. Already, sir, have you found it? Lo thee, Abel!
  Sub. And in right way towards riches——
  Face. Sir!
  Sub. This summer
He will be of the clothing of his company,
And next spring call'd to the scarlet; spend what he can.
  Face. What, and so little beard?
  Sub. Sir, you must think,
He may have a receipt to make hair come:
But he'll be wise, preserve his youth, and fine for't;
His fortune looks for him another way.
  Face. 'Slid, doctor, how canst thou know this so soon?
I am amused at that!
  Sub. By a rule, captain,
In metoposcopy, which I do work by;
A certain star in the forehead, which you see not.
Your chestnut or your olive-colour'd face
Does never fail: and your long ear doth promise.
I knew't by certain spots, too, in his teeth,
And on the nail of his mercurial finger.
  Face. Which finger's that?
  Sub. His little finger. Look.
You were born upon a Wednesday?
  Drug. Yes, indeed, sir.
  Sub. The thumb, in chiromancy, we give Venus;
The forefinger, to Jove; the midst, to Saturn;
The ring, to Sol; the least, to Mercury,

Who was the lord, sir, of his horoscope,
His house of life being Libra ; which fore-show'd,
He should be a merchant, and should trade with balance.
   Face. Why, this is strange !　Is it not, honest Nab ?
   Sub. There is a ship now, coming from Ormus,
That shall yield him such a commodity
Of drugs——This is the west, and this the south ?
[*Pointing to the Plan.*

   Drug. Yes, sir.
   Sub. And those are your two sides ?
   Drug. Ay, sir.
   Sub. Make me your door, then, south; your broad
      side, west:
And on the east side of your shop, aloft,
Write Mathlai, Tarmiel, and Baraborat ;
Upon the north part, Rael, Velel, Thiel.
They are the names of those mercurial spirits,
That do fright flies from boxes.
   Drug. Yes, sir.
   Sub. And
Beneath your threshold, bury me a load-stone
To draw in gallants that wear spurs ; the rest,
They'll seem to follow.
   Face. That's a secret, Nab !
   Sub. And, on your stall, a puppet, with a vice
And a court-fucus to call city dames :
You shall deal much with minerals.
   Drug. Sir, I have
At home, already——
   Sub. Ay, I know you have arsenic,
Vitriol, sal-tartar, argaile, alkali,
Cinoper : I know all.—This fellow, captain,
Will come, in time, to be a great distiller,
And give a say—I will not say directly,
But very fair—at the philosopher's stone.

Face. Why, how now, Abel ! is this true ?
Drug. Good captain,
What must I give ?   [*Aside to* FACE.
Face. Nay, I'll not counsel thee.
Thou hearest what wealth (he says, spend what thou
    canst)
Thou'rt like to come to.
Drug. I would gi' him a crown.
Face. A crown ! and toward such a fortune ? heart,
Thou shalt rather gi' him thy shop.   No gold about thee ?
Drug. Yes, I have a portague, I have kept this half
                year,
Face. Out on thee, Nab ! 'Slight, there was such an
                offer—
Shalt keep't no longer, I'll give't him for thee.   Doctor,
Nab prays your worship to drink this, and swears
He will appear more grateful, as your skill
Does raise him in the world.
Drug. I would entreat
Another favour of his worship.
Face. What is't, Nab ?
Drug. But to look over, sir, my almanack,
And cross out my ill days, that I may neither
Bargain, nor trust upon them.
Face. That he shall, Nab ;
Leave it, it shall be done, 'gainst afternoon.
Sub. And a direction for his shelves.
Face. Now, Nab,
Art thou well pleased, Nab ?
Drug. 'Thank, sir, both your worships.
Face. Away.—   [*Exit* DRUGGER.
Why, now, you smoaky persecutor of nature !
Now do you see, that something's to be done,
Beside your beech-coal, and your corsive waters,
Your crosslets, crucibels, and cucurbites !

You must have stuff brought home to you, to work on :
And yet you think, I am at no expense
In searching out these veins, then following them,
Then trying them out. 'Fore God, my intelligence
Costs me more money, than my share oft comes to,
In these rare works.
    Sub. You are pleasant, sir.—

Re-enter DOL.

                              How now !
What says my dainty Dolkin ?
    Dol. Yonder fish-wife
Will not away.   And there's your giantess,
The bawd of Lambeth.
    Sub. Heart, I cannot speak with them.
    Dol. Not afore night, I have told them in a voice,
Thorough the trunk, like one of your familiars.
But I have spied sir Epicure Mammon——
    Sub. Where ?
    Dol. Coming along, at far end of the lane,
Slow of his feet, but earnest of his tongue
To one that's with him.
    Sub. Face, go you and shift.   [*Exit* FACE
Dol, you must presently make ready, too.
    Dol. Why, what's the matter ?
    Sub. O, I did look for him
With the sun's rising : 'marvel he could sleep,
This is the day I am to perfect for him
The magisterium, our great work, the stone ;
And yield it, made, into his hands : of which
He has, this month, talk'd as he were possess'd.
And now he's dealing pieces on't away.—
Methinks I see him entering into ordinaries,
Dispensing for the pox, and plaguy houses,
Reaching his dose, walking Moorfields for lepers,

And offering citizens' wives pomander-bracelets,
As his preservative, made of the elixir ;
Searching the spittal, to make old bawds young ;
And the highways, for beggars to make rich :
I see no end of his labours.   He will make
Nature asham'd of her long sleep : when art,
Who's but a step-dame, shall do more than she,
In her best love to mankind, ever could :
If his dream lasts, he'll turn the age to gold.   [*Exeunt.*

ACT II.

Scene I.—*An outer Room in* Lovewit's *House:*

Enter Sir Epicure Mammon *and* Surly.

Mam. Come on, sir.   Now, you set your foot on shere
In *Novo Orbe;* here's the rich Peru :
And there within, sir, are the golden mines,
Great Solomon's Ophir ! he was sailing to't,
Three years, but we have reach'd it in ten months.
This is the day, wherein, to all my friends,
I will pronounce the happy word, Be rich ;
This day you shall be spectatissimi.
You shall no more deal with the hollow dye,
Or the frail card.   No more be at charge of keeping
The livery-punk for the young heir, that must
Seal, at all hours, in his shirt : no more,
If he deny, have him beaten to't, as he is
That brings him the commodity.   No more
Shall thirst of satin, or the covetous hunger
Of velvet entrails for a rude-spun cloke,
To be display'd at madam Augusta's make
The sons of Sword and Hazard fall before
The golden calf, and on their knees, whole nights
Commit idolatry with wine and trumpets :

Or go a-feasting after drum and ensign.
No more of this.   You shall start up young viceroys,
And have your punks, and punketees, my Surly.
And unto thee I speak it first, BE RICH.
Where is my Subtle, there?   Within, ho !
   Face. [*Within.*] Sir, he'll come to you by and by.
   Mam. That is his fire-drake,
His Lungs, his Zephyrus, he that puffs his coals,
Till he firk nature up, in her own centre.
You are not faithful, sir.   This night I'll change
All that is metal, in my house, to gold :
And, early in the morning, will I send
To all the plumbers and the pewterers,
And buy their tin and lead up ; and to Lothbury
For all the copper.
   Sur. What, and turn that too ?
   Mam. Yes, and I'll purchase Devonshire and Cornwall,
And make them perfect Indies ! you admire now ?
   Sur. No, faith.
   Mam. But when you see th' effects of the Great
         Medicine,
Of which one part projected on a hundred
Of Mercury, or Venus, or the moon,
Shall turn it to as many of the sun ;
Nay, to a thousand, so ad infinitum :
You will believe me.
   Sur. Yes, when I see't, I will.
But if my eyes do cozen me so, and I
Giving them no occasion, sure I'll have
A whore, shall piss them out next day.
   Mam. Ha ! why ?
Do you think I fable with you ? I assure you,
He that has once the flower of the sun,
The perfect ruby, which we call elixir,
Not only can do that, but, by its virtue,

Can confer honour, love, respect, long life ;
Give safety, valour, yea, and victory,
To whom he will.   In eight and twenty days,
I'll make an old man of fourscore, a child.
    Sur. No doubt ; he's that already.
    Mam. Nay, I mean,
Restore his years, renew him, like an eagle,
To the fifth age ; make him get sons and daughters,
Young giants ; as our philosophers have done,
The ancient patriarchs, afore the flood,
But taking, once a week, on a knife's point,
The quantity of a grain of mustard of it ;
Become stout Marses, and beget young Cupids.
    Sur. The decay'd vestals of Pict-hatch would thank you,
That keep the fire alive, there.
    Mam. 'Tis the secret
Of nature naturiz'd 'gainst all infections,
Cures all diseases coming of all causes ;
A month's grief in a day, a year's in twelve :
And, of what age soever, in a month :
Past all the doses of your drugging doctors.
I'll undertake, withall, to fright the plague
Out of the kingdom in three months.
    Sur. And I'll
Be bound, the players shall sing your praises, then,
Without their poets.
    Mam. Sir, I'll do't.   Mean time,
I'll give away so much unto my man,
Shall serve the whole city, with preservative,
Weekly ; each house his dose, and at the rate——
    Sur. As he that built the Water-work, does with water ?
    Mam. You are incredulous.
    Sur. Faith I have a humour,
I would not willingly be gull'd.   Your stone
Cannot transmute me.

Mam. Pertinax, [my] Surly,
Will you believe antiquity ? records ?
I'll shew you a book where Moses and his sister,
And Solomon have written of the art ;
Ay, and a treatise penn'd by Adam—
　Sur. How !
　Mam. Of the philosopher's stone, and in High Dutch.
　Sur. Did Adam write, sir, in High Dutch ?
　Mam. He did ;
Which proves it was the primitive tongue.
　Sur. What paper ?
　Mam. On cedar board.
　Sur. O that, indeed, they say,
Will last 'gainst worms.
　Mam. 'Tis like your Irish wood,
'Gainst cob-webs.　I have a piece of Jason's fleece, too,
Which was no other than a book of alchemy,
Writ in large sheep-skin, a good fat ram-vellum.
Such was Pythagoras' thigh, Pandora's tub,
And, all that fable of Medea's charms,
The manner of our work ; the bulls, our furnace,
Still breathing fire ; our argent-vive, the dragon :
The dragon's teeth, mercury sublimate,
That keeps the whiteness, hardness, and the biting ;
And they are gather'd into Jason's helm,
The alembic, and then sow'd in Mars his field,
And thence sublimed so often, till they're fix'd.
Both this, the Hesperian garden, Cadmus' story,
Jove's shower, the boon of Midas, Argus' eyes,
Boccace his Demogorgon, thousands more,
All abstract riddles of our stone.—

　　　　　Enter FACE, *as a Servant.*
　　　　　　　　　　How now !
Do we succeed ?　Is our day come ? and holds it ?

Face. The evening will set red upon you, sir ;
You have colour for it, crimson : the red ferment
Has done his office ; three hours hence prepare you
To see projection.
    Mam. Pertinax, my Surly,
Again I say to thee, aloud, Be rich.
This day, thou shalt have ingots ; and, to-morrow,
Give lords th' affront.—Is it, my Zephyrus, right ?
Blushes the bolt's-head ?
    Face. Like a wench with child, sir,
That were but now discover'd to her master.
    Mam. Excellent witty Lungs !—my only care is,
Where to get stuff enough now, to project on ;
This town will not half serve me.
    Face. No, sir ! buy
The covering off o' churches.
    Mam That's true.
    Face. Yes.
Let them stand bare, as do their auditory ;
Or cap them, new, with shingles.
    Mam. No, good thatch :
That will lie light upon the rafters, Lungs.—
Lungs, I will manumit thee from the furnace :
I will restore thee thy complexion, Puffe,
Lost in the embers ; and repair this brain,
Hurt with the fume o' the metals.
    Face. I have blown, sir,
Hard for your worship ; thrown by many a coal,
When 'twas not beech ; weigh'd those I put in, just,
To keep your heat still even ; these bleared eyes
Have wak'd to read your several colours, sir,
Of the pale citron, the green lion, the crow,
The peacock's tail, the plumed swan.
    Mam. And, lastly,
Thou hast descry'd the flower, the sanguis agni ?

Face. Yes, sir.
Mam. Where's master ?
Face. At his prayers, sir, he ;
Good man, he's doing his devotions
For due success.
  Mam. Lungs, I will set a period
To all thy labours ; thou shalt be the master
Of my seraglio.
  Face. Good, sir.
  Mam. But do you hear ?
I'll geld you, Lungs.
  Face. Yes, sir.
  Mam. For I do mean
To have a list of wives and concubines,
Equal with Solomon, who had the stone
Alike with me ; and I will make me a back
With the elixir, that shall be as tough
As Hercules, to encounter fifty a night.—
Thou art sure thou saw'st it blood ?
  Face. Both blood and spirit, sir.
  Mam. I will have all my beds blown up, not stuft ·
Down is too hard : and then, mine oval room
Fill'd with such pictures as Tiberius took
From Elephantis, and dull Aretine
But coldly imitated.   Then, my glasses
Cut in more subtle angles, to disperse
And multiply the figures, as I walk
Naked between my succubæ.   My mists
I'll have of perfume, vapour'd 'bout the room,
To lose ourselves in ; and my baths, like pits
To fall into ; from whence we will come forth,
And roll us dry in gossamer and roses.—
Is it arrived at ruby ?——Where I spy
A wealthy citizen, or [a] rich lawyer,
Have a sublimed pure wife, unto that fellow

I'll send a thousand pound to be my cuckold.
  Face. And I shall carry it?
  Mam. No.   I'll have no bawds,
But fathers and mothers : they will do it best,
Best of all others.   And my flatterers
Shall be the pure and gravest of divines,
That I can get for money.   My mere fools,
Eloquent burgesses, and then my poets
The same that writ so subtly of the fart,
Whom I will entertain still for that subject.
The few that would give out themselves to be
Court and town-stallions, and, each-where, bely
Ladies who are known most innocent for them ;
Those will I beg, to make me eunuchs of :
And they shall fan me with ten estrich tails
A-piece, made in a plume to gather wind.
We will be brave, Puffe, now we have the med'cine.
My meat shall all come in, in Indian shells,
Dishes of agat set in gold, and studded
With emeralds, sapphires, hyacinths, and rubies.
The tongues of carps, dormice, and camels' heels,
Boil'd in the spirit of sol, and dissolv'd pearl,
Apicius' diet, 'gainst the epilepsy :
And I will eat these broths with spoons of amber,
Headed with diamond and carbuncle.
My foot-boy shall eat pheasants, calver'd salmons,
Knots, godwits, lampreys : I myself will have
The beards of barbels served, instead of sallads ;
Oil'd mushrooms ; and the swelling unctuous paps
Of a fat pregnant sow, newly cut off,
Drest with an exquisite, and poignant sauce ;
For which, I'll say unto my cook, *There's gold,*
Go forth, and be a knight.
  Face. Sir, I'll go look
A little, how it heightens.   [*Exit.*

Mam. Do.—My shirts
I'll have of taffeta-sarsnet, soft and light
As cobwebs ; and for all my other raiment,
It shall be such as might provoke the Persian,
Were he to teach the world riot anew.
My gloves of fishes and birds' skins, perfumed
With gums of paradise, and eastern air——
   Sur. And do you think to have the stone with this ?
   Mam. No, I do think t' have all this with the stone.
   Sur. Why, I have heard, he must be *homo frugi*,
A pious, holy, and religious man,
One free from mortal sin, a very virgin.
   Mam. That makes it, sir ; he is so : but I buy it ;
My venture brings it me.   He, honest wretch,
A notable, superstitious, good soul,
Has worn his knees bare, and his slippers bald,
With prayer and fasting for it : and, sir, let him
Do it alone, for me, still.   Here he comes.
Not a profane word afore him : 'tis poison.—

Enter SUBTLE.

Good morrow, father.
   Sub. Gentle son, good morrow.
And to your friend there.   What is he, is with you ?
   Mam. An heretic, that I did bring along,
In hope, sir, to convert him.
   Sub. Son, I doubt
You are covetous, that thus you meet your time
In the just point : prevent your day at morning.
This argues something, worthy of a fear
Of importune and carnal appetite.
Take heed you do not cause the blessing leave you,
With your ungovern'd haste.   I should be sorry
To see my labours, now even at perfection,
Got by long watching and large patience,

Not prosper where my love and zeal hath placed them,
Which (heaven I call to witness, with your self,
To whom I have pour'd my thoughts) in all my ends,
Have look'd no way, but unto public good,
To pious uses, and dear charity,
Now grown a prodigy with men.   Wherein
If you, my son, should now prevaricate,
And, to your own particular lusts employ
So great and catholic a bliss, be sure
A curse will follow, yea, and overtake
Your subtle and most secret ways.
    Mam. I know, sir ;
You shall not need to fear me : I but come,
To have you confute this gentleman.
    Sur. Who is,
Indeed, sir, somewhat costive of belief
Toward your stone ; would not be gull'd.
    Sub. Well, son,
All that I can convince him in, is this,
The WORK IS DONE, bright sol is in his robe.
We have a medicine 'of the triple soul,
The glorified spirit.   Thanks be to heaven,
And make us worthy of it !—Ulen Spiegel !
    Face. [*within.*] Anon, sir.
    Sub. Look well to the register,
And let your heat still lessen by degrees,
To the aludels.
    Face. [*within.*] Yes, sir.
    Sub. Did you look
On the bolt's-head yet ?
    Face. [*within.*] Which ? on D, sir ?
    Sub. Ay ;
What's the complexion ?
    Face. [*within.*] Whitish.
    Sub. Infuse vinegar,

To draw his volatile substance and his tincture :
And let the water in glass E be filter'd,
And put into the gripe's egg.   Lute him well ;
And leave him closed in balneo.
    Face. [*within.*] I will, sir.
    Sur. What a brave language here is ! next to canting.
    Sub. I have another work, you never saw, son,
That three days since past the philosopher's wheel
In the lent heat of Athanor ; and's become
Sulphur of Nature.
    Mam. But 'tis for me ?
    Sub. What need you ?
You have enough in that is perfect.
    Mam. O but——
    Sub. Why, this is covetise !
    Mam. No, I assure you,
I shall employ it all in pious uses,
Founding of colleges and grammar schools,
Marrying young virgins, building hospitals,
And now and then a church.

Re-enter FACE.

    Sub. How now !
    Face. Sir, please you,
Shall I not change the filter ?
    Sub. Marry, yes ;
And bring me the complexion of glass B.   [*Exit* FACE.
    Mam. Have you another ?
    Sub. Yes, son ; were I assured—
Your piety were firm, we would not want
The means to glorify it ; but I hope the best.—
I mean to tinct C in sand-heat to-morrow,
And give him imbibition.
    Mam. Of white oil ?
    Sub. No, sir, of red.   F is come over the helm too,

I thank my Maker, in S. Mary's bath,
And shews *lac virginis.*   Blessed be heaven !
I sent you of his fæces there calcined ;
Out of that calx, I have won the salt of mercury.
  Mam. By pouring on your rectified water ?
  Sub. Yes, and reverberating in Athanor.

Re-enter FACE.

How now ! what colour says it ?
  Face. The ground black, sir.
  Mam. That's your crow's head ?
  Sur. Your cock's-comb's, is it not ?
  Sub. No, 'tis not perfect.   Would it were the crow !
That work wants something.
  Sur. O, I look'd for this.
The hay's a pitching.   [*Aside.*
  Sub. Are you sure you loosed them
In their own menstrue ?
  Face. Yes, sir, and then married them,
And put them in a bolt's-head nipp'd to digestion,
According as you bade me, when I set
The liquor of Mars to circulation
In the same heat.
  Sub. The process then was right.
  Face. Yes, by the token, sir, the retort brake,
And what was saved was put into the pelican,
And sign'd with Hermes' seal.
  Sub. I think 'twas so.
We should have a new amalgama.
  Sur. O, this ferret
Is rank as any pole-cat.   [*Aside.*
  Sub. But I care not :
Let him e'en die ; we have enough beside,
In embrion.   H has his white shirt on ?
  Face. Yes, sir,

He's ripe for inceration, he stands warm,
In his ash-fire.   I would not you should let
Any die now, if I might counsel, sir
For luck's sake to the rest : it is not good.
  Mam. He says right.
  Sur. Ay, are you bolted ?   [*Aside.*
  Face, Nay, I know't, sir.
I have seen the ill-fortune.   What is some three ounces
Of fresh materials ?
  Mam. Is't no more ?
  Face. No more, sir,
Of gold, t'amalgame with some six of mercury.
  Mam. Away, here's money.   What will serve ?
  Face. Ask him, sir.
  Mam. How much ?
  Sub. Give him nine pound :—you may give him ten.
  Sur. Yes, twenty, and be cozen'd, do.
  Mam. There 'tis.   [*Gives* FACE *the money.*
  Sub. This needs not ; but that you will have it so,
To see conclusions of all : for two
Of our inferior works are at fixation,
A third is in ascension.   Go your ways.
Have you set the oil of luna in kemia ?
  Face. Yes, sir.
  Sub. And the philosopher's vinegar ?
  Face. Ay,   [*Exit.*
  Sur. We shall have a sallad !
  Mam. When do you make projection ?
  Sub. Son, be not hasty, I exalt our med'cine,
By hanging him in *balnco vaporoso,*
And giving him solution ; then congeal him ;
And then dissolve him ; then again congeal him :
For look, how oft I iterate the work,
So many times I add unto his virtue.
As, if at first one ounce convert a hundred,

After his second loose, he'll turn a thousand;
His third solution, ten ; his fourth, a hundred :
After his fifth, a thousand thousand ounces
Of any imperfect metal, into pure
Silver or gold, in all examinations,
As good as any of the natural mine.
Get you your stuff here against afternoon,
Your brass, your pewter, and your andirons.
   Mam. Not those of iron ?
   Sub. Yes, you may bring them too :
We'll change all metals.
   Sur. I believe you in that.
   Mam. Then I may send my spits ?
   Sub. Yes, and your racks.
   Sur. And dripping pans, and pot-hangers, and hooks.
Shall he not ?
   Sub. If he please.
   Sur. —To be an ass.
   Sub. How, sir !
   Mam. This gentleman you must bear withal :
I told you he had no faith.
   Sur. And little hope, sir ;
But much less charity, should I gull myself.
   Sub. Why, what have you observ'd, sir, in our art,
Seems so impossible ?
   Sur. But your whole work, no more.
That you should hatch gold in a furnace, sir,
As they do eggs in Egypt !
   Sub. Sir, do you
Believe that eggs are hatch'd so ?
   Sur. If I should ?
   Sub. Why, I think that the greater miracle.
No egg but differs from a chicken more
Than metals in themselves.
   Sur. That cannot be.

The egg's ordain'd by nature to that end,
And is a chicken *in potentia*.
   Sub. The same we say of lead and other metals,
Which would be gold, if they had time.
   Mam. And that
Our art doth further.
   Sub. Ay, for 'twere absurd
To think that nature in the earth bred gold
Perfect in the instant: something went before.
There must be remote matter.
   Sur. Ay, what is that ?
   Sub. Marry, we say——
   Mam. Ay, now it heats : stand, father ;
Pound him to dust.
   Sub. It is, of the one part,
A humid exhalation, which we call
Materia liquida, or the unctuous water ;
On the other part, a certain crass and vicious
Portion of earth ; both which, concorporate,
Do make the elementary matter of gold ;
Which is not yet *propria materia*,
But common to all metals and all stones ;
For, where it is forsaken of that moisture,
And hath more driness, it becomes a stone :
Where it retains more of the humid fatness,
It turns to sulphur, or to quicksilver,
Who are the parents of all other metals.
Nor can this remote matter suddenly
Progress so from extreme unto extreme,
As to grow gold, and leap o'er all the means.
Nature doth first beget the imperfect, then
Proceeds she to the perfect.   Of that airy
And oily water, mercury is engender'd ;
Sulphur of the fat and earthy part : the one,
Which is the last, supplying the place of male,

The other of the female, in all metals.
Some do believe hermaphrodeity,
That both do act and suffer.   But these two
Make the rest ductile, malleable, extensive.
And even in gold they are; for we do find
Seeds of them, by our fire, and gold in them ;
And can produce the species of each metal
More perfect thence, than nature doth in earth.
Beside, who doth not see in daily practice
Art can beget bees, hornets, beetles, wasps,
Out of the carcasses and dung of creatures ;
Yea, scorpions of an herb, being rightly placed ?
And these are living creatures, far more perfect
And excellent than metals.
    Mam. Well said, father !
Nay, if he take you in hand, sir, with an argument,
He'll bray you in a mortar.
    Sur. Pray you, sir, stay.
Rather than I'll be bray'd, sir, I'll believe
That Alchemy is a pretty kind of game,
Somewhat like tricks o' the cards, to cheat a man
With charming.
    Sub. Sir ?
    Sur. What else are all your terms,
Whereon no one of your writers 'grees with other ?
Of your elixir, your *lac virginis,*
Your stone, your med'cine, and your chrysosperme,
Your sal, your sulphur, and your mercury,
Your oil of height, your tree of life, your blood,
Your marchesite, your tutie, your magnesia,
Your toad, your crow, your dragon, and your panther ;
Your sun, your moon, your firmament, your adrop,
Your lato, azoch, zernich, chibrit, heautarit,
And then your red man, and your white woman,
With all your broths, your menstrues, and materials,

Of piss and egg-shells, women's terms, man's blood,
Hair o' the head, burnt clouts, chalk, merds, and clay,
Powder of bones, scalings of iron, glass,
And worlds of other strange ingredients,
Would burst a man to name ?
   Sub. And all these named,
Intending but one thing : which art our writers
Used to obscure their art.
   Mam. Sir, so I told him—
Because the simple idiot should not learn it,
And make it vulgar.
   Sub. Was not all the knowledge
Of the Ægyptians writ in mystic symbols ?
Speak not the scriptures oft in parables ?
Are not the choicest fables of the poets,
That were the fountains and first springs of wisdom,
Wrapp'd in perplexed allegories ?
   Mam. I urg'd that,
And cleared to him, that Sysiphus was damn'd
To roll the ceaseless stone, only because
He would have made Ours common. [Dol *appears at the
        door.*]—Who is this ?   [lady,
   Sub. 'Sprecious !—What do you mean ? go in, good
Let me entreat you. [Dol *retires.*]—Where's this
      varlet ?

Re-enter FACE.

   Face. Sir.
   Sub. You very knave ! do you use me thus?
   Face. Wherein, sir ?
   Sub. Go in and see, you traitor. Go !   [*Exit* FACE.
   Mam. Who is it, sir ?
   Sub. Nothing, sir ; nothing.
   Mam. What's the matter, good sir ?
I have not seen you thus distemper'd : who is't !

Sub. All arts have still had, sir, their adversaries,
But ours the most ignorant.—

Re-enter FACE.

What now?
 Face. 'Twas not my fault, sir; she would speak with
   you.
 Sub. Would she, sir! Follow me.   [*Exit.*
 Mam. [*stopping him.*] Stay, Lungs.
 Face. I dare not, sir.
 Mam. Stay, man; what is she?
 Face. A lord's sister, sir.
 Mam. How! pray thee, stay.
 Face. She's mad, sir, and sent hither—
He'll be mad too—
 Mam. I warrant thee.—
Why sent hither?
 Face. Sir, to be cured.
 Sub. [*within.*] Why, rascal!
 Face. Lo you!—Here, sir!   [*Exit.*
 Mam. 'Fore God, a Bradamante, a brave piece.
 Sur. Heart, this is a bawdy-house! I will be burnt
   else.
 Mam. O, by this light, no; do not wrong him. He's
Too scrupulous that way; it is his vice.
No, he's a rare physician, do him right,
An excellent Paracelsian, and has done
Strange cures with mineral physic. He deals all
With spirits, he; he will not hear a word
Of Galen, or his tedious recipes.—

Re-enter FACE.

How now, Lungs!
 Face. Softly, sir; speak softly. I meant.
To have told your worship all. This must not hear.

Mam. No, he will not be " gull'd : " let him alone.

Facc. You are very right, sir, she is a most rare
    scholar,
And is gone mad with studying Broughton's works.
If you but name a word touching the Hebrew,
She falls into her fit, and will discourse
' So learnedly of genealogies,
As you would run mad too, to hear her, sir.

Mam. How might one do t' have conference with her,
     Lungs?

Face. O divers have run mad upon the conference :
I do not know, sir. I am sent in haste,
To fetch a vial.

Sur. Be not gull'd, sir Mammon.

Mam. Wherein ? pray ye, be patient.

Sur. Yes, as you are,
And trust confederate knaves and bawds and whores.

Mam. You are too foul, believe it.—Come here, Ulen,
One word.

Face. I dare not, in good faith.   [*Going.*

Mam. Stay, knave.

Face. He is extreme angry that you saw her, sir.

Mam. Drink that. [*Gives him money.*] What is she
    when she's out of her fit ?

Face. O, the most affablest creature, sir ! so merry !
So pleasant ! she'll mount you up, like quicksilver,
Over the helm ; and circulate like oil,
A very vegetal : discourse of state,
Of mathematics, bawdry, any thing——

Mam. Is she no way accessible ? no means,
No trick to give a man a taste of her——wit——
Or so ?

Sub. [*within.*] Ulen !

Face. I'll come to you again, sir.   [*Exit.*

Mam. Surly, I did not think one of your breeding
Would traduce personages of worth.
　Sur. Sir Epicure,
Your friend to use ; yet still loth to be gull'd :
I do not like your philosophical bawds.
Their stone is letchery enough to pay for,
Without this bait.
　Mam. 'Heart, you abuse yourself.
I know the lady, and her friends, and means,
The original of this disaster.　Her brother
Has told me all.
　Sur. And yet you never saw her
Till now ?
　Mam. O yes, but I forgot.　I have, believe it,
One of the treacherousest memories, I do think,
Of all mankind.
　Sur. What call you her brother ?
　Mam. My lord——
He will not have his name known, now I think on't.
　Sur. A very treacherous memory !
　Mam. On my faith——
　Sur. Tut, if you have it not about you, pass it,
Till we meet next.
　Mam. Nay, by this hand, 'tis true.
He's one I honour, and my noble friend ;
And I respect his house.
　Sur. Heart, can it be,
That a grave sir, a rich, that has no need,
A wise sir, too, at other times, should thus,
With his own oaths, and arguments, make hard means
To gull himself ?　An this be yuor elixir,
Your *lapis mineralis*, and your lunary,
Give me your honest trick yet at primero,
Or gleek ; and take your *lutum sapientis*,
Your *menstruum simplex !*　I'll have gold before you,

And with less danger of the quicksilver,
Or the hot sulphur.

Re-enter FACE.

Face. Here's one from captain Face, sir,   [*to* SURLY.]
Desires you meet him in the Temple-church,
Some half hour hence, and upon earnest business.
Sir, [*whispers* MAMMON.] if you please to quit us, now ;
          and come
Again within two hours, you shall have
My master busy examining o' the works ;
And I will steal you in, unto the party,
That you may see her converse.—Sir, shall I say,
You'll meet the captain's worship ?
    Sur. Sir, I will.—   [*Walks aside.*
But, by attorney, and to a second purpose.
Now, I am sure it is a bawdy-house ;
I'll swear it, were the marshal here to thank me :
The naming this commander doth confirm it.
Don Face ! why he's the most authentic dealer
In these commodities, the superintendant
To all the quainter traffickers in town !
He is the visitor, and does appoint,
Who lies with whom, and at what hour ; what price ;
Which gown, and in what smock ; what fall ; what tire.
Him will I prove, by a third person, to find
The subtleties of this dark labyrinth ;
Which if I do discover, dear sir Mammon,
You'll give your poor friend leave, though no
          philosopher,
To laugh : for you that are, 'tis thought, shall weep.
    Face. Sir, he does pray, you'll not forget.
    Sur. I will not, sir.
Sir Epicure, I shall leave you.   [*Exit.*
    Mam. I follow you, straight.

Face. But do so, good sir, to avoid suspicion. This
    gentleman has a parlous head.
Mam. But wilt thou, Ulen,
Be constant to thy promise ?
    Face. As my life, sir.   [me,
Mam. And wilt thou insinuate what I am, and praise
And say, I am a noble fellow ?
    Face. O, what else, sir ?
And that you'll make her royal with the stone,
An empress ; and yourself, king of Bantam.
    Mam. Wilt thou do this ?
    Face. Will I, sir !
    Mam. Lungs, my Lungs !
I love thee.
    Face. Send your stuff, sir, that my master
May busy himself about projection.
    Mam. Thou hast witch'd me, rogue : take, go.
                           [*Gives him money.*
    Face. Your jack, and all, sir.
    Mam. Thou art a villain—I will send my jack,
And the weights too. Slave, I could bite thine ear.
Away, thou dost not care for me.
    Face. Not I, sir !
    Mam. Come, I was born to make thee, my good
    weasel,
Set thee on a bench, and have thee twirl a chain
With the best lord's vermin of 'em all.
    Face. Away, sir.
    Mam. A count, nay, a count palatine——
    Face. Good, sir, go.
    Mam. Shall not advance thee better: no, nor
    faster.   [*Exit.*

Re-enter SUBTLE *and* DOL.

Sub. Has he bit ! has he bit ?

Face. And swallowed too, my Subtle.
I have given him line, and now he plays, i' faith.
  Sub. And shall we twitch him ?
  Face. Thorough both the gills.
A wench is a rare bait, with which a man
No sooner's taken, but he straight firks mad.
  Sub. Dol, my lord What'ts'hums sister, you must now
Bear yourself *statelich.*
  Dol. O let me alone.
I'll not forget my race, I warrant you.
I'll keep my distance, laugh and talk aloud ;
Have all the tricks of a proud scurvy lady,
And be as rude as her woman.
  Face. Well said, sanguine !
  Sub. But will he send his andirons ?
  Face. His jack too.
And's iron shoeing horn ; I have spoke to him.   Well,
I must not lose my wary gamester yonder.
  Sub. O monsieur Caution, that *will not be gull'd.*
  Face. Ay,
If I can strike a fine hook into him, now !
The Temple-church, there I have cast mine angle.
Well, pray for me.   I'll about it.   [*Knocking without.*
  Sub. What, more gudgeons !
Dol, scout, scout ! [Dol *goes to the window.*] Stay,
        Face, you must go to the door.
'Pray God it be my anabaptist.—Who is't, Dol ?
  Dol. I know him not : he looks like a gold-end-man.
  Sub. Ods so ! 'tis he, he said he would send what call
        you him ?
The sanctified elder, that should deal
For Mammon's jack and andirons.   Let him in.
Stay, help me off, first, with my gown. [*Exit* Face
        with the gown.]   Away,   [Now,
Madam, to your withdrawing chamber. [*Exit* Dol.]

In a new tune, new gesture, but old language.—
This fellow is sent from one negociates with me
About the stone too ; for the holy brethren
Of Amsterdam, the exiled saints ; that hope
To raise their discipline by it.   I must use him
In some strange fashion, now, to make him admire
       me.—

Enter ANANIAS.

Where is my drudge ?   [*Aloud.*

Re-enter FACE.

   Face. Sir !
   Sub. Take away the recipient,
And rectify your menstrue from the phlegma.
Then pour it on the Sol, in the cucurbite,
And let them macerate together.
   Face. Yes, sir.
And save the ground ?
   Sub. No : *terra damnata*
Must not have entrance in the work.—Who are you ?
   Ana. A faithful brother, if it please you.
   Sub. What's that ?
A Lullianist ? a Ripley ? *Filius artis?*
Can you sublime and dulcify ? calcine ?
Know you the sapor pontic ? sapor stiptic !
Or what is homogene, or heterogene ?
   Ana. I understand no heathen language, truly.
   Sub. Heathen ! you Knipper-doling ? is Ars sacra,
Or chrysopœia, or spagyrica,
Or the pamphysic, or panarchic knowledge,
A heathen language ?
   Ana. Heathen Greek, I take it.
   Sub. How ! heathen Greek ?
   Ana. All's heathen but the Hebrew.

   Sub. Sirrah, my varlet, stand you forth and speak to
       him,
Like a philosopher : answer in the language.
Name the vexations, and the martyrizations
Of metals in the work.
   Face. Sir, putrefaction,
Solution, ablution, sublimation,
Cohobation, calcination, ceration, and
Fixation.
   Sub. This is heathen Greek to you, now !—
And when comes vivification ?
   Face. After mortification.
   Sub. What's cohobation ?
   Face. 'Tis the pouring on
Your aqua regis, and then drawing him off,
To the trine circle of the seven spheres.
   Sub. What's the proper passion of metals ?
   Face. Malleation.
   Sub. What's your *ultimum supplicium auri* ?
   Face. Antimonium.   [mercury ?
   Sub. This is heathen Greek to you !—And what's your
   Face. A very fugitive, he will be gone, sir.
   Sub. How know you him ?
   Face. By his viscosity,
His oleosity, and his suscitability.
   Sub. How do you sublime him ?
   Face. With the calce of egg-shells,
White marble, talc.
   Sub. Your magisterium, now,
What's that ?
   Face. Shifting, sir, your elements,
Dry into cold, cold into moist, moist into hot,
Hot into dry.
   Sub. This is heathen Greek to you still !
Your *lapis philosophicus* ?

Face. 'Tis a stone,
And not a stone; a spirit, a soul, and a body:
Which if you do dissolve, it is dissolved;
If you coagulate, it is coagulated;
If you make it to fly, it flieth.
 Sub. Enough.   [*Exit* Face.
This is heathen Greek to you! What are you, sir?
 Ana. Please you, a servant of the exiled brethren,
That deal with widows and with orphans' goods;
And make a just account unto the saints:
A deacon.
 Sub. O, you are sent from master Wholsome,
Your teacher?
 Ana. From Tribulation Wholsome,
Our very zealous pastor.
 Sub. Good, I have
Some orphans' goods to come here.
 Ana. Of what kind, sir.
 Sub. Pewter and brass, andirons and kitchen-ware,
Metals, that we must use our medicine on:
Wherein the brethren may have a pennyworth,
For ready money.
 Ana. Were the orphans' parents
Sincere professors?
 Sub. Why do you ask?
 Ana. Because
We then are to deal justly, and give, in truth,
Their utmost value.
 Sub. 'Slid, you'd cozen else,
And if their parents were not of the faithful!—
I will not trust you, now I think on it,
'Till I have talk'd with your pastor. Have you brought
  money
To buy more coals?
 Ana. No, surely.

Sub. No ! how so ?
Ana. The brethren bid me say unto you, sir,
Surely they will not venture any more,
Till they may see projection.
    Sub. How !
    Ana. You have had,
For the instruments, as bricks, and lome, and glasses,
Already thirty pound ; and for materials,
They say, some ninety more : and they have heard
       since,
That one at Heidelberg made it of an egg,
And a small paper of pin-dust.
    Sub. What's your name ?
    Ana. My name is Ananias.
    Sub. Out, the varlet
That cozen'd the apostles ! Hence, away !
Flee, mischief ! had your holy consistory
No name to send me, of another sound,
Than wicked Ananias ? send your elders
Hither to make atonement for you quickly,
And give me satisfaction ; or out goes
The fire ; and down th' alembics, and the furnace,
Piger Henricus, or what not. Thou wretch !
Both sericon and bufo shall be lost,
Tell them. All hope of rooting out the bishops
Or the anti-christian hierarchy, shall perish,
If they stay threescore minutes : the aqueity,
Terreity, and sulphureity
Shall run together again, and all be annull'd,
Thou wicked Ananias ! [*Exit* ANANIAS.] This will fetch
       'em,
And make them haste towards their gulling more.
A man must deal like a rough nurse, and fright
Those that are froward, to an appetite.

Re-enter FACE *in his uniform, followed by* DRUGGER.

Face. He is busy with his spirits, but we'll upon him.
Sub. How now! what mates, what Baiards have we
      here?
Face. I told you, he would be furious.—Sir, here's
      Nab,
Has brought you another piece of gold to look on :
—We must appease him. Give it me,—and prays you,
.You would devise—what is it, Nab?
Drug. A sign, sir.
Face. Ay, a good lucky one, a thriving sign, doctor.
Sub. I was devising now.
Face. 'Slight, do not say so,
He will repent he gave you any more—
What say you to his constellation, doctor,
The Balance?
Sub. No, that way is stale, and common.
A townsman born in Taurus, gives the bull,
Or the bull's-head : in Aries, the ram,
A poor-device ! No, I will have his name
Form'd in some mystic character ; whose radii,
Striking the senses of the passers by,
Shall, by a virtual influence, breed affections,
That may result upon the party owns it :
As thus——
Face. Nab !
Sub. He shall have *a bel*, that's *Abel ;*
And by it standing one whose name is *Dee*,
In a *rug* gown, there's *D*, and *Rug*, that's *drug :*
And right anenst him a dog snarling *er ;*
There's *Drugger*, Abel Drugger. That's his sign.
And here's now mystery and hieroglyphic !
Face. Abel, thou art made.
Drug. Sir, I do thank his worship.

Face. Six o' thy legs more will not do it, Nab.
He has brought you a pipe of tobacco, doctor.
  Drug. Yes, sir :
I have another thing I would impart——
  Face. Out with it, Nab.
  Drug. Sir, there is lodged, hard by me,
A rich young widow——
  Face. Good ! a bona roba ?
  Drug. But nineteen, at the most.
  Face. Very good, Abel.
  Drug. Marry, she's not in fashion yet ; she wears
A hood, but it stands a cop.
  Face. No matter, Abel.
  Drug. And I do now and then give her a fucus——
  Face. What ! dost thou deal, Nab ?
  Sub. I did tell you, captain.   [trusts me
  Drug. And physic too, sometime, sir ; for which she
With all her mind. She's come up here of purpose
To learn the fashion.
  Face. Good (his match too !)—On, Nab.
  Drug. And she does strangely long to know her
        fortune.
  Face. Ods lid, Nab, send her to the doctor, hither.
  Drug. Yes, I have spoke to her of his worship already;
But she's afraid it will be blown abroad,
And hurt her marriage.
  Face. Hurt it ! 'tis the way
To heal it, if 'twere hurt ; to make it more
Follow'd and sought : Nab, thou shalt tell her this.
She'll be more known, more talk'd of; and your
        widows
Are ne'er of any price till they be famous ;
Their honour is their multitude of suitors :
Send her, it may be thy good fortune. What !
Thou dost not know.

Drug. No, sir, she'll never marry
Under a knight : her brother has made a vow.
  Face. What ! and dost thou despair, my little Nab,
Knowing what the doctor has set down for thee,
And seeing so many of the city dubb'd ?
One glass o' thy water, with a madam I know,
Will have it done, Nab : what's her brother, a knight ?
  Drug. No, sir, a gentleman newly warm in his laud,
      sir,
Scarce cold in his one and twenty, that does govern
His sister here ; and is a man himself
Of some three thousand a year, and is come up
To learn to quarrel, and to live by his wits,
And will go down again, and die in the country.
  Face. How ! to quarrel ?
  Drug. Yes, sir, to carry quarrels,
As gallants do ; to manage them by line.
  Face. 'Slid, Nab, the doctor is the only man
In Christendom for him.   He has made a table,
With mathematical demonstrations,
Touching the art of quarrels : he will give him
An instrument to quarrel by.   Go, bring them both,
Him and his sister.   And, for thee, with her
The doctor happ'ly may persuade.   Go to :
'Shalt give his worship a new damask suit
Upon the premises.
  Sub. O, good captain !
  Face. He shall ;
He is the honestest fellow, doctor.—Stay not,
No offers ; bring the damask, and the parties.
  Drug. I'll try my power, sir.
  Face. And thy will too, Nab.
  Sub. 'Tis good tobacco, this ! what is't an ounce ?
  Face. He'll send you a pound, doctor.
  Sub. O no.

Face. He will do't.
It is the goodest soul !—Abel, about it.
Thou shalt know more anon.   Away, be gone.—
                                             [*Exit* ABEL.
A miserable rogue, and lives with cheese,
And has the worms.   That was the cause, indeed,
Why he came now : he dealt with me in private,
To get a med'cine for them.
    Sub. And shall, sir.   This works.
    Face. A wife, a wife for one of us, my dear Subtle !
We'll e'en draw lots, and he that fails, shall have
The more in goods, the other has in tail.
    Sub. Rather the less : for she may be so light
She may want grains.
    Face. Ay, or be such a burden,
A man would scarce endure her for the whole.   [mine.
    Sub. Faith, best let's see her first, and then deter-
    Face. Content : but Dol must have no breath on't.
    Sub. Mum.
Away you, to your Surly yonder, catch him.
    Face. 'Pray God I have not staid too long.
    Sub. I fear it.   [*Exeunt.*

ACT III.

SCENE I.—*The Lane before* LOVEWIT'S *House.*

Enter TRIBULATION, WHOLESOME, *and* ANANIAS.

Tri. These chastisements are common to the saints,
And such rebukes, we of the separation
Must bear with willing shoulders, as the trials
Sent forth to tempt our frailties.
    Ana. In pure zeal,
I do not like the man, he is a heathen,
And speaks the language of Canaan, truly.

Tri. I think him a profane person indeed.
    Ana. He bears
The visible mark of the beast in his forehead.
And for his stone, it is a work of darkness,
And with philosophy blinds the eyes of man.
    Tri. Good brother, we must bend unto all means
That may give furtherance to the holy cause.
    Ana. Which his cannot: the sanctified cause
Should have a sanctified course.
    Tri. Not always necessary:
The children of perdition are oft-time
Made instruments even of the greatest works:
Beside, we should give somewhat to man's nature,
The place he lives in, still about the fire,
And fume of metals, that intoxicate
The brain of man, and make him prone to passion.
Where have you greater atheists than your cooks?
Or more profane, or choleric, than your glass-men?
More anti-christian than your bell-founders?
What makes the devil so devilish, I would ask you,
Sathan, our common enemy, but his being
Perpetually about the fire, and boiling
Brimstone and arsenic? We must give, I say,
Unto the motives, and the stirrers up
Of humours in the blood. It may be so,
When as the work is done, the stone is made,
This heat of his may turn into a zeal,
And stand up for the beauteous discipline,
Against the menstruous cloth and rag of Rome.
We must await his calling, and the coming
Of the good spirit. You did fault, t'upbraid him
With the brethren's blessing of Heidelberg, weighing
What need we have to hasten on the work,
For the restoring of the silenced saints,
Which ne'er will be, but by the philosopher's stone.

And so a learned elder, one of Scotland,
Assured me ; *aurum potabile* being
The only med'cine, for the civil magistrate,
T' incline him to a feeling of the cause ;
And must be daily used in the disease.

   Ana. I have not edified more, truly, by man ;
Not since the beautiful light first shone on me :
And I am sad my zeal hath so offended.

   Tri. Let us call on him then.

   Ana. The motion's good,
And of the spirit ; I will knock first.　[*Knocks.*]　Peace
   be within !

       [*The door is opened, and they enter.*]

SCENE II.—*A Room in* LOVEWIT'S *House.*

Enter SUBTLE, *followed by* TRIBULATION *and* ANANIAS.

   Sub. O, are you come ? 'twas time.　Your threescore
     minutes
Were at last thread, you see ; and down had gone
Furnus acediæ, turris circulatorius :
Lembec, bolt's-head, retort and pelican
Had all been cinders.—Wicked Ananias !
Art thou return'd ? nay then, it goes down yet.

   Tri. Sir, be appeased ; he is come to humble
Himself in spirit, and to ask your patience,
If too much zeal hath carried him aside
From the due path.

   Sub. Why, this doth qualify !

   Tri. The brethren had no purpose, verily,
To give you the least grievance : but are ready
To lend their willing hands to any project
The spirit and you direct.

Sub. This qualifies more !
Tri. And for the orphan's goods, let them be valued,
Or what is needful else to the holy work,
It shall be numbered ; here, by me, the saints,
Throw down their purse before you.
Sub. This qualifies most !
Why, thus it should be, now you understand.
Have I discours'd so unto you of our stone,
And of the good that it shall bring your cause ?
Shew'd you (beside the main of hiring forces
Abroad, drawing the Hollanders, your friends,
From the Indies, to serve you, with all their fleet)
That even the med'cinal use shall make you a faction,
And party in the realm ?   As, put the case,
That some great man in state, he have the gout,
Why, you but send three drops of your elixir,
You help him straight : there you have made a friend.
Another has the palsy or the dropsy,
He takes of your incombustible stuff,
He's young again : there you have made a friend.
A lady that is past the feat of body,
Though not of mind, and hath her face decay'd
Beyond all cure of paintings, you restore,
With the oil of talc : there you have made a friend ;
And all her friends.   A lord that is a leper,
A knight that has the bone-ache, or a squire
That hath both these, you make them smooth and sound,
With a bare fricace of your med'cine : still
You increase your friends.
Tri. Ay, it is very pregnant.
Sub. And then the turning of this lawyer's pewter
To plate at Christmas.——
Ana. Christ-tide, I pray you.
Sub. Yet, Ananias !
Ana. I have done.

Sub. Or changing
His parcel gilt to massy gold.   You cannot
But raise you friends.   Withal, to be of power
To pay an army in the field, to buy
The king of France out of his realms, or Spain
Out of his Indies.   What can you not do
Against lords spiritual or temporal,
That shall oppone you ?
   Tri. Verily, 'tis true.
We may be temporal lords ourselves, I take it.
   Sub. You may be any thing, and leave off to make
Long-winded exercises ; or suck up
Your *ha!* and *hum!* in a tune.   I not deny,
But such as are not graced in a state,
May, for their ends, be adverse in religion,
And get a tune to call the flock together :
For, to say sooth, a tune does much with women,
And other phlegmatic people ; it is your bell.
   Ana. Bells are profane ; a tune may be religious.
   Sub. No warning with you !   then   farewell   my
            patience.
 Slight, it shall down : I will not be thus tortured.
   Tri. I pray you, sir.
   Sub. All shall perish.   I have spoke it.
   Tri. Let me find grace, sir, in your eyes ; the man
He stands corrected : neither did his zeal,
But as your self, allow a tune somewhere.
Which now, being tow'rd the stone, we shall not need.
   Sub. No, nor your holy vizard, to win widows
To give you legacies ; or make zealous wives
To rob their husbands for the common cause ;
Nor take the start of bonds broke but one day,
And say, they were forfeited by providence.
Nor shall you need o'er night to eat huge meals,
To celebrate your next day's fast the better ;

The whilst the brethren and the sisters humbled,
Abate the stiffness of the flesh.   Nor cast
Before your hungry hearers scrupulous bones ;
As whether a Christian may hawk or hunt,
Or whether matrons of the holy assembly
May lay their hair out, or wear doublets,
Or have that idol starch about their linen.
   Ana. It is indeed an idol.
   Tri. Mind him not, sir.
I do command thee, spirit of zeal, but trouble,
To peace within him !   Pray, you, sir, go on.
   Sub. Nor shall you need to libel 'gainst the prelates,
And shorten so your ears against the hearing
Of the next wire-drawn grace.   Nor of necessity
Rail against plays, to please the alderman
Whose daily custard you devour : nor lie
With zealous rage till you are hoarse.   Not one
Of these so singular arts.   Nor call your selves
By names of Tribulation, Persecution,
Restraint, Long-patience, and such like, affected
By the whole family or wood of you,
Only for glory, and to catch the ear
Of the disciple.
   Tri. Truly, sir, they are
Ways that the godly brethren have invented,
For propagation of the glorious cause,
As very notable means, and whereby also
Themselves grow soon, and profitably, famous.
   Sub. O, but the stone, all's idle to it ! nothing !
The art of angels' nature's miracle,
The divine secret that doth fly in clouds
From east to west ; and whose tradition
Is not from men, but spirits.
   Ana. I hate traditions ;
I do not trust them.——

Tri. Peace !
Ana. They are popish all.
I will not peace : I will not——
   Tri. Ananias !
   Ana. Please the profane, to grieve the godly ; I may
      not.
   Sub. Well, Ananias, thou shalt overcome.
   Tri. It is an ignorant zeal that haunts him, sir ;
But truly, else, a very faithful brother,
A botcher, and a man, by revelation,
That hath a competent knowledge of the truth.
   Sub. Has he a competent sum there in the bag
To buy the goods within ?   I am made guardian,
And must, for charity, and conscience sake,
Now see the most be made for my poor orphan ;
Though I desire the brethren too good gainers :
There they are within.   When you have view'd, and
      bought 'em,
And ta'en the inventory of what they are,
They are ready for projection ; there's no more
To do : cast on the med'cine, so much silver
As there is tin there, so much gold as brass,
I'll give't you in by weight.
   Tri. But how long time,
Sir, must the saints expect yet ?
   Sub. Let me see,
How's the moon now ?   Eight, nine, ten days hence,
He will be silver potate ; then three days
Before he citronise :   Some fifteen days,
The magisterium will be perfected.
   Ana. About the second day of the third week,
In the ninth month ?
   Sub. Yes, my good Ananias.
   Tri. What will the orphan's goods arise to, think
      you ?

Sub. Some hundred marks, as much as fill'd three cars,
Unladed now : you'll make six millions of them.—
But I must have more coals laid in.
  Tri. How !
  Sub. Another load,
And then we have finish'd.   We must now increase
Our fire to *ignis ardens*, we are past
Fimus equinus, balnei, cincris,
And all those lenter heats.   If the holy purse
Should with this draught fall low, and that the saints
Do need a present sum, I have a trick
To melt the pewter, you shall buy now, instantly.
And with a tincture make you as good Dutch dollars
As any are in Holland.
  Tri. Can you so ?
  Sub. Ay, and shall 'bide the third examination.
  Ana. It will be joyful tidings to the brethren.
  Sub. But you must carry it secret.
  Tri. Ay ; but stay,
This act of coining, is it lawful ?
  Ana. Lawful !
We know no magistrate ; or, if we did,
This is foreign coin.
  Sub. It is no coining, sir.
It is but casting.
  Tri. Ha ! you distinguish well :
Casting of money may be lawful.
  Ana. 'Tis sir.
  Tri. Truly, I take it so.
  Sub. There is no scruple,
Sir, to be made of it ; believe Ananias :
This case of conscience he is studied in.
  Tri. I'll make a question of it to the brethren.
  Ana. The brethren shall approve it lawful, doubt not.
Where shall it be done ?   *[Knocking without.*

Sub. For that we'll talk anon.
There's some to speak with me.   Go in, I pray you,
And view the parcels.   That's the inventory.
I'll come to you straight.   [*Exeunt* TRIB. *and* ANA.]
    Who is it ?—Face ! appear.

Enter FACE, *in his uniform.*
How now ! good prize ?
    Face. Good pox ! yond' costive cheater
Never came on.
    Sub. How then ?
    Face. I have walk'd the round
Till now, and no such thing.
    Sub. And have you quit him ?
    Face. Quit him ! an hell would quit him too, he were
        happy.
Slight ! would you have me stalk like a mill-jade,
All day, for one that will not yield us grains ?
I know him of old.
    Sub. O, but to have gull'd him,
Had been a mastery.
    Face. Let him go, black boy !
And turn thee, that some fresh news may possess thee.
A noble count, a don of Spain, my dear
Delicious compeer, and my party-bawd,
Who is come hither private for his conscience,
And brought munition with him, six great slops,
Bigger than three Dutch hoys, beside round trunks,
Furnished with pistolets, and pieces of eight,
Will straight be here, my rogue, to have thy bath,
(That is the colour) and to make his battery
Upon our Dol, our castle, our cinque-port,
Our Dover pier, our what thou wilt.   Where is she ?
She must prepare perfumes, delicate linen,
The bath in chief, a banquet, and her wit,

For she must milk his epididimis.
Where is the doxy ?
  Sub. I'll send her to thee :
And but dispatch my brace of little John Leydens,
And come again my self.
  Face. Are they within then ?
  Sub. Numbering the sum.
  Face. How much ?
  Sub. A hundred marks, boy.   *[Exit.*
  Face. Why, this is a lucky day. Ten pounds of
      Mammon !
Three of my clerk ! a portague of my grocer !
This of the brethren ! beside reversions,
And states to come in the widow, and my count !
My share to-day will not be bought for forty——

Enter Dol.

  Dol. What ?
  Face. Pounds, dainty Dorothy ! art thou so near ?
  Dol. Yes ; say, lord general, how fares our camp ?
  Face. As with the few that had entrench'd themselves
Safe, by their discipline, against a world, Dol,
And laugh'd within those trenches, and grew fat
With thinking on the booties, Dol, brought in
Daily by their small parties.   This dear hour,
A doughty don is taken with my Dol ;
And thou mayst make his ransom what thou wilt,
My Dousabel ; he shall be brought here fetter'd
With thy fair looks, before he sees thee ; and thrown
In a down-bed, as dark as any dungeon ;
Wherein thou shalt keep him waking with thy drum :
Thy drum, my Dol, thy drum ; till he be tame
As the poor blackbirds were in the great frost,
Or bees are with a bason ; and so hive him

In the swan-skin coverlid, and cambric sheets,
Till he work honey and wax, my little God's-gift.
  Dol. What is he, general?
  Face. An adalantado,
A grandee, girl,   Was not my Dapper here yet?
  Dol. No.
  Face. Nor my Drugger?
  Sub. A pox on 'em,
They are so long a furnishing! such stinkards
Would not be seen upon these festival days.—

Re-enter SUBTLE.

How now! have you done?
  Sub. Done.   They are gone: the sum
Is here in bank, my Face.   I would we knew
Another chapman now would buy 'em outright.
  Face. 'Slid, Nab shall do't against he have the widow,
To furnish household.
  Sub. Excellent, well thought on:
Pray God he come!
  Face. I pray he keep away
Till our new business be o'erpast.
  Sub. But, Face,
How cam'st thou by this secret don?
  Face. A spirit
Brought me th' intelligence in a paper here,
As I was conjuring yonder in my circle
For Surly; I have my flies abroad.   Your bath
Is famous, Subtle, by any means.   Sweet Dol,
You must go tune your virginal, no losing
O' the least time: and, do you hear? good action.
Firk, like a flounder; kiss, like a scallop, close;
And tickle him with thy mother-tongue.   His great
Verdugoship has not a jot of language;
So much the easier to be cozen'd, my Dolly.
...12...

He will come here in a hired coach, obscure,
And our own coachman, whom I have sent as guide,
No creature else. [*Knocking without.*] Who's that?
             [*Exit* DOL.

 Sub. Is it not he?
 Face. O no, not yet this hour.

      Re-enter DOL.

 Sub. Who is't?
 Dol. Dapper,
Your clerk.
 Face. God's will then, queen of Fairy,
On with your tire; [*Exit* DOL.] and, doctor, with your
  robes.
Let's dispatch him for God's sake.
 Sub. 'Twill be long.
 Face. I warrant you, take but the cues I give you,
It shall be brief enough. [*Goes to the window.*] Slight,
  here are more!
Abel, and I think the angry boy, the heir,
That fain would quarrel,
 Sub. And the widow?
 Face. No,
Not that I see. Away!   [*Exit* SUB.

      Enter DAPPER.
        —O sir, you are welcome.
The doctor is within a moving for you;
I have had the most ado to win him to it!—
He swears you'll be the darling of the dice:
He never heard her highness dote till now.
Your aunt has given you the most gracious words
That can be thought on,
 Dap. Shall I see her grace?
 Face. See her, and kiss her too.—

Enter ABEL, *followed by* KASTRIL.

       What, honest Nab !
Hast brought the damask ?
 Drug. No, sir ; here's tobacco.
 Face. 'Tis well done, Nab : thou'lt bring the damask
  too ?
 Drug. Yes : here's the gentleman, captain, master
  Kastril,
I have brought to see the doctor.
 Face. Where's the widow ?
 Drug. Sir, as he likes, his sister, he says, shall come.
 Face. O, is it so ? good time. Is your name Kastril,
  sir ?   [else,
 Kas. Ay, and the best of the Kastrils, I'd be sorry
By fifteen hundred a year. Where is the doctor ?
My mad tobacco-boy, here, tells me of one
That can do things : has he any skill ?
 Face. Wherein, sir ?
 Kas. To carry a business, manage a quarrel fairly,
  t terms.
 Face. It seems, sir, you are but young
About the town, that can make that a question.
 Kas. Sir, not so young, but I have heard some speech
Of the angry boys, and seen them take tobacco ;
And in his shop ; and I can take it too.
And I would fain be one of 'em, and go down
And practise in the country.
 Face. Sir, for the duello,
The doctor, I assure you, shall inform you,
To the least shadow of a hair ; and show you
An instrument he has of his own making,
Wherewith no sooner shall you make report
Of any quarrel, but he will take the height on't
Most instantly, and tell in what degree

Of safety it lies in, or mortality,
And how it may be borne, whether in a right line,
Or a half circle ; or may else be cast
Into an angle blunt, if not acute :
All this he will demonstrate.   And then, rules
To give and take the lie by.
    Kas. How ! to take it ?
    Face. Yes, in oblique he'll show you, or in circle ;
But never in diameter.   The whole town
Study his theorems, and dispute them ordinarily
At the eating academics.
    Kas. But does he teach
Living by the wits too ?
    Face. Anything whatever.
You cannot think that sublety, but he reads it.
He made me a captain.   I was a stark pimp,
Just of your standing, 'fore I met with him ;
It is not two months since.   I'll tell you his method :
First, he will enter you at some ordinary.
    Kas. No, I'll not come there : you shall pardon me.
    Face. For why, sir ?
    Kas. There's gaming there, and tricks.
    Face. Why, would you be
A gallant, and not game ?
    Kas. Ay, 'twill spend a man.   [spent :
    Face. Spend you ! it will repair you when you are
How do they live by their wits there, that have vented
Six times your fortunes ?
    Kas. What, three thousand a-year !
    Face. Ay, forty thousand.
    Kas. Are there such ?
    Face. Ay, sir,
And gallants yet.   Here's a young gentleman
Is born to nothing.—[*Points to* DAPPER.] forty marks
    a-year,

Which I count nothing :—he is to be initiated,
And have a fly of the doctor.   He will win you,
By unresistible luck, within this fortnight,
Enough to buy a barony.   They will set him
Upmost, at the groom porters, all the Christmas :
And for the whole year through, at every place,
Where there is play, present him with the chair ;
The best attendance, the best drink ; sometimes
Two glasses of Canary, and pay nothing ;
The purest linen, and the sharpest knife,
The partridge next his trencher : and somewhere
The dainty bed, in private, with the dainty.
You shall have your ordinaries bid for him,
As play-houses for a poet ; and the master
Pray him aloud to name what dish he affects,
Which must be butter'd shrimps : and those that drink
To no mouth else, will drink to his, as being
The goodly president mouth of all the board.
    Kas. Do you not gull one ?
    Face. 'Ods my life ! do you think it ?
You shall have a cast commander (can but get
In credit with a glover, or a spurrier,
For some two pair of either's ware aforehand),
Will, by most swift posts, dealing [but] with him,
Arrive at competent means to keep himself,
His punk and naked boy, in excellent fashion,
And be admired for't.
    Kas. Will the doctor teach this ?
    Face. He will do more, sir : when your land is gone,
As men of spirit hate to keep earth long,
In a vacation, when small money is stirring,
And ordinaries suspended till the term,
He'll show a perspective, where on one side
You shall behold the faces and the persons
Of all sufficient young heirs in town.

Whose bonds are current for commodity ;
On th' other side, the merchant's forms, and others,
That without help of any second broker,
Who would expect a share, will trust such parcels :
In the third square, the very street and sign
Where the commodity dwells, and does but wait
To be deliver'd, be it pepper, soap,
Hops, or tobacco, oatmeal, woad, or cheeses.
All which you may so handle, to enjoy
To your own use, and never stand obliged.
   Kas. I'faith ! is he such a fellow ?
   Face. Why, Nab here knows him.
And then for making matches for rich widows,
Young gentlewomen, heirs, the fortunat'st man !
He's sent to, far and near, all over England,
To have his counsel, and to know their fortunes.
   Kas. God's will, my suster shall see him.
   Face. I'll tell you, sir.
What he did tell me of Nab.   It's a strange thing :—
By the way, you must eat no cheese, Nab, it breeds
    melancholy,
And that same melancholy breeds worms ; but pass it :—
He told me, honest Nab here was ne'er at tavern
But once in's life !
   Drug. Truth, and no more I was not.
   Face. And then he was so sick—
   Drug. Could he tell you that, too ?
   Face. How should I know it ?
   Drug. In troth we had been a shooting,
And had a piece of fat ram-mutton to supper,
That lay so heavy o' my stomach——
   Face. And he has no head
To bear any wine ; for what with the noise of the fiddlers,
And care of his shop, for he dares keep no servants——
   Drug. My head did so ach——

Face. As he was fain to be brought home,
The doctor told me : and then a good old woman——
 Drug. Yes, faith, she dwells in Sea-coal-lane,—did
      cure me,
With sodden ale, and pellitory of the wall ;
Cost me but twopence.   I had another sickness
Was worse than that.
 Face. Ay, that was with the grief
Thou took'st for being cess'd at eighteenpence,
For the water-work.
 Drug. In truth, and it was like
T' have cost me almost my life.
 Face. Thy hair went off ?
 Drug. Yes, sir ; 'twas done for spight.
 Face. Nay, so says the doctor.
 Kas. Pray thee, tobacco-boy, go fetch my suster ;
I'll see this learned boy before I go ;
And so shall she.
 Face. Sir, he is busy now :
But if you have a sister to fetch hither,
Perhaps your own pains may command her sooner ;
And he by that time will be free.
 Kas. I go.   [*Exit.*
 Face. Drugger, she's thine :—the damask !—[*Exit
      ABEL.*] Subtle and I   [*Dapper,*
Must wrestle for her. [*Aside.*]—Come on, master
You see how I turn clients here away,
To give your cause dispatch ; have you perform'd
The ceremonies were enjoin'd you ?
 Dap. Yes, of the vinegar,
And the clean shirt,
 Face. 'Tis well : that shirt may do you
More worship than you think.   Your aunt's a-fire,
But that she will not show it, 't have a sight of you.
Have you provided for her grace's servants ?

Dap. Yes, here are six score Edward shillings.
Face. Good !
Dap. And an old Harry's sovereign.
Face. Very good !
Dap. And three James shillings, and an Elizabeth
    groat,
Just twenty nobles.
  Face. O, you are too just.
I would you had had the other noble in Maries.
  Dap. I have some Philip and Maries.
  Face. Ay, those same
Are best of all : where are they ?   Hark, the doctor.

Enter SUBTLE, *disguised like a priest of Fairy, with a
stripe of cloth.*

  Sub. [*In a feigned voice.*] Is yet her grace's cousin
    come ?
  Face. He is come.
  Sub. And is he fasting ?
  Face. Yes.
  Sub. And hath cried hum ?
  Face. Thrice, you must answer.
  Dap. Thrice.
  Sub. And as oft buz ?
  Face. If you have, say.
  Dap. I have.
  Sub. Then, to her cuz,
Hoping that he hath vinegar'd his senses,
As he was bid, the Fairy queen dispenses,
By me, this robe, the petticoat of fortune ;
Which that he straight put on, she doth importune.
And though to fortune near be her petticoat,
Yet nearer is her smock, the queen doth note :
And therefore, ev'n of that a piece she hath sent,
Which, being a child, to wrap him in was rent ;

And prays him for a scarf he now will wear it,
With as much love as then her grace did tear it,
About his eyes, [*They blind him with the rag*] to shew
  he is fortunate.
And, trusting unto her to make his state,
He'll throw away all worldly pelf about him ;
Which that he will perform, she doth not doubt him.
  Face. She need not doubt him, sir. Alas, he has
    nothing.
But what he will part withal as willingly,
Upon her grace's word—throw away your purse—
As she would ask it ;—handkerchiefs and all—
              [*He throws away, as they bid him.*
She cannot bid that thing, but he'll obey.—
If you have a ring about you, cast it off,
Or a silver seal at your wrist ; her grace will send
Her fairies here to search you, therefore deal
Directly with her highness : if they find
That you conceal a mite, you are undone.
  Dap. Truly, there's all.
  Face. All what?
  Dap. My money ; truly.
  Face. Keep nothing that is transitory about you.
Bid Dol play music. [*Aside to* SUBTLE.]—Look, the
  elves are come
                [DOL *plays on the cittern within.*
To pinch you, if you tell not truth. Advise you.
                    [*They pinch him.*
  Dap. O ! I have a paper with a spur-ryal in't.
  Face Ti, ti.
They knew't, they say.
  Sub. Ti, ti, ti, ti. He has more yet.
  Face. Ti, ti-ti-ti. In the other pocket.
                    [*Aside to* SUB.

Sub. *Titi, titi, titi, titi, titi.*
They must pinch him or he will never confess, they say.
>   [*They pinch him again.*
Dap. O, O !
Face. Nay, pray you hold : he is her grace's nephew.
Ti, ti, ti? What care you ? good faith, you shall care.—
Deal plainly, sir, and shame the fairies.   Shew
You are innocent.
Dap. By this good light, I have nothing.
Sub. *Ti, ti, ti, ti, to, ta.*   He does equivocate, she
          says :
Ti, ti do ti, ti ti do, ti da ; and swears by the *light* when
          he is blinded.
Dap. By this good *dark,* I have nothing but a
          half-crown
Of gold about my wrist, that my love gave me ;
And a leaden heart I wore since she forsook me.
Face. I thought 'twas something.   And would you
          incur
Your aunt's displeasure for these trifles ?   Come,
I had rather you had thrown away twenty half-crowns.
>   [*Takes it off.*
You may wear your leaden heart still.—

Enter DOL, *hastily.*

>   How now !
Sub. What news, Dol ?
Dol. Yonder's your knight, sir Mammon.
Face. 'Ods lid, we never thought of him till now !
Where is he ?
Dol. Here hard by : he is at the door.
Sub. And you are not ready, now !   Dol, get his suit.
>   [*Exit* DOL.
He must not be sent back.

Face. O by no means.
What shall we do with this same puffin here,
Now he's on the spit ?
    Sub. Why, lay him back awhile,
With some device.

              Re-enter DOL, *with* FACE'S *clothes.*
--*Ti, ti, ti, ti, ti, ti.*   Would her grace speak with me ?
I come.—Help, Dol !   [*Knocking without.*
    Face. [*Speaks through the key-hole.*]   Who's there ?
              sir Epicure,
My master's in the way.   Please you to walk
Three or four turns, but till his back be turn'd,
And I am for you.—Quickly, Dol !
    Sub. Her grace
Commends her kindly to you, master Dapper.
    Dap. I long to see her grace.
    Sub. She now is set,
At dinner in her bed, and she has sent you
From her own private trencher, a dead mouse,
And a piece of ginger-bread, to be merry withal,
And stay your stomach, lest you faint with fasting ;
Yet if you could hold out till she saw you, she says,
It would be better for you.
    Face. Sir, he shall
Hold out, an 'twere this two hours, for her highness :
I can assure you that.   We will not lose
All we have done.——
    Sub. He must not see, nor speak
To any body, till then.
    Face. For that we'll put, sir,
A stay in's mouth.
    Sub. Of what ?
    Face. Of ginger-bread.
Make you it fit.   He that hath pleas'd her grace

Thus far, shall not now crincle for a little.—
Gape sir, and let him fit you.
        [*They thrust a gag of ginger-bread in his mouth.*
    Sub. Where shall we now
Bestow him ?
    Dol. In the privy.
    Sub. Come along, sir,
I now must shew you Fortune's privy lodgings.
    Face. Are they perfum'd, and his bath ready ?
    Sub. All :
Only the fumigation's somewhat strong.
    Face. [*Speaking through the key-hole.*] Sir Epicure,
        I am yours, sir, by and by.
                        [*Exeunt with* DAPPER.

ACT IV.

SCENE I.—*A Room in* LOVEWIT'S *House.*

Enter FACE *and* MAMMON.

    Face. O sir, you are come in the only finest time.—
    Mam. Where's master ?
    Face. Now preparing for projection, sir.
Your stuff will be all changed shortly.
    Mam. Into gold ?
    Face. To gold and silver, sir.
    Mam. Silver I care not for.
    Face. Yes, sir, a little to give beggars.
    Mam. Where's the lady ?
    Face. At hand here. I have told her such brave
        things of you,
Touching your bounty, and your noble spirit—
    Mam. Hast thou ?
    Face. As she is almost in her fit to see you.
But, good sir, no divinity in your conference,
For fear of putting her in rage.—

Mam. I warrant thee.
Face. Six men [sir] will not hold her down ; and then,
If the old man should hear or see you——
Mam. Fear not.
Face. The very house, sir, would run mad. You
        know it,
How scrupulous he is, and violent,
'Gainst the least act of sin. Physic, or mathematics,
Poetry, state, or bawdry, as I told you,
She will endure, and never startle ; but
No word of controversy.
Mam. I am school'd, good Ulen.
Face. And you must praise her house, remember that,
And her nobility.
Mam. Let me alone :
No herald, no, nor antiquary, Lungs,
Shall do it better. Go.
Face. Why, this is yet
A kind of modern happiness, to have
Dol Common for a great lady.   [*Aside and exit.*
Mam. Now, Epicure,
Heighten thyself, talk to her all in gold ;
Rain her as many showers as Jove did drops
Unto his Danäe ; shew the god a miser,
Compared with Mammon. What ! the stone will do't.
She shall feel gold, taste gold, hear gold, sleep gold ;
Nay, we will *concumbere* gold : I will be puissant,
And mighty in my talk to her.—

    Re-enter FACE, *with* DOL *richly dressed.*

                Here she comes.
Face. To him, Dol, suckle him.—This is the noble
        knight,
I told your ladyship——

Mam. Madam, with your pardon,
1 kiss your vesture.
   Dol. Sir, I were uncivil
If I would suffer that ; my lip to you, sir.
   Mam. I hope my lord your brother be in health,
      lady.
   Dol. My lord, my brother is, though I no lady, sir.
   Face. Well said, my Guinea bird.   [*Aside.*
   Mam. Right noble madam——
   Face. O, we shall have most fierce idolatry.   [*Aside.*
   Mam. 'Tis your prerogative.
   Dol. Rather your courtesy.
   Mam. Were there nought else to enlarge your virtues
      to me,
These answers speak your breeding and your blood.
   Dol. Blood we boast none, sir, a poor baron's
      daughter.
   Mam. Poor ! and gat you ? profane not. Had your
      father
Slept all the happy remnant of his life
After that act, lien but there still, and panted,
He had done enough to make himself, his issue,
And his posterity noble.
   Dol. Sir, although
We may be said to want the gilt and trappings,
The dress of honour, yet we strive to keep
The seeds and the materials.
   Mam. I do see
The old ingredient, virtue, was not lost,
Nor the drug money used to make your compound.
There is a strange nobility in your eye,
This lip, that chin ! methinks you do resemble
One of the Austriac princes.
   Face. Very like !
Her father was an Irish costarmonger.   [*Aside.*

Mam. The house of Valois just had such a nose,
And such a forehead yet the Medici
Of Florence boast.
    Dol. Troth, and I have been liken'd
To all these princes.
    Face. I'll be sworn, I heard it.
    Mam. I know not how ! it is not any one,
But e'en the very choice of all their features.
    Face. I'll in, and laugh.   [*Aside and exit.*
    Mam. A certain touch, or air,
That sparkles a divinity, beyond
An earthly beauty !
    Dol. O, you play the courtier.
    Mam. Good lady, give me leave——
    Dol. In faith, I may not,
To mock me, sir.
    Mam. To burn in this sweet flame ;
The phœnix never knew a nobler death.
    Dol. Nay, now you court the courtier, and destroy
What you would build : this art, sir, in your words,
Calls your whole faith in question.
    Mam. By my soul——
    Dol. Nay, oaths are made of the same air, sir.
    Mam. Nature
Never bestow'd upon mortality
A more unblamed, a more harmonious feature ;
She play'd the step-dame in all faces else :
Sweet Madam, let me be particular——
    Dol. Particular, sir ! I pray you know your distance.
    Mam. In no ill sense, sweet lady ; but to ask
How your fair graces pass the hours ? I see
You are lodg'd here, in the house of a rare man,
An excellent artist ; but what's that to you ?
    Dol. Yes, sir ; I study here the mathematics,
And distillation.

Mam. O, I cry your pardon.
He's a divine instructor ! can extract
The souls of all things by his **art** ; call all
The virtues, and the miracles of the sun,
Into a temperate furnace ; teach dull nature
What her own forces are. A man, the emperor
Has courted above Kelly ; sent his medals
And chains, to invite him.
  Dol. Ay, and for his physic, sir——
  Mam. Above the art of Æsculapius,
That drew the envy of the thunderer !
I know all this, and more.
  Dol. Troth, I am taken, sir,
Whole with these studies, that contemplate nature.
  Mam. It is a noble humour ; but this form
Was not intended to so dark a use.
Had you been crooked, foul, of some coarse mould,
A cloister had done well ; but such a feature
That might stand up the glory of a kingdom,
To live recluse ! is a mere solœcism,
Though in a nunnery. It must not be.
I muse, my lord your brother will permit it :
You should spend half my land first, were I he.
Does not this diamond better on my finger,
Than in the quarry.
  Dol. Yes.
  Mam. Why, you are like it.
You were created, lady, for the light.
Here, you shall wear it ; take it, the first pledge
Of what I speak, to bind you to believe me.
  Dol. In chains of adamant ?
  Mam. Yes, the strongest bands.
And take a secret too—here, by your side,
Doth stand this hour, the happiest man in Europe.
  Dol. You are contented, sir !

Mam. Nay, in true being,
The envy of princes and the fear of states.
    Dol. Say, you so, sir Epicure ?
    Mam. Yes, and thou shalt prove it,
Daughter of honour.   I have cast mine eye
Upon thy form, and I will rear this beauty
Above all styles.
    Dol. You mean no treason, sir ?
    Mam. No, I will take away that jealousy.
I am the lord of the philosopher's stone,
And thou the lady.
    Dol. How sir ! have you that ?
    Mam. I am the master of the mastery.
This day the good old wretch here o' the house
Has made it for us ; now he's at projection.
Think therefore thy first wish now, let me hear it ;
And it shall rain into thy lap, no shower,
But floods of gold, whole cataracts, a deluge,
To get a nation on thee.
    Dol. You are pleased, sir,
To work on the ambition of our sex.
    Mam. I am pleased the glory of her sex should know,
This nook, here, of the Friers is no climate
For her to live obscurely in, to learn
Physic and surgery, for the constable's wife
Of some odd hundred in Essex ; but come forth,
And taste the air of palaces ; eat, drink
The toils of empirics, and their boasted practice ;
Tincture of pearl, and coral, gold and amber ;
Be seen at feasts and triumphs ; have it ask'd,
What miracle she is ? set all the eyes
Of court a-fire, like a burning glass,
And work them into cinders, when the jewels
Of twenty states adorn thee, and the light
Strikes out the stars ! that when thy name is mention'd,

Queens may look pale ; and we but shewing our love,
Nero's Poppæa may be lost in story !
Thus will we have it.
 Dol. I could well consent, sir,
But, in a monarchy, how will this be ?
The prince will soon take notice, and both seize
You and your stone, it being a wealth unfit
For any private subject.
 Mam. If he knew it.
 Dol. Yourself do boast it, sir.
 Mam. To thee, my life.
 Dol. O, but beware, sir ! you may come to end
The remnant of your days in a loth'd prison,
By speaking of it.
 Mam. 'Tis no idle fear :
We'll therefore go withall, my girl, and live
In a free state, where we will eat our mullets,
Soused in high-country wines, sup pheasants' eggs,
And have our cockles boil'd in silver shells ;
Our shrimps to swim again, as when they liv'd,
In a rare butter made of dolphin's milk,
Whose cream does look like opals ; and with these
Delicate meats set ourselves high for pleasure,
And take us down again, and then renew
Our youth and strength with drinking the elixir,
And so enjoy a perpetuity
Of life and lust ! And thou shalt have thy wardrobe
Richer than nature's, still to change thy self,
And vary oftener, for thy pride, than she,
Or art, her wise and almost-equal servant.

Re-enter FACE.

 Face. Sir, you are too loud. I hear you every word
Into the laboratory. Some fitter place ;
The garden, or great chamber above. How like you her ?

Mam. Excellent ! Lungs.   There's for thee.
> [*Gives him money.*

Face. But do you hear ?
Good sir, beware, no mention of the rabbins.
Mam. We think not on 'em.
> [*Exeunt* MAM. *and* DOL.

Face. O, it is well, sir.—Subtle !

Enter SUBTLE.

Dost thou not laugh ?
Sub. Yes ; are they gone ?
Face. All's clear.
Sub. The widow is come.
Face. And your quarrelling disciple ?
Sub. Ay.
Face. I must to my captainship again then.
Sub. Stay, bring them in first.
Face. So I meant.   What is she ?
A bonnibel ?
Sub. I know not.
Face. We'll draw lots !
You'll stand to that ?
Sub. What else ?
Face. O, for a suit,
To fall now like a curtain, flap !
Sub. To the door, man.
Face. You'll have the first kiss, 'cause I am not ready.
> [*Exit.*

Sub. Yes, and perhaps hit you through both the
    nostrils.
Face. [*within.*] Who would you speak with ?
Kas. [*within.*] Where's the captain ?
Face. [*within.*] Gone, sir,
About some business.
Kas. [*within.*] Gone !

Face. [*within.*] He'll return straight.
But master doctor, his lieutenant, is here.

Enter KASTRIL, *followed by* Dame PLIANT.

Sub. Come near, my worshipful boy, my *terræ fili*,
That is, my boy of land ; make thy approaches :
Welcome ; I know thy lusts, and thy desires,
And I will serve and satisfy them. Begin,
Charge me from thence, or thence, or in this line ;
Here is my centre : ground thy quarrel.
Kas. You lie.
Sub. How, child of wrath and anger ! the loud lie ?
For what, my sudden boy ?
Kas. Nay, that look you to,
I am afore-hand.
Sub. O, this is no true grammar,
And as ill logic ! You must render causes, child,
Your first and second intentions, know your canons
And your divisions, moods, degrees, and differences,
Your predicaments, substance, and accident,
Series, extern and intern, with their causes,
Efficient, material, formal, final,
And have your elements perfect ?
Kas. What is this !
The angry tongue he talks in ?   [*Aside.*
Sub. That false precept,
Of being afore-hand, has deceived a number,
And made them enter quarrels, often-times,
Before they were aware ; and afterward,
Against their wills.
Kas. How must I do then, sir ?
Sub. I cry this lady mercy : she should first
Have been saluted. [*Kisses her.*] I do call you lady,
Because you are to be one, ere't be long,
My soft and buxom widow.

Kas. Is she, i'faith !
Sub. Yes, or my art is an egregious liar.
Kas. How know you ?
Sub. By inspection on her forehead,
And subtlety of her lip, which must be tasted
Often, to make a judgment. [*Kisses her again.*] 'Slight,
    she melts
Like a myrobolane :—here is yet a line,
In *rivo frontis*, tells me he is no knight.
  Dame P. What is he then, sir ?
  Sub. Let me see your hand.
O, your *linea fortunæ* makes it plain ;
And stella here *in monte Veneris*.
But, most of all, *junctura annularis*.
He is a soldier, or a man of art, lady,
But shall have some great honour shortly.
  Dame P. Brother,
He's a rare man, believe me !

       Re-enter FACE, *in his uniform.*

  Kas. Hold your peace.
Here comes the t' other rare man.—'Save you, captain.
  Face. Good master Kastril ! Is this your sister ?
  Kas. Ay, sir.
Please you to kuss her, and be proud to know her.
  Face. I shall be proud to know you, lady.
                    [*Kisses her.*

  Dame P. Brother,
He calls me lady too.
  Kas. Ay, peace : I heard it.   [*Takes her aside.*
  Face. The count is come.
  Sub. Where is he ?
  Face. At the door.
  Sub. Why, you must entertain him.

Face. What will you do
With these the while ?
    Sub. Why, have them up, and shew them
Some fustian book, or the dark glass.
    Face. Fore God,
She is a delicate dab-chick !   I must have her.   [*Exit.*
    Sub. Must you ! ay, if your fortune will, you must.—
Come, sir, the captain will come to us presently :
I'll have you to my chamber of demonstrations,
Where I will shew you both the grammar, and logic,
And rhetoric of quarrelling ; my whole method
Drawn out in tables ; and my instrument,
That hath the several scales upon't, shall make you
Able to quarrel at a straw's-breadth by moonlight.
And, lady, I'll have you look in a glass,
Some half an hour, but to clear your eyesight,
Against you see your fortune ; which is greater,
Than I may judge upon the sudden, trust me.
            [*Exit, followed by* KAST. *and* Dame P.

                Re-enter FACE.

    Face. Where are you, doctor ?
    Sub. [*within.*] I'll come to you presently.
    Face. I will have this same widow, now I have seen
        her,
On any composition.

                Re-enter SUBTLE.

    Sub. What do you say ?
    Face. Have you disposed of them.
    Sub. I have sent them up.
    Face. Subtle, in troth, I needs must have this widow.
    Sub. Is that the matter ?
    Face. Nay, but hear me.

Sub. Go to.
If you rebel once, Dol shall know it all :
Therefore be quiet, and obey your chance.
    Face. Nay, thou art so violent now—Do but conceive,
Thou art old, and canst not serve——
    Sub. Who cannot ? I ?
'Slight, I will serve her with thee, for a——
    Face. Nay,
But understand : I'll give you composition.
    Sub. I will not treat with thee ; what ! sell my
        fortune ?
'Tis better than my birth-right.   Do not murmur :
Win her, and carry her.   If you grumble, Dol
Knows it directly.
    Face. Well, sir, I am silent.
Will you go help to fetch in Don in state ?   [*Exit.*
    Sub. I follow you, sir : we must keep Face in awe,
Or he will overlook us like a tyrant.

     Re-enter FACE, *introducing* SURLY *disguised as a*
                Spaniard.

Brain of a tailor ! who comes here ?   Don John !
    Sur. Señores, beso las manos a vuestras mercedes.
    Sub. Would you had stoop'd a little, and kist our
        anos !
    Face. Peace, Subtle.
    Sub. Stab me ; I shall never hold, man.
He looks in that deep ruff like a head in a platter,
Serv'd in by a short cloke upon two trestles.   [down
    Face. Or, what do you say to a collar of brawn, cut
Beneath the souse, and wriggled with a knife ?
    Sub. 'Slud, he does look too fat to be a Spaniard.
    Face. Perhaps some Fleming or some Hollander got
        him
In d'Alva's time ; count Egmont's bastard.

Sub. Don,
Your scurvy, yellow, Madrid face is welcome.
Sur. Gratia.
Sub. He speaks out of a fortification.
Pray God he have no squibs in those deep sets.
Sur. Por dios, señores, muy linda casa!
Sub. What says he?
Face. Praises the house, I think;
I know no more but's action.
Sub. Yes, the *casa,*
My precious Diego, will prove fair enough
To cozen you in. Do you mark? you shall
Be cozen'd, Diego.
Face. Cozen'd, do you see,
My worthy Donzel, cozen'd.
Sur. Entiendo.
Sub. Do you intend it? so do we, dear Don.
Have you brought pistolets, or portagues,
My solemn Don?—Dost thou feel any?
Face. [*Feels his pockets.*] Full.
Sub. You shall be emptied, Don, pumped and drawn
Dry, as they say.
Face. Milked, in troth, sweet Don.
Sub. See all the monsters; the great lion of all, Don.
Sur. Con licencia, se puede ver a esta señora?
Sub. What talks he now?
Face. Of the sennora.
Sub. O, Don,
That is the lioness, which you shall see
Also, my Don.
Face. 'Slid, Subtle, how shall we do?
Sub. For what?
Face. Why Dol's employ'd, you know.
Sub. That's true.
'Fore heaven, I know not: he must stay, that's all.

Face. Stay ! that he must not by no means.
Sub. No ! why ?
Face. Unless you'll mar all.   'Slight, he will suspect
 it :
And then he will not pay, not half so well.
This is a travelled punk-master, and does know
All the delays : a notable hot rascal,
And looks already rampant.
 Sub. 'Sdeath, and Mammon
Must not be troubled.
 Face. Mammon ! in no case.
 Sub. What shall we do then ?
 Face. Think : you must be sudden.
 *Sur. Entiendo que la señora es tan hermosa, que
codicio tan verla, como la bien aventuranza de mi vida.*
 Face. Mi vida ! 'Slid, Subtle, he puts me in mind o'
 the widow.
What dost thou say to draw her to it, ha !
And tell her 'tis her fortune ? all our venture
Now lies upon't.   It is but one man more,
Which of us chance to have her : and beside,
There is no maidenhead to be fear'd or lost.
What dost thou think on't, Subtle ?
 Sub. Who, I ? why——
 Face. The credit of our house too is engaged.
 Sub. You made me an offer for my share erewhile.
What wilt thou give me, i' faith ?
 Face. O, by that light
I'll not buy now : You know your doom to me.
E'en take your lot, obey your chance, sir ; win her,
And wear her out, for me.
 Sub. 'Slight, I'll not work her then.
 Face. It is the common cause ; therefore bethink you.
Dol else must know it, as you said.
 Sub. I care not.

Sur. *Señores, porque se tarda tanto?*
Sub. Faith, I am not fit, I am old.
Face. That's now no reason, sir.
Sur. *Puede ser de hazer burla de mi amor?*
Face. You hear the Don too ? by this air, I call,
And loose the hinges : Dol !
Sub. A plague of hell——
Face. Will you then do ?
Sub. You are a terrible rogue !
I'll think of this : will you, sir, call the widow ?
Face. Yes, and I'll take her too with all her faults,
Now I do think on't better.
Sub. With all my heart, sir ;
Am I discharged o' the lot ?
Face. As you please.
Sub. Hands.   [*They take hands.*
Face. Remember now, that upon any change,
You never claim her.
Sub. Much good joy, and health to you, sir.
Marry a whore ! fate, let me wed a witch first.
Sur. *Por estas honradas barbas——*
Sub. He swears by his beard.
Dispatch, and call the brother too.   [*Exit* FACE.
Sur. *Tengo duda, señores, que no me hagan alguna*
         traycion.
Sub. How, issue on ? yes, præsto, sennor. Please
         you
Enthratha the *chambrata,* worthy don :
Where if you please the fates, in your *bathada,*
You shall be soked, and stroked, and tubb'd, and rubb'd,
And scrubb'd, and fubb'd, dear don, before you go.
You shall in faith, my scurvy baboon don,
Be curried, claw'd, and flaw'd, and taw'd, indeed.
I will the heartlier go about it now,
And make the widow a punk so much the sooner,

To be revenged on this impetuous Face :
The quickly doing of it, is the grace.
[Exeunt Sub. and Surly.

SCENE II.—Another Room in the same.

Enter Face, Kastril, and Dame Pliant.

Face. Come, lady : I knew the Doctor would not leave,
Till he had found the very nick of her fortune.
  Kas. To be a countess, say you, a Spanish countess, sir ?
  Dame P. Why, is that better than an English countess ?
  Face. Better ! 'Slight, make you that a question, lady ?
  Kas. Nay, she is a fool, captain, you must pardon her.
  Face. Ask from your courtier, to your inns-of-court-man,
To your mere milliner ; they will tell you all,
Your Spanish gennet is the best horse ; your Spanish
Stoup is the best garb : your Spanish beard
Is the best cut ; your Spanish ruffs are the best
Wear ; your Spanish pavin the best dance ;
Your Spanish titillation in a glove
The best perfume : and for your Spanish pike,
And Spanish blade, let your poor captain speak—
Here comes the doctor.

Enter Subtle, with a paper.

  Sub. My most honour'd lady,
For so I am now to style you, having found
By this my scheme, you are to undergo
An honourable fortune, very shortly.
What will you say now, if some——

Face. I have told her all, sir;
And her right worshipful brother here, that she shall be
A countess: do not delay them, sir: a Spanish countess.
   Sub. Still, my scarce-worshipful captain, you can keep
No secret! Well, since he has told you, madam,
Do you forgive him, and I do.
   Kas. She shall do that, sir:
I'll look to't, 'tis my charge.
   Sub. Well then: nought rests
But that she fit her love now to her fortune.
   Dame P. Truly I shall never brook a Spaniard.
   Sub. No!
   Dame P. Never since eighty-eight could I abide them,
And that was some three years afore I was born, in truth.
   Sub. Come, you must love him, or be miserable;
Choose which you will.
   Face. By this good rush, persuade her,
She will cry strawberries else within this twelvemonth.
   Sub. Nay, shads and mackarel, which is worse.
   Face. Indeed, sir?
   Kas. Ods lid, you shall love him, or I'll kick you.
   Dame P. Why,
I'll do as you will have me, brother.
   Kas. Do,
Or by this hand I'll maul you.
   Face. Nay, good sir,
Be not so fierce.
   Sub. No, my enraged child;
She will be ruled. What, when she comes to taste
The pleasures of a countess! to be courted——
   Face. And kiss'd, and ruffled!
   Sub. Ay, behind the hangings.

Face. And then come forth in pomp!

Sub. And know her state!

Face. Of keeping all the idolators of the chamber
Barer to her, than at their prayers!

Sub. Is serv'd
Upon the knee!

Face. And has her pages, ushers,
Footmen, and coaches——

Sub. Her six mares——

Face. Nay, eight!

Sub. To hurry her through London, to the Exchange,
Bethlem, the china-houses——

Face. Yes, and have
The citizens gape at her, and praise her tires,
And my lord's goose-turd bands, that ride with her.

Kas. Most brave! By this hand, you are not my
　　　 suster
If you refuse.

Dame P. I will not refuse, brother.

Enter Surly.

Sur. Que es esto, señores, que no venga? Esta
tardanza me mata!

Face. It is the count come:
The doctor knew he would be here, by his art.

Sub. En gallanta madama, Don! gallantissima!

Sur. Por todos los dioses, la mas acabada hermosura,
que he visto en mi vida!

Face. Is't not a gallant language that they speak?

Kas. An admirable language! Is't not French?

Face. No, Spanish, sir.

Kas. It goes like law-French,
And that, they say, is the courtliest language.

Face. List, sir.

Sur. *El sol ha perd:do su lumbre, con el esplandor que trae esta dama! Valyame dios!*
  Face. He admires your sister.
  Kas. Must not she make curt'sy?
  Sub. Ods will, she must go to him, man, and kiss
      him!
It is the Spanish fashion, for the women
To make first court.
  Face. 'Tis true he tells you, sir:
His art knows all.
  Sur. *Porque no se acude?*
  Kas. He speaks to her, I think.
  Face. That he does, sir.
  Sur. *Por el amor de dios, que es esto que se tarda?*
  Kas. Nay, see: she will not understand him! gull,
Noddy.
  Dame P. What say you, brother?
  Kas. Ass, my suster.
Go kuss him, as the cunning man would have you;
I'll thrust a pin in your buttocks else.
  Face. O no, sir.
  Sur. *Señora mia, mi persona esta muy indigna de allegar a tanta hermosura.*
  Face. Does he not use her bravely?
  Kas. Bravely, i'faith!
  Face. Nay, he will use her better.
  Kas. Do you think so?
  Sur. *Señora, si sera servida entremonos.*
                      [*Exit with* Dame PLIANT.
  Kas. Where does he carry her?
  Face. Into the garden, sir;
Take you no thought: I must interpret for her.
  Sub. Give Dol the word. [*Aside to* FACE, *who goes
      out.*]—Come, my fierce child, advance,
We'll to our quarrelling lesson again.

Kas. Agreed.
I love a Spanish boy with all my heart.
   Sub. Nay, and by this means, sir, you shall be
      brother
To a great count.
   Kas. Ay, I knew that at first.
This match will advance the house of the Kastrils.
   Sub. 'Pray God your sister prove but pliant !
   Kas. Why,
Her name is so, by her other husband.
   Sub. How !
   Kas. The widow Pliant.   Knew you not that ?
   Sub. No faith, sir ;
Yet, by erection of her figure, I guest it.
Come, let's go practise.
   Kas. Yes, but do you think, doctor,
I e'er shall quarrel well ?
   Sub. I warrant you.   *[Exeunt.*

SCENE III.—*Another Room in the same.*

Enter DOL *in her fit of raving, followed by* MAMMON.

Dol. For after Alexander's death——
Mam. Good lady——
Dol. That Perdiccas and Antigonus were slain,
The two that stood, Seleuc', and Ptolomee——
Mam. Madam.
Dol. Made up the two legs, and the fourth beast,
That was Gog-north, and Egypt-south : which after
Was call'd Gog-iron-leg, and South-iron-leg——
Mam. Lady——
Dol. And then Gog-horned.   So was Egypt, too :
Then Egypt-clay-leg, and Gog-clay-leg——
Mam. Sweet madam.

Dol. *And last Gog-dust, and Egypt-dust, which fall*
In the last link of the fourth chain.   *And these*
Be stars in story, which none see, or look at——
   Mam. What shall I do.
   Dol. *For,* as he says, *except*
We call the rabbins, and the heathen Greeks——
   Mam. Dear lady.
   Dol. *To come from Salem, and from Athens,*
And teach the people of Great Britain——

     Enter FACE, *hastily, in his Servant's Dress.*

   Face. What's the matter, sir?
   Dol. *To speak the tongue of Eber, and Javan——*
   Mam. O,
She's in her fit.
   Dol. *We shall know nothing——*
   Face. Death, sir,
We are undone !
   Dol. *Where then a learned linguist*
Shall see the ancient used communion
Of vowels and consonants——
   Face. My master will hear !
   Dol. *A wisdom, which Pythagoras held most high——*
   Mam. Sweet honourable lady !
   Dol. *To comprise*
All sounds of voices, in few marks of letters——
   Face. Nay, you must never hope to lay her now.
                [They all speak together
   Dol. *And so we may arrive by Talmud skill,*
And profane Greek, to raise the building up
Of Helen's house against the Ismaelite,
King of Thogarma, and his habergions
Brimstony, blue, and fiery ; and the force
Of king Abaddon, and the beast of Cittim :

Which rabbi David Kimchi, Onkelos,
And Aben Ezra do interpret Rome.
    Face. How did you put her into't ?
    Mam. Alas ! I talk'd
Of a fifth monarchy I would erect,
With the philosopher's stone, by chance, and she
Falls on the other four straight.
    Face. Out of Broughton !
I told you so. 'Slid, stop her mouth.
    Mam. Is't best ?
    Face. She'll never leave else. If the old man hear
        her,
We are but fæces, ashes.
    Sub. [*Within.*] What's to do there ?
    Face. O, we are lost ! Now she hears him, she is
        quiet.

      Enter SUBTLE, *they run different ways.*
    Mam. Where shall I hide me !
    Sub. How ! what sight is here ?
Close deeds of darkness, and that shun the light !
Bring him again. Who is he ? What, my son !
O, I have lived too long.
    Mam. Nay, good, dear father,
There was no unchaste purpose.
    Sub. Not ! and flee me,
When I come in ?
    Mam. That was my error.
    Sub. Error !   [marvel,
Guilt, guilt, my son : give it the right name. No
If I found check in our great work within,
When such affairs as these were managing !
    Mam. Why, have you so ?
    Sub. It has stood still this half hour :
And all the rest of our less works gone back.
        ...14...

Where is the instrument of wickedness,
My lewd false drudge?
  Mam. Nay, good sir, blame not him;
Believe me, 'twas against his will or knowledge:
I saw her by chance.
  Sub. Will you commit more sin,
To excuse a varlet?
  Mam. By my hope, 'tis true, sir.
  Sub. Nay, then I wonder less, if you, for whom
The blessing was prepared, would so tempt heaven,
And lose your fortunes.
  Mam. Why, sir?
  Sub. This will retard
The work, a month at least.
  Mam. Why, if it do,
What remedy? But think it not, good father:
Our purposes were honest.
  Sub. As they were,
So the reward will prove.—[*A loud explosion within.*]
    How now! ah me!
God, and all saints be good to us.—

Re-Enter FACE.

                    What's that?
  Face. O, sir, we are defeated! all the works
Are flown *in fumo*, every glass is burst:
Furnace, and all rent down! as if a bolt
Of thunder had been driven through the house.
Retorts, receivers, pelicans, bolt-heads,
All struck in shivers!
                [SUBTLE *falls down as in a swoon.*
                Help, good sir! alas,
Coldness, and death invades him. Nay, sir Mammon,
Do the fair offices of a man! you stand,
As you were readier to depart than he. [*Knocking within.*

Who's there ? my lord her brother is come.
   Mam. Ha, Lungs !
   Face. His coach is at the door.   Avoid his sight,
For he's as furious as his sister's mad.
   Mam. Alas !
   Face. My brain is quite undone with the fume, sir,
I ne'er must hope to be mine own man again.
   Mam. Is all lost, Lungs ? will nothing be preserv'd
Of all our cost ?
   Face. Faith, very little, sir ;
A peck of coals or so, which is cold comfort, sir.
   Mam. O my voluptuous mind !   I am justly punish'd.
   Face. And so am I, sir.
   Mam. Cast from all my hopes——
   Face. Nay, certainties, sir.
   Mam. By mine own base affections.
   Sub. [*Seeming to come to himself.*] O, the curst fruits
       of vice and lust !
   Mam. Good father,
It was my sin.   Forgive it.
   Sub. Hangs my roof
Over us still, and will not fall, O justice
Upon us, for this wicked man !
   Face. Nay, look, sir,
You grieve him now with staying in his sight :
Good sir, the nobleman will come too, and take you,
And that may breed a tragedy.
   Mam. I'll go.
   Face. Ay, and repent at home, sir.   It may be,
For some good penance you may have it yet ;
A hundred pound to the box at Bethlem——
   Mam. Yes.
   Face. For the restoring such as—have their wits.
   Mam. I'll do't.
   Face. I'll send one to you to receive it.

Mam. Do.
Is no projection left !
    Face. All flown, or stinks, sir.   [think'st thou ?
    Mam. Will nought be sav'd that's good for med'cine,
    Face. I cannot tell, sir.   There will be perhaps,
Something about the scraping of the shards,
Will cure the itch,—though not your itch of mind, sir.
                                              [*Aside.*
It shall be saved for you, and sent home.   Good sir,
This way, for fear the lord should meet you.
                                              [*Exit* MAMMON.

    Sub. [*Raising his head.*] Face !
    Face. Ay.
    Sub. Is he gone ?
    Face. Yes, and as heavily
As all the gold he hoped for were in's blood.
Let us be light though.
    Sub. [*Leaping up.*] Ay, as balls, and bound
And hit our heads against the roof for joy :
There's so much of our care now cast away.
    Face. Now to our don.
    Sub. Yes, your young widow by this time
Is made a countess, Face ; she has been in travail
Of a young heir for you.
    Face. Good sir.
    Sub. Off with your case,
And greet her kindly, as a bridegroom should,
After these common hazards.
    Face. Very well, sir.
Will you go fetch don Diego off, the while ?
    Sub. And fetch him over too, if you'll be pleased, sir :
Would Dol were in her place, to pick his pockets now !
    Face. Why, you can do't as well, if you would set to't.
I pray you prove your virtues.
    Sub. For your sake, sir.   [*Exeunt.*

SCENE IV.—*Another Room in the same.*

Enter SURLY *and* Dame PLIANT.

Sur. Lady, you see into what hands you are fall'n ;
'Mongst what a nest of villains ! and how near
Your honour was t'have catch'd a certain clap,
Through your credulity, had I but been
So punctually forward, as place, time,
And other circumstances would have made a man ;
For you're a handsome woman : would you were wise too !
I am a gentleman come here disguised,
Only to find the knaveries of this citadel ;
And where I might have wrong'd your honour, and have
    not,
I claim some interest in your love.   You are,
They say, a widow, rich ; and I'm a batchelor,
Worth nought : your fortunes may make me a man,
As mine have preserv'd you a woman.   Think upon it,
And whether I have deserv'd you or no.
    Dame P. I will, sir.
    Sur. And for these household-rogues, let me alone
To treat with them.

Enter SUBTLE.

Sub. How doth my noble Diego,
And my dear madam countess ? hath the count
Been courteous, lady ? liberal, and open ?
Donzel, methinks you look melancholic,
After your coitum, and scurvy : truly,
I do not like the dulness of your eye ;
It hath a heavy cast, 'tis upsee Dutch,
And says you are a lumpish whore-master.
Be lighter, I will make your pockets so.
                    [Attempts to pick them.

Sur. [*Throws open his cloak.*] Will you, don bawd
    and pick-purse? [*strikes him down.*] how now!
    reel you?
Stand up, sir, you shall find, since I am so heavy,
I'll give you equal weight.
    Sub. Help! murder!
    Sur. No, sir,
There's no such thing intended: a good cart,
And a clean whip shall ease you of that fear.
I am the Spanish don *that should be cozen'd,*   .
Do you see, cozen'd! Where's your captain Face,
That parcel broker, and whole-bawd, all rascal!

    Enter FACE, *in his uniform.*
    Face. How, Surly!
    Sur. O, make your approach, good captain.
I have found from whence your copper rings and spoons
Come, now, wherewith you cheat abroad in taverns.
'Twas here you learn'd t' anoint your boot with brim-
    stone,
Then rub men's gold on't for a kind of touch,
And say 'twas naught, when you had changed the
    colour,
That you might have't for nothing. And this doctor,
Your sooty, smoky-bearded compeer, he
Will close you so much gold, in a bolt's-head,
And, on a turn, convey in the stead another
With sublimed mercury, that shall burst in the heat,
And fly out all *in fumo!* Then weeps Mammon;
Then swoons his worship. [FACE *slips out.*] Or, he is
    the Faustus,
That casteth figures and can conjure, cures
Plagues, piles, and pox, by the ephemerides,
And holds intelligence with all the bawds
And midwives of three shires: while you send in—

Captain—what ! is he gone ?—damsels with child,
Wives that are barren, or the waiting-maid
With the green sickness.

> [*Seizes* SUBTLE *as he is retiring.*

Nay, sir, you must tarry,
Though he be scaped ; and answer by the ears, sir.

Re-enter FACE, *with* KASTRIL.

Face. Why, now's the time, if ever you will quarrel
Well, as they say, and be a true-born child :
The doctor and your sister both are abused.

Kas. Where is he ? which is he ? he is a slave,
Whate'er he is, and the son of a whore.—Are you
The man, sir, I would know ?

Sur. I should be loth, sir,
To confess so much.

Kas. Then you lie in your throat.

Sur. How !

Face. [*to* KASTRIL.] A very errant rogue, sir, and a
      cheater,
Employ'd here by another conjurer
That does not love the doctor, and would cross him,
If he knew how.

Sur. Sir, you are abused.

Kas. You lie :
And 'tis no matter.

Face. Well said, sir !   He is
The impudent'st rascal——

Sur. You are indeed : Will you hear me, sir ?

Face. By no means : bid him be gone.

Kas. Begone, sir, quickly.

Sur. This 's strange !—Lady, do you inform your
      brother.

Face. There is not such a foist in all the town,
The doctor had him presently ; and finds yet,

The Spanish count will come here.—Bear up, Subtle.

[*Aside.*

 Sub. Yes, sir, he must appear within this hour.
 Face. And yet this rogue would come in a disguise,
By the temptation of another spirit,
To trouble our art, though he could not hurt it !
 Kas. Ay,
I know—Away, [*to his Sister.*] you talk like a foolish
  mauther.
 Sur. Sir, all is truth she says.
 Face. Do not believe him, sir.
He is the lying'st swabber !　Come your ways, sir.
 Sur. You are valiant out of company !
 Kas. Yes, how then, sir ?

Enter DRUGGER, *with a piece of damask.*

 Face. Nay, here's an honest fellow, too, that knows
  him.
And all his tricks.　Make good what I say, Abel,
This cheater would have cozen'd thee o' the widow.—

[*Aside to* DRUG.

He owes this honest Drugger here, seven pound,
He has had on him, in twopenny'orths of tobacco.
 Drug. Yes, sir.
And he has damn'd himself three terms to pay me.
 Face. And what does he owe for lotium ?
 Drug. Thirty shillings, sir ;
And for six syringes.
 Sur. Hydra of villainy !
 Face. Nay, sir, you must quarrel him out o' the house.
 Kas. I will :
—Sir, if you get not out o' doors, you lie ;
And you are a pimp.
 Sur. Why, this is madness, sir,
Not valour in you ; I must laugh at this.

Kas. It is my humour: you are a pimp and a trig,
And an *Amadis de Gaul,* or a Don Quixote.

Drug. Or a knight o' the curious coxcomb, do you
see ?

Enter ANANIAS.

Ana. Peace to the household !
Kas. I'll keep peace for no man.
Ana. Casting of dollars is concluded lawful.
Kas. Is he the constable ?
Sub. Peace, Ananias.
Face. No, sir.
Kas. Then you are an otter, and a shad, a whit,
A very tim.

Sur. You'll hear me, sir ?
Kas. I will not.
Ana. What is the motive ?
Sub. Zeal in the young gentleman,
Against his Spanish slops.

Ana. They are profane,
Lewd, superstitious, and idolatrous breeches.

Sur. New rascals !
Kas. Will you begone, sir ?
Ana. Avoid, Sathan !
Thou art not of the light: That ruff of pride
About thy neck, betrays thee ; and is the same
With that which the unclean birds, in seventy-seven,
Were seen to prank it with on divers coasts :
Thou look'st like anti-christ, in that lewd hat.

Sur. I must give way.
Kas. Be gone, sir.
Sur. But I'll take
A course with you——

Ana. Depart, proud Spanish fiend !
Sur. Captain and Doctor.

Ana. Child of perdition !

Kas. Hence, sir !   [*Exit* SURLY.
Did I not quarrel bravely ?

Face. Yes, indeed, sir.

Kas. Nay, an I give my mind to't, I shall do't.

Face. O, you must follow, sir, and threaten him tame:
He'll turn again else.

Kas. I'll re-turn him then.   [*Exit.*
                              [SUBTLE *takes* ANANIAS *aside.*

Face. Drugger, this rogue prevented us for thee :
We had determin'd that thou should'st have come
In a Spanish suit, and have carried her so : and he,
A brokerly slave ! goes, puts it on himself.
Hast brought the damask ?

Drug. Yes, sir.

Face. Thou must borrow
A Spanish suit : hast thou no credit with the players !

Drug. Yes, sir ; did you never see me play the Fool ?

Face. I know not, Nab :—Thou shalt, if I can help
          it.—   [*Aside.*
Hieronimo's old cloak, ruff, and hat will serve ;
I'll tell thee more when thou bring'st 'em.
                                       [*Exit* DRUGGER.

Ana. Sir, I know
The Spaniard hates the brethren, and hath spies
Upon their actions : and that this was one
I make no scruple.—But the holy synod
Have been in prayer and meditation for it ;
And 'tis reveal'd no less to them than me,
That casting of money is most lawful.

Sub. True,
But here I cannot do it ; if the house
Shou'd chance to be suspected, all would out,
And we be lock'd up in the Tower for ever,

To make gold there for the state, never come out ;
And then are you defeated.
    Ana. I will tell
This to the elders and the weaker brethren,
That the whole company of the separation
May join in humble prayer again.
    Sub. And fasting.
    Ana. Yea, for some fitter place.   The peace of mind
Rest with these walls !   [*Exit.*
    Sub. Thanks, courteous Ananias.
    Face. What did he come for ?
    Sub. About casting dollars,
Presently out of hand.   And so I told him,
A Spanish minister came here to spy,
Against the faithful——
    Face. I conceive.   Come, Subtle,
Thou art so down upon the least disaster !
How wouldst thou ha' done, if I had not help't thee out ?
    Sub. I thank thee, Face, for the angry boy, i' faith.
    Face. Who would have look'd it should have been that
               rascal,
Surly ? he had dyed his beard and all.   Well, sir,
Here's damask come to make you a suit.
    Sub. Where's Drugger ?
    Face. He is gone to borrow me a Spanish habit ;
I'll be the count, now.
    Sub. But where's the widow ?
    Face. Within, with my lord's sister : madam Dol
Is entertaining her.
    Sub. By your favour, Face,
Now she is honest, I will stand again.
    Face. You will not offer it.
    Sub. Why ?
    Face. Stand to your word,
Or—here comes Dol, she knows——

Sub. You are tyrannous still.

          Enter DOL, *hastily.*
Face. Strict for my right.—How now, Dol. Hast
    [thou] told her,
The Spanish count will come ?
  Dol. Yes ; but another is come,
You little look'd for !
  Face. Who is that ?
  Dol. Your master ;
The master of the house.
  Sub. How, Dol !
  Face. She lies,
This is some trick.   Come, leave your quiblins, Dorothy.
  Dol. Look out and see.   [FACE *goes to the window.*
  Sub. Art thou in earnest ?
  Dol. 'Slight.
Forty o' the neighbours are about him, talking.
  Face. 'Tis he, by this good day.
  Dol. 'Twill prove ill day
For some on us.
  Face. We are undone, and taken.
  Dol. Lost, I'm afraid.
  Sub. You said he would not come,
While there died one a week within the liberties.
  Face. No : 'twas within the walls.
  Sub. Was't so ! cry you mercy.
I thought the liberties.   What shall we do now, Face ?
  Face. Be silent : not a word, if he call or knock.
I'll into mine old shape again and meet him,
Of Jeremy, the butler.   In the mean time,
Do you two pack up all the goods and purchase,
That we can carry in the two trunks.   I'll keep him
Off for to-day, if I cannot longer : and then
At night, I'll ship you both away to Ratcliff,

Where we will meet to-morrow, and there we'll share.
Let Mammon's brass and pewter keep the cellar ;
We'll have another time for that.   But, Dol,
'Prythee go heat a little water quickly ;
Subtle must shave me : all my captain's beard
Must off, to make me appear smooth Jeremy.
You'll do it ?
    Sub. Yes, I'll shave you, as well as I can.
    Face. And not cut my throat, but trim me ?
    Sub. You shall see, sir.   [*Exeunt.*

ACT V.

SCENE I.—*Before* LOVEWIT'S *Door.*

Enter LOVEWIT, *with several of the* Neighbours.

    Love. Has there been such resort, say you ?
1 *Nei.* Daily, sir.
2 *Nei.* And nightly, too.
3 *Nei.* Ay, some as brave as lords.
4 *Nei.* Ladies and gentlewomen.
5 *Nei.* Citizens' wives.
1 *Nei.* And knights.
6 *Nei.* In coaches.
2 *Nei.* Yes, and oyster women.
1 *Nei.* Beside other gallants.
3 *Nei.* Sailors' wives.
4 *Nei.* Tobacco men.
5 *Nei.* Another Pimlico !
    Love. What should my knave advance,
To draw this company ? he hung out no banners
Of a strange calf with five legs to be seen,
Or a huge lobster with six claws ?
    6 *Nei.* No, sir.
    3 *Nei.* We had gone in then, sir.

Love. He has no gift
Of teaching in the nose that e'er I knew of.
You saw no bills set up that promised cure
Of ague, or the tooth-ach ?
   2 *Nei.* No such thing, sir.
   Love. Nor heard a drum struck for baboons or puppets ?
   5 *Nei.* Neither, sir.
   Love. What device should he bring forth now ?
I love a teeming wit as I love my nourishment :
'Pray God he have not kept such open house,
That he hath sold my hangings, and my bedding !
I left him nothing else.   If he have eat them,
A plague o' the moth, say I !   Sure he has got
Some bawdy pictures to call all this ging !
The friar and the nun ; or the new motion
Of the knight's courser covering the parson's mare ;
The boy of six year old with the great thing :
Or't may be, he has the fleas that run at tilt
Upon a table, or some dog to dance.
When saw you him ?
   1 *Nei.* Who, sir, Jeremy ?
   2 *Nei.* Jeremy Butler ?
We saw him not this mouth.
   Love. How !
   4 *Nei.* Not these five weeks, sir.
   6 *Nei.* These six weeks at the least.
   Love. You amaze me, neighbours !
   5 *Nei.* Sure, if your worship know not where he is,
He's slipt away.
   6 *Nei.* Pray God, he be not made away.
   Love. Ha ! it's no time to question, then.
                                   [*Knocks at the Door.*
   6 *Nei.* About
Some three weeks since, I heard a doleful cry,
As I sat up a mending my wife's stockings.

Love. 'Tis strange that none will answer !   Didst thou
    hear
A cry, sayst thou ?
  6 *Nei.* Yes, sir, like unto a man
That had been strangled an hour, and could not speak.
  2 *Nei.* I heard it too, just this day three weeks, at
    two o'clock
Next morning.
  Love. These be miracles, or you make them so !
A man an hour strangled, and could not speak,
And both you heard him cry ?
  3 *Nei.* Yes, downward, sir.
  Love. Thou art a wise fellow.   Give me thy hand, I
    pray thee,
What trade art thou on ?
  3 *Nei.* A smith, an't please your worship.
  Love. A smith ! then lend me thy help to get this
    door open.
  3 *Nei.* That I will presently, sir, but fetch my
    tools——   [*Exit.*
  1 *Nei.* Sir, best to knock again, afore you break it.
  Love. [*Knocks again.*] I will.

        Enter FACE, *in his butler's livery.*

  Face. What mean you, sir ?
  1, 2, 4 *Nei.* O, here's Jeremy !
  Face. Good sir, come from the door.
  Love. Why, what's the matter ?
  Face. Yet farther, you are too near yet.
  Love. In the name of wonder,
What means the fellow !
  Face. The house, sir, has been visited.
  Love. What, with the plague? stand thou then farther.
  Face. No. sir,
I had it not.

Love. Who had it then ? I left
None else but thee in the house.
    Face. Yes, sir, my fellow,
The cat that kept the buttery, had it on her
A week before I spied it ; but I got her
Convey'd away in the night : and so I shut
The house up for a month——
    Love. How !
    Face. Purposing then, sir,
T'have burnt rose-vinegar, treacle, and tar,   [known it ;
And have made it sweet, that you shou'd ne'er have
Because I knew the news would but afflict you, sir.
    Love. Breathe less, and farther off ! Why this is
               stranger :
The neighbours tell me all here that the doors
Have still been open——
    Face. How, sir !
    Love. Gallants, men and women,
And of all sorts, tag-rag, been seen to flock here
In threaves, these ten weeks, as to a second Hogsden,
In days of Pimlico and Eye-bright.
    Face, Sir,
Their wisdoms will not say so.
    Love. To-day they speak
Of coaches and gallants : one in a French hood
Went in, they tell me ; and another was seen
In a velvet gown at the window : divers more
Pass in and out.
    Face. They did pass through the doors then,
Or walls, I assure their eye-sights, and their spectacles ;
For here, sir, are the keys, and here have been,
In this my pocket, now above twenty days ;
And for before, I kept the fort alone there.
But that 'tis yet not deep in the afternoon,
I should believe my neighbours had seen double

Through the black pot, and made these apparitions !
For, on my faith to your worship, for these three weeks
And upwards the door has not been open'd.
 Love. Strange !
 1 *Nei.* Good faith, I think I saw a coach.
 2 *Nei.* And I too,
I'd have been sworn.
 Love. Do you but think it now ?
And but one coach ?
 4 *Nei.* We cannot tell, sir: Jeremy
Is a very honest fellow.
 Face. Did you see me at all ?
 1 *Nei.* No ; that we are sure on.
 2 *Nei.* I'll be sworn o' that.
 Love. Fine rogues to have your testimonies built on !

Re-enter Third Neighbour, *with his Tools.*

 3 *Nei.* Is Jeremy come !
 1 *Nci.* O, yes ; you may leave your tools ;
We were deceived, he says.
 2 *Nei.* He has had the keys ;
And the door has been shut these three weeks.
 3 *Nei.* Like enough.
 Love. Peace and get hence, you changelings.

Enter SURLY *and* MAMMON.

 Face. Surly come !
And Mammon made acquainted ! they'll tell all.
How shall I beat them off ? what shall I do ?
Nothing's more wretched than a guilty conscience.
[*Aside.*

 Sur. No, sir, he was a great physician. This,
It was no bawdy house, but a mere chancel !
You knew the lord and his sister.
 Mam. Nay, good Surly——

...15...

Sur. The happy word, BE RICH——
Mam. Play not the tyrant.——
Sur. Should be to-day pronounced to all your friends.
And where be your andirons now? and your brass pots,
That should have been golden flagons, and great
     wedges?
Mam. Let me but breathe. What, they have shut
     their doors,
Methinks!
Sur. Ay, now 'tis holiday with them.
Mam. Rogues,   [*He and* SURLY *knock.*
Cozeners, impostors, bawds!
Face. What mean you, sir?
Mam. To enter if we can.
Face. Another man's house!
Here is the owner, sir: turn you to him,
And speak your business.
Mam. Are you, sir, the owner?
Love. Yes, sir.
Mam. And are those knaves within your cheaters?
Love. What knaves, what cheaters?
Mam. Subtle and his Lungs.
Face: The gentleman is distracted, sir! No lungs,
Nor lights have been seen here these three weeks, sir,
Within these doors, upon my word.
Sur. Your word,
Groom arrogant!
Face. Yes, sir, I am the housekeeper,
And know the keys have not been out of my hands.
Sur. This is a new Face.
Face. You do mistake the house, sir:
What sign was't at?
Sur. You rascal! this is one
Of the confederacy. Come, let's get officers,
And force the door.

Love. 'Pray you stay, gentlemen.
Sur. No, sir, we'll come with warraut.
Mam. Ay, and then
We shall have your doors open.

         [*Exeunt* MAM. *and* SUR.

Love. What means this ?
Face. I cannot tell, sir.
1 *Nei.* These are two of the gallants
That we do think we saw.
Face. Two of the fools !
You talk as idly as they. Good faith, sir,
I think the moon has crazed 'em all.—O me,

Enter KASTRIL.

The angry boy come too ! He'll make a noise,
And ne'er away till he have betray'd us all. [*Aside.*
 Kas. [*knocking.*] What, rogues, bawds, slaves, you'll
    open the door, anon !
Punk, cockatrice, my suster ! By this light
I'll fetch the marshal to you. You are a whore
To keep your castle——
 Face. Who would you speak with, sir ?
 Kas. The bawdy doctor, and the cozening captain,
And puss my suster.
 Love. This is something sure.
 Face. Upon my trust, the doors were never open, sir.
 Kas. I have heard all their tricks told me twice over,
By the fat knight and the lean gentleman.
 Love. Here comes another.

Enter ANANIAS *and* TRIBULATION.

Face. Ananias too !
And his pastor !
 Tri. [*beating at the door.*] The doors are shut against
   us.

Ana. Come forth, you seed of sulphur, sons of fire !
Your stench it is broke forth ; abomination
Is in the house.
  Kas. Ay, my suster's there.
  Ana. The place,
It is become a cage of unclean birds.
  Kas. Yes, I will fetch the scavenger, and the
      constable.
  Tri. You shall do well.
  Ana. We'll join to weed them out.   [sister !
  Kas. You will not come then, punk devise, my
  Ana. Call her not sister : she's a harlot verily.
  Kas. I'll raise the street.
  Love. Good gentleman, a word.
  Ana. Satan avoid, and hinder not our zeal !
                    [*Exuent* ANA., TRIB., *and* KAS.
  Love. The world's turn'd Bethlem.
  Face. These are all broke loose,
Out of St. Katherine's, where they use to keep
The better sort of mad-folks.
  1 *Nei.* All these persons
We saw go in and out here.
  2 *Nei.* Yes, indeed, sir.
  3 *Nei.* These were the parties.
  Face. Peace, you drunkards ! Sir,
I wonder at it : please you to give me leave
To touch the door, I'll try an the lock be chang'd.
  Love. It mazes me !
  Face. [*Goes to the door.*] Good faith, sir, I believe
There's no such thing : 'tis all *deceptio visus*—
Would I could get him away.   [*Aside.*
  Dap. [*within.*] Master captain ! master doctor !
  Love. Who's that ?
  Face. Our clerk within, that I forgot ! [*Aside.*] I know
      not, sir.

Dap. [*within.*] For God's sake, when will her grace be
    at leisure ?
    Face. Ha!
Illusions, some spirit o' the air !—His gag is melted,
And now he sets out the throat.   [*Aside.*
    Dap. [*within.*] I am almost stifled——
    Face. Would you were altogether.   [*Aside.*
    Love. 'Tis in the house.
Ha ! list.
    Face. Believe it, sir, in the air.
    Love. Peace, you.
    Dap. [*within.*] Mine aunt's grace does not use me
    well.
    Sub. [*within.*] You fool,
Peace, you'll mar all.
    Face. [*speaks through the key-hole, while* LOVEWIT
      advances to the door unobserved.] Or you will
      else, you rogue.
    Love. O, is it so ? then you converse with spirits !—
Come, sir. No more of your tricks, good Jeremy,
The truth, the shortest way.
    Face. Dismiss this rabble, sir.—
What shall I do ? I am catch'd.   [*Aside.*
    Love. Good neighbours,
I thank you all. You may depart. [*Exuent* Neigh-
    bours.]—Come, sir,
You know that I am an indulgent master ;
And therefore conceal nothing. What's your medicine,
To draw so many several sorts of wild fowl ?
    Face. Sir, you were wont to affect mirth and wit—
But here's no place to talk on't in the street.
Give me but leave to make the best of my fortune,
And only pardon me the abuse of your house :
It's all I beg. I'll help you to a widow,
In recompence, that you shall give me thanks for,

Will make you seven years younger, and a rich one.
'Tis but your putting on a Spanish cloak :
I have her within.   You need not fear the house ;
It was not visited.
 Love. But by me, who came
Sooner than you expected
 Face. It is true, sir.
'Pray you forgive me.
 Love. Well : let's see your widow.   [*Exeunt.*

Scene II.—A Room in the same.

Enter Subtle, *leading in* Dapper, *with his eyes bound
as before.*

 Sub. How ! have you eaten your gag ?
 Dap. Yes faith, it crumbled
Away in my mouth.
 Sub. You have spoil'd all, then.
 Dap. No !
I hope my aunt of Fairy will forgive me.
 Sub. Your aunt's a gracious lady ; but in troth
You were to blame.
 Dap. The fume did overcome me,
And I did do't to stay my stomach.   'Pray you
So satisfy her grace.

Enter Face, in his uniform.

      Here comes the captain.
 Face. How now ! is his mouth down ?
 Sub. Ay, he has spoken !
 Face. A pox, I heard him, and you too.—He's undone,
   then.—
I have been fain to say, the house is haunted
With spirits, to keep churl back.
 Sub. And hast thou done it ?

Face. Sure, for this night.
Sub. Why, then triumph and sing
Of Face so famous, the precious king
Of present wits.
Face. Did you not hear the coil
About the door ?
Sub. Yes, and I dwindled with it.
Face. Shew him his aunt, and let him be dispatch'd :
I'll send her to you.   [*Exit* Face.
Sub. Well, sir, your aunt her grace
Will give you audience presently, on my suit,
And the captain's word that you did not eat your gag
In any contempt of her highness.   [*Unbinds his eyes.*
Dap. Not I, in troth, sir.

Enter Dol, *like the Queen of Fairy.*

Sub. Here she is come. Down o' your knees and
        wriggle :
She has a stately presence, [Dapper *kneels, and shuffles*
        towards her.] Good ! Yet nearer,
And bid, God save you !
Dap. Madam !
Sub. And your aunt.
Dap. And my most gracious aunt, God save your
        grace.
Dol. Nephew, we thought to have been angry with
        you ;
But that sweet face of yours hath turn'd the tide,
And made it flow with joy, that ebb'd of love.
Arise, and touch our velvet gown.
Sub. The skirts,
And kiss 'em. So !
Dol. Let me now stroke that head.
Much, nephew, shalt thou win, much shalt thou spend,
Much shalt thou give away, much shalt thou lend.

Sub. Ay, much ! indeed. [*Aside.*] Why do you not
thank her grace ?
Dap. I cannot speak for joy.
Sub. See the kind wretch !
Your grace's kinsman right.
Dol. Give me the bird.
Here is your fly in a purse, about your neck, cousin ;
Wear it, and feed it about this day sev'n-night,
On your right wrist——
Sub. Open a vein with a pin,
And let it suck but once a week ; till then,
You must not look on't.
Dol. No : and kinsman,
Bear yourself worthy of the blood you come on.
Sub. Her grace would have you eat no more Woolsack
pies,
Nor Dagger frumety.
Dol. Nor break his fast
In Heaven and Hell.
Sub. She's with you every where !
Nor play with costarmongers, at mum-chance, tray-trip.
God make you rich ; (when as your aunt has done it) ;
But keep
The gallant'st company, and the best games——
Dap. Yes, sir.
Sub. Gleek and primero : and what you get, be true
to us.
Dap. By this hand, I will.
Sub. You may bring a thousand pound
Before to-morrow night, if but three thousand
Be stirring, an you will.
Dap. I swear I will then.
Sub. Your fly will learn you all games.
Face. [*within.*] Have you done there ?
Sub. Your grace will command him no more duties ?

Dol. No:
But come, and see me often.   I may chance
To leave him three or four hundred chests of treasure,
And some twelve thousand acres of fairy land,
If he game well and comely with good gamesters.
   Sub. There's a kind aunt ! kiss her departing part.—
But you must sell your forty mark a year, now.
   Dap. Ay, sir, I mean.
   Sub. Or, give 't away ; pox on't !
   Dap. I'll give 't mine aunt: I'll go and fetch the
      writings.   [*Exit.*
   Sub. 'Tis well—away !

Re-enter FACE.

Face. Where's Subtle ?
   Sub. Here: what news ?
   Face. Drugger is at the door, go take his suit,
And bid him fetch a parson, presently ;
Say, he shall marry the widow.   Thou shalt spend
A hundred pound by the service ! [*Exit* SUBTLE.] Now,
      queen Dol,
Have you pack'd up all ?
   Dol. Yes.
   Face. And how do you like
The lady Pliant ?
   Dol. A good dull innocent.

Re-enter SUBTLE.

Sub. Here's your Hieronimo's cloak and hat.
   Face. Give me them.
   Sub. And the ruff too ?
   Face. Yes ; I'll come to you presently.   [*Exit.*
   Sub. Now he is gone about his project, Dol,
I told you of, for the widow.

Dol. 'Tis direct
Against our articles.

 Sub. Well, we will fit him, wench.
Hast thou gull'd her of her jewels or her bracelets?

 Dol. No; but I will do't.

 Sub. Soon at night, my Dolly,
When we are shipp'd, and all our goods aboard,
Eastward for Ratcliff: we will turn our course
To Brainford, westward, if thou sayst the word,
And take our leaves of this o'er-weening rascal,
This peremptory Face.

 Dol. Content, I'm weary of him.

 Sub. Thou'st cause, when the slave will run a wiving,
   Dol,
Against the instrument that was drawn between us.

 Dol. I'll pluck his bird as bare as I can.

 Sub. Yes, tell her,
She must by any means address some present
To the cunning man, make him amends for wronging
His art with her suspicion; send a ring
Or chain of pearl; she will be tortured else
Extremely in her sleep, say, and have strange things
Come to her.　Wilt thou?

 Dol. Yes.

 Sub. My fine flitter-mouse,
My bird o' the night! we'll tickle it at the Pigeons,
When we have all, and may unlock the trunks,
And say, this's mine, and thine: and thine, and mine.
         [*They kiss.*

Re-enter FACE.

 Face. What now! a billing?

 Sub. Yes, a little exalted
In the good passage of our stock-affairs.

Face. Drugger has brought his parson ; take him in,
    Subtle,
And send Nab back again to wash his face.
    Sub. I will : and shave himself.   [*Exit.*
    Face. If you can get him.
    Dol. You are hot upon it, Face, whate'er it is !
    Face. A trick that Dol shall spend ten pound a month
    by.

Re-enter SUBTLE.

Is he gone ?
    Sub. The chaplain waits you in the hall, sir.
    Face. I'll go bestow him.   [*Exit.*
    Dol. He'll now marry her, instantly.
    Sub. He cannot yet, he is not ready.   Dear Dol,
Cozen her of all thou canst.   To deceive him
Is no deceit, but justice, that would break
Such an inextricable tie as ours was.
    Dol. Let me alone to fit him.

Re-enter FACE.

    Face. Come, my venturers,
You have pack'd up all ? where be the trunks ? bring
    forth.
    Sub. Here.
    Face. Let us see them.   Where's the money ?
    Sub. Here,
In this.
    Face. Mammon's ten pound ; eight score before :
The brethren's money, this.   Drugger's and Dapper's.
What paper's that ?
    Dol. The jewel of the waiting-maid's,
That stole it from her lady, to know certain——
    Face. If she should have precedence of her mistress ?
    Dol. Yes.

Face. What box is that ?
Sub. The fish-wives' rings, I think.
And the ale-wives' single-money. Is't not, Dol?
Dol. Yes ; and the whistle that the sailor's wife
Brought you to know an her husband were with Ward.
Face. We'll wet it to-morrow ; and our silver-beakers,
And tavern cups. Where be the French petticoats,
And girdles and hangers ?
Sub. Here, in the trunk,
And the bolts of lawn.
Face. Is Drugger's damask there,
And the tobacco ?
Sub. Yes.
Face. Give me the keys.
Dol. Why you the keys ?
Sub. No matter, Dol ; because
We shall not open them before he comes.
Face. 'Tis true, you shall not open them, indeed ;
Nor have them forth, do you see ? not forth, Dol.
Dol. No !
Face. No, my smock rampant. The right is, my
      master
Knows all, has pardon'd me, and he will keep them ;
Doctor, 'tis true—you look—for all your figures :
I sent for him indeed. Wherefore, good partners,
Both he and she be satisfied ; for here
Determines the indenture tripartite
'Twixt Subtle, Dol, and Face. All I can do
Is to help you over the wall, o' the back-side,
Or lend you a sheet to save your velvet gown, Dol.
Here will be officers presently, bethink you
Of some course suddenly to 'scape the dock :
For thither you will come else. [*Loud knocking.*] Hark
    you, thunder.
Sub. You are a precious fiend !

Offi. [*without.*] Open the door.
  Face. Dol, I am sorry for thee, i' faith ; but hear'st
      thou ?
It shall go hard but I will place thee somewhere :
Thou shalt have my letter to mistress Amo——
  Dol. Hang you !
  Face. Or madam Cæsarean.
  Dol. Pox upon you, rogue,
Would I had but time to beat thee !
  Face. Subtle,
Let's know where you set up next ; I will send you
A customer now and then, for old acquaintance :
What new course have you ?
  Sub. Rogue, I'll hang myself ;
That I may walk a greater devil than thou,
And haunt thee in the flock-bed and the buttery.
                            [*Exeunt.*

Scene III.—*An outer Room in the same.*

Enter Lovewit *in the Spanish dress, with the Parson.*

[*Loud knocking at the door.*]

  Love. What do you mean, my masters ?
  Mam. [*without.*] Open your door,
Cheaters, bawds, conjurers.
  Offi. [*without.*] Or we will break it open.
  Love. What warrant have you ?
  Offi. [*without.*] Warrant enough, sir, doubt not,
If you'll not open it.
  Love. Is there an officer, there ?
  Offi. [*without.*] Yes, two or three for failing.
  Love. Have but patience,
And I will open it straight.

Enter FACE, *as butler.*

Face. Sir, have you done?
Is it a marriage? perfect?
Love. Yes, my brain.   [sir.
Face. Off with your ruff and cloak then ; be yourself,
Sur. [*without.*] Down with the door.
Kas. [*without.*] 'Slight, ding it open.
Love. [*opening the door.*] Hold,
Hold, gentlemen, what means this violence?

MAMMON, SURLY, KASTRIL, ANANIAS, TRIBULATION,
and Officers, *rush in.*

Mam. Where is this collier?
Sur. And my captain Face?
Mam. These day owls.
Sur. That are birding in men's purses.
Mam. Madam suppository,
Kas. Doxy, my suster.
Ana. Locusts,
Of the foul pit.
Tri. Profane as Bel and the dragon.
Ana. Worse than the grasshoppers, or the lice of
        Egypt.
Love. Good gentlemen, hear me.   Are you officers,
And cannot stay this violence?
1 *Offi.* Keep the peace.
Love. Gentlemen, what is the matter? whom do you
        seek?
Mam. The chemical cozener.
Sur. And the captain pander..
Kas. The nun my suster.
Mam. Madam Rabbi.
Ana. Scorpions,
And caterpillars.

Love. Fewer at once, I pray you.
2 *Off.* One after another, gentlemen, I charge you,
By virtue of my staff.
    Ana. They are the vessels
Of pride, lust, and the cart.
    Love. Good zeal, lie still
A little while.
    Tri. Peace, deacon Ananias.   [open ;
    Love. The house is mine here, and the doors are
If there be any such persons as you seek for,
Use your authority, search on o' God's name.
I am but newly come to town, and finding
This tumult 'bout my door, to tell you true,
It somewhat mazed me ; till my man, here, fearing
My more displeasure, told me he had done
Somewhat an insolent part, let out my house
(Belike, presuming on my known aversion
From any air o' the town while there was sickness)
To a doctor and a captain : who, what they are
Or where they be, he knows not.
    Mam. Are they gone ?
    Love. You may go in and search, sir. [MAMMON,
        ANA., *and* TRIB. *go in.*] Here, I find
The empty walls worse than I left them, smoak'd.
A few crack'd pots, and glasses, and a furnace :
The ceiling fill'd with poesies of the candle,
And madam with a dildo writ o' the walls :
Only one gentlewoman, I met here,
That is within, that said she was a widow——
    Kas. Ay, that's my suster ; I'll go thump her. Where
      is she ?   [*Goes in.*
    Love. And should have married a Spanish count,
      but he,
When he came to't, neglected her so grossly,
That I, a widower, am gone through with her.

Sur. How ! have I lost her then ?
Love. Were you the don, sir ?
Good faith, now, she does blame you extremely, and
     says
You swore, and told her you had taken the pains
To dye your beard, and umbre o'er your face,
Borrowed a suit, and ruff, all for her love ;
And then did nothing, What an oversight,
And want of putting forward, sir, was this !
Well fare an old harquebuzier, yet,
Could prime his powder, and give fire, and hit,
All in a twinkling !

Re-enter MAMMON.

Mam. The whole nest are fled !
Love. What sort of birds were they ?
Mam. A kind of choughs,
Or thievish daws, sir, that have pick'd my purse
Of eight score and ten pounds within these five weeks,
Besides my first materials ; and my goods,
That lie in the cellar, which I am glad they have left,
I may have home yet.
Love. Think you so, sir ?
Mam. Ay.
Love. By order of law, sir, but not otherwise.
Mam. Not mine own stuff !
Love. Sir, I can take no knowledge
That they are yours, but by public means.
If you can bring certificate that you were gull'd of them,
Or any formal writ out of a court,
That you did cozen your self, I will not hold them
Mam. I'll rather loose them.
Love. That you shall not, sir,
By me, in troth : upon these terms, they are yours.
What ! should they have been, sir, turn'd into gold, all !

Mam. No,
I cannot tell—It may be they should—What then ?
  Love. What a great loss in hope have you sustain'd !
  Mam. Not I, the common-wealth has.
  Face. Ay, he would have built
The new city ; and made a ditch about it
Of silver, should have run with cream from Hogsden ;
That, every Sunday, in Moor-fields, the younkers,
And tits and tom-boys should have fed on, gratis.
  Mam. I will go mount a turnip-cart, and preach
The end of the world, within these two months.   Surly,
What ! in a dream ?
  Sur. Must I needs cheat myself,
With that same foolish vice of honesty !
Come, let us go and hearken out the rogues :
That Face I'll mark for mine, if e'er I meet him.
  Face. If I can hear of him, sir, I'll bring you word,
Unto your lodging ; for in troth, they were strangers   ·
To me, I thought them honest as my self, sir.
                              [*Exeunt* Mam. *and* Sur.

Re-enter Ananias *and* Tribulation.
  Tri. 'Tis well, the saints shall not lose all yet.   Go,
And get some carts——
  Love. For what, my zealous friends ?
  Ana. To bear away the portion of the righteous
Out of this den of thieves.
  Love. What is that portion ?
  Ana. The goods sometimes the orphan's, that the
          brethren
Bought with their silver pence.
  Love. What, those in the cellar,
The knight Sir Mammon claims ?
  Ana. I do defy.
The wicked Mammon, so do all the brethren,
                    ...16...

Thou profane man ! I ask thee with what conscience
Thou canst advance that idol against us,
That have the scal ? were not the shillings number'd,
That made the pounds ; were not the pounds told out,
Upon the second day of the fourth week,
In the eighth month, upon the table dormant,
The year of the last patience of the saints,
Six hundred and ten ?

 Love.　Mine earnest vehement botcher,
And deacon also, I cannot dispute with you :
But if you get you not away the sooner,
I shall confute you with a cudgel.

 Ana.　Sir !

 Tri.　Be patient, Ananias.

 Ana.　I am strong.
And will stand up, well girt, against an host
That threaten Gad in exile.

 Love.　I shall send you
To Amsterdam to your cellar.

 Ana　I will pray there,
Against thy house : may dogs defile thy walls,
And wasps and hornets breed beneath thy roof,
This seat of falsehood, and this cave of cozenage !

[Exeunt ANA. and TRIB.

Enter DRUGGER.

 Love.　Another too ?

 Drug.　Not I, sir, I am no brother.

 Love.　[*beats him.*]　Away, you Harry Nicholas !　do
  you talk ?　　　　　　　　　　　　　　[*Exit* DRUG.

 Face.　No, this was Abel Drugger.　Good sir, go,

[To the Parson.

And satisfy him ; tell him all is done :
He staid too long a washing of his face.
The doctor, he shall hear of him at West-chester ;

And of the captain, tell him, at Yarmouth, or
Some good port-town else, lying for a wind.

[*Exit* Parson.

If you can get off the angry child, now, sir——

Enter KASTRIL, *dragging in his sister.*

Kas. Come on, you ewe, you have match'd most
    sweetly, have you not?
Did not I say, I would never have you tupp'd
But by a dubb'd boy, to make you a lady-tom?
'Slight, you are a mammet! O, I could touse you, now.
Death, mun' you marry, with a pox!
Love. You lie, boy;
As sound as you; and I'm aforehand with you.
Kas. Anon!
Love. Come, will you quarrel? I will feize you,
    sirrah;
Why do you not buckle to your tools?
Kas. Od's light,
This is a fine old boy as e'er I saw!
Love. What, do you change your copy now? proceed,
Here stands my dove: stoop at her, if you dare.
Kas. 'Slight, I must love him! I cannot choose,
    i' faith,
An I should be hang'd for't! Suster, I protest,
I honour thee for this match.
Love. O, do you so, sir?
Kas. Yes, an thou canst take tobacco and drink, old
    boy,
I'll give her five hundred pound more to her marriage,
Than her own state.
Love. Fill a pipe full, Jeremy.
Face. Yes; but go in and take it, sir.
Love. We will—
I will be ruled by thee in anything, Jeremy.

Kas. 'Slight, thou art not hide-bound, thou art a jovy
      boy !
Come, let us in, I pray thee, and take our whiffs.
   Love. Whiff in with your sister, brother boy. [*Exeunt*
      KAS. *and* Dame P.] That master.
That had received such happiness by a servant,
In such a widow, and with so much wealth,
Were very ungrateful, if he would not be
A little indulgent to that servant's wit,
And help his fortune, though with some small strain
Of his own candour. [*advancing.*]—*Therefore, gentle-
      men,*
And kind spectators, if I have outstript
An old man's gravity, or strict canon, think
What a young wife and a good brain may do ;
Stretch age's truth sometimes, and crack it too.
Speak for thy self, knave.
   Face. So I will, sir. [advancing to the front of the
      stage.] *Gentlemen,*
My part a little fell in this last scene.
Yet 'twas decorum.   And though I am clean
Got off from Subtle, Surly, Mammon, Dol,
Hot Ananias, Dapper, Drugger, all
With whom I traded : yet I put my self
On you, that are my country : and this pelf,
Which I have got, if you do quit me, rests
To feast you often, and invite new guests.   [Exeunt.

THE FIRST ACT

OF

Catiline: His Conspiracy.

CATILINE: HIS CONSPIRACY.

SCENE I.—*A room in* CATILINE'S *House.*

The Ghost of SYLLA *rises.*

Dost thou not feel me, Rome? not yet! is night
So heavy on thee, and my weight so light?
Can Sylla's ghost arise within thy walls,
Less threatening than an earthquake, the quick fails
Of thee and thine?   Shake not the frighted heads
Of thy steep towers, or shrink to their first beds?
Or, as their ruin the large Tyber fills,
Make that swell up, and drown thy seven proud hills?
What sleep is this doth seize thee so like death,
And is not it? wake, feel her in my breath:
Behold, I come, sent from the Stygian sound,
As a dire vapour that had cleft the ground.
To ingender with the night, and blast the day;
Or like a pestilence that should display
Infection through the world: which thus I do.—
    [The curtain draws, and CATILINE is discovered in his
        study.
Pluto be at thy counsels, and into
Thy darker bosom enter Sylla's spirit!

All that was mine, and bad, thy breast inherit.
Alas, how weak is that for Catiline!
Did I but say—vain voice!—all that was mine?—
All that the Gracchi, Cinna, Marius would,
What now, had I a body again, I could,
Coming from hell, what fiends would wish should be,
And Hannibal could not have wish'd to see,
Think thou, and practise.   Let the long-hid seeds
Of treason in thee, now shoot forth in deeds
Ranker than horror ; and thy former facts
Not fall in mention, but to urge new acts,
Conscience of them provoke thee on to more :
Be still thy incests, murders, rapes, before
Thy sense ; thy forcing first a vestal nun ;
Thy parricide, late, on thine own only son,
After his mother, to make empty way
For thy last wicked nuptials ; worse than they,
That blaze that act of thy incestuous life,
Which got thee at once a daughter and a wife.
I leave the slaughters that thou didst for me,
Of senators , for which, I hid for thee
Thy murder of thy brother, being so bribed,
And writ him in the list of my proscribed
After thy fact, to save thy little shame ;
Thy incest with thy sister, I not name:
These are too light ; fate will have thee pursue
Deeds, after which no mischief can be new ;
The ruin of thy country : Thou wert built
For such a work, and born for no less guilt.
What though defeated once thou'st been, and known,
Tempt it again : That is thy act, or none.
What all the several ills that visit earth,
Brought forth by night with a sinister birth,
Plagues, famine, fire, could not reach unto,
The sword, nor surfeits ; let thy fury do:

Make all past, present, future ill thine own ;
And conquer all example in thy one.
Nor let thy thought find any vacant time
To hate an old, but still a fresher crime
Drown the remembrance ; let not mischief cease,
But while it is in punishing, increase,
Conscience and care die in thee ; and be free
Not heaven itself from thy impiety :
Let night grow blacker with thy plots, and day,
At shewing but thy head forth, start away
From this half-sphere ; and leave Rome's blinded walls
To embrace lusts, hatreds, slaughters, funerals,
And not recover sight till their own flames
Do light them to their ruins!   All the names
Of thy confederates too be no less great
In hell than here : that when we would repeat
Our strengths in muster, we may name you all,
And furies upon you for furies call !
Whilst what you do may strike them into fears,
Or make them grieve, and wish your mischief theirs.
[Sinks.

CATILINE *rises and comes forward.*

Cat. It is decreed : nor shall thy fate, O Rome,
Resist my vow.   Though hills were set on hills,
And seas met seas to guard thee, I would through ;
Ay, plough up rocks, steep as the Alps, in dust,
And lave the Tyrrhene waters into clouds,
But I would reach thy head, thy head, proud city !
The ills that I have done cannot be safe
But by attempting greater ; and I feel
A spirit within me chides my sluggish hands,
And says, they have been innocent too long.
Was I a man bred great as Rome herself,
One form'd for all her honours, all her glories,

Equal to all her titles ; that could stand
Close up with Atlas, and sustain her name
As strong as he doth heaven ! and was I,
Of all her brood, mark'd out for the repulse
By her no-voice, when I stood candidate
To be commander in the Pontic war !
I will hereafter call her step-dame ever.
If she can lose her nature, I can lose
My piety, and in her stony entrails
Dig me a seat ; where I will live again,
The labour of her womb, and be a burden
Weightier than all the prodigies and monsters
That she hath teem'd with, since she first knew Mars—

Enter AURELIA ORESTILLA.

Who's there ?
   Aur. 'Tis I.
   Cat. Aurelia ?
   Aur. Yes.
   Cat. Appear,
And break like day, my beauty, to this circle :
Upbraid thy Phœbus, that he is so long
In mounting to that point, which should give thee
Thy proper splendour.   Wherefore frowns my sweet ?
Have I too long been absent from these lips,
This cheek, these eyes ? [*Kisses them.*] What is my
     trespass, speak ?
   Aur. It seems you know, that can accuse your self.
   Cat. I will redeem it.
   Aur. Still you say so.   When ?
   Cat. When Orestilla, by her bearing well
These my retirements, and stol'n times for thought,
Shall give their effects leave to call her queen
Of all the world, in place of humbled Rome.
   Aur. You court me now.

Cat. As I would always, love,
By this ambrosiac kiss, and this of nectar,
Wouldst thou but hear as gladly as I speak.
Could my Aurelia think I meant her less,
When, wooing her, I first removed a wife,
And then a son, to make my bed and house
Spacious and fit to embrace her ? these were deeds
Not to have begun with, but to end with more
And greater : He that, building, stays at one
Floor, or the second, hath erected none.
'Twas how to raise thee I was meditating,
To make some act of mine answer thy love ;
That love, that, when my state was now quite sunk,
Came with thy wealth and weigh'd it up again,
And made my emergent fortune once more look
Above the main ; which now shall hit the stars,
And stick my Orestilla there amongst them,
If any tempest can but make the billow,
And any billow can but lift her greatness.
But I must pray my love, she will put on
Like habits with myself ; I have to do
With many men, and many natures : Some
That must be blown and sooth'd ; as Lentulus,
Whom I have heav'd with magnifying his blood,
And a vain dream out of the Sybil's books,
That a third man of that great family
Whereof he is descended, the Cornelii,
Should be a king in Rome : which I have hired
The flattering augurs to interpret Him,
Cinna and Sylla dead.   Then bold Cethegus,
Whose valour I have turn'd into his poison,
And praised so into daring, as he would
Go on upon the gods, kiss lightning, wrest
The engine from the Cyclops, and give fire
At face of a full cloud, and stand his ire,

When I would bid him move.   Others there are,
Whom envy to the state draws, and puts on
For contumelies received (and such are sure ones),
As Curius, and the forenamed Lentulus,
Both which have been degraded in the senate,
And must have their disgraces still new rubb'd,
To make them smart, and labour of revenge.
Others whom mere ambition fires, and dole
Of provinces abroad, which they have feign'd
To their crude hopes, and I as amply promised :
These, Lecca, Vargunteius, Bestia, Autronius.
Some whom their wants oppress, as the idle captains
Of Sylla's troops ; and divers Roman knights,
The profuse wasters of their patrimonies,
So threaten'd with their debts, as they will now
Run any desperate fortune for a change.
These, for a time, we must relieve, Aurelia,
And make our house their safeguard : like for those
That fear the law, or stand within her gripe,
For any act past or to come ; such will,
From their own crimes, be factious, as from ours.
Some more there be, slight airlings, will be won
With dogs and horses, or perhaps a whore ;
Which must be had : and if they venture lives
For us, Aurelia, we must hazard honours
A little.   Get thee store and change of women,
As I have boys ; and give them time and place,
And all connivance : be thy self, too, courtly ;
And entertain and feast, sit up, and revel ;
Call all the great, the fair, and spirited dames
Of Rome about thee ; and begin a fashion
Of freedom and community : some will thank thee,
Though the sour senate frown, whose heads.must ache
In fear and feeling too.   We must not spare
Or cost or modesty : It can but shew

Like one of Juno's or of Jove's disguise,
In either thee or me : and will as soon,
When things succeed, be thrown by, or let fall,
As is a veil put off, a visor changed,
Or the scene shifted in our theatres—   [*Noise within.*
Who's that ?   It is the voice of Lentulus.
  Aur. Or of Cethegus.
  Cat. In, my fair Aurelia,
And think upon these arts : they must not see
How far you're trusted with these privacies,
Though on their shoulders, necks and heads you rise.
                                        [*Exit* AURELIA.

Enter LENTULUS, *in discourse with* CETHEGUS.

  Lent. It is, methinks, a morning full of fate !
It riseth slowly, as her sullen car
Had all the weights of sleep and death hung at it !
She is not rosy-finger'd, but swoll'n black ;
Her face is like a water turn'd to blood,
And her sick head is bound about with clouds,
As if she threaten'd night ere noon of day !
It does not look as it would have a hail
Or health wish'd in it, as on other morns.
  Cet. Why, all the fitter, Lentulus ; our coming
Is not for salutation, we have business.
  Cat. Said nobly, brave Cethegus ! Where's Autronius ?
  Cet. Is he not come ?
  Cat. Not here.
  Cet. Nor Vargunteius ?
  Cat. Neither.
  Cet. A fire in their beds and bosoms,
That so will serve their sloth rather than virtue !
They are no Romans,—and at such high need
As now !

Len. Both they, Longinus, Lecca, Curius,
Fulvius, Gabinus, gave me word, last night,
By Lucius Bestia, they would all be here,
And early.
  Cet. Yes ; as you, had I not call'd you.
Come, we all sleep, and are mere dormice ; flies
A little less than dead : more dulness hangs
On us than on the morn.   We are spirit-bound
In ribs of ice, our whole bloods are one stone,
And honour cannot thaw us, nor our wants,
Though they burn hot as fevers to our states.
  Cat. I muse they would be tardy at an hour
Of so great purpose.
  Cet. If the gods had call'd
Them to a purpose, they would just have come
With the same tortoise speed ; that are thus slow
To such an action, which the gods will envy,
As asking no less means than all their powers,
Conjoin'd, to effect ! I would have seen Rome burn
By this time, and her ashes in an urn ;
The kingdom of the senate rent asunder,
And the degenerate talking gown run frighted
Out of the air of Italy.
  Cat. Spirit of men !
Thou heart of our great enterprise ! how much
I love these voices in thee !
  Cet. O, the days
Of Sylla's sway, when the free sword took leave
To act all that it would !
  Cat. And was familiar
With entrails, as our augurs.
  Cet. Sons kill'd fathers,
Brothers their brothers.
  Cat. And had price and praise.
All hate had license given it, all rage reins.

Cet. Slaughter bestrid the streets, and stretch'd him-
    self
To seem more huge ; whilst to his stained thighs
The gore he drew flow'd up, and carried down
Whole heaps of limbs and bodies through his arch.
No age was spared, no sex.
   Cat. Nay, no degree.
   Cet. Not infants in the porch of life were free.
The sick, the old, that could but hope a day
Longer by nature's bounty, not let stay,
Virgins, and widows, matrons, pregnant wives,
All died.
   Cat. 'Twas crime enough, that they had lives :
To strike but only those that could do hurt,
Was dull and poor : some fell to make the number,
As some the prey.
   Cet. The rugged Charon fainted,
And ask'd a navy, rather than a boat,
To ferry over the sad world that came :
The maws and dens of beasts could not receive
The bodies that those souls were frighted from ;
And e'en the graves were fill'd with men yet living,
Whose flight and fear had mix'd them with the dead.
   Cat. And this shall be again, and more, and more,
Now Lentulus, the third Cornelius,
Is to stand up in Rome.
   Lent. Nay, urge not that
Is so uncertain.
   Cat. How !
   Lent. I mean, not clear'd,
And therefore not to be reflected on.
   Cat. The Sybil's leaves uncertain ! or the comments
Of our grave, deep, divining men not clear.
   Lent. All prophecies, you know, suffer the torture.

Cat. But this already hath confess'd, without :
And so been weigh'd, examined and compared,
As 'twere malicious ignorance in him
Would faint in the belief.
　　Lent. Do you believe it ?
　　Cat. Do I love Lentulus, or pray to see it ?
　　Lent. The augurs all are constant I am meant.
　　Cat. They had lost their science else.
　　Lent. They count from Cinna.
　　Cat. And Sylla next, and so make you the third ;
All that can say the sun is risen, must think it.
　　Lent. Men mark me more of late, as I come forth.
　　Cat. Why, what can they do less ?　Cinna and Sylla
Are set and gone ; and we must turn our eyes
On him that is, and shines.　Noble Cethegus,
But view him with me here ? he looks already
As if he shook a sceptre o'er the senate,
And the awed purple dropp'd their rods and axes :
The statues melt again, and household gods
In groans confess the travail of the city ;
The very walls sweat blood before the change,
And stones start out to ruin ere it comes.
　　Cet. But he, and we, and all are idle still.
　　Lent. I am your creature, Sergius ; and whate'er
The great Cornelian name shall win to be,
It is not augury nor the Sybil's books,
But Catiline that makes it.
　　Cat. I am a shadow
To honour'd Lentulus, and Cethegus here,
Who are the heirs of Mars.
　　Cet. By Mars himself,
Cataline is more my parent ; for whose virtue
Earth cannot make a shadow great enough,　　[they are.
Though envy should come too. [*Noise within.*] O, here
Now we shall talk more, though we yet do nothing.

Enter AUTRONIUS, VARGUNTEIUS, LONGINUS, CURIUS,
LECCA, BESTIA, FULVIUS, GABINIUS, etc. *and* Servants.

Aut. Hail, Lucius Catiline.
Var. Hail, noble Sergius.
Lon. Hail, Publius Lentulus.
Cur. Hail, the third Cornelius.
Lec. Caius Cethegus, hail.
Cet. Hail, sloth and words,
Instead of men and spirits !
Cat. Nay, dear Caius——
Cet. Are your eyes yet unseel'd ? dare they look day
In the dull face ?
Cat. He's zealous for the affair,
And blames your tardy coming, gentlemen.
Cet. Unless we had sold ourselves to sleep and ease,
And would be our slaves' slaves——
Cat. Pray you forbear,
Cet. The north is not so stark and cold.
Cat. Cethegus——
Bes. We shall redeem all if your fire will let us.
Cat. You are too full of lightning, noble Caius.
Boy, see all doors be shut, that none approach us   [bid
On this part of the house. [*Exit* Servant.] Go you, and
The priest, he kill the slave I mark'd last night,
And bring me of his blood, when I shall call him :
Till then, wait all without.   [*Exeunt* Servants.
Var. How is't, Autronius ?
Aut. Longinus ?
Lon. Curius ?
Cur. Lecca ?
Var. Feel you nothing ?
Lon. A strange unwonted horror doth invade me,
I know not what it is.
              [*A darkness comes over the place.*
              ...17...

Lec. The day goes back,
Or else my senses!
  Cur. As at Atreus' feast!
  Ful. Garkness grows more and more!
  Len. The vestal flame,
I think, be out.
          [*A groan of many people is heard under ground.*
  Gab. What groan was that?
  Cet. Our phant'sies:
Strike fire out of ourselves, and force a day.
                              [*A second groan.*

  Aut. Again it sounds.
  Bes. As all the city gave it!
  Cet. We fear what ourselves feign.
                        [*A fiery light appears.*

  Var. What light is this?
  Cur. Look forth.
  Len. It still grows greater!
  Lec. From whence comes it?
  Lon. A bloody arm it is that holds a pine
Lighted above the capitol! and now
It waves unto us!
  Cat. Brave and ominous!
Our enterprise is seal'd.
  Cet. In spite of darkness,
That would discountenance it.   Look no more!
We lose time and ourselves.   To what we came for.—
Speak Lucius, we attend you.
  Cat. Noblest Romans,
If you were less, or that your faith and virtue
Did not hold good that title, with your blood,
I should not now unprofitably spend
Myself in words, or catch at empty hopes,
By airy ways, for solid certainties;
But since in many, and the greatest dangers,

I still have known you no less true than valiant,
And that I taste in you the same affections,
To will or nil, to think things good or bad,
Alike with me, which argues your firm friendship ;
I dare the boldlier with you set on foot,
Or lead unto this great and goodliest action.
What I have thought of it afore, you all
Have heard apart : I then express'd my zeal
Unto the glory ; now, tho need inflames me.
When I forethink the hard conditions
Our states must undergo, except in time
We do redeem our selves to liberty,
And break the iron yoke forged for our necks ;
For what less can we call it, when we see,
The commonwealth engross'd so by a few,
The giants of the state, that do by turns
Enjoy her, and defile her ! all the earth,
Her kings and tetrachs, are their tributaries ;
People and nations pay them hourly stipends ;
The riches of the world flow to their coffers,
And not to Rome's.   While, (but those few) the rest,
However great we are, honest, and valiant,
Are herded with the vulgar, and so kept,
As we were only bred to consume corn,
Or wear out wool ; to drink the city's water :
Ungraced, without authority or mark,
Trembling beneath their rods ; to whom, if all
Were well in Rome, we should come forth bright
    axes ;
All places, honours, offices are theirs,
Or where they will confer them : they leave us
The dangers, the repulses, judgments, wants ;
Which how long will you bear, most valiant spirits ?
Were we not better to fall once with virtue,
Than draw a wretched and dishonour'd breath,

To lose with shame, when these men's pride will
    laugh ?
I call the faith of Gods and men to question,
The power is in our hands, our bodies able,
Our minds as strong ; o' the contrary, in them
All things grown aged, with their wealth and years :
There wants but only to begin the business,
The issue is certain.
   Cet. Lon. On ! let us go on !
   Cur. Bes. Go on, brave Sergius !
   Cat. It doth strike my soul,
And who can scape the stroke, that hath a soul,
Or but the smallest air of man within him ?
To see them swell with treasure, which they pour
Out in their riots, eating, drinking, building,
Ay, in the sea ! planing of hills with valleys,
And raising valleys above hills ! whilst we
Have not to give our bodies necessaries.
They have their change of houses, manors, lordships ;
We scarce a fire, or a poor household Lar !
They buy rare Attic statues, Tyrian hangings,
Ephesian pictures, and Corinthian plate,
Attalic garments, and now new-found gems,
Since Pompey went for Asia, which they purchase
At price of provinces ! the river Phasis
Cannot afford them fowl, nor Lucrine lake
Oysters enow : Circei too is search'd,
To please the witty gluttony of a meal !
Their ancient habitations they neglect,
And set up new ; then, if the echo like not
In such a room, they pluck down those, build newer,
Alter them too ; and by all frantic ways,
Vex their wild wealth, as they molest the people,
From whom they force it ! Yet they cannot tame,
Or overcome their riches ! not by making

Baths, orchards, fish-pools, letting in of seas
Here, and then there forcing them out again
With mountainous heaps, for which the earth hath lost
Most of her ribs, as entrails ; being now
Wounded no less for marble, than for gold ?
We, all this while, like calm benumb'd spectators,
Sit till our seats do crack, and do not hear
The thund'ring ruins ; whilst at home our wants,
Abroad, our debts do urge us ; our states daily
Bending to bad, our hopes to worse : and what
Is left but to be crush'd ?   Wake, wake, brave friends,
And meet the liberty you oft have wish'd for.
Behold, renown, riches, and glory court you !
Fortune holds these out to you, as rewards.
Methinks, though I were dumb, the affair itself,
The opportunity, your needs, and dangers,
With the brave spoil the war brings, should invite you.
Use me, your general, or soldier : neither
My mind nor body shall be wanting to you :
And, being consul, I not doubt to effect
All that you wish, if trust not flatter me,
And you'd not rather still be slaves, than free.
 Cet. Free, Free !
 Lon. 'Tis Freedom.
 Cur. Freedom we all stand for.
 Cat. Why, these are noble voices !   Nothing wants,
  then,
But that we take a solemn sacrament,
To strengthen our design.
 Cet. And most to act it :
Deferring hurts, where powers are so prepared.
 Aut. Yet, ere we enter into open act,
With favour, 'twere no loss, if't might be inquired,
What the condition of these arms would be.
 Var. Ay, and the means to carry us through.

Cat. How, friends !
Think you that I would bid you grasp the wind
Or call you to th' embracing of a cloud !
Put your known valours on so dear a business,
And have no other second than the danger,
Nor other garland than the loss ?   Become
Your own assurances.   And for the means,
Consider, first, the stark security
The commonwealth is in now ; the whole senate
Sleepy, and dreaming no such violent blow ;
Their forces all abroad ; of which the greatest,
That might annoy us most, is farthest off,
In Asia, under Pompey, ; those near hand,
Commanded by our friends ; one army in Spain,
By Cneus Piso ; the other in Mauritania,
By Nucerinus ; both which I have firm
And fast unto our plot.   My self, then, standing
Now to be consul, with my hoped colleague
Caius Antonius, one no less engaged
By his wants, than we ; and whom I've power to melt,
And cast in any mould : beside, some others,
That will not yet be named, both sure, and great ones,
Who, when the time comes, shall declare themselves
Strong for our party ; so that no resistance
In nature can be thought.   For our reward then,
First, all our debts are paid ; dangers of law,
Actions, decrees, judgments against us, quitted ;
The rich men, as in Sylla's times, proscribed,
And publication made of all their goods :
That house is yours ; that land is his ; those waters,
Orchards, and walks, a third's ; he has that honour,
And he that office : such a province falls
To Varguntcius ; this to Autronius ; that
To bold Cethegus ; Rome to Lentulus.
You share the world, her magistracies, priesthoods,

Wealth and felicity, amongst you, friends ;
And Catiline your servant.   Would you, Curius,
Revenge the contumely stuck upon you,
In being removed from the senate ? now,
Now is your time.   Would Publius Lentulus
Strike for the like disgrace ? now is his time.
Would stout Longinus walk the streets of Rome,
Facing the Prætor ? now has he a time
To spurn and tread the fasces into dirt,
Made of the usurers' and the lictors' brains.
Is there a beauty here in Rome you love ?
An enemy you would kill ? what head's not your's ?
Whose wife, which boy, whose daughter, of what race,
That the husband, or glad parents, shall not bring you,
And boasting of the office ? only spare
Yourselves, and you have all the earth beside,
A field to exercise your longings in.
I see you raised, and read your forward minds
High in your faces.   Bring the wine and blood
You have prepared there.

Enter Servants, *with a bowl.*

Lon. How !
Cat. I have kill'd a slave,
And of his blood caused to be mix'd with wine :
Fill every man his bowl.   There cannot be.
A fitter drink to make this sauction in.
Here I begin the sacrament to all.
O for a clap of thunder now, as loud
As to be heard throughout the universe,
To tell the world the fact, and to applaud it !
Be firm, my hand, not shed a drop ; but pour
Fierceness into me with it, and fell thirst
Of more and more, till Rome be left as bloodless
As ever her fears made her, or the sword.

And when I leave to wish this to thee, step-dame,
Or stop to affect it, with my powers fainting,
So may my blood be drawn, and so drunk up,
As is this slave's.　　　　　　　　　*[Drinks.*
　　Lon. And so be mine.
　　Len. And mine.
　　Aut. And mine.
　　Var. And mine.　　　　　　　　*[They drink.*
　　Cct. Swell me my bowl yet fuller.
Here, I do drink this, as I would do Cato's,
Or the new fellow Cicero's, with that vow
Which Catiline hath given.　　　　　*[Drinks.*
　　Cur. So do I.
　　Lec. And I.
　　Bes. And I.
　　Ful. And I.
　　Gab. And all of us.　　　　　　*[They drink.*
　　Cat. Why, now's the business safe, and each man
　　　　　strengthen'd—
Sirrah, what ail you?
　　Page. Nothing.
　　Bes. Somewhat modest.
　　Cat. Slave, I will strike your soul out with my foot,
Let me but find you again with such a face:
You whelp——
　　Bes. Nay, Lucius.
　　Cat. Are you coying it.
When I command you to be free, and general
To all?
　　Bes. You'll be observed.
　　Cat. Arise! and shew
But any least aversion in you look
To him that bourds you next; and your throat opens—
Noble confederates, thus far is perfect.
Only your suffrages I will expect

At the assembly for the choosing consuls,
And all the voices you can make by friends
To my election : then let me work out
Your fortunes and mine own.   Meanwhile, all rest
Seal'd up and silent, as when rigid frosts
Have bound up brooks and rivers, forced wild beasts
Unto their caves, and birds into the woods,
Clowns to their houses, and the country sleeps :
That, when the sudden thaw comes, we may break
Upon them like a deluge, bearing down
Half Rome before us, and invade the rest
With cries, and noise, able to wake the urns
Of those are dead, and make their ashes fear.
The horrors that do strike the world, should come
Loud, and unlook'd for ; till they strike, be dumb.
  Cet. Oraculous Sergius !
  Len. God-like Catiline !   [*Exeunt.*

CHORUS.

Can nothing great, and at the height,
Remain so long, but its own weight
Will ruin it ? or is't blind chance,
That still desires new states to advance,
And quit the old ? else why must Rome
Be by itself now overcome ?
Hath she not foes enow of those
Whom she hath made such, and enclose
Her round about ? or are they none,
Except she first become her own :
O wretchedness of greatest states,
To be obnoxious to these fates !
That cannot keep what they do gain ;
And what they raise so ill sustain !
Rome now is mistress of the whole
World, sea and land, to either pole ;
And even that fortune will destroy
The pow'r that made it : she doth joy
So much in plenty, wealth, and ease,
As now th' excess is her disease.

She builds in gold, and to the stars,
As if she threaten'd heav'n with wars ;
And seeks for hell in quarries deep,
Giving the fiends, that there do keep,
A hope of day.   Her women wear
The spoils of nations in an ear,
Changed for the treasure of a shell ;
And in their loose attires do swell,
More light than sails, when all winds play :
Yet are the men more loose than they
More kemb'd, and bath'd, and rubb'd, and trimm'd,
More sleek, more soft, and slacker limb'd ;
As prostitute ; so much, that kind
May seek itself there, and not find.
They eat on beds of silk and gold,
At ivory tables, or wood sold
Dearer than it ; and leaving plate,
Do drink in stone of higher rate.
They hunt all grounds, and draw all seas,
Fowl every brook and bush, to please
Their wanton taste ; and in request
Have new and rare things, not the best.
Hence comes that wild and vast expense,
That hath enforced Rome's virtue thence,
Which simple poverty first made :
And now ambition doth invade
Her state, with eating avarice,
Riot, and every other vice.
Decrees are bought, and laws are sold,
Honours, and offices, for gold ;
The people's voices, and the free
Tongues in the senate, bribed be :
Such ruin of her manners Rome
Doth suffer now, as she's become
(Without the gods it soon gainsay)
Both her own spoiler, and own prey.
So, Asia, art thou cru'lly even
With us, for all the blows thee given ;
When we, whose virtue conquer'd thee,
Thus, by thy vices, ruin'd be.

FROM THE FIRST ACT

OF

Volpone; or, The Fox.

THE DEDICATION

OF

VOLPONE; OR, THE FOX.

———————

TO THE MOST NOBLE AND MOST EQUAL SISTERS,

THE TWO FAMOUS UNIVERSITIES,

FOR THEIR LOVE AND ACCEPTANCE SHEWN TO HIS POEM IN
THE PRESENTATION ;

BEN JONSON,

THE GRATEFUL ACKNOWLEDGER,

DEDICATES BOTH IT AND HIMSELF.

NEVER, most equal Sisters, had any man a wit so presently excellent, as that it could raise itself; but there must come both matter, occasion, commenders, and favourers to it. If this be true, and that the fortune of all writers doth daily prove it, it behoves the careful to provide well towards these accidents ; and, having acquired them, to preserve that part of reputation most tenderly, wherein the benefit of a friend is also defended. Hence is it, that I now render myself grateful, and am studious to justify the bounty of your act ; to which, though your mere authority were satisfying, yet it being an age wherein poetry and the professors of it hear so ill on all sides, there will a reason be looked for in the subject. It is certain, nor can it with any forehead be opposed, that the too much license of poetasters in this time, hath much deformed their mistress; that, every day, their manifold and manifest ignorance doth stick unnatural reproaches upon her: but for their petulancy, it were an act of the greatest injustice, either to let the learned suffer, or so divine a skill (which indeed should not be attempted with unclean hands) to fall under the least contempt. For, if men will impartially, and not asquint, look toward the offices and function of a poet, they will easily conclude to themselves the impossibility of any man's being the good poet, without first being a good man.   He that is said to be able to inform young men to all good disciplines, inflame grown men to all great virtues, keep old men in their best and supreme state, or, as they decline to childhood, recover them to their first strength; that comes forth the interpreter and arbiter of nature, a teacher of things divine no less than human, a master in manners; and can alone, or with a few, effect the business of mankind : this, I take him, is no subject for pride and ignorance to exercise their railing rhetoric upon.   But it will here be hastily answered, that the writers of these days are other things; that not only their manners, but their natures, are inverted, and nothing remaining with them of the dignity of poet, but the abused name, which every scribe usurps; that now, especially in dramatic, or, as they term it, stage-poetry, nothing but ribaldry, profanation, blasphemy, all license of offence to God and man is practised.   I dare not deny a great part of this, and am sorry I dare not, because in some men's abortive features (and would they had never boasted the light) it is over true : but that all are embarked in this bold adventure for hell, is a most uncharitable thought, and, uttered, a more malicious slander.   For my particular, I can, and from a most clear conscience, affirm, that I have ever trembled to think toward the least profaneness; have loathed the use of such foul and unwashed bawdry, as is now made the food of the scene : and, howsoever I cannot escape from some, the imputation of sharpness, but that they will say, I have taken a pride, or lust, to be bitter, and not my youngest infant but hath come into the world with all his teeth; I would ask of these supercilious politics, what nation, society, or general order or state, I have provoked? What public person? Whether I have not in all these preserved their dignity, as mine own person, safe? My works are read, allowed, (I speak of those that are intirely mine), look into them, what broad reproofs have I used? where have I been particular? where personal? except to a mimic, cheater, bawd, or buffoon, creatures, for their insolencies, worthy to be taxed? yet to which of these so pointingly, as he might not either ingenuously have confest, or wisely dissembled his disease? But it is not rumour can make men guilty, much less entitle me to other men's crimes. I know, that nothing can be so innocently writ or carried, but may be made obnoxious to construction ; marry, whilst I bear mine innocence about me, I fear it not.   Application is now grown a trade with many; and

there are that profess to have a key for the decyphering of
every thing: but let wise and noble persons take heed how they
be too credulous, or give leave to these invading interpreters to
be over-familiar with their fames, who cunningly, and often,
utter their own virulent malice, under other men's simplest
meanings. As for those that will (by faults which charity hath
raked up, or common honesty concealed) make themselves a
name with the multitude, or, to draw their rude and beastly
claps, care not whose living faces they intrench with their
petulant styles, may they do it without a rival, for me! I
choose rather to live graved in obscurity, than share with them
in so preposterous a fame. Nor can I blame the wishes of
those severe and wise patriots, who providing the hurts these
licentious spirits may do in a state, desire rather to see fools
and devils, and those antique relics of barbarism retrieved,
with all other ridiculous and exploded follies, than behold the
wounds of private men, of princes and nations: for, as Horace
makes Trebatius speak among these,

"Sibi quisque timet, quanquam est intactus, et odit,"

and men may justly impute such rages, if continued, to the
writer, as his sports. The increase of which lust in liberty,
together with the present trade of the stage, in all their mis-
celline interludes, what learned or liberal soul doth not already
abhor? where nothing but the filth of the time is uttered, and
with such impropriety of phrase, such plenty of solecisms, such
dearth of sense, so bold prolepses, so racked metaphors, with
brothelry, able to violate the ear of a pagan, and blasphemy, to
turn the blood of a Christian to water. I cannot but be serious
in a cause of this nature, wherein my fame, and the reputation
of divers honest and learned are the question; when a name so
full of authority, antiquity, and all great mark, is, through
their insolence, become the lowest scorn of the age; and those
men subject to the petulancy of every vernaculous orator, that
were wont to be the care of kings and happiest monarchs. This
it is that hath not only rapt me to present indignation, but
made me studious heretofore, and by all my actions, to stand off
from them; which may most appear in this my latest work,
which you, most learned Arbitresses, have seen, judged, and to
my crown, approved; wherein I have laboured for their
instruction and amendment, to reduce not only the ancient
forms, but manners of the scene, the easiness, the propriety, the
innocence, and last, the doctrine, which is the principal end of
poesie, to inform men in the best reason of living. And though

my catastrophe may, in the strict rigour of comic law, meet
with censure, as turning back to my promise; I desire the
learned and charitable critic, to have so much faith in me,
to think it was done of industry: for, with what ease I could
have varied it nearer his scale (but that I fear to boast my own
faculty) I could here insert. But my special aim being to put
the snaffle in their mouths, that cry out, We never punish vice
in our interludes, etc., I took the more liberty; though not
without some lines of example, drawn even in the ancients
themselves, the goings out of whose comedies are not always
joyful, but ofttimes the bawds, the servants, the rivals, yea,
and the masters are mulcted; and fitly, it being the office of a
comic poet to imitate justice, and instruct to life, as well as
purity of language, or stir up gentle affections; to which I shall
take the occasion elsewhere to speak.

For the present, most reverenced Sisters, as I have cared to
be thankful for your affections past, and here made the understanding acquainted with some ground of your favours; let me
not despair their continuance, to the maturing of some worthier
fruits; wherein, if my muses be true to me, I shall raise the
despised head of poetry again, and stripping **her** out of those
rotten and base rags wherewith the times have adulterated her
form, restore her to her primitive habit, feature, and majesty,
and render her worthy to be embraced and kist of all the great
and master-spirits of our world. As for the vile and slothful,
who never affected an act worthy of celebration, or are so
inward with their own vicious natures, as they worthily fear her,
and think it an high point of policy to keep her in contempt,
with their declamatory and windy invectives; she shall out of
just rage incite her servants (who are *genus irritabile*) to spout
ink in their faces, that shall eat farther than their marrow into
their fames; and not Cinnamus the barber, with his art, shall
be able to take out the brands: but they shall live, and be read
till the wretches die, as things worst deserving of themselves in
chief, and then of all mankind.

From my House in the Black-Friars,
   this 11th day of February 1607.

FROM THE FIRST ACT

OF

VOLPONE; OR, THE FOX.

[Volpone, a Venetian nobleman, rich and childless, pretends to be dying, in order to draw presents of plate, jewels, etc., from the covetous persons who seek his inheritance. Mosca, his parasite and accomplice, aids him by persuading each legacy-hunter in turn that his name alone is inscribed upon Volpone's will.]

SCENE I.—*A room in* VOLPONE'S *House.*

Enter VOLPONE *and* MOSCA.

Volp. Good morning to the day; and next, my
      gold !—
Open the shrine, that I may see my saint.
      [MOSCA *withdraws the curtain, and discovers*
        piles of gold, plate, jewels, etc.
Hail the world's soul, and mine ! more glad than is
The teeming earth to see the long'd-for sun
Peep through the horns of the celestial Ram,
Am I, to view thy splendour darkening his ;
That lying here, amongst my other hoards,

Shew'st like a flame by night, or like the day
Struck out of chaos, when all darkness fled
Unto the centre. O thou son of Sol,
But brighter than thy father, let me kiss,
With adoration, thee, and every relick
Of sacred treasure in this blessed room.
Well did wise poets, by thy glorious name,
Title that age which they would have the best ;
Thou being the best of things, and far transcending
All style of joy, in children, parents, friends,
Or any other waking dream on earth :
Thy looks when they to Venus did ascribe,
They should have given her twenty thousand Cupids ;
Such are thy beauties and our loves ! Dear saint,
Riches, the dumb god, that giv'st all men tongues,
Thou canst do nought, and yet mak'st men do all things;
The price of souls ; even hell, with thee to boot,
Is made worth heaven. Thou art virtue, fame,
Honour, and all things else. Who can get thee,
He shall be noble, valiant, honest, wise——
  Mos. And what he will, sir. Riches are in fortune
A greater good than wisdom is in nature.
  Volp. True, my beloved Mosca. Yet I glory
More in the cunning purchase of my wealth,
Than in the glad possession, since I gain
No common way ; I use no trade, no venture ;
I wound no earth with plough-shares, fat no beasts,
To feed the shambles ; have no mills for iron,
Oil, corn, or men, to grind them into powder :
I blow no subtle glass, expose no ships
To threat'nings of the furrow-faced sea ;
I turn no monies in the public bank,
Nor usure private.
  Mos. No, sir, nor devour
Soft prodigals. You shall have some will swallow

A melting heir as glibly as your Dutch
Will pills of butter, and ne'er purge for it ;
Tear forth the fathers of poor families
Out of their beds, and coffin them alive
In some kind clasping prison, where their bones
May be forthcoming, when the flesh is rotten :
But your sweet nature doth abhor these courses ;
You lothe the widow's or the orphan's tears
Should wash your pavements, or their piteous cries
Ring in your roofs, and beat the air for vengeance,
   Volp. Right, Mosca ; I do lothe it.
   Mos. And besides, sir,
You are not like the thresher that doth stand
With a huge flail, watching a heap of corn,
And, hungry, dares not taste the smallest grain,
But feeds on mallows, and such bitter herbs ;
Nor like the merchant, who hath fill'd his vaults
With Romagnia, and rich Candian wines,
Yet drinks the lees of Lombard's vinegar ;
You will lie not in straw, whilst moths and worms
Feed on your sumptuous hangings and soft beds ;
You know the use of riches, and dare give now
From that bright heap, to me, your poor observer,
Or to your dwarf, or your hermaphrodite,
Your eunuch, or what other household trifle
Your pleasure allows maintenance——
   Volp. Hold thee, Mosca,   [*Gives him money.*
Take of my hand ; thou strik'st on truth in all,
And they are envious term thee parasite.
Call forth my dwarf, my eunuch, and my fool,
And let them make me sport. [*Exit* Mos.] What should I
     do,
But cocker up my genius, and live free
To all delights my fortune calls me to ?
I have no wife, no parent, child, ally,

To give my substance to ; but whom I make
Must be my heir : and this makes men observe me :
This draws new clients daily to my house,
Women and men of every sex and age,
That bring me presents, send me plate, coin, jewels,
With hope that when I die (which they expect
Each greedy minute) it shall then return
Ten-fold upon them ; whilst some, covetous
Above the rest, seek to engross me whole,
And counter-work the one unto the other,
Contend in gifts, as they would seem in love :
All which I suffer, playing with their hopes,
And am content to coin them into profit,
And look upon their kindness, and take more,
And look on that ; still bearing them in hand,
Letting the cherry knock against their lips,
And draw it by their mouths, and back again.—
How now !   [*Knocking without.*
Who's that ?   Away !   Look, Mosca.
   Mos. 'Tis Signior Voltore, the advocate ;
I know him by his knock,
   Volp. Fetch me my gown,
My furs and night-caps ; say, my couch is changing,
And let him entertain himself awhile
Without i' the gallery. [*Exit* Mosca.] Now, now, my
    clients
Begin their visitation ! Vulture, kite,
Raven, and gorcrow, all my birds of prey,
That think me turning carcase, now they come ;
I am not for them yet—

      Re-enter Mosca, *with the gown, etc.*
           How now, the news ?

   Mos. A piece of plate, sir.
   Volp. Of what bigness ?

Mos. Huge,
Massy, and antique, with your name inscribed,
And arms engraven.
    Volp. Good ! and not a fox
Stretch'd on the earth, with fine delusive sleights,
Mocking a gaping crow ? ha, Mosca !
    Mos. Sharp, sir.
    Volp. Give me my furs. [*Puts on his sick dress.*] Why
        dost thou laugh so, man ?
    Mos. I cannot choose, sir, when I apprehend
What thoughts he has without now, as he walks :
That this might be the last gift he should give ;
That this would fetch you ; if you died to-day,
And gave him all, what he should be to-morrow ;
What large return would come of all his ventures ;
How he should worship'd be, and reverenced ;
Ride with his furs, and foot-cloths ; waited on
By herds of fools, and clients ; have clear way
Made for his mule, as letter'd as himself ;
Be call'd the great and learn'd advocate :
And then concludes, there's nought impossible.
    Volp. Yes, to be learned, Mosca.
    Mos. O, no : rich
Implies it. Hood an ass with reverend purple,
So you can hide his two ambitious ears,
And he shall pass for a cathedral doctor.
    Volp. My caps, my caps, good Mosca. Fetch him in.
    Mos. Stay, sir ; your ointment for your eyes.
    Volp. That's true ;
Dispatch, dispatch : I long to have possession
Of my new present.
    Mos. That, and thousands more,
I hope to see you lord of.
    Volp. Thanks, kind Mosca.

Mos. And that, when I am lost in blended dust,
And hundred such as I am, in succession——
　Volp. Nay, that were too much, Mosca.
　Mos. You shall live,
Still, to delude these harpies.
　Volp. Loving Mosca !
'Tis well : my pillow now, and let him enter.
　　　　　　　　　　　　　　　[*Exit* Mosca.
Now, my feign'd cough, my phthisic, and my gout,
My apoplexy, palsy, and catarrhs,
Help, with your forced functions, this my posture,
Wherein, this three year, I have milk'd their hopes.
He comes ; I hear him—Uh ! [*coughing.*] uh ! uh ! uh !
　　O——

Re-enter Mosca, *introducing* Voltore, *with a piece of Plate.*

　Mos. You still are what you were, sir.　Only you,
Of all the rest, are he commands his love,
And you do wisely to preserve it thus,
With early visitation, and kind notes
Of your good meaning to him, which, I know,
Cannot but come most grateful.　Patron ! sir !
Here's signior Voltore is come——
　Volp. [*faintly.*] What say you ?
　Mos. Sir, signior Voltore is come this morning
To visit you.
　Volp. I thank him.
　Mos. And hath brought
A piece of antique plate, bought of St. Mark,
With which he here presents you.
　Volp. He is welcome.
Pray him to come more often.
　Mos. Yes,
　Volt. What says he ?

Mos. He thanks you, and desires you see him often.
Volp. Mosca.
Mos. My patron !
Volp. Bring him near, where is he ?
I long to feel his hand.
Mos. The plate is here, sir.
Volt. How fare you, sir ?
Volp. I thank you, signior Voltore ;
Where is the plate ? mine eyes are bad.
Volt. [*putting it into his hands.*] I'm sorry,
To see you still thus weak.
Mos. That he's not weaker.   [*Aside.*
Volp. You are too munificent.
Volt. No, sir, would to heaven,
I could as well give health to you, as that plate !
Volp. You give, sir, what you can : I thank you.
                 Your love
Hath taste in this, and shall not be unanswer'd :
I pray you see me often.
Volt. Yes, I shall, sir.
Volp. Be not far from me.
Mos. Do you observe that, sir !
Volp. Hearken unto me still ; it will concern you.
Mos. You are a happy man, sir ; know your good.
Volp. I cannot now last long——
Mos. You are his heir, sir.
Volt. Am I ?
Volp. I feel me going ; Uh ! uh ! uh ! uh !
I'm sailing to my port, Uh ! uh ! uh ! uh !
And I am glad I am so near my haven.
Mos. Alas, kind gentleman ! Well, we must all go——
Volt. But, Mosca——
Mos. Age will conquer.
Volt. 'Pray thee, hear me :
Am I inscribed his heir for certain?

Mos. Are you !
I do beseech you, sir, you will vouchsafe
To write me in your family.   All my hopes
Depend upon your worship : I am lost,
Except the rising sun do shine on me.
   Volt. It shall both shine, and warm thee, Mosca.
   Mos. Sir,
I am a man, that hath not done your love
All the worst offices : here I wear your keys,
See all your coffers and your caskets lock'd,
Keep the poor inventory of your jewels,
Your plate and monies ; am your steward, sir,
Husband your goods here.
   Volt. But am I sole heir ?
   Mos. Without a partner, sir ; confirm'd this morning :
The wax is warm yet, and the ink scarce dry
Upon the parchment.
   Volt. Happy, happy, me !
By what good chance, sweet Mosca ?
   Mos. Your desert, sir ;
I know no second cause.
   Volt. Thy modesty.
Is not to know it ; well, we shall requite it.
   Mos. He ever liked your course, sir ; that first took
       him.
I oft have heard him say, how he admired
Men of your large profession, that could speak
To every cause, and things mere contraries,
Till they were hoarse again, yet all the law ;
That, with most quick agility, could turn,
And [re-] return ; [could] make knots, and undo them ;
Give forked counsel ; take provoking gold
On either hand, and put it up : these men,
He knew, would thrive with their humility.
And, for his part, he thought he should be blest

To have his heir of such a suffering spirit,
So wise, so grave, of so perplex'd a tongue,
And loud withal, that would not wag, nor scarce
Lie still, without a fee ; when every word
Your worship but lets fall, is a chequin !—
                              [*Knocking without.*
Who's that ? one knocks; I would not have you seen, sir.
And yet—pretend you came, and went in haste :
I'll fashion an excuse——and, gentle sir,
When you do come to swim in golden lard,
Up to the arms in honey, that your chin
Is borne up stiff, with fatness of the flood,
Think on your vassal ; but remember me :
I have not been your worst of clients.
     Volt. Mosca !——
     Mos. When will you have your inventory brought, sir ?
Or see a copy of the will ?——Anon !—
I'll bring them to you, sir.   Away, be gone,
Put business in your face.   [*Exit* VOLTORE.
     Volp. [*springing up.*] Excellent Mosca !
Come hither, let me kiss thee.
     Mos. Keep you still, sir.
Here is Corbaccio.
     Volp. Set the plate away :
The vulture's gone, and the old raven's come !
     Mos. Betake you to your silence, and your sleep.
Stand there and multiply. [*Putting the plate to the rest.*]
     Now, shall we see
A wretch who is indeed more impotent
Than this can feign to be ; yet hopes to hop
Over his grave—

              Enter CORBACCIO.
                    Signior Corbaccio !
You're very welcome, sir.

Corb. How does your patron ?
Mos. Troth, as he did, sir ; no amends.
Corb. What ! mends he ?
Mos. No, sir : he's rather worse.
Corb. That's well.   Where is he ?
Mos. Upon his couch, sir, newly fall'n asleep.
Corb. Does he sleep well ?
Mos. No wink, sir, all this night.
Nor yesterday ; but slumbers.
Corb. Good ! he should take
Some counsel of physicians : I have brought him
An opiate here, from mine own doctor.
Mos. He will not hear of drugs.
Corb. Why ? I myself
Stood by while it was made, saw all the ingredients :
And know, it cannot but most gently work :
My life for his, 'tis but to make him sleep.
Volp. Ay, his last sleep, if he would take it.   [*Aside.*
Mos. Sir,
He has no faith in physic.
Corb. Say you, say you ?
Mos. He has no faith in physic : he does think
Most of your doctors are the greater danger,
And worse disease, to escape.   I often have
Heard him protest, that your physician
Should never be his heir.
Corb. Not I his heir ?
Mos. Not your physician, sir.
Corb. O, no, no, no,
I do not mean it.
Mos. No, sir, nor their fees
He cannot brook : he says, they flay a man,
Before they kill him.
Corb. Right, I do conceive you.

Mos. And then they do it by experiment :
For which the law not only doth absolve them,
But gives them great reward : and he is loth
To hire his death, so.
  Corb. It is true, they kill
With as much license as a judge.
  Mos. Nay, more ;
For he but kills, sir, where the law condemns,
And these can kill him too.
  Corb. Ay, or me ;
Or any man.   How does his apoplex ?
Is that strong on him still ?
  Mos. Most violent.
His speech is broken, and his eyes are set,
His face drawn longer than 'twas wont——
  Corb. How ! how !
Stronger than he was wont !
  Mos. No, sir : his face
Drawn longer than 'twas wont.
  Corb. O, good !
  Mos. His mouth
Is ever gaping, and his eyelids hang.
  Corb. Good.
  Mos. A freezing numbness stiffens all his joints,
And makes the colour of his flesh like lead.
  Corb. 'Tis good.
  Mos. His pulse beats slow, and dull.
  Corb. Good symptoms still.
  Mos. And from his brain——
  Corb. I conceive you : good.
  Mos. Flows a cold sweat, with a continual rheum,
Forth the resolved corners of his eyes.
  Corb. Is't possible ? Yes, I am better, ha !
How does he, with the swimming of his head ?

Mos. O, sir, 'tis past the scotomy ; he now
Hath lost his feeling, and hath left to snort :
You hardly can perceive him, that he breathes.
    Corb. Excellent, excellent ! sure I shall outlast him ;
This makes me young again, a score of years.
    Mos. I was a coming for you, sir.
    Corb. Has he made his will ?
What has he given me ?
    Mos. No, sir.
    Corb. Nothing, ha !
    Mos. He has not made his will, sir.
    Corb. Oh, oh, oh !
What then did Voltore, the lawyer, here ?
    Mos. He smelt a carcase, sir, when he but heard
My master was about his testament ;
As I did urge it to him for your good——
    Corb. He came unto him, did he ? I thought so.
    Mos. Yes, and presented him this piece of plate.
    Corb. To be his heir ?
    Mos. I do not know, sir.
    Corb. True :
I know it too.
    Mos. By your own scale, sir.   [*Aside.*
    Corb. Well,
I shall prevent him, yet. See, Mosca, look,
Here, I have brought a bag of bright chequines,
Will quite weigh down his plate.
    Mos. [*Taking the bag.*] Yea, marry sir,
This is true physic, this your sacred medicine ;
No talk of opiates, to this great elixir !
    Corb. 'Tis aurum palpabile, if not potabile.
    Mos. It shall be minister'd to him, in his bowl.
    Corb. Ay, do, do, do.
    Mos. Most blessed cordial !
This will recover him.

Corb. Yes, do, do, do.
Mos. I think it were not best, sir.
Corb. What ?
Mos. To recover him.
Corb. O, no, no, no ; by no means.
Mos. Why, sir, this
Will work some strange effect, if he but feel it.
   Corb. 'Tis true, therefore forbear ; I'll take my
        venture :
Give me it again.
   Mos. At no hand ; pardon me :
You shall not do yourself that wrong, sir.   I
Will so advise you, you shall have it all.
   Corb. How ?
   Mos. All, sir ; 'tis your right, your own : no man
Can claim a part : 'tis yours, without a rival,
Decreed by destiny.
   Corb. How, how, good Mosca ?
   Mos. I'll tell you, sir.   This fit he shall recover.
   Corb. I do conceive you.
   Mos. And, on first advantage
Of his gain'd sense, will I re-importune him
Unto the making of his testament :
And shew him this.   *[Pointing to the money.*
   Corb. Good, good.
   Mos. 'Tis better yet,
If you will hear, sir.
   Corb. Yes, with all my heart.   [speed ;
   Mos. Now, would I counsel you, make home with
There, frame a will ; whereto you shall inscribe
My master your sole heir.
   Corb. And disinherit
My son !
   Mos. O, sir, the better : for that colour
Shall make it much more taking.

Corb. O, but colour?

Mos. This will, sir, you shall send it unto me.
Now, when I come to inforce, as I will do,
Your cares, your watchings, and your many prayers,
Your more than many gifts, your this day's present,
And last, produce your will; where, without thought,
Or least regard, unto your proper issue,
A son so brave, and highly meriting,
The stream of your diverted love hath thrown you
Upon my master, and made him your heir:
He cannot be so stupid, or stone-dead,
But out of conscience, and mere gratitude——

Corb. He must pronounce me his?

Mos. 'Tis true.

Corb. This plot
Did I think on before.

Mos. I do believe it.

Corb. Do you not believe it?

Mos. Yes, sir.

Corb. Mine own project.

Mos. Which, when he hath done, sir——

Corb. Publish'd me his heir?

Mos. And you so certain to survive him——

Corb. Ay.

Mos. Being so lusty a man——

Corb. 'Tis true.

Mos. Yes, sir——

Corb. I thought on that too. See, how he
should be
The very organ to express my thoughts!

Mos. You have not only done yourself a good——

Corb. But multiplied it on my son.

Mos. 'Tis right, sir.

Corb. Still, my invention.

Mos. 'Las, sir ! heaven knows,
It hath been all my study, all my care,
(I e'en grow gray withal) how to work things——
   Corb. I do conceive, sweet Mosca.
   Mos. You are he,
For whom I labour here.
   Corb. Ay, do, do, do :
I'll straight about it.   *[Going.*
   Mos. Rook go with you, raven !
   Corb. I know thee honest.
   Mos. You do lie, sir !   *[Aside.*
   Corb. And——
   Mos. Your knowledge is no better than your ears, sir.
   Corb. I do not doubt, to be a father to thee.
   Mos. Nor I to gull my brother of his blessing.
   Corb. I may have my youth restored to me, why not ?
   Mos. Your worship is a precious ass !
   Corb. What say'st thou ?
   Mos. I do desire your worship to make haste, sir.
   Corb. 'Tis done, 'tis done ; I go.   *[Exit.*
   Volp. [*leaping from his couch.*] O, I shall burst !
Let out my sides, let out my sides——
   Mos. Contain
Your flux of laughter, sir : you know this hope
Is such a bait, it covers any hook.
   Volp. O, but thy working, and thy placing it !
I cannot hold ; good rascal, let me kiss thee :
I never knew thee in so rare a humour.
   Mos. Alas, sir, I but do as I am taught ;
Follow your grave instructions ; give them words ;
Pour oil into their ears, and send them hence.
   Volp. 'Tis, true, 'tis true. What a rare punishment
Is avarice to itself !
   Mos. Ay, with our help, sir.

Volp. So many cares, so many maladies,
So many fears attending on old age,
Yea, death so often call'd on, as no wish
Can be more frequent with them, their limbs faint,
Their senses dull, their seeing, hearing, going,
All dead before them ; yea, their very teeth,
Their instruments of eating, failing them :
Yet this is reckon'd life ! nay, here was one,
Is now gone home, that wishes to live longer !
Feels not his gout, nor palsy ; feigns himself
Younger by scores of years, flatters his age
With confident belying it, hopes he may,
With charms, like Æson, have his youth restored :
And with these thoughts so battens, as if fate
Would be as easily cheated on, as he,   [now ? a third !
And all turns air ! [*Knocking within.*] Who's that there,
  Mos. Close, to your couch again ; I hear his voice :
It is Corvino, our spruce merchant.
  Volp. [*lies down as before.*] Dead.
  Mos. Another bout, sir, with your eyes.   [*Anointing
    them.*]—Who's there ?

Enter CORVINO.

Signior Corvino ! come most wish'd for !   O,
How happy were you, if you knew it, now !
  Corv. Why ? what ? wherein ?
  Mos. The tardy hour is come, sir.
  Corv. He is not dead ?
  Mos. Not dead, sir, but as good ;
He knows no man.
  Corv. How shall I do then ?
  Mos. Why, sir ?
  Corv. I have brought him here a pearl.
  Mos. Perhaps he has
So much remembrance left, as to know you, sir :

He still calls on you ; nothing but your name
Is in his mouth.   Is your pearl orient, sir ?
  Corv. Venice was never owner of the like.
  Volp. [*faintly.*] Signior Corvino !
  Mos. Hark.
  Volp. Signior Corvino !
  Mos. He calls you ; step and give it him.—
      He's here, sir,
And he has brought you a rich pearl.
  Corv. How do you, sir ?
Tell him, it doubles the twelfth caract.
  Mos. Sir,
He cannot understand, his hearing's gone ;
And yet it comforts him to see you——
  Corv. Say,
I have a diamond for him, too.
  Mos. Best shew it, sir ;
Put it into his hand ; 'tis only there
He apprehends : he has his feeling, yet.
See how he grasps it !
  Corv. 'Las, good gentleman !
How pitiful the sight is !
  Mos. Tut ! forget, sir.
The weeping of an heir should still be laughter
Under a visor.
  Corv. Why, am I his heir ?
  Mos. Sir, I am sworn, I may not shew the will
Till he be dead ; but here has been Corbaccio,
Here has been Voltore, here were others too,
I cannot number 'em, they were so many ;
All gaping here for legacies : but I,
Taking the vantage of his naming you,
Signior Corvino, Signior Corvino, took
Paper, and pen, and ink, and there I asked him,
Whom he would have his heir ?   *Corvino.*   Who

Should be executor? *Corvino.*   And,
To any question he was silent to,
I still interpreted the nods he made,
Through weakness, for consent: and sent home th'
    others,
Nothing bequeath'd them, but to cry and curse.
   Corv. O, my dear Mosca! [*They embrace.*] Does he
    not perceive us?   [man,
   Mos. No more than a blind harper.   He knows no
No face of friend, nor name of any servant,
Who 'twas that fed him last, or gave him drink:
Not those he hath begotten, or brought up,
Can he remember.
   Corv. Has he children?
   Mos. Bastards,
Some dozen, or more, that he begot on beggars,
Gypsies, and Jews, and blackmoors, when he was
    drunk.
Knew you not that, sir? 'tis the common fable.
The dwarf, the fool, the eunuch, are all his;
He's the true father of his family,
In all, save me:—but he has given them nothing.
   Corv. That's well, that's well!   Art sure he does not
    hear us?
   Mos. Sure, sir! why, look you, credit your own sense.
                        [*Shouts in* VOL.'s *ear.*
The pox approach, and add to your diseases,
If it would send you hence the sooner, sir,
For your incontinence, it hath deserv'd it
Thoroughly, and thoroughly, and the plague to boot!—
You may come near, sir.—Would you would once close
Those filthy eyes of yours, that flow with slime,
Like two frog-pits; and those same hanging cheeks,
Cover'd with hide instead of skin—Nay, help, sir—
That look like frozen dish-clouts set on end!

Corv. [*aloud.*] Or like an old smoke wall, ou which
    the rain
Ran down in streaks !
  Mos. Excellent, sir ! speak out :
You may be louder yet ; a culverin
Discharged in his ear would hardly bore it.
  Corv. His nose is like a common sewer, still running.
  Mos. 'Tis good ! And what his mouth ?
  Corv. A very draught.
  Mos. O, stop it up——
  Corv. By no means.
  Mos. 'Pray you, let me :
Faith I could stifle him rarely with a pillow,
As well as any woman that should keep him.
  Corv. Do as you will ; but I'll begone.
  Mos. Be so :
It is your presence makes him last so long.
  Corv. I pray you, use no violence.
  Mos. No, sir ! why ?
Why should you be thus scrupulous, pray you, sir ?
  Corv. Nay, at your discretion.
  Mos. Well, good sir, begone.
  Corv. I will not trouble him now, to take my pearl.
  Mos. Puh ! not your diamond. What a needless care
Is this afflicts you ? Is not all here yours ?
Am not I here, whom you have made your creature ?
That owe my being to you ?
  Corv. Grateful Mosca !
Thou art my friend, my fellow, my companion,
My partner, and shalt share in all my fortunes.
  Mos. Excepting one.
  Corv. What's that ?
  Mos. Your gallant wife, sir,——   [*Exit* Corv.
Now is he gone : we had no other means
To shoot him hence, but this.

Volp. My divine Mosca !
Thou hast to-day outgone thyself.   [*Knocking within.*]
    —Who's there ?
I will be troubled with no more.   Prepare
Me music, dances, banquets, all delights ;
The Turk is not more sensual in his pleasures,
 Then will Volpone.   [*Exit* Mos.]   Let me see ; a pearl !
1   diamond ! plate ! chequines !   Good   morning's
    purchase.
Why, this is better than rob churches, yet ;
Or fat, by eating, once a month a man.

Bartholomew Fair.

THE PURITANS.

Scenes selected from *Bartholomew Fair*, in illustration of the manners of a Puritan Family and their Pastor.

DRAMATIS PERSONÆ.

John Littlewit, *a Proctor*.
Zeal-of-the-Land Busy, *Suitor to* Dame.
Purecraft, *a Banbury Man*.
Win-the-Fight, *Wife of* Littlewit.
Dame Purecraft, *her Mother, and a Widow*.

The other personages in these scenes are too numerous to be described, and their action will serve only to bring the Puritan family into play.

BARTHOLOMEW FAIR.

SCENE I.

[Mr. Littlewit persuades his wife to manifest a carnal longing for roast pig in the Bartholomew Fair. He desires himself to be present at an Interlude on the Tragical History of *Hero and Leander,* which he has written for a booth at the fair. Zeal-of-the-Land Busy, their Pastor, has to settle the casuistical question of eating pig in Smithfield before the Littlewits can take their pleasure.]

Lit. Win, you see 'tis in fashion to go to the Fair, Win; we must to the Fair too, you and I, Win. I have an affair in the Fair, Win, a puppet-play of mine own making, say nothing, that I writ for the motion-man, which you must see, Win.

Mrs. Lit. I would I might, John; but my mother will never consent to such a profane motion, she will call it.

Lit. Tut, we'll have a device, a dainty one. Now Wit, help at a pinch, good Wit come, come good Wit, au it be thy will! I have it, Win, I have it i'faith, and 'tis a fine one. Win, long to eat of a pig, sweet Win, in the Fair, do you see, in the heart of the Fair, not at Pye-corner. Your mother will do any thing, Win, to

satisfy your longing, you know ; pray thee long presently ; and be sick o' the sudden, good Win. I'll go
in and tell her; cut thy lace in the mean time, and play
the hypocrite, sweet Win.

Mrs. Lit. No, I'll not make me unready for it : I can
be hypocrite enough, though I were never so strait-
laced.

Lit. You say true, you have been bred in the family,
and brought up to't. Our mother is a most elect hypocrite, and has maintained us all this seven year with it,
like gentlefolks.

Mrs. Lit. Ay, let her alone, John, she is not a wise
wilful widow for nothing ; nor a sanctified sister for a
song. And let me alone too, I have somewhat of the
mother in me, you shall see ; fetch her, fetch her—[*Exit*
LITTLEWIT.] Ah ! ah !   [*Seems to swoon.*

Re-enter LITTLEWIT *with* Dame PURECRAFT.

Pure. Now, the blaze of the beauteous discipline,
fright away this evil from our house ! how now, Win-
the-fight, child ! how do you ? sweet child, speak to me.

Mrs. Lit. Yes, forsooth.

Pure. Look up, sweet Win-the-fight, and suffer not
the enemy to enter you at this door, remember that your
education has been with the purest : What polluted
one was it, that named first the unclean beast, pig, to
you, child ?

Mrs. Lit. Uh, uh !

Lit. Not I, on my sincerity, mother ? she longed
above three hours ere she would let me know it.—Who
was it, Win ?

Mrs. Lit. A profane black thing with a beard, John.

Pure. O, resist it, Win-the-fight, it is the tempter,
the wicked tempter, you may know it by the fleshly
motion of pig ; be strong against it, and its foul tempta-

tions, in these assaults, whereby it broacheth flesh and blood, as it were on the weaker side ; and pray against its carnal provocations ; good child, sweet child, pray.

Lit. Good mother, I pray you, that she may eat some pig, and her belly full too ; and do not you cast away your own child, and perhaps one of mine, with your tale of the tempter.   How do you do, Win, are you not sick ?

Mrs. Lit. Yes, a great deal, John, uh, uh !

Pure. What shall we do ?   Call our zealous brother Busy hither, for his faithful fortification in this charge of the adversary.   [*Exit* LITTLEWIT.]   Child, my dear child, you shall eat pig ; be comforted, my sweet child.

Mrs. Lit. Ay, but in the Fair, mother.

Pure. I mean in the Fair, if it can be any way made or found lawful.—

Re-enter LITTLEWIT.

Where is our brother Busy ? will he not come ?   Look up, child.

Lit. Presently, mother, as soon as he has cleansed his beard.   I found him fast by the teeth in the cold-turkey pie in the cupboard, with a great white loaf on his left hand, and a glass of malmsey on his right.

Pure. Slander not the brethren, wicked one.

Lit. Here he is now, purified, mother.

Enter ZEAL-OF-THE-LAND BUSY.

Pure. O brother Busy ! your help here, to edify and raise us up in a scruple : my daughter Win-the-fight is visited with a natural disease of women, called a longing to eat pig.

Lit. Ay sir, a Bartholomew pig ; and in the Fair.

Pure. And I would be satisfied from you, religiously-wise, whether a widow of the sanctified assembly, or a widow's daughter, may commit the act without offence to the weaker sisters.

Busy. Verily, for the disease of longing, it is a disease, a carnal disease, or appetite, incident to women ; and as it is carnal and incident, it is natural, very natural : now pig, it is a meat, and a meat that is nourishing and may be longed for, and so consequently eaten ; it may be eaten ; very exceeding well eaten ; but in the Fair, and as a Bartholomew pig, it cannot be eaten ; for the very calling it a Bartholomew pig, and to eat it so, is a spice of idolatry, and you make the Fair no better than one of the high-places. This, I take it, is the state of the question : a high-place.

Lit. Ay, but in state of necessity, place should give place, master Busy. I have a conceit left yet.

Pure. Good brother Zeal-of-the-land, think to make it as lawful as you can.

Lit. Yes, sir, and as soon as you can ; for it must be, sir : you see the danger my little wife is in, sir.

Pure. Truly, I do love my child dearly, and I would not have her miscarry, or hazard her first-fruits, if it might be otherwise.

Bus. Surely, it may be otherwise, but it is subject to construction, subject, and hath a face of offence with the weak, a great face, a foul face ; but that face may have a veil put over it, and be shadowed as it were ; it may be eaten, and in the Fair, I take it, in a booth, the tents of the wicked : the place is not much, not very much, we may be religious in the midst of the profane, so it be eaten with a reformed mouth, with sobriety and humbleness ; not gorged in with gluttony or greediness, there's the fear : for, should she go there, as taking pride in the place, or delight in the unclean dressing, to feed the vanity of the eye, or lust of the palate, it were not well, it were not fit, it were abominable, and not good.

Lit. Nay, I knew that afore, and told her on't; but courage, Win, we'll be humble enough, we'll seek out the homeliest booth in the Fair, that's certain ; rather than fail, we'll eat it on the ground.

Pure. Ay, and I'll go with you myself, Win-the-fight, and my brother Zeal-of-the-land shall go with us too, for our better consolation.

Mrs. Lit. Uh, uh !

Lit. Ay, and Solomon too, Win, the more the merrier. Win, we'll leave Rabbi Busy in a booth.   [*Aside to Mrs.* LIT.]—Solomon ! my cloak.

Enter SOLOMON *with the cloak.*

Sol. Here, sir.

Bus. In the way of comfort to the weak, I will go and eat.   I will eat exceedingly, and prophesy ; there may be a good use made of it too, now I think on't: by the public eating of swine's flesh, to profess our hate and loathing of Judaism, whereof the brethren stand tax'd.   I will therefore eat, yea, I will eat exceedingly.

Lit. Good, i'faith, I will eat heartily too, because I will be no Jew, I could never away with that stiff-necked generation : and truly, I hope my little one will be like me, that cries for pig so in the mother's belly.

Bus. Very likely, exceeding likely, very exceeding likely.   [*Exeunt.*

SCENE II.

[The Puritans enter Smithfield and walk up between the booths.]

Enter Rabbi BUSY, Dame PURECRAFT, JOHN LITTLEWIT, *and* Mrs. LITTLEWIT.

Busy. So, walk on in the middle way, fore-right, turn neither to the right hand nor to the left ; let not your eyes be drawn aside with vanity, nor your ear with noises.

Quar. O, I know him by that start.

Leath. What do you lack, what do you buy, mistress ? a fine hobby-horse, to make your son a tilter ? a drum to make him a soldier ? a fiddle to make him a reveller ? what is't you lack ? little dogs for your daughters ? or babies, male or female ?

Busy. Look not toward them, hearken not ; the place is Smithfield, or the field of smiths, the grove of hobby-horses and trinkets, the wares are the wares of devils, and the whole Fair is the shop of Satan : they are hooks and baits, very baits, that are hung out on every side, to catch you, and to hold you, as it were, by the gills, and by the nostrils, as the fisher doth ; therefore you must not look nor turn toward them.—The heathen man could stop his ears with wax against the harlot of the sea ; do you the like with your fingers against the bells of the beast.

Winw. What flashes come from him !

Quar. O, he has those of his oven ; a notable hot baker 'twas when he plied the peel ; he is leading his flock into the Fair now.

Winw. Rather driving them to the pens, for he will let them look upon nothing.

Enter KNOCKEM *and* WHIT *from* URSULA's *booth.*

Knock. Gentlewomen, the weather's hot ; whither walk you ? have a care of your fine velvet caps, the Fair is dusty. Take a sweet delicate booth, with boughs, here in the way, and cool yourselves in the shade: you and your friends. The best pig and bottle-ale in the Fair, sir. Old Ursula is cook, there you may read ; [*Points to the sign, a pig's head, with a large writing under it.*] the pig's head speaks it. Poor soul,

she has had a string-halt, the maryhinchco ; but she's
prettily amended.

Whit. A delicate show-pig, little mistress, with shweet
sauce, and crackling, like de bay-leaf i' de fire, la ! tou
shalt ha' de clean side o' de table-clot, and di glass
vash'd with phatersh of dame Annesh Cleare.

Lit. [*Gazing at the inscription.*] This is fine verily.
*Here be the best pigs, and she docs roast them as well as
ever she did*, the pig's head says.

Knock. Excellent, excellent, mistress ; with fire o'
juniper and rosemary branches ! the oracle of the pig's
head, that, sir.

Pure. Son, were you not warn'd of the vanity of the
eye ? have you forgot the wholesome admonition so
soon ?

Lit. Good mother, how shall we find a pig, if we do
not look about for't : will it run off o' the spit, into our
mouths, think you, as in Lubberland, and cry, *wee,
wee !*

Busy. No, but your mother, religiously-wise, con-
ceiveth it may offer itself by other means to the sense,
as by way of steam, which I think it doth here in this
place—huh, huh—yes, it doth. [*He scents after it like a
hound.*] And it were a sin of obstinacy, great obstinacy,
high and horrible obstinacy, to decline or resist the
good titillation of the famelic sense, which is the smell.
Therefore be bold—huh, huh, huh—follow the scent :
enter the tents of the unclean, for once, and satisfy your
wife's frailty. Let your frail wife be satisfied ; your
zealous mother, and my suffering self, will also be
satisfied.

Lit. Come, Win, as good winny here as go farther, and
see nothing.

Busy. We scape so much of the other vanities, by our
early entering.

Pure. It is an edifying consideration.

Mrs. Lit. This is scurvy, that we must come into the Fair, and not look on't.

Lit. Win, have patience, Win, I'll tell you more anon.

[*Exeunt into the booth*, LITTLEWIT, Mrs. LITTLEWIT, BUSY, *and* PURECRAFT.

Knock. Mooncalf, entertain within there, the best pig in the booth, a pork-like pig. These are Banbury-bloods, o' the sincere stud, come a pig-hunting. Whit, wait, Whit, look to your charge.   *Exit* WHIT.

Busy. [*within.*] A pig prepare presently, let a pig be prepared to us.   [*The Puritans enter Ursula's booth.*

SCENE III.

[Brother Zeal-of-the-Land Busy protests against the Idols of the Fair, throws down the stalls of Toymen and Ginger-bread-Sellers, and is sent off to the stocks.]

Enter LITTLEWIT *from* URSULA'S *booth, followed by* Mrs. LITTLEWIT.

Lit. Do you hear, Win, Win ?

Mrs. Lit. What say you, John ?

Lit. While they are paying the reckoning, Win, I'll tell you a thing, Win ; we shall never see any sights in the Fair, Win, except you long still, Win : good Win, sweet Win, long to see some hobby-horses, and some drums, and rattles, and dogs, and fine devices, Win. The bull with the five legs, Win ; and the great hog. Now you have begun with pig, you may long for any thing, Win, and so for my motion, Win.

Mrs. Lit. But we shall not eat of the bull and the hog, John ; how shall I long then ?

Lit. O yes, Win : you may long to see, as well as to

taste, Win: how did the pothecary's wife, Win, that longed to see the anatomy, Win? or the lady, Win, that desired to spit in the great lawyer's mouth, after an eloquent pleading? I assure you, they longed, Win; good Win, go in, and long.

[*Exeunt* LITTLEWIT *and* Mrs. LITTLEWIT.

Trash. I think we are rid of our new customer, brother Leatherhead, we shall hear no more of him.

Leath. All the better; let's pack up all and begone, before he find us.

Trash. Stay a little, yonder comes a company; it may be we may take some more money.

Enter KNOCKEM *and* BUSY.

Knock. Sir, I will take your counsel, and cut my hair, and leave vapours: I see that tobacco, and bottle-ale, and pig, and Whit, and very Ursla herself, is all vanity.

Busy. Only pig was not comprehended in my admonition, the rest were: for long hair, it is an ensign of pride, a banner; and the world is full of those banners, very full of banners. And bottle-ale is a drink of Satan's, a diet-drink of Satan's, devised to pull us up, and make us swell in this latter age of vanity; as the smoke of tobacco, to keep us in mist and error: but the fleshly woman, which you call Ursla, is above all to be avoided, having the marks upon her of the three enemies of man; the world, as being in the Fair; the devil, as being in the fire; and the flesh, as being herself.

Enter Mrs. PURECRAFT.

Pure. Brother Zeal-of-the-land! what shall we do? my daughter Win-the-fight is fallen into her fit of longing again.

Busy, For more pig! there is no more, is there?

Pure. To see some sights in the Fair.

Busy. Sister, let her fly the impurity of the place swiftly, lest she partake of the pitch thereof. Thou art the seat of the beast, O Smithfield, and I will leave thee! Idoltary peepeth out on every side of thee.

[*Goes forward.*

Knock. An excellent right hypocrite! now his belly is full, he falls a railing and kicking, the jade. A very good vapour! I'll in, and joy Ursla, with telling how her pig works; two and a half he eat to his share; and he has drunk a pailfull. He eats with his eyes, as well as his teeth. [*Exit.*

Leath. What do you lack, gentlemen? what is't you buy? rattles, drums, babies——

Busy. Peace, with thy apocryphal wares, thou profane publican; thy bells, thy dragons, and thy Tobie's dogs. Thy hobby-horse is an idol, a very idol, a fierce and rank idol; and thou, the Nebuchadnezzar, the proud Nebuchadnezzar of the Fair, that sett'st it up, for children to fall down to, and worship.

Leath. Cry you mercy, sir; will you buy a fiddle to fill up your noise?

Re-enter LITTLEWIT *and his* Wife.

Lit. Look, Win, do, look a God's name, and save your longing. Here be fine sights.

Pure. Ay, child, so you hate them, as our brother Zeal does, you may look on them.

Leath. Or what do you say to a drum, sir?

Busy. It is the broken belly of the beast, and thy bellows there are his lungs, and these pipes are his throat, those feathers are of his tail, and thy rattles the gnashing of his teeth.

Trash. And what's my ginger-bread, I pray you?

Busy. The provender that pricks him up. Hence with thy basket of popery, thy nest of images, and whole legend of ginger-work.

Leath. Sir, if you be not quiet the quicklier, I'll have you clapp'd fairly by the heels, for disturbing the Fair.

Busy. The sin of the Fair provokes me, I cannot be silent.

Pure. Good brother Zeal !

Leath. Sir, I'll make you silent, believe it.

Lit. I'd give a shilling you could, i'faith, friend.

[Aside to LEATHERHEAD.

Leath. Sir, give me your shilling, I'll give you my shop, if I do not; and I'll leave it in pawn with you in the mean time.

Lit. A match, i'faith ; but do it quickly then.

[Exit LEATHERHEAD.

Busy. [*to* Mrs. PURECRAFT]. Hinder me not, woman. I was moved in spirit, to be here this day, in this Fair, this wicked and foul Fair ; and fitter may it be called a Foul than a Fair ; to protest against the abuses of it, the foul abuses of it, in regard of the afflicted saints, that are troubled, very much troubled, exceedingly troubled, with the opening of the merchandise of Babylon again, and the peeping of popery upon the stalls here, here, in the high places. See you not Goldylocks, the purple strumpet there, in her yellow gown and green sleeves ? the profane pipes, the tinkling timbrels? a shop of relicks ! [Attempts to seize the toys.

Lit. Pray you forbear, I am put in trust with them.

Busy. And this idolatrous grove of images, this flasket of idols, which I will pull down——

[Overthrows the ginger-bread basket.

Trash. O my ware, my ware ! God bless it !

Busy. In my zeal, and glory to be thus exercised.

...20...

Re-enter LEATHERHEAD, *with* BRISTLE, HAGGISE, *and other* Officers.

Leath. Here he is, pray you lay hold on his zeal ; we cannot sell a whistle for him in tune. Stop his noise first.

Busy. Thou canst not ; 'tis a sanctified noise : I will make a loud and most strong noise, till I have daunted the profane enemy. And for this cause——

Leath. Sir, here's no man afraid of you, or your cause. You shall swear it in the stocks, sir.

Busy. I will thrust myself into the stocks, upon the pikes of the land.   [*They seize him.*

Leath. Carry him away.

Pure. What do you mean, wicked men ?

Busy. Let them alone, I fear them not.

                    [*Exeunt* Officers *with* BUSY, *followed by* Dame PURECRAFT.]

SCENE IV.

[Rabbi Busy is put into the stocks, and finds singular companions in adversity.

[*As they open the stocks,* WASPE *puts his shoe on his hand, and slips it in for his leg.*

Waspe. I shall put a trick upon your Welsh diligence perhaps.   [*Aside.*

Bri. Put in your leg, sir.   [*To* BUSY.

Quar. What, rabbi Busy ! is he come ?

Busy. I do obey thee ; the lion may roar, but he cannot bite. I am glad to be thus separated from the heathen of the land, and put apart in the stocks, for the holy cause.

Waspe. What are you, sir ?

Busy. One that rejoiceth in his affliction, and sitteth here to prophesy the destruction of fairs and May-games, wakes and Whitson-ales, and doth sigh and groan for the reformation of these abuses.

Waspe. [*to* OVERDO.] And do you sigh and groan too, or rejoice in your affliction?

Over. I do not feel it, I do not think of it, it is a thing without me : Adam, thou art above these batteries, these contumelies. *In te manca ruit fortuna,* as thy friend Horace says ; thou art one, *Quem neque pauperies, neque mors, neque vincula, terrent.* And therefore, as another friend of thine says, I think it be thy friend Persius, *Non te quæsiveris extra.*

Quar. What's here ! a stoic in the stocks ? the fool is turn'd philosopher.

Busy. Friend, I will leave to communicate my spirit with you, if I hear any more of those superstitious relics, those lists of Latin, the very rags of Rome, and patches of popery.

Waspe. Nay, an you begin to quarrel, gentlemen, I'll leave you. I have paid for quarrelling too lately : look you, a device, but shifting in a hand for a foot. God be wi' you.   [*Slips out his hand.*

Busy. Wilt thou then leave thy brethren in tribula-tion ?

Waspe. For this once, sir.   [*Exit, running.*

Busy. Thou art a halting neutral ; stay him there, stop him, that will not endure the heat of persecution ?

Bri. How now, what's the matter ?

Busy. He is fled, he is fled, and dares not sit it out.

Bri. What, has he made an escape ! which way ? follow, neighbour Haggise.

       [*Exeunt* HAGGISE *and* WATCH.

Enter Dame PURECRAFT.

Pure. O me, in the stocks ! have the wicked prevail'd ?

Busy. Peace, religious sister, it is my calling, comfort yourself ; an extraordinary calling, and done for my better standing, my surer standing, hereafter.

SCENE V.

[Rabbi Busy, unexpectedly delivered from the stocks, blunders into a booth where Mr. Littlewit's Interlude of *Hero and Leander* is being played. On this occasion also he displays his zeal, which is subdued by arguments.]

Rabbi BUSY *rushes in.*

Busy. Down with Dagon ! down with Dagon ! 'tis I, I will no longer endure your profanations.

Leath. What mean you, sir ?

Busy. I will remove Dagon there, I say, that idol, that heathenish idol, that remains, as I may say, a beam, a very beam,—not a beam of the sun, nor a beam of the moon, nor the beam of a balance, neither a house-beam, nor a weaver's beam, but a beam in the eye, in the eye of the brethren ; a very great beam, an exceeding great beam ; such as are your stage-players, rimers, and morrice-dancers, who have walked hand in hand, in contempt of the brethren, and the cause ; and been born out by instruments of no mean countenance.

Leath. Sir, I present nothing but what is licensed by authority.

Busy. Thou art all license, even licentiousness itself, Shimei !

Leath. I have the master of the revels' hand for't, sir.

Busy. The master of the rebels' hand thou hast. Satan's ! hold thy peace, thy scurrility, shut up thy mouth, thy profession is damnable, and in pleading for

it thou dost plead for Baal. I have long opened my
mouth wide, and gaped ; I have gaped as the oyster for
the tide, after thy destruction: but cannot compass it by
suit or dispute ; so that I look for a bickering, ere long,
and then a battle.

Knock. Good Banbury vapours !

Cokes. Friend, you'd have an ill match on't, if you
bicker with him here ; though he be no man of the fist,
he has friends that will to cuffs for him. Numps, will
not you take our side ?

Edg. Sir, it shall not need ; in my mind he offers
him a fairer course, to end it by disputation : hast thou
nothing to say for thyself, in defence of thy quality ?

Leath. Faith, sir, I am not well-studied in these controversies, between the hypocrites and us. But here's
one of my motion, puppet Dionysius, shall undertake
him, and I'll venture the cause on't.

Cokes. Who, my hobby-horse ! will he dispute with
him ?

Leath. Yes, sir, and make a hobby-ass of him, I hope.

Cokes. That's excellent ! indeed he looks like the best
scholar of them all. Come, sir, you must be as good as
our word now.

Busy. I will not fear to make my spirit and gifts
known : assist me zeal, fill me, fill me, that is, make me
full !

Winw. What a desperate, profane wretch is this ! is
there any ignorance or impudence like his, to call his
zeal to fill him against a puppet ?

Quar. I know no fitter match than a puppet to
commit with an hypocrite !   [calling.

Busy. First, I say unto thee, idol, thou hast no

Dion. *You lie, I am call'd Dionysius.*

Leath. The motion says, you lie, he is call'd Dionysius
in the matter, and to that calling he answers.

Busy. I mean no vocation, idol, no present lawful calling.

Dion. *Is yours a lawful calling?*

Leath. The motion asketh, if yours be a lawful calling.

Busy. Yes, mine is of the spirit.

Dion. *Then idol is a lawful calling.*

Leath. He says, then idol is a lawful calling ; for you call'd him idol, and your calling is of the spirit.

Cokes. Well disputed, hobby-horse.

Busy. Take not part with the wicked, young gallant : he neigheth and hinnieth ; all is but hinnying sophistry. I call him idol again ; yet, I say, his calling, his profession is profane, it is profane, idol.

Dion. *It is not profane.*

Leath. It is not profane, he says.

Busy. It is profane.

Dion. *It is not profane.*

Busy. It is profane.

Dion. *It is not profane.*

Leath. Well said, confute him with *Not,* still. You cannot bear him down with your base noise, sir.

Busy. Nor he me, with his treble crecking, though he creek like the chariot wheels of Satan ; I am zealous for the cause——

Leath. As a dog for a bone.

Busy. And I say, it is profane, as being the page of Pride, and the waiting-woman of Vanity.

Dion. *Yea ! what say you to your tire-women, then ?*

Leath. Good.

Dion. *Or feather-makers in the Friers, that are of your faction of faith ? are not they with their perukes, and their puffs, their fans, and their huffs, as much pages of Pride, and waiters upon Vanity ? What say you, what say you, what say you ?*

Busy. I will not answer for them.

Dion. Because you cannot, because you cannot. Is a bugle-maker a lawful calling? or the confect-makers? such you have there; or your French fashioner? you would have all the sin within yourselves, would you not, would you not?

Busy. No, Dagon.

Dion. What then, Dagonet? is a puppet worse than these?

Busy. Yes, and my main argument against you is, that you are an abomination; for the male, among you, putteth on the apparel of the female, and the female of the male.

Dion. You lie, you lie, you lie abominably.

Cokes. Good, by my troth, he has given him the lie thrice.

Dion. It is your old stale argument against the players, but it will not hold against the puppets; for we have neither male nor female amongst us. And that thou may'st see, if thou wilt, like a malicious purblind zeal as thou art. [*Takes up his garment.*

Edg. By my faith, there he has answer'd you, friend, a plain demonstration.

Dion. Nay, I'll prove, against e'er a Rabbin of them all, that my standing is as lawful as his; that I speak by inspiration, as well as he; that I have as little to do with learning as he; and do scorn her helps as much as he.

Busy. I am confuted, the cause hath failed me.

Dion. Then be converted, be converted.

Leath. Be converted, I pray you, and let the play go on!

Busy. Let it go on; for I am changed, and will become a beholder with you.

THE HUE AND CRY AFTER CUPID.

———

[THE worthy custom of honouring worthy marriages, with these noble solemnities, hath of late years advanced itself frequently with us; to the reputation no less of our court, than nobles; expressing besides (through the difficulties of expense and travel, with the cheerfulness of undertaking) a most real affection in the personaters, to those, for whose sake they would sustain these persons. It behoves then us, that are trusted with a part of their honour in these celebrations, to do nothing in them beneath the dignity of either. With this proposed part of judgment, I adventure to give that abroad, which in my first conception I intended honourably fit: and, though it hath labour'd since, under censure, I, that know truth to be always of one stature, and so like a rule, as who bends it the least way, must needs do an injury to the right, cannot but smile at their tyrannous ignorance, that will offer to slight me (in these things being an artificer) and give themselves a peremptory license to judge who have never touched so much as to the bark, or utter shell of any knowledge. But their daring dwell with them. They have found a place to pour out their follies; and I a seat, to sleep out the passage.]

THE HUE AND CRY AFTER CUPID.

The scene to this Masque was a high, steep, red cliff,
advancing itself into the clouds, figuring the place, from
whence (as I have been, not fabulously, informed) the
honourable family of the Radcliffs first took their name,
a clivo rubro, and is to be written with that orthography ; as I have observed out of master Camden, in
his mention of the earls of Sussex.   This cliff was also a
note of height, greatness, and antiquity.   Before which,
on the two sides, were erected two pilasters, charged with
spoils and trophies of Love and his mother, consecrate
to marriage : amongst which, were old and young persons
figured, bound with roses, the wedding garments, rocks
and spindles, hearts transfixed with arrows, others
flaming, virgins' girdles, garlands, and worlds of such
like : all wrought round and bold : and over head two
personages, Triumph and Victory, in flying postures,
and twice so big as the life, in place of the arch, and
holding a garland of myrtle for the key.   All which,
with the pillars, seemed to be of burnished gold, and
embossed out of the metal.   Beyond the cliff was seen

nothing but clouds, thick and obscure; till on the
sudden, with a solemn music, a bright sky breaking
forth, there were discovered first two doves,* then two
swans * with silver geers, drawing forth a triumphant
chariot; in which Venus sat, crowned with her star,
and beneath her the three Graces, or Charites, Aglaia,
Thalia, Euphrosyne, all attired according to their
antique figures.   These, from their chariot, alighted on
the top of the cliff, and descending by certain abrupt and
winding passages, Venus having left her star only
flaming in her seat, came to the earth, the Graces
throwing garlands all the way, and began to speak.

Ven. It is no common cause, ye will conceive,
My lovely Graces, makes your goddess leave
Her state in heaven, to-night, to visit earth.
Love late is fled away, my eldest birth,
Cupid, whom I did joy to call my son ;
And whom long absent, Venus is undone.
   Spy, if you can, his footsteps on this green ;
For here, as I am told, he late hath been,
With divers of his brethren,† lending light
From their best flames, to gild a glorious night ;
Which I not grudge at, being done for her,
Whose honours, to my own, I still prefer.
But he not yet returning, I'm in fear,
Some gentle Grace, or innocent Beauty here,
Be taken with him : or he hath surprised
A second Psyche, and lives here disguised.
Find ye no track of his stray'd feet ?

* Both doves and swans were sacred to this goddess, and as
well with the one as the other, her chariot is induced by Ovid.
lib. 10 and 11 Metamor.
   † Alluding to the Loves (the torch-bearers) in the Queen's
Masque before.

1 *Gra.* Not I.

2 *Gra.* Nor I.

3 *Gra.* Nor I.

Ven. Stay, nymphs, we then will try
A nearer way.   Look all these ladies' eyes,
And see if there be not concealed lies ;
Or in their bosoms, 'twixt their swelling breasts ;
The wag affects to make himself such nests :
Perchance he hath got some simple heart, to hide
His subtle shape in ; I will have him cry'd,
And all his virtues told ! that, when they'd know
What sprite he is, she soon may let him go,
That guards him now ; and think herself right blest,
To be so timely rid of such a guest.
Begin, soft GRACES, and proclaim reward
To her that brings him in.   Speak to be heard.

1 *Grace.* Beauties, have ye seen this toy,
          Called Love, a little boy, *
          Almost naked, wanton, blind ;
          Cruel now, and then as kind ?
          If he be amongst ye, say ?
          He is Venus' runaway.

2 *Grace.* She that will but now discover
          Where the winged wag doth hover,
          Shall to-night receive a kiss,
          How, or where herself would wish :
          But, who brings him to his mother,
          Shall have that kiss, and another.

3 *Grace.* He hath marks about him plenty :
          You shall know him among twenty.

   * In this Love, I express Cupid, as he is Veneris filius, and
owner of the following qualities, ascribed him by the antique
and later poets.

All his body is a fire,
And his breath a flame entire,
That being shot, like lightning, in,
Wounds the heart, but not the skin.

1 *Grace.* At his sight, the sun hath turn'd,[*]
    Neptune in the waters burn'd;
    Hell hath felt a greater heat;[†]
    Jove himself forsook his seat:
    From the centre to the sky,
    Are his trophies reared high.[‡]

2 *Grace.* Wings he hath, which though ye clip,
    He will leap from lip to lip,
    Over liver, lights, and heart,
    But not stay in any part;
    And, if chance his arrow misses,
    He will shoot himself, in kisses.

3 *Grace.* He doth bear a golden bow,
    And a quiver, hanging low,
    Full of arrows, that outbrave
    Dian's shafts; where, if he have
    Any head more sharp than other,
    With that first he strikes his mother.

1 *Grace.* Still the fairest are his fuel,
    When his days are to be cruel,
    Lovers' hearts are all his food;
    And his baths their warmest blood:

[*] See Lucian. Dial. Deor.
[†] And Claud. in raptu Proserp.
[‡] Such was the power ascrib'd him, by all the ancients: whereof there is extant an elegant Greek epigram. Phil. Poe, wherein he makes all the other deities despoiled by him, of their ensigns; Jove of his thunder, Phœbus of his arrows, Hercules of his club, etc.

Nought but wounds his hand doth season,
And he hates none like to Reason.

2 *Grace.* Trust him not ; his words, though sweet,
    Seldom with his heart do meet.
    All his practice is deceit ;
    Every gift it is a bait ;
    Not a kiss but poison bears ;
    And most treason in his tears.

3 *Grace.* Idle minutes are his reign ;
    Then, the straggler makes his gain,
    By presenting maids with toys,
    And would have ye think them joys ;
    'Tis the ambition of the elf,
    To have all childish as himself.

1 *Grace.* If by these ye please to know him,
    Beauties, be not nice, but show him.

2 *Grace.* Though ye had a will to hide him,
    Now, we hope, ye'll not abide him.

3 *Grace.* Since you hear his falser play ;
    And that he's Venus' runaway.

At this, from behind the trophies, CUPID *discovered
himself, and came forth armed ; attended with twelve
boys, most antickly attired, that represented the
Sports, and pretty Lightnesses that accompany Love,
under the titles of Joci and Risus ; and are said to
wait on Venus as she is Prefect of Marriage.**

* Which Horat. consents to, Car. lib. 1. ode 2,

———Erycina ridens,
Quam Jocus circum volat, et Cupido.

Cup. Come, my little jocund Sports,
    Come away ; the time now sorts
    With your pastime : this same night
    Is Cupid's day.   Advance your light.
    With your revel fill the room,
    That our triumphs be not dumb.

*Wherewith they fell into a subtle capricious dance, to as
odd a music, each of them bearing two torches, and
nodding with their antic faces, with other variety of
ridiculous gesture, which gave much occasion of mirth
and delight to the spectators.   The dance ended,
Cupid went forward.*

Cup. Well done, anticks ! now my bow,
    And my quiver bear to show ;
    That these beauties, here, may know,
    By what arms this feat was done,
    That hath so much honour won
    Unto Venus and her son.

*At which, his mother apprehended him : and circling him
in, with the Graces, began to demand.*

Ven. What feat, what honour is it that you boast,
My little straggler ?   I had given you lost,
With all your games, here.
    Cup. Mother !
    Ven. Yes, sir, she.
What might your glorious cause of triumph be ?
Have you shot Minerva* or the Thespian dames ?
Heat aged Ops again,† with youthful flames ?

   * She urges these as miracles, becauses Pallas, and the
Muses, are most contrary to Cupid.   See Luc. Dial. Ven. et
Cupid.
   † Rhea, the mother of the gods, whom Lucian, in that place,
makes to have fallen franticly in love by Cupid's means, with
Atys.   So of the Moon, with Endymion, Hercules, etc.

Or have you made the colder Moon to visit
Once more, a sheepcote? Say, what conquest is it
Can make you hope such a renown to win ?
Is there a second Hercules brought to spin ?
Or, for some new disguise, leaves Jove his thunder?
   Cup. Nor that, nor those, and yet no less a
       wonder——*   [*He espies* HYMEN.
Which to tell, I may not stay :
Hymen's presence bids away ;
'Tis, already, at his night,
He can give you further light.
You, my Sports, may here abide,
Till I call to light the bride.   [*Slips from her.*

Enter HYMEN.

   Hy. Venus, is this a time to quit your car ?
To stoop to earth, to leave alone your star,
Without your influence, and, on such a night †
Which should be crown'd with your most cheering sight.
As you were ignorant of what were done
By Cupid's hand, your all-triumphing son ?
Look on this state ; and if you yet not know,
What crown there shines, whose sceptre here doth grow ;
Think on thy loved Æneas, and what name,
Maro, the golden trumpet of his fame,
Gave him, read thou in this. A prince that draws
By example more, than others do by laws :‡

   * Here Hymen, the god of marriage, entered ; and was so
induced here, as you have described in my Hymenæi.
   † When she is nuptiis præfecta, with Juno, Suadela, Diana,
and Jupiter himself. Paus. in Messeniac. et Plut. in Problem.
   ‡ Æneas, the son of Venus, Virgil makes throughout, the
most exquisite pattern of piety, justice, prudence, and all other
princely virtues, with whom (in way of that excellence) I confer
my sovereign, applying in his description his own word usurped
of that poet, Parcere subjectis, et debellare superbos.
...21...

That is so just to his great act, and thought,
To do, not what kings may, but what kings ought.
Who, out of piety, unto peace is vow'd,
To spare his subjects, yet to quell the proud ;
And dares esteem it the first fortitude,
To have his passions, foes at home, subdued.
That was reserv'd, until the Parcæ spun
Their whitest wool ; and then his thread begun,
Which thread, when treason would have burst,* a soul
To-day renown'd, and added to my roll,†
Opposed ; and, by that act, to his name did bring
The honour to be saver of his king.
This king whose worth, if gods for virtue love,
Should Venus with the same affections move,
As her Æneas ; and no less endear
Her love to his safety, than when she did cheer,
After a tempest,‡ long-afflicted Troy,
Upon the Lybian shore ; and brought them joy.

Ven. I love, and know his virtues, and do boast
Mine own renown, when I renown him most.
My Cupid's absence I forgive, and praise,
That me to such a present grace could raise.
His champion shall, hereafter, be my care :
But speak his bride, and what her virtues are.

Hy. She is a noble virgin, styled, The Maid
Of the Red-cliff, and hath her dowry weigh'd
No less in virtue, blood, and form, than gold ;
Thence, where my pillar's rear'd, you may behold,
Fill'd with love's trophies, doth she take her name.

* In that monstrous conspiracy of E. Gowry.

† Titulo tunc crescere posses,
    Nunc per te titulus.

‡ Virg. Æneid. lib. 1.

Those pillars did uxorious Vulcan frame,*
Against this day, and underneath that hill,
He, and his Cyclopes, are forging still
Some strange and curious piece, to adorn the night,
And give these graced nuptials greater light.

> *Here* VULCAN *presented himself, as overhearing Hymen,
> attired in a cassock girt to him, with bare arms, his
> hair and beard rough ; his hat of blue, and ending in
> a cone ; in his hand a hammer and tongs, as coming
> from the forge.*

Vul. Which I have done ; the best of all my life ;
And have my end, if it but please my wife,
And she commend it, to the labour'd worth.
Cleave, solid rock ! and bring the wonder forth.

> *At which, with a loud and full music, the cliff parted
> in the midst, and discovered an illustrious concave,
> filled with an ample and glistering light, in which
> an artificial sphere was made of silver, eighteen feet
> in the diameter, that turned perpetually : the coluri
> were heightened with gold ; so were the arctic and
> antarctic circles, the tropics, the equinoctial, the
> meridian and horizon ; only the zodiac was of pure
> gold : in which the masquers, under the characters of
> the twelve signs, were placed, answering them in
> number ; whose offices, with the whole frame, as it
> turned, Vulcan went forward to describe.*

* The ancient poets, whensoever they would intend any thing
to be done with great mastery, or excellent art, made Vulcan
the artificer, as Hom. Il Σ. in the forging of Achilles's armour,
and Virg. for Æneas, Æneid. 8. He is also said to be the god of
fire and light. Sometime taken for the purest beam : and by
Orph. in Hym. celebrated for the sun and moon. But more
especially by Eurip. in Troad. he is made Facifer in Nuptiis.
Which present office we give him here, as being Calor Naturæ,
and Præses Luminis. See Plat. in Cratyl. For his description,
read Pausan. in Eliac.

It is a sphere, I've formed round and even,
In due proportion to the sphere of heaven,
With all his lines and circles ; that compose
The perfect'st form, and aptly do disclose
The heaven of marriage : which I title it :
Within whose zodiac, I have made to sit,
In order of the signs, twelve sacred powers,
That are presiding at all nuptial hours :

The first, in Aries' place, respecteth pride
Of youth, and beauty ; graces in the bride.

In Taurus, he loves strength and manliness ;
The virtues which the bridegroom should profess.

In Gemini, that noble power is shown,
That twins their hearts, and doth of two make one.

In Cancer, he that bids the wife give way
With backward yielding to her husband's sway.

In Leo, he that doth instil the heat
Into the man : which from the following seat

Is temper'd so, as he that looks from thence
Sees yet they keep a Virgin innocence.

In Libra's room, rules he that doth supply
All happy beds with sweet equality.

The Scorpion's place he fills, that makes the jars,
And stings in wedlock ; little strifes and wars :

Which he, in th' Archer's throne, doth soon remove,
By making, with his shafts, new wounds of love.

And those the follower with more heat inspires,
As, in the Goat, the sun renews his fires.

In wet Aquarius' stead, reigns he that showers
Fertility upon the genial bowers.

Last, in the Fishes place, sits he doth say,
In married joys, all should be dumb as they.

And this hath Vulcan for his Venus done,
To grace the chaster triumph of her son.

Ven. And for this gift, will I to heaven return,
And vow for ever, that my lamp shall burn
With pure and chastest fire ; or never shine,*
But when it mixeth with thy sphere and mine.

*Here Venus returned to her chariot, with the Graces ;
while Vulcan, calling out the priests of Hymen, who
were the musicians, was interrupted by* PYRACMON.†

Vul. Sing, then, ye priests.

Pyrac. Stay, Vulcan, shall not these
Come forth and dance ?

Vul. Yes, my Pyracmon, please
The eyes of these spectators with our art.‡

---

* As Catul. hath it in nup. Jul. et Manl. without Hymen,
which is marriage, Nil potest Venus, fama quod bona comprobet,
etc.

† One of the Cyclops, of whom, with the other two, Brontes
and Steropes, see Virg. Æneid.

Ferrum exercebant vasto Cyclopes in antro,
Brontesque, Steropesque et nudus membra Pyracmon, etc.

‡ As when Hom. Iliad. Σ, makes Thetis for her son Achilles,
to visit Vulcan's house, he feigns that Vulcan had made twenty
tripods, or stools with golden wheels, to move of themselves
miraculously, and go out and return fitly. To which the invention of our dance alludes, and is in the poet a most elegant
place, and worthy the tenth reading.

Pyrac. Come here then, Brontes, bear a Cyclop's part,
And Steropes, both with your sledges stand,
And strike a time unto them as they land ;
And as they forwards come, still guide their paces,
In musical and sweet proportion'd graces ;
While I upon the work and frame attend,
And Hymen's priests forth, at their seasons, send
To chaunt their hymns ; and make this square admire
Our great artificer, the god of fire.

*Here the musicians, attired in yellow, with wreaths of
marjoram, and veils like Hymen's priests, sung the
first staff of the following Epithalamion : which,
because it was sung in pieces between the dances,
shewed to be so many several songs ; but was made to
be read an entire poem. After the song, they came
(descending in an oblique motion) from the Zodiac,
and danced their first dance ; then music interposed,
(but varied with voices, only keeping the same chorus)
they danced their second dance. So after, their third
and fourth dances, which were all full of elegancy
and curious device. And thus it ended.**

 * The two latter dances were made by master Thomas Giles,
the two first by master Hier. Herne : who, in the persons of
the two Cyclopes, beat a time to them with their hammers.
The tunes were master Alphonso Ferrabosco's. The device and
act of the scene master Inigo Jones's, with addition of the
trophies. For the invention of the whole, and the verses,
Assertor qui dicat esse meos, imponet plagiario pudorem.
 The attire of the masquers throughout was most graceful and
noble ; partaking of the best both ancient and later figure. The
colours carnation and silver, enriched both with embroidery and
lace. The dressing of their heads, feathers and jewels ; and so
excellently ordered to the rest of the habit, as all would suffer
under any description, after the shew. Their performance of

Epithalamion.

Up, youths and virgins, up, and praise
  The god, whose nights outshine his days;
  Hymen, whose hallowed rites
Could never boast of brighter lights;
  Whose bands pass liberty.
Two of your troop, that with the morn were free,
  Are now waged to his war.
    And what they are,
  If you'll perfection see,
    Yourselves must be.
Shine, Hesperus, shine forth, thou wished star!

  What joy or honours can compare
  With holy nuptials, when they are
    Made out of equal parts
  Of years of states, of hands, of hearts?
    When in the happy choice,
The spouse and spoused have the foremost voice!
    Such, glad of Hymen's war,
      Live what they are,
    And long perfection see:
      And such ours be,
Shine, Hesperus, shine forth, thou wished star!

    The solemn state of this one night
    Were fit to last an age's light;

all, so magnificent and illustrious, that nothing can add to the
seal of it, but the subscription of their names:—

The Duke of LENOX,	Lord of WALDEN,
Earl of ARUNDELL,	Lord HAY,
Earl of PEMBROKE,	Lord SANKRE,
Earl of MONTGOMERY,	Sir Ro. RICHE,
Lord D'AUBIGNY,	Sir Jo. KENNETHIE,

Master ERSKINE.

But there are rights behind
Have less of state, but more of kind :
Love's wealthy crop of kisses,
And fruitful harvest of his mother's blisses.
Sound then to Hymen's war :
That what these are,
Who will perfection see,
May haste to be.
Shine, Hesperus, shine forth, thou wished sta: !

Love's commonwealth consists of toys ;
His council are those antic boys,
Games, Laughter, Sports, Delights,
That triumph with him on these nights :
To whom we must give way,
For now their reign begins, and lasts till day.
They sweeten Hymen's war,
And, in that jar,
Make all, that married be,
Perfection see.
Shine, Hesperus, shine forth, thou wished star !

Why stays the bridegroom to invade
Her, that would be a matron made ?
Good-night, whilst yet we may
Good-night, to you, a virgin, say :
To-morrow rise the same
Your mother is,* and use a nobler name.
Speed well in Hymen's war,
That, what you are,
By your perfection, we
And all may see.
Shine, Hesperus, shine forth, thou wished star !

* A wife or matron : which is a name of more dignity than
Virgin. D. Heins. in Nup. Ottonis Heurnii, Cras matri similis
tuæ redibis.

To-night is Venus' vigil kept.
This night no bridegroom ever slept ;
  And if the fair bride do,
The married say, 'tis his fault too.
  Wake then, and let your lights
Wake too ; for they'll tell nothing of your nights
    But, that in Hymen's war,
      You perfect are.
    And such perfection, we
      Do pray should be.
Shine, Hesperus, shine forth, thou wished star !

    That, ere the rosy-finger'd morn
    Behold nine moons, there may be born
      A babe, t'uphold the fame
    Of Ratcliffe's blood, and Ramsey's name :
      That may, in his great seed,
Wear the long honours of his father's deed.
    Such fruits of Hymen's war
      Most perfect are :
    And all perfection, we
      Wish you should see.
Shine, Hesperus, shine forth, thou wished star !

Lyrics and Occasional Pieces.

LYRICS AND OCCASIONAL PIECES.

ECHO'S SONG.

(FROM CYNTHIA'S REVELS.)

SLOW, slow, fresh fount, keep time with my salt tears :
  Yet, slower, yet ; O faintly, gentle springs :
List to the heavy part the music bears,
  Woe weeps out her division, when she sings.
        Droop herbs and flowers,
        Fall grief in showers,
        Our beauties are not ours ;
        O, I could still,
Like melting snow upon some craggy hill,
        Drop, drop, drop, drop,
Since nature's pride is now a wither'd daffodil.

THE KISS.

(FROM CYNTHIA'S REVELS.)

O, THAT joy so soon should waste !
　　Or so sweet a bliss
　　As a kiss
Might not for ever last !
So sugar'd, so melting, so soft, so delicious,
　　The dew that lies on roses,
　　When the morn herself discloses,
　　　Is not so precious.
O rather than I would it smother,
Were I to taste such another ;
　　　It should be my wishing
　　　That I might die with kissing.

HESPER'S SONG TO CYNTHIA.

(FROM CYNTHIA'S REVELS.)

QUEEN and huntress, chaste and fair,
Now the sun is laid to sleep,
Seated in thy silver chair,
State in wonted manner keep :
　　Hesperus entreats thy light,
　　Goddess, excellently bright.

Earth, let not thy envious shade
Dare itself to interpose ;
Cynthia's shining orb was made
Heav'n to clear, when day did close :
　　Bless us then with wished sight,
　　Goddess excellently bright.

Lay thy bow of pearl apart,
And thy crystal shining quiver ;
Give unto the flying hart
Space to breathe, how short soever :
    Thou that mak'st a day of night,
    Goddess excellently bright.

HORACE, HIS DRINKING SONG.

(From the Poetaster.)

Swell me a bowl with lusty wine,
  Till I may see the plump Lyæus swim
    Above the brim :
I drink as I would write
In flowing measure filled with flame and sprite.

SONG.—TO CELIA.

Drink to me only with thine eyes,
  And I will pledge with mine;
Or leave a kiss but in the cup,
  And I'll not look for wine.
The thirst, that from the soul doth rise,
  Doth ask a drink divine :
But might I of Jove's nectar sup,
  I would not change for thine.

I sent thee late a rosy wreath,
  Not so much honouring thee,
As giving it a hope, that there
  It could not wither'd be.
But thou thereon didst only breathe,
  And sent'st it back to me :
Since when it grows, and smells, I swear,
  Not of itself, but thee.

SONG.—TO CELIA.

Come, my Celia, let us prove,
While we may, the sports of love ;
Time will not be ours for ever :
He at length our good will sever.
Spend not then his gifts in vain.
Suns that set, may rise again ;
But if once we lose this light,
'Tis with us perpetual night.
Why should we defer our joys ?
Fame and rumour are but toys.
Cannot we delude the eyes
Of a few poor household spies ;
Or his easier ears beguile,
So removèd by our wile ?
'Tis no sin love's fruit to steal,
But the sweet theft to reveal :
To be taken, to be seen,
These have crimes accounted been.

Kiss me, sweet ; the wary lover
Can you favours keep, and cover,
When the common courting jay
All your bounties will betray.
Kiss again : no creature comes.
Kiss, and score up wealthy sums
On my lips thus hardly sundred,
While you breathe.   First give a hundred,
Then a thousand, then another
Hundred, then unto the other
Add a thousand, and so more :
Till you equal with the store,
All the grass that Rumney yields,
Or the sands in Chelsea fields,

Or the drops in silver Thames,
Or the stars that gild his streams,
In the silent Summer-nights,
When youths ply their stolen delights ;
That the curious may not know
How to tell 'em as they flow,
And the envious, when they find
What their number is, be pined.

THAT WOMEN ARE BUT MEN'S SHADOWS.

FOLLOW a shadow, it still flies you,
  Seem to fly it, it will pursue :
So court a mistress, she denies you ;
  Let her alone, she will court you.
Say are not women truly, then,
Styl'd but the shadows of us men ?

At morn and even shades are longest ;
  At noon they are or short, or none :
So men at weakest, they are strongest,
  But grant us perfect, they're not known.
Say are not women truly, then,
Styl'd but the shadows of us men ?

FOR CHARIS.

HER TRIUMPH.

SEE the chariot at hand here of Love,
  Wherein my Lady rideth !
Each that draws is a swan or a dove,
  And well the car Love guideth.
As she goes, all hearts do duty
            Unto her beauty ;
      ...22...

And enamour'd, do wish, so they might
           But enjoy such a sight,
That they still were to run by her side,   [ride.
Through swords, through seas, whither she would

Do but look on her eyes, they do light
   All that Love's world compriseth !
Do but look on her hair, it is bright
   As Love's star when it riseth !
Do but mark, her forehead's smoother
           Than words that soothe her :
And from her arched brows, such a grace
           Sheds itself through the face,
As alone there triumphs to the life
All the gain, all the good of the elements' strife.

Have you seen but a bright lily grow,
   Before rude hands have touch'd it ?
Have you mark'd but the fall of the snow
   Before the soil hath smutch'd it ?
Have you felt the wool of the bever ?
           Or swan's down ever ?
Or have smelt o' the bud of the briar ?
           Or the nard in the fire ?
Or have tasted the bag of the bee ?
O so white | O so soft | O so sweet is she !

BEGGING ANOTHER KISS, ON COLOUR OF
MENDING THE FORMER.

For Love's sake, kiss me once again,
I long, and should not beg in vain,
   Here's none to spy, or see ;

Why do you doubt or stay ?
I'll taste as lightly as the bee,
That doth but touch his flower, and flies away.

Once more, and, faith, I will be gone,
Can he that loves ask less than one ?
  Nay, you may err in this,
    And all your bounty wrong :
  This could be call'd but half a kiss ;
What we're but once to do, we should do long.

I will but mend the last, and tell
Where, how, it would have relish'd well ;
  Join lip to lip, and try :
    Each suck the other's breath,
    And whilst our tongues perplexed lie,
Let who will think us dead, or wish our death.

A SONG.

Oʜ do not wanton with those eyes,
  Lest I be sick with seeing ;
Nor cast them down, but let them rise,
  Lest shame destroy their being.

Oh be not angry with those fires,
  For then their threats will kill me ;
Nor look too kind on my desires,
  For then my hopes will spill me.

Oh do not steep them in thy tears,
  For so will sorrow stay me ;
Nor spread them as distract with fears ;
  Mine own enough betray me.

INVITING A FRIEND TO SUPPER.

To-night, grave sir, both my poor house and I
Do equally desire your company :
Not that we think us worthy such a guest,
But that your worth will dignify our feast,
With those that come ; whose grace may make that
    seem
Something, which else would hope for no esteem.
It is the fair acceptance, sir, creates
The entertainment perfect, not the cates.
Yet shall you have, to rectify your palate,
An olive, capers, or some better sallad
Ushering the mutton : with a short-legg'd hen,
If we can get her full of eggs, and then,
Limons, and wine for sauce : to these, a coney
Is not to be despair'd of for our money ;
And though fowl now be scarce, yet there are clerks,
The sky not falling, think we may have larks.
I'll tell you of more, and lie, so you will come :
Of partridge, pheasant, woodcock, of which some
May yet be there ; and godwit if we can ;
Knat, rail, and ruff too.   Howsoe'er, my man
Shall read a piece of Virgil, Tacitus,
Livy, or of some better book to us,
Of which we'll speak our minds, amidst our meat ;
And I'll profess no verses to repeat :
To this if aught appear, which I not know of,
That will the pastry, not my paper, show of,
Digestive cheese, and fruit there sure will be ;
But that which most doth take my muse and me,
Is a pure cup of rich Canary wine,
Which is the Mermaid's now, but shall be mine :
Of which had Horace or Anacreon tasted,
Their lives, as do their lines, till now had lasted.

Tobacco, nectar, or the Thespian spring,
Are all but Luther's beer, to this I sing.
Of this we will sup free, but moderately,
And we will have no Pooly', or Parrot by ;
Nor shall our cups make any guilty men :
But at our parting, we will be, as when
We innocently met.   No simple word,
That shall be utter'd at our mirthful board,
Shall make us sad next morning ; or affright
The liberty, that we'll enjoy to-night.

TO PENSHURST.

Thou art not, Penshurst, built to envious show
Of touch or marble ; nor canst boast a row
Of polish'd pillars, or a roof of gold :
Thou hast no lantern, whereof tales are told ;
Or stair, or courts ; but stand'st an ancient pile,
And these grudg'd at, art reverenced the while.
Thou joy'st in better marks, of soil, of air,
Of wood, of water ; therein thou art fair.
Thou hast thy walks for health, as well as sport ;
Thy mount, to which thy Dryads do resort,
Where Pan and Bacchus their high feasts have made,
Beneath the broad beech, and the chestnut shade ;
That taller tree, which of a nut was set,
At his great birth, where all the Muses met.
There, in the writhed bark, are cut the names
Of many a sylvan, taken with his flames ;
And thence the ruddy satyrs oft provoke
The lighter fauns, to reach thy lady's oak.
Thy copse, too, named of Gamage, thou hast there,
That never fails to serve thee, season'd deer,
When thou wouldst feast or exercise thy friends.
The lower land, that to the river bends,

Thy sheep, thy bullocks, kine, and calves do feed ;
The middle grounds thy mares and horses breed.
Each bank doth yield thee conies ; and the tops
Fertile of wood, Ashore and Sydneys copp's,
To crown thy open table, doth provide
The purpled pheasant, with the speckled side
The painted partridge lies in ev'ry field,
And for thy mess is willing to be kill'd.
And if the high-swoln Medway fail thy dish,
Thou hast thy ponds, that pay thee tribute fish,
Fat aged carps that run into thy net,
And pikes, now weary their own kind to eat,
As loth the second draught or cast to stay,
Officiously at first themselves betray.
Bright eels that emulate them, and leap on land,
Before the fisher, or into his hand.
Then hath thy orchard fruit, thy garden flowers,
Fresh as the air, and new as are the hours.
The early cherry, with the later plum,
Fig, grape, and quince, each in his time doth come ;
The blushing apricot, and woolly peach
Hang on thy walls, that every child may reach.
And though thy walls be of the country stone,
They're reared with no man's ruin, no man's groan ;
There's none, that dwell about them, wish them down ;
But all come in, the farmer and the clown ;
And no one empty-handed, to salute
Thy lord and lady, though they have no suit.
Some bring a capon, some a rural cake,
Some nuts, some apples ; some that think they make
The better cheeses, bring them ; or else send
By their ripe daughters, whom they would commend
This way to husbands ; and whose baskets bear
An emblem of themselves in plum, or pear.
But what can this (more than express their love)

Add to thy free provisions, far above
The need of such ? whose liberal board doth flow,
With all that hospitality doth know !
Where comes no guest, but is allowed to eat,
Without his fear, and of thy lord's own meat :
Where the same beer and bread, and self-same wine,
That is his lordship's, shall be also mine.
And I not fain to sit (as some this day,
At great men's tables) and yet dine away.
Here no man tells my cups ; nor standing by,
A waiter, doth my gluttony envý :
But gives me what I call, and lets me eat,
He knows, below, he shall find plenty of meat ;
Thy tables hoard not up for the next day,
Nor, when I take my lodging, need I pray
For fire, or lights, or livery ; all is there ;
As if thou then wert mine, or I reign'd here :
There's nothing I can wish, for which I stay.
That found king JAMES, when hunting late, this way,
With his brave son, the prince ; they saw thy fires
Shine bright on every hearth, as the desires
Of thy Penates had been set on flame,
To entertain them ; or the country came,
With all their zeal, to warm their welcome here.
What (great, I will not say, but) sudden chear
Didst thou then make 'em ! and what praise was
    heap'd
On thy good lady, then ! who therein reap'd
The just reward of her high huswifry ;
To have her linen, plate, and all things nigh,
When she was far ; and not a room, but drest,
As if it had expected such a guest !
These, Penshurst, are thy praise, and yet not all
Thy lady's noble, fruitful, chaste withal.
His children thy great lord may call his own :

A fortune, in this age, but rarely known.
They are, and have been taught religion ; thence
Their gentler spirits have suck'd innocence.
Each morn, and even, they are taught to pray,
With the whole houschold, and may, every day,
Read in their virtuous parents' noble parts,
The mysteries of manners, arms, and arts.
Now, Penshurst, they that will proportion thee
With other edifices, when they see
Those proud ambitious heaps, and nothing else,
May say, their lords have built, but thy lord dwells.

TO WILLIAM CAMDEN.

CAMDEN ! most reverend head, to whom I owe
All that I am in arts, all that I know ;
(How nothing's that ?) to whom my country owes
The great renown, and name wherewith she goes !
Than thee the age sees not that thing more grave,
More high, more holy, that she more would crave.
What name, what skill, what faith hast thou in things !
What sight in searching the most antique springs !
What weight, and what authority in thy speech !
Men scarce can make that doubt, but thou canst teach.
Pardon free truth, and let thy modesty,
Which conquers all, be once o'ercome by thee.
Many of thine, this better could, than I ;
But for their powers, accept my piety.

ON LORD BACON'S BIRTHDAY.

HAIL, happy GENIUS of this ancient pile !
How comes it all things so about thee smile ?
The fire, the wine, the men ! and in the midst
Thou stand'st as if some mystery thou didst !

Pardon, I read it in thy face, the day
For whose returns, and many, all these pray ;
And so do I.   This is the sixtieth year,
Since BACON, and thy lord was born, and here ;
Son to the grave wise Keeper of the Seal,
Fame and foundation of the English weal.
What then his father was, that since is he,
Now with a title more to the degree ;
England's high Chancellor : the destin'd heir,
In his soft cradle, to his father's chair :
Whose even thread the fates spin round and full,
Out of their choicest and their whitest wool.
    'Tis a brave cause of joy, let it be known,
For 'twere a narrow gladness, kept thine own.
Give me a deep-crown'd bowl, that I may sing,
In raising him, the wisdom of my king.

TO JOHN DONNE.

DONNE, the delight of Phœbus and each Muse,
Who, to thy one, all other brains refuse ;
Whose every work, of thy most early wit,
Came forth example, and remains so, yet :
Longer a knowing than most wits do live,
And which no' affection praise enough can give !
To it, thy language, letters, arts, best life,
Which might with half mankind maintain a strife ;
All which I meant to praise, and yet I would ;
But leave, because I cannot as I should !

TO FRANCIS BEAUMONT.

How I do love thee, Beaumont, and thy Muse,
That unto me dost such religion use !
How I do fear myself, that am not worth
The least indulgent thought thy pen drops forth !
At once thou mak'st me happy, and unmak'st ;
And giving largely to me, more thou tak'st !
What fate is mine, that so itself bereaves ?
What art is thine, that so thy friend deceives ?
When even there, where most thou praisest me,
For writing better, I must envy thee.

ON THE PORTRAIT OF SHAKESPEARE.

TO THE READER.

This figure that thou here seest put,
It was for gentle Shakespeare cut,
Wherein the graver had a strife
With nature, to out-do the life :
O could he but have drawn his wit
As well in brass, as he has hit
His face ; the print would then surpass
All that was ever writ in brass :
But since he cannot, reader, look
Not on his picture, but his book.

TO THE MEMORY OF MY BELOVED MASTER, WILLIAM SHAKESPEARE, AND WHAT HE HATH LEFT US.

To draw no envy, SHAKESPEARE, on thy name,
Am I thus ample to thy book and fame ;
While I confess thy writings to be such,
As neither man, nor Muse, can praise too much.
'Tis true, and all men's suffrage.   But these ways
Were not the paths I meant unto thy praise ;
For silliest ignorance on these may light,
Which, when it sounds at best, but echoes right ;
Or blind affection, which doth ne'er advance
The truth, but gropes, and urgeth all by chance ;
Or crafty malice might pretend this praise,
And think to ruin, where it seem'd to raise.
These are, as some infámous bawd, or whore,
Should praise a matron ; what could hurt her more ?
But thou art proof against them, and, indeed,
Above the ill fortune of them, or the need.
I therefore will begin : Soul of the age !
The applause ! delight ! the wonder of our stage !
My SHAKESPEARE rise ! I will not lodge thee by
Chaucer, or Spenser, or bid Beaumont lie
A little further off, to make thee room :
Thou art a monument without a tomb,
And art alive still, while thy book doth live,
And we have wits to read, and praise to give.
That I not mix thee so, my brain excuses,
I mean with great, but disproportion'd Muses :
For if I thought my judgment were of years,
I should commit thee surely with thy peers,
And tell how far thou didst our Lily outshine,
Or sporting Kyd, or Marlow's mighty line.

And though thou hadst small Latin and less Greek,
From thence to honour thee, I will not seek
For names : but call forth thund'ring Eschylus,
Euripides, and Sophocles to us,
Pacuvius, Accius, him of Cordoua dead,
To live again, to hear thy buskin tread,
And shake a stage : or when thy socks were on,
Leave thee alone for the comparison
Of all, that insolent Greece, or haughty Rome
Sent forth, or since did from their ashes come.
Triumph, my Britain, thou hast one to show,
To whom all scenes of Europe homage owe.
He was not of an age, but for all time !
And all the Muses still were in their prime,
When, like Apollo, he came forth to warm
Our ears, or like a Mercury to charm !
Nature herself was proud of his designs,
And joyed to wear the dressing of his lines !
Which were so richly spun, and woven so fit,
As, since, she will vouchsafe no other wit.
The merry Greek, tart Aristophanes,
Neat Terence, witty Plautus, now not please ;
But antiquated and deserted lie,
As they were not of nature's family.
Yet must I not give nature all ; thy art,
My gentle Shakespeare, must enjoy a part.
For though the poet's matter nature be,
His art doth give the fashion : and, that he
Who casts to write a living line, must sweat,
(Such as thine are) and strike the second heat
Upon the Muses' anvil ; turn the same,
And himself with it, that he thinks to frame ;
Or for the laurel, he may gain a scorn ;
For a good poet's made, as well as born.
And such wert thou ! Look how the father's face

Lives in his issue, even so the race
Of Shakespeare's mind and manners brightly shines
In his well torned, and true filed lines ;
In each of which he seems to shake a lance,
As brandish'd at the eyes of ignorance.
Sweet Swan of Avon ! what a sight it were
To see thee in our water yet appear,
And make those flights upon the banks of Thames,
That so did take Eliza, and our James !
But stay, I see thee in the hemisphere
Advanced, and made a constellation there !
Shine forth, thou Star of poets, and with rage,
Or influence, chide, or cheer the drooping stage,
Which, since thy flight from hence, hath mourn'd like
   night,
And despairs day, but for thy volume's light.

AN EPITAPH ON SALATHIEL PAVY, A CHILD OF QUEEN ELIZABETH'S CHAPEL.

Weep with me, all you that read
   This little story :
And know, for whom a tear you shed
   Death's self is sorry.
'Twas a child that so did thrive
   In grace and feature,
As heaven and nature seem'd to strive
   Which own'd the creature.
Years he number'd scarce thirteen
   When fates turn'd cruel,
Yet three fill'd zodiacs had he been
   The stage's jewel ;
And did act, what now we moan,
   Old men so duly,

As, sooth, the Parcæ thought him one,
    He play'd so truly.
So, by error to his fate
    They all consented ;
But viewing him since, alas, too late !
    They have repented ;
And have sought, to give new birth,
    In baths to steep him ;
But being so much too good for earth,
    Heaven vows to keep him.

EPITAPH ON THE COUNTESS OF PEMBROKE.

UNDERNEATH this sable herse
Lies the subject of all verse,
SIDNEY'S sister, PEMBROKE'S mother ;
Death ! ere thou hast slain another,
Learn'd and fair, and good as she,
Time shall throw a dart at thee.

THE TRUE MEASURE OF LIFE.

IT is not growing like a tree
In bulk, doth make men better be ;
Or standing long an oak, three hundred year,
To fall a log at last, dry, bald, and scar :
    A lily of a day,
    Is fairer far, in May,
Although it fall and die that night ;
It was the plant and flower of light.
In small proportions we just beauties see ;
And in short measures, life may perfect be.

ON MY FIRST DAUGHTER.

Here lies, to each her parents ruth,
Mary, the daughter of their youth ;
Yet all heaven's gifts being heaven's due,
It makes the father less to rue.
At six months end she parted hence
With safety of her innocence ;
Whose soul heaven's Queen, whose name she bears,
In comfort of her mother's tears,
Hath placed amongst her virgin-train :
Where while that, severed, doth remain,
This grave partakes the fleshly birth ;
Which cover lightly, gentle earth !

ON MY FIRST SON.

Farewell, thou child of my right hand, and joy ;
My sin was too much hope of thee, lov'd boy :
Seven years thou wert lent to me, and I thee pay,
Exacted by thy fate, on the just day.
O, could I lose all father, now ! for why,
Will man lament the state he should envy ?
To have so soon 'scaped world's, and flesh's rage,
And, if no other misery, yet age !
Rest in soft peace, and ask'd, say here doth lie
Ben Jonson his best piece of poetry :
For whose sake henceforth all his vows be such,
As what he loves may never like too much.

AN ODE.—TO HIMSELF.

Wʜᴇʀᴇ dost Thou carless lie
　　Buried in ease and sloth ?
Knowledge, that sleeps, doth die ;
And this security,
　　It is the common moth,
That eats on wits and arts, and [so] destroys them
　　both :

Are all the Aonian springs
　　Dried up ? lies Thespia waste ?
Doth Clarius' harp want strings,
That not a nymph now sings ;
　　Or droop they as disgrac'd,
To see their seats and bowers by chattering pies
　　defac'd ?

If hence thy silence be,
　　As 'tis too just a cause ;
Let this thought quicken thee :
Minds that are great and free
　　Should not on fortune pause,
'Tis crown enough to virtue still, her own applause.

What though the greedy fry
　　Be taken with false baits
Of worded balladry
And think it poesy ?
　　They die with their conceits,
And only piteous scorn upon their folly waits.

Then take in hand thy lyre,
    Strike in thy proper strain,
With Japhet's line, aspire
Sol's chariot for new fire,
    To give the world again :
Who aided him, will thee, the issue of Jove's brain.

And since our dainty age
    Cannot endure reproof,
Make not thyself a page,
    To that strumpet the stage,
    But sing high and aloof,
Safe from the wolf's black jaw, and the dull ass's hoof.

THE JUST INDIGNATION THE AUTHOR TOOK AT THE
    VULGAR CENSURE OF HIS PLAY, "THE NEW INN,"
    BY SOME MALICIOUS SPECTATORS, BEGAT THIS
    FOLLOWING

ODE

(TO HIMSELF).

COME leave the loathed stage,
    And the more loathsome age ;
Where pride and impudence, in faction knit,
    Usurp the chair of wit !
Indicting and arraigning every day,
    Something they call a play.
    Let their fastidious, vain
    Commission of the brain
Run on and rage, sweat, censure, and condemn ;
They were not made for thee, less thou for them.
...23...

Say that thou pour'st them wheat,
And they will acorns eat ;
'Twere simple fury still thyself to waste
On such as have no taste !
To offer them a surfeit of pure bread,
Whose appetites are dead !
No, give them grains their fill,
Husks, draff to drink and swill :
If they love lees, and leave the lusty wine,
Envy them not, their palate's with the swine.

No doubt some mouldy tale,
Like Pericles, and stale
As the shrieve's crusts, and nasty as his fish—
Scraps, out of every dish
Thrown forth, and raked into the common tub,
May keep up the Play-club ;
There, sweepings do as well
As the best-order'd meal ;
For who the relish of these guests will fit,
Needs set them but the alms-basket of wit.

And much good do't you then :
Brave plush and velvet-men,
Can feed on orts ; and, safe in your stage-clothes,
Dare quit, upon your oaths,
The stagers and the stage-wrights too, your peers,
Of larding your large ears
With their foul comic socks,
Wrought upon twenty blocks ;
Which, if they are torn, and turn'd, and patch'd
    enough,
The gamesters share your gilt, and you their stuff.—

Leave things so prostitute
And take the Alcaic lute ;
Or thine own Horace, or Anacreon's lyre ;
Warm thee by Pindar's fire :
And though thy nerves be shrunk, and blood be cold
Ere years have made thee old,
Strike that disdainful heat
Throughout, to their defeat,
As curious fools, and envious of thy strain,
May, blushing, swear no palsy's in thy brain.

But when they hear thee sing
The glories of thy king,
His zeal to God, and his just awe o'er men :
They may, blood-shaken then,
Feel such a flesh-quake to possess their powers
As they shall cry, " Like ours,
In sound of peace or wars,
No harp e'er hit the stars,
In tuning forth the acts of his sweet reign ;
And raising Charles his chariot 'bove his Wain."

Printed by WALTER SCOTT, *Felling, Newcastle-on-Tyne.*